The Stone

Claire Nolan

Published by YouWriteOn.com, 2011

Acknowledgements

A very big thank you to Mum, Dad and all the clan in Kilkenny.
Also thanks to Mark for keeping me going.
Thanks to everyone at the School of Information and Library Studies, UCD
Dublin, Ireland, for their help, encouragement, support, and suggestions.
A very big thank you to Susan Lanigan and Nicole Murphy for reading the
early drafts and finding enough there to keep going with.
Finally, thank you to all the readers and writers on **www.youwriteon.com**
for making any of this possible.

Foreword

Alice Kyteler was a real woman who lived in extraordinary times. However, her own reaction to those times is not recorded.

What I have written is a work of fiction that attempts to interpret her and those people around her. I've plundered the available sources as much as I am able, but much of what you are about to read is speculation. Therefore, where I am inaccurate, incorrect or have simply changed the story to suit myself, I beg the reader's indulgence.

Chapter One

The Year 1280

Alice rolled her eyes. "When?"

"Soon! Soon now. Wait a little longer." Still, the Nurse knew to move, they all did.

They were at home, in the hall, Alice waiting for them. It was morning, only a few candles lit. On the stone over the hall door was a small decoration, not grand: in truth, the dark blue of the stone had just a white line across it for relief.

Alice could remember that stone from the day they moved here. The country had opened up with the siege of Strongbow across Ireland a hundred or so years before. Alice's father had moved and adapted, eventually, and the Hibernia had seemed utter brutes. Time, however, lessened everything. It was home now, as much as anywhere else. Of course, the Irish natives themselves were savages, but some of the neighbours were civilised enough.

Finally ready, the Nurse and she were walking down the steps, opening the small oak door.

"Why can I never go out by myself, Nurse? I see other children by themselves all the time."

"Why! Because the world is full of killers and thieves who want nothing more than to cut your throat! And most of them are those very children you see! You may be safe behind that door my Lady, but you're not safe against those who would like nothing more than to see Master Kyteler's daughter in trouble. Imagine you, held to ransom while a debt ticks away. Even just to see you harmed, because of the trade of your father!"

"What's my father's trade got to with it?"

"A moneylender! They would cut his neck rather than repay their debt to him! The Lord in the Castle might wring his hands at any misfortune of us, but we're neither Nobility nor Church, so no help will come for the likes of us!"

"But is this town so vicious?"

The Nurse pointed to figures in the street.

"Look at him, drunk in his cups. He might cut you down and not remember it in the morning. Or her! Hungry and bitter and with no soul left but to fight or to die. And only a few days ago they found a woman and child murdered. Need I say more?"

5

The Nurse closed the door as she spoke. Their world was bedlam. Everywhere there were shouts and screams as people called out their wares, cursed their beasts of burden, greeted one another, sang out the hourly news, or fought their enemies.

"Good morrow, Sir Thomas!"

"Move your wart encrusted backside, you pest!"

"God save you, move yours first!"

Alice and the Nurse kept their eyes low as they moved quickly up the street. The choking smell would soak into your clothes and hair.

One of the locals, a large man with an unsheathed knife in his belt which showed he was a soldier, but not a knight, stood tall and straight before them.

"Please, good sir, let my Lady go past."

"I give way to the betters of mine, to the Holy Father and to those above me, not to those that deny God's law each day."

A pause.

Alice spoke.

"Then please move past for those who must depend on the strong for safety, and grant that safety to one who cannot but submit."

She sounded almost bored. The man, surprised, stood by and let them pass, his eyes wide.

After a moment:

"To address him in such a fashion, my Lady! It would go badly for you if your father knew!"

"I would rather face my father than face him."

Alice used the silence to compose herself.

At the end of the street was a small carriage waiting for them. Their own street was too narrow, so they had to make the short walk.

Alice gladly stepped out of the squelching dirt and sat in, the Nurse following. They made sure the blind was lowered and Alice sat back.

"How far again is it, Nurse?"

"God's breath if I can remember...It will be a degree of travelling, say it will be half the morning."

"And no one knows?"

"No one."

They moved into the countryside. The landscape was rough and untended. Great trees went past, their branches hanging overhead, reaching out to brush the roof of the carriage. There was only a small dirt path to follow.

They passed people of all ages working in the fields. How innocently happy such people must be, with no curiosity! They were most happy when kept in their place. It was cruel to test a fool. How would they cope with her life! She looked at her hands, clean and pale and untouched by work.

Suddenly the carriage lurched to a stop. Alice was thrown to the other side, while the Nurse ended up on the floor.

The driver's grinning face appeared around the door.   "God's wounds, the roads get worse every year! Everyone still enjoying the glorious morning?"

"Quit your joviality. When we return, your insolence will be rewarded." She stood to her full height.

His smile faded.

"Help her up," she said, indicating the Nurse.

He went to help.

Alice sat down, and looked at the man.

"Now, onwards. And no more bumps."

The carriage slowly moved on. Alice felt something wet on her right temple; blood! She had a small cut on her forehead. The Nurse let out a squawk, and pressed a piece of cloth to it as they travelled along. Alice sighed.

"How much longer?"

"Not much longer now. Look, we're at the woods."

Alice glanced out the window and thought she was seeing things. A small figure made of twigs hung from a tree. The trees were filling up with figurines, with dolls, with images and rags and all manner of things.

The sky got darker. The wet smell reached them. The wood swallowed them up.

"We're here."

They had stopped at a clearing that was covered with fallen leaves. The trees around them were filled with rags and filth from the superstitious. Calls could be heard above them in the trees. Alice and the Nurse slowly made their way out and stood, the sound of their skirts loud in the stillness. On the other side of the clearing there was what looked like a grotto, or cave.

The Nurse looked bashful.

"I will need to lead the way in."

Alice blinked, but after a moment, nodded.

The two women set off. The Nurse moved differently, Alice noticed. She seemed to gain a sort of limber walk. Alice did not know it but it was also a stance for defence. She looked around them as they walked. As they passed one low branch, she saw something small, burnt black and bent over in agony, tied to the tree. A dog? A child? She could not tell, only that it had died burning. She walked on.

7

The Nurse walked in. Alice stood back for a moment. The smell was dreadful, but there was more. She was afraid. It looked most unholy, most intemperate.

Alice swallowed, and entered.

The smell was of something boiling, a thick hard substance that had been burning for days and would burn days more before it was done. The air was wet and warm and she had to blink to see. To her right the Nurse sat on a stool at a low table, getting out something from her pocket. Everywhere were rags, the dirty tied rags she had seen outside, with the figurines made from the trees, each one showing a man or a woman, a child or an adult.

The floor was dirt and the roof was low. The smoke and steam curled around them. The Nurse had a red face. The older woman was at the other side of the table, and she did not look like any woman Alice had seen before. She was tall, with a straight back and a high chin, hair dark but going grey. She wore a cloth as poor as any serf. She wore no jewels in her hair and did not have any form of formality about her. Alice knew, though, she was in the presence of her senior.

The woman gestured to the third stool at the table. Alice sat, and the woman turned to the Nurse.

"Did you bring them?"

The Nurse lifted the several strips of cloth from her lap, and made to hand them into the older woman's hands.

"Not yet, not yet," she said, and getting up from the table, went to the fireplace and poured light green liquid into three wooden cups. She gave one to Alice and one to the Nurse. Alice lifted the cup and sniffed. She couldn't tell what it was.

"So, what did your Nurse tell you of me? Or of why you are here?"

"She told me very little, only that we could see how many children I might bear."

"I see. Drink up."

She lifted the cup and took a sip, and then another. The liquid was sweet but not unpleasantly so. Alice found she was thirsty.

"The days are changing, as is right and proper. But will the change include us? Or was it meant to live without us, to leave us here while it travels on without us? Change can be part of us, or it can be something external where we don't survive it. Will change include you, my noble lady, hmm?"

"I'm not a noble."

The Nurse leaned forward.

"What do the signs say?"

8

The old woman looked at her, an eyebrow raised.

"The signs? The signs say many things, good for some, worse for others. Such as it was, such as it always will be...we will see change, though, here, soon."

The Nurse looked afraid.

"What type of change?"

"The type that means to do well, but only for itself. The type that is only for the others, but the rest is destruction." She shook her head. "Change, change, all is change..."

Alice put her cup down.

"Ah, so you're finished already! A good sign. Would you like some more, me Deary?"

"She wouldn't. One is enough."

"I'd like more."

"A strong one! So be it."

The old woman got another cup. The smell of the room was invading Alice's nostrils, making it hard to concentrate. She watched as the old woman slowly sat down again.

"Now," the woman gestured to the Nurse, "let us have a look."

The Nurse produced the pieces of cloth again, and Alice could see there was a small egg included in the bundle as well. Why the egg, she wondered? The old woman pointed at Alice.

"You, hold this for a while."

Alice carefully picked up the egg and looked at it. It wasn't a hen's egg, but was a small green egg, with strong black dots on it. She lifted it to her nose and sniffed. It smelt of remembered heat. All dead and cold now, alas.

The old woman lifted up the rags, and spread each of them flat on the table. Alice looked with shock at the Nurse as she recognised them. They were her undergarments, with her first bloods on them from a few weeks back. Why were they spread out on this stranger's table?

The woman leaned in close and looked at each of the three cloths in turn. The first one had a dark black stain, the second a green brown discharge, the third a lighter red blood colour. Alice swallowed back her distaste.

The expression on the woman's face was that of an eager hungry bird.

"She's got a temper, and it will get worse, not better. She'll spread other blood because of it."

The Nurse frowned.

"Do you know who?"

9

"No, but it won't be yours, don't worry."

The old woman went back to examining the cloths.

"Not many children …. just the one. She's no taste for it herself, she'll need leading to it, but it will always be little to her."

The old woman lifted the cup from Alice's hand and spread a few drops on to the green discharge.

"Not much for family, is she? Though I see many families, just not connected by blood…strange. You may not make much of a wife, my dear, but of marriages I see plenty."

Marriages? More than one? But what of William, her betrothed? The holy bond consecrated in a Church in the eyes of God? Well, maybe that bond wasn't so important. The smell was awful, the blood seemed to awaken again and Alice could smell it.

The old woman lifted the third cloth up, and, pulling up a small bowl, put it inside. Then she added in some of the liquid and set it alight. All there watched the flames. The cloth burned poorly, folding over on itself when it reached the liquid at the bottom of the bowl.

The old woman gestured to Alice to hold out her hand with the egg, then suddenly closed Alice's fist around it, and snapped the egg open. The yoke and white slid down her hand and onto the cloth.

Then something very strange happened.

The cloth caught fire again. The blue flame rose once and then became a white one that curved over the cloth. The three of burned while the three of them stared.

"What does it mean?" the Nurse asked.

It took the witch a moment to answer.

"What it means is that something very bad is going to happen to you. Something you cannot avoid, something you cannot foresee, will greet you once in your life and will not let you go. You might think you can escape it, but you cannot. You will not die from it, but someone near you will, and you will be the reason they die. That is what this, all this means."

The cloth continued burning silently in the gathering dark.

Time to go. The Nurse stood up. Slowly, Alice followed.

They made their way out of the grotto, to the carriage. The Nurse sat back on the seat with exhaustion.

And back in the grotto, back into the dank reaches where the light would not reach, the old woman lifted the first of the two remaining clothes off the table, and reached down from the floor. She began to twist the twigs with her fingers, and soon the rags were taking the shape of another figure to place about her. Her eyes watched the entrance, and in the darkness they glittered, gleeful.

Someone was shaking Alice awake. She was in the coach, back at the House.

"Wake up my Lady!"

The Nurse stood above her. Alice sat up, surprised. She had slept all the way home in the darkness, not even waking when the city gates had shut behind them.

"Oh my Lady, something terrible has happened!"

Alice struggled for her composure, answered.

"What? What is it?"

"It's your father, my Lady!"

"My father? What of him, yes?"

"He's missing my Lady! The Houseman was so worried, he thought you were both missing, and now we're back but without him!"

Her father? Missing? He would not venture out at night by himself. Had he been missing since noon? Alice looked out the window. The black night was no place to be by yourself. She made a decision.

"Tell the town watcher to call for others to be on their look out for him."

The Nurse nodded and bustled out, helping Alice from the seat as she went. There was no reason for her father would be out of house so late. No reason that would give her comfort, in any case.

Alice's wedding was held in the newly finished Canice's Cathedral, high on one of the hills overlooking the town. The Castle occupied the other hill. The treadmills with their blind men were nearly all gone and just the last few masons were needed. She stood at the top of the aisle beside William. Minus her father, of course, but that was the sorrow in the midst of all this.

William was pragmatic. She had seen him wash a horse down with that attitude, and supposed it was the best way. She blinked at the slightly drunk figure of the Bishop in front of her.

The Cathedral was quiet, lit by candles and torches, the Bishop's Latin winding around them like the wind around the cathedral. The local populace weren't allowed in, today or any day.

Alice let herself think on the Business. She had sat down with the clerk yesterday and gone through everything.

"Here you are, m'Lady," he had said, handing her the ledger.

Alice had been silent for a long time, taking it in. He had watched her face reading the figures, she had given nothing away, except becoming a little pale.

"The properties in Kilkenny, seven now, soon to be ten, are doing well, and have developed into nice little businesses, especially since the staff have been improved. There is much less money being pocketed by the house masters in the brothels, for example."

A pause, and he went on.

"There is a large volume of cash being made in the lending house. If I may say, when such a sum of money is being managed, then it has a way of taking care of itself."

That was a sentiment not worth a pig's bollix, thought Alice that night. Money stood still by itself, lost its glitter all by itself. She had looked at it a long time, those numbers written down in front of her, and its volume and gleam had faded the longer she had looked. It was a large amount of money, but there was more out there. They could do better, they could always do better. She thought again about the Castle. Imagine having them take a loan! She would be able to charge any interest she wanted! Take care of itself! That clerk should be thrown out in the street as her wedding present!

She decided she was going to enjoy being married, with more freedom to enjoy. She would be raised to the eyes of Society now. There was a cough from somewhere behind her from the guests, all this new nobility. All duly invited, of course. The Earl of Ulster, even.

These men had apparently served with the King on the battlefields against the infidels in the Holy City. They had led battalions, planned strategy and watched from the hills. Now settled on their estates, they sought to maintain their holdings and to show their wealth and status. There was a very large chance that war would break out with France. There was always a call for it, particularly with the French causing strife. All of these newly rich would need money, with interest. She could supply it, lots of it, and would be very happy to do so.

And after that, what would there be to stop her being great, and staying that way? "Dame" Alice, even?

William's hand rubbed against hers and she chanced a quick glance at him. Tall, like her father. Fair haired, fleshy. Blue eyes that did not seem deep, but not watery. His hand on hers was warm. His thumb ran down her curled forefinger, then made its way slowly back up, until it hid itself in the warm darkness of her palm. She aimed to speak to the clerk before the week was out, aiming to set out terms of lending to the nobility, and to see if business might be engorged that way. Their world would expand. Oh yes. Money and marriage; she was going to enjoy her new life.

Alice and her household stood at the front door to bid William welcome. He brought five servants, two men, two women and a boy, horses and their saddles, plate and pearl, and several cloths that would be useful for warming the house. Alice was regal and solemn. Her hair was tied back in a new style. As he came up the steps she and the household bowed low and long.

Kneeling, Alice saw only his feet on her floor, placed firmly with confidence. The shoes were pale tanned leather, soft and unstained from the rain outside.

"I say to you my wife, rise and welcome me."

Alice slowly rose to her full height, such as it was, and her grey eyes looked into his blue ones.

"Were it the will of God, my father would be here to bid you welcome to this house. In his place, I give that which was his to give."

She held out the large key, which was for the front door, and the ring of her father's.

When she took it off his cold white hand, she could not cry. Only later, alone, had she felt. But she was soon to be a wife, so she could not feel for long.

"Take the key of this house, of which you are now master. Take the ring of my beloved Father, that in his place, your place may now be."

William took the items with due solemnity and the parties bowed again. The husband and wife, rising, looked at each other. William reached down and took her hand. Alice nodded and led him to the centre of the hall, where food and drink were waiting.

The servants mixed and moved around them to settle in the new lord. Alice and William sat down to the best of the plate that the house had to offer. William cut the meat from the bone for Alice, and she acknowledged his husbandry with a quiet smile. He leaned forward and spoke quietly into her ear, so that he could be heard over the noise.

"How goes the house, my Lady?"

Alice saw the question, rightly, as one of management. She began.

"The tavern here is well attended and has a full cellar for the next three months, with taxes and tithes paid for four weeks to come. There were four girls for the customers but one has died of the pox two days ago, none of the others show any signs of it however and word of the death has not spread. This house has a full pantry and cellar. We have plate preserved in the attic, as well as some mother of pearl, much silver and some gold. The pantry holds meat for three days at any one time, with wine and beer for five days. There are sheets and bedding so that we may provide lodging for 20 people if it should be seen to be necessary. There are five books of my father's in our native language to be had in his old bedroom, now our room." She looked at him, unsure. "Is there anything further, my lord?"

"I will need to speak to the…"

Alice lifted her index figure to the First Clerk, who was waiting a few feet away. He walked over to William's left and produced several ledgers, speaking quietly.

"Be sure," Alice had instructed him, "to mention the benefits of giving loans to the King's men for the Scottish war. Let there be no doubt in his mind that it is the best path."

She didn't eavesdrop, as it would be unladylike. Instead she lifted her goblet and found her eyes watching the new staff.

William listened to the clerk, who skilfully gave the major details. It was promising, indeed, but not as promising as he had hoped.

"If I may please be so bold, Sir, is this not to your liking?"

"I had been of the impression that the manner of the loans was to personages of greater…. renown."

"Sir, there is talk about among circles that there will soon be increased warfare by the King's troops in Scotland. Should this prove to be the case, there will be an increased need for funds, a need we are," he gestured to the ledger, "in an excellent position to facilitate."

Alice had heard the word Scotland. She paused to listen. Say yes. Come on, come on, say yes.

William was not expecting this idea, but now that it was put before him, it seemed astute. He slowly nodded.

"Examine your figures fully and let me have more indications in the morning."

"Aye, Sire," said the clerk and bowed away.

William turned back to his wife.

"An excellent man, that clerk. Your father must have found him a great asset."

Alice smiled.

"To be honest, he never mentioned him."

William sat in the house by the fire, with a cup of wine beside him. His place was set at the dormant table, with other tables set up for the others. The room was small, warm and dark, with furnishings to soften it. The place was comfortable, but he didn't feel the Master here.

When they had found Alice's father, he had suffered a broken bone outside the city gates. Seeing as no one found him until the morning, he was

14

already doomed, and had a bad week before being called to his Maker. William frowned in the dark. Kyteler was a superb businessman and a skilled negotiator. His ability to get money out of those tight-fisted pox ridden sons of whores was a gift. It was to be handed over to William as the inheritor of the business. The intention had been to have him slowly introduced.

But this was not to be. Kyteler was gone, his stone engraved and stamped, and so the smooth handover was lost. Good for them both that the marriage had been arranged before the death, otherwise the wedding would have been delayed and much more precarious. As it was, all went from her father to William, with no leave to take of King or country other than the usual fees upon marriage.

The house was quieter without him. His manner had been to rule without saying anything. His presence would have changed the rhythm of the house just by being in it, and now that was gone. At least Alice had been able to be strong of character. She had not cried for days, she had not taken to her room and refused to eat, she had not shunned visitors nor her duties as lady of the house, she had been all to him she had been before. But she was different in some way.

William was not a man for delicate dealing. His way was to say as he saw and to suit himself accordingly. But Alice's soul seemed more silent. Secretive.

The fire glittered beside him, and Alice entered.

She took her seat. He watched as she kept her eyes lowered and took up her sewing. It was growing dark – she would not be able to do much in the gathering dusk, but she would be here for a little while. Watching that quiet face, he wondered again what she was thinking.

Alice pierced the needle though the fabric again and again, concentrating on getting clean thread and keeping the pattern. She watched as it grew in her hands. Were her Nurse here, she could expect a slap on the hands for any inattention. But the Nurse was not here. The Nurse was old and had taken to her bed earlier and earlier in an effort to ward off the chill. It had reached her hair, made it white. Alice kept her lines straight and true.

She was well able to sit with her husband now. The first night she had sat with her him, she had been unsure.

"How is my husband?" she had asked.

"I am well, my wife," William had replied. He had spoken about his day in town, and looked back at her.

Alice looked back at him, then down at her sewing.

After five minutes of silence, William had sat back into his seat.

After days of this, she finally became aware of his anger. He sat with an air of furious anticipation, awaiting her lack of response. She had been amazed; what should she be doing?

On the sixth day, the tables were put away and they sat again at the dormant.

"...written as it was in the document."

"In what, my Lord?" asked Alice.

"The document, the one produced earlier that day."

Alice smiled a smile, free from all artifice or guile and asked another question. Before long her husband's anger was all smoothed and another problem was solved. She sat beside him tonight with no worry of him.

"So how does this evening find you, my lord?"

"It finds me well, my wife. This afternoon's meeting went well with the clerk, in that the deeds are confirmed for the building. However, the dates were another matter."

The matter in question was a mortgage between the Kytelers and another family, the Fitzroys. They had granted the mortgage to them about 20 years ago. The payment details of a mortgage were harsh: there was no concept of partial ownership, and property could revert to the lenders up to and including the last day of payment, which was a time of great fear.

Alice knew the Fitzroys; they spoke Norman French too and kept a French house. She had had social calls to and from their young daughter, Louisa, who soon would be married herself. Louisa was very pretty. She lifted her head.

"The dates, my Lord?"

"The dates on the mortgage were as clear as day, instead of following anything like a lunar or unclear method. There's no chance of misunderstanding."

The house owned by the Fitzroys was at Kieran's Lane, just off the main thoroughfare of the town. Anyone who had such a house would have access to all those who walked on down the lane, and also on the main thoroughfare as the house bordered on to the main street as well. Alice bit her lip. She liked that house, very much. She had seen it when calling onto the girl, especially to thank her for gifts received on her wedding. Also, that house was as near to the riverbank as their home here.

"You're sure there is no possibility of confusion? The dates are as clear as can be?"

"Yes, there's no confusion, on the Sabbath it returns to them."

"Is there no way they might be persuaded to forgo their last payment? No way at all?"

He looked at her.

"What has occurred to you?"

Alice sewed on, her lines strong.

16

On Sabbath day, the morning was bright and clear. The air was cold and untouched by smell yet. Louisa and her family dressed in their highest finery and made their way to Church. She wanted very much to have her mother sitting beside her this morning, for likely it was for her betrothed William de Percival, the young son of a Norman knight to be there. It was rare for a betrothed to see the lass before the wedding, but William's father was still unsure regarding the dowry, and so the matter dragged on.

The sermon seemed to go on and on. Eventually, leaving the Cathedral, the family carriage was making its way down the hill, when it came across a man lying across the dirt path. The driver made to stop, and her father put his head out the door.

"What is it, man?"

"A beggar man, Sir. He's lying in my way, Sir."

"Is he alive or dead?"

"Happen I don't know, Sir. Should I drive over him?"

"Certainly not! We are civilised people; we do not ignore the unfortunate in that way. Please get down and pull him to one side."

The driver slowly made his way down the carriage and approached the beggar.

"How now, let's be having ye!"

Quicksilver quick, there was a blade between his collarbone and his flesh. He gave out a roar and fell back. The beggar man got up, all recovered, and quickly took the reins.

"What on earth is this?" squawked the head of the household. And as the driver used the whip, the carriage soon sped up and the family disappeared from sight.

Their disappearance caused a stir. Eventually news of them reached the City.

"So what happened?" asked one old woman to her neighbour.

"They were found, a good two day walk from the city. The thief had thrown them out of the carriage, the parents, maid and child."

"Not Miss Louisa?"

"No he kept her! Held her at knife point he did, drove around with her in the back for a few hours, she says, then just dropped her back!"

"Just dropped her back! With no infringement on her honour! A likely story!"

"What you mean?"

"I think she's been tupped, well and truly, and she's being a mind to hide it to preserve her honour!"

"No!"

"She's betrothed to that Percival fellow, isn't she? Stands to reason, with her honour at stake she'll do all she can to keep the standard up!"

"But to lie about such a thing!"

"I heard, that she was no modest maiden, but instead had a blush raised before he was done with her!"

"No! So she just... well I never!"

Nothing had happened to Louisa, not a thing. She had been deposited back to the spot where her family was, untouched and unharmed, just as she said. But now she and her family were 'bad luck'. Not a single person believed her. They all believed she had been raped and was shameful enough to still pass herself off as a virgin. Disgraceful!

Louisa's father read the letter from the Kytelers, with a trembling hand. The end payment of the house had not been kept. This was the last payment of the mortgage on the house. Until every payment was received, the house belonged to the Kytelers. If the payment was not received on the right date as stipulated by the agreement, the house could and did return in ownership to the Kytelers. Therefore they would give notice to them that failure to pay meant that ownership of the house was reverting to them immediately. No appeal would meet with success. It was true that the family had been excellent debtors, of that there could be no doubt. But the terms of the indenture mortgage were more than clear. And the date had been passed by approximately two days. The matter would not be allowed rest. Also, please pass on my compliments to Miss Louisa on this most trying time.

Louisa was beside herself. The news had reached her both publicly and privately that William de Percival was not willing to continue with the betrothal. Publicly had been by a strong message received by their houseman (their houseman! The shame of it). Privately had been by a whispered conversation with William de Percival near a corner of the Church garden soon after morning matins.

"I cannot," he whispered.

"But!"

"I cannot! Do not ask it of me, if you were true you would not ask it of me," he said, his hand shaking on the tombstone, before disappearing into the shadows of his watery love.

This meant that she had no safety net, no expectation of security and almost certain destitution. It also meant that there was no chance of his family paying a penalty clause for the late payment and thus retaining their home. Within a matter of a few weeks the security her parents had worked years for was gone. Their home lost, their family lost, their future lost. Her father sent messages to all they knew. None could offer money. Many

18

offered board and assistance. After an evening spent bitter by the fireside, letters of refusal clutched in his hand, he had been obliged to write to the most generous one, accepting. The family were to leave, the house to return to the original owners, the Kytelers. Louisa left the house, head held high, but smelled on the air a finished life.

Alice had a small banquet that evening on their departure, a small affair. William was quiet beside her. A little afraid. He noticed William de Percival and his family in attendance, and did not have courage to wonder. When he held her that night in their bed, he felt her still and waiting, as always, and let her sleep. He had no taste for her that night, and for days afterwards. If she noticed, she gave no sign.

Chapter Two

The Year 1317

With a final shove from the men, the boat docked in the port of Kilkenny. Ropes were thrown from ship to shore, and the sailors quickly tied the vessel into place. The stevedores called out their usual greeting.

"What ho, how goes she?"

"She goes well enough, but not well for some!" laughed the men. The sea was a mighty force, enough to steal a Bishop's dignity.

A door onto the top deck opened. Bishop Richard Le Drede stepped out with his two priests, and surveyed the small port before him. He took a deep breath, and silently prayed.

Oh Lord, I thank you for my safe arrival. Grant that I may spread your sanctity and holy judgement upon these people. Let the Law of the most Holy Father go forth and be heard throughout the – what on earth?

"Sorry Father, mind if I get past?" the sailor said, carrying a huge box in front of him.

"Yes I do, you heathen! Stay where you are and know your place!"

The rest of the crew burst out laughing. Furious, he turned and stomped down the gangway, a small man with little feet, little hands and a furiously large belief in himself.

So it was that the Bishop first set foot in Ireland.

"Come Brothers," he said, recovering himself. "Let us to the Palace."

A fellow priest at the port met the three men. The clean-shaven young man greeted his new Bishop with at least some show of respect. He knelt on one knee and bowed his head.

"Most Holy Father, may I welcome you most humbly to Kilkenny."

The Bishop looked with a smile he hoped was friendly, but in truth was thin and prissy.

"Thank you my son. What is your name?"

The young man lifted his head.

"Friar John Clyn, my lord."

"Friar John, I thank you for your kind welcome."

The Friar gave an enormous smile and stood, quickly walking them to a waiting carriage.

The Bishop and the two men sat inside. He looked with surprise as the young Friar sat down beside him. Familiar!

He looked out the window as it moved through the streets and frowned.

"You are unhappy, my Grace?"

"Utterly disgraceful, the people living in filth, as usual. Their poor moral states and their poor living states are one and the same."

"Oh, we have many attempts to assist these poor souls from their fallen state, your Grace."

"Yes, I know. Working with them. Living with them. Praying with them. And even fighting for them! Of course, that will soon be put to a halt, but still."

A pause.

"Are you from France, your Grace?"

"I am English, Friar Clyn, I came to the Papal Court on foot of my scholastic achievements."

"Indeed your Grace! Well done!"

"Oh, it was not my humble nature, but God's, that brought me to his Holiness's attention. Some advice for you Friar Clyn; never give up on an argument, but stay and continue until the battle is won. It is a tactic that has impressed many, I can assure you."

"I do not doubt it, your Grace."

"Of course, we must always be mindful of the power the Church needs to save men's souls," said the Bishop, lifting a gloved hand to his nose to block out the smell.

It was so different at the Court. There, the magnificence of the Holy Father was visible for all to see. Temporal power was nothing before it. Heaven and salvation were its gift to give. Crucial to all this, however, was its power. If they did not have that, then the Church was like a lamb against the wolf.

The carriage hit a massive bump in the road. Dear Heart, where had he arrived!

Later that day, the Bishop sat in the Cathedral while mass went on. The Cathedral was the jewel in the crown of the diocese. He was horrified by it. Firstly, it was small, and squat, at least compared to what he had left behind. The windows were small and the Rose window was ugly. There was an actual round tower outside which was so quaint and stupid Richard had laughed out loud. The entrance commonly used was not good enough for him. The larger west door, he was told, was only used on the morning of Easter Sunday. That would have to change.

"Isn't it beautiful?" whispered Friar Clyn. The Bishop didn't answer.

Added to that, the Cathedral was not well kept. There were beggars outside the Church door. They were for some reason permitted onto the Church grounds. Could you imagine? He knew he was far from civilisation but not this far!

All these people were ugly. Richard sat on his throne and sulked. If he was back at Court the pews would be filled with nobility in finery, all attentive. But all he could see here were scurvy-ridden merchants and a few barons. There was a cough somewhere about him as the singers finished one song and started another. If he were home, he would be hearing singers above him pouring out their worship. Instead, here, he…what was it he was hearing?

It wasn't a hymn, at least not in Latin. French! They sang hymns in French! Disgraceful! A foul, sick language to be presenting to God's ears. He put a hand to his mouth and shook his head.

He felt a wave of grief. They have soiled the face of the Mother Church, he thought. They have made her a stained maid, with dirt on her face and soil on her feet. They will seek to reduce my strength too, to harm her further. No. No! I will not stand idly by and see her wounded! I will not permit her to be disgraced or humiliated! I will see her proud again! I will not be weak! I will stand; I will defy! I will defend her! I will make her powerful again, and see to it that she and I rule among these men!

He stood up.

"Your Grace?"

The Bishop was not listening. He walked out of the Cathedral, followed quickly by the two priests and Friar Clyn. The singers continued on.

The Bishop stood at the entrance to the Castle, its tall grey towers high above him. This was the administrative centre for the Church in Kilkenny. Hence, Bishop Le Drede had custody of the Castle when he arrived. Now, he thought, I will rebuild the Church's power.

He stomped in, his small stature making him look like a little boy.

The guards standing at the door looked with alarm at the man who approached them, flanked by the three Franciscan priests. The man came to a halt and looked at them. After a moment's silence, he spoke.

"I am the Bishop Le Drede, and you will open the door!"

All right, thought one of the guards. All you had to do was ask. He leaned over and opened it; it wasn't locked.

Richard walked into the stone flagged entrance and turned to Friar Clyn.

"You will show me around the Castle."

It was not a request. Friar Clyn nodded, and began to lead the Bishop and the entourage out of the foyer and into the Castle proper.

Eventually they came to a solid oak door.

"What have we here?"

"These, your Grace, are the rooms of Administration."

"And what happens here?"

"This is where the Church records births, deaths, marriages, tithes, collections, cases against sinners, court dates, all matters of records."

"Ah, very good. Lead on."

Friar Clyn opened the door. Immediately the noise of men talking and arguing could be heard. Bishop Le Drede swept in, and the room went silent. Who was this?

"I am Bishop Le Drede, and I will speak to the scribe here."

A figure in black scurried forward. Le Drede regarded the bent head before him.

"You will bring to me all your current records, and all of the recent receipts for entries."

The figure at his feet looked up with a frightened look in his eye, but then scurried away out of view. While he was waiting, the Bishop examined the other occupants about him. A sorry looking bunch, he thought. He singled out one fellow in particular.

"You there, what is your name?"

The man lifted his head at the question.

"I? Why, I am Arnold Le Poer."

"And is it normally your custom, Le Poer, to take your wine so early in the day?"

"Huh? And what business is it of yours?"

The Bishop opened his mouth to answer, when the clerk returned. He handed to Le Drede two slim volumes.

"What is this?"

The clerk gestured mutely.

The Bishop slowly realised. These were the records? Only this, for a vast and complicated sea like Kilkenny? He turned the pages in front of him, horrified.

"You are not happy, your Grace?" asked Friar Clyn.

"Not happy? There is almost no record system at all!"

The Bishop could forgive poor or half-hearted records, but this was terrible. But he did not want to make a fuss in front of these men. Lord knows what a loose tongue would do in a room like this. But wait... why was he attempting to placate these men in the first place! They should be made leave immediately, to earn an audience with the Bishop. Away with them!

"I want this room emptied," he announced to all about him. "You are to leave immediately!"

Shock ran across the faces about him, and the Bishop was delighted to see their anger. Money-changers in the Temple, indeed!

With rumbling complaints, they left the room. Friar Clyn leaned forward to the Bishop.

"Your Grace, some of these men are important to the Church, and their disgruntlement may tell badly against us!"

"Let them! They are not as important as the Church my good man and need to learn a sharp lesson!" he said, watching that Le Poer fellow leave his place slowly, with many a complaining look. Eventually the room was empty.

Richard looked at the room, to the overturned seats and wine covered benches.

"Now! That's better. Money-changers out of the temple, hey?" he said. Friar Clyn nodded, miserable.

The best part of an hour was then spent reviewing the papers that were there. The registering of judgements in particular was paltry. The Bishop understood that the last Bishop was a Royal Appointee, and a former Treasurer of Ireland. How did such a man call this a standard? How? They would not even know the judgement of their own courts, never mind how much they had collected, or needed to collect. The records of collection of tithes were poor to say the least. The Bishop did not care so much about that, so long as the money was collected, he knew it was all right. But his position was made more difficult by the fact that he did not know who had given what. To collect without this knowledge next year would make his job very difficult.

Eventually the Bishop had risen from his chair.

"And now my brothers, we will visit the dungeons."

Friar Clyn sounded frantic as they all made their way down the stone steps.

"You see, your Grace, the dungeons contain all those guilty of offences."

"You mean sacrilege, heresy, patronage and perjury, as well as, ahem, other unsavoury matters."

"Yes, your Grace. Therefore these men and women may be very unpleasant to see and hear!"

They were down the spiral steps now, into the dungeon proper. The Bishop let the guard open and close the gate behind them before he spoke, giving Friar John a look of calm patience.

"We are here to do the Lord's work on earth," he said. "Therefore I cannot be afraid, for I have on my side-"

"Hello my lover! Come, watch me sleep with the devil's cock!"

screamed a woman.

"-Christ!"

The hag threw herself against the bars of the cell, her eyes wild, her teeth black in her mouth. She reached out her arms to the Bishop, who merely raised his chin at this fallen thing, and ignored her.

"My lover!"

"Indeed," he said dryly, and turned to Friar John. "The rest?"

"Over there," said Clyn his hand over his mouth. The bodies, of which there were three, hung in various positions.

"This one," said Le Drede, pointing to a girl of twelve years of age.

"She stole from a chapel, your Grace," said the jailer, lowering the knife.

"This one?" he said, standing beside a man of about forty, who was held in irons, including one around his mouth that he had to hold up with both hands or his jaw would have been slowly ripped off.

"Guilty of adultery your Grace."

"This one?" he said, looking at an old man of indeterminate age, but with grey hair.

"Questioned the Holy Trinity."

"Very good. Carry on!"

He swept from the room.

And made it back up the stairs and into the reception rooms before he threw up. The smell, the smell! He could stand the sight and the sound but the smell was always too much for him. He hoped very much no one had seen, but felt somehow that it was. He made himself sit up straight in the chair and sniffed. He must be strong. Upon such things was authority built. He would now go to his Palace on the outskirts and see the way of things there. They would all be looking to him for guidance. He would need to be strong.

Watching his departure from a window, Friar Clyn sighed. Lord help you, he thought, because you certainly are unable to help yourself.

The Palace was near the Cathedral. A guard stood outside it. The Bishop sat in the carriage for a moment, looking at the building. It appeared acceptable enough. He and the two priests descended and stood. At this point, a door opened and a manservant, also a priest, exited.

"Your Excellency," he said, and knelt.

The Bishop gave the man his ring to kiss.

"This way, please Sire," said the man, gesturing inside.

Thus did Richard enter his new home. He first made his way to the library of his predecessor; his library now. The room was small. Books of accounts were on one side, with religious works on the other. At least, he hoped they were religious.

"What is this?"

"I believe it is a book of Norman Verse, Your Grace."

"And this?"

"Poems, Your Grace?"

Richard frowned, and began pulling books down from the shelves and dropping them on the floor.

The man behind him cleared his throat gently.

"May I ask your instructions with regard to these books, my Lord?"

"You are to use them to start a fire in this room, in that grate," he said, pointing to the fireplace, "immediately."

The man swallowed once, but did not hesitate. Each book on the wall was a year's salary, and cost an enormous amount of hours to produce. So be it.

"At once your Grace." He turned and began to add the texts, page by page, to the fire.

Richard turned from the shelves, and walked from the room. The manservant, seeing this, called out to a boy to continue burning the books, while he ran after the Bishop.

The Bishop walked into the main reception room, and stopped.

"This room is far too small! How can I impress a visitor with the might and power of the Lord's Church if I fail to show might and power?"

"Yes your Grace."

The Bishop pointed to the tapestry on the wall.

"That is a most unholy and irreligious image!"

"But, your Grace-,"

He reached out and ripped off the tapestry from the wall. It tore in half when he did so, and he reminded himself of the Curtain in the Temple. I do the Lord's work!

"Bring me the accounts! I will see all the account books of this Palace immediately!"

The manservant moved to obey.

"But first bring me pen and paper. I will need to extend my authority on the fallen brothers of our order. I will need to show them who is in control."

The manservant looked at him.

"And how will you do that, your Grace?"

Bishop Le Drede stood in the middle of the room and heard his voice ring out.

"I am God's man on earth! I will call a Synod, where the priests will gather and hear my voice, and know my judgement. I will visit every Church in the land, and let them know that they are being watched."

The manservant nodded, and made, again, a move to obey.

"But first, get someone in here to light a fire with those books. It's cold in here."

The Bishop watched the flames in the fire and planned. His entire life, he had succeeded where others had failed. He had seen the trials of the Templars, the Pope's beloved. They had grown so assured, so confident, but unprotected from the Unholy One. The Church had used the Inquisitorial system against them. Evil must have no defence, no refuge. If it could seek out the beloved of the Holy Father, where else could it make its home?

Richard still found it hard to believe the signed confessions he had read. They would have gone to their graves with their secrets but for the torture. They would have died with their souls black. Torture had been the only way to get them to talk. Torture sanctioned by the Church was pure, he knew. It was the only way that a soul could be saved at all, sometimes. But it was such a hard thing to do. He had such a hard life. Self-pity touched him, and he watched the books burn, morose.

He knew the ways of the Church and he knew it was his home. He owed it all his devotion and valour, all of him. When he had been appointed to the Papal Court, it had been the happiest day of his life. He had sent word back to his father in England, and had received no reply. In the end, he had been glad. He had never liked the man anyway.

Chapter Three

The Year 1281

Alice discovered she was pregnant the day she lost a maid.

She woke with a start that morning. All were sleeping around her, still and dark before the dawn. What had woken her? William lay asleep beside her, his hair over his eyes. Then she heard it again. A bird call outside the window.

Why was it startling? She was afraid, she was afraid to move, it seemed so threatening.

When a moment later William had stirred and had pulled her close to him in his sleep, she gasped with relief. She had made the day start then so she could brush off the foolishness. She did not dress in her usual black, but instead a pale floral dress and matching headdress. She wore more colour on her face than usual. She was always pale, but seemed more so this morning.

They were all leaving the house today, to attend the Lord's celebration of May Day. Nobles and merchants were going out of the city gates for a few hours to enjoy the sun. Hence her floral dress. Alice and William took the carriage, with a maid and a houseman walking along with them. The City gates were crowded, as always. Alice glanced out the window, and saw the particularly fine carriage of the Le Poers, merchants of the city, and marked the man for further associations. The journey took them past the river, towards the new township of Callan.

When they arrived, the area was a flat piece of grassland, with excellent exposure to the sun, near the river and surrounded by trees. She could smell marigolds and honeysuckle, and the sun shone with a real strength. Everyone seemed happy in the sunlight, and the air smelled of milk. There were as promised minstrels and music and jugglers, with mead and beer being served and a large number of families enjoying the day.

They came to a stop near the trees and alighted, the maid and the houseman arriving at a trot shortly afterwards.

"Will you come for a walk with me, Wife?"

"I will indeed, my husband."

They headed away, strolling across the grass. Alice thought it delightful, she had never seen some of it before. She saw a ring game, and William and she watched the players for a short while. There were also hen fights and cock fights. Alice was in a good mood, good enough to forget her earlier fragility.

The day was a blue brightness, with the air sweet and fresh. Alice wondered to herself that they were there outside. Was not disease and illness on the air? Still, it might be all right.

The couple reached the carriage, the maid serving the food.

As they sat there, Alice noticed a bird land near the cloth. Before she could speak, the bird quickly hopped forward and took one of their good silver knives.

"That bird stole our knife!"

"What, a bird?"

"Yes, and it flew into there!" she said, pointing to the wood. She called to the maid.

"You! Go in there and get that knife back, and be quick about it!" she snarled, almost baring her teeth. The pair of them watched as the young girl nodded and began running into the woods.

The girl's name was Deirdre, and she was fourteen years old. She hadn't seen the bird, she hadn't seen where it had flown off to, but she had to just smile and nod in front of the Lady, who despised everyone who did not follow immediately what she was saying. The idea of the Lady being her mistress for the rest of her life was a nightmare. Especially at night, when in the dark, she would imagine what the next day would bring, panic could drown her.

She rushed into a clearing, and began searching the trees for any signs of silver or sparkle to let her know where the bird might have taken the knife. She scanned the trees above. Nothing here... no, nothing here. Did it seem that she had been here before? No, no not at all, for there was the fair proper, with all the jugglers and the cock fight, and her lady and her husband were sitting further down to her left. She continued scanning the trees, and moved back the way she came from. Alice was directly in front of her now, but she was hidden from the trees and so couldn't be heard. She could hear her mistress's voice but not what she was saying. Deirdre, knowing she wasn't observed, took the time to look at her boldly. Floral headdress,

29

sharp eyes that stared accusingly, thin mouth that rarely smiled, pointed unpleasant face, with a slim build to her that spoke of agitation. Deirdre felt her lip curl slightly at her, and then turned back when she saw Dame Alice lift her head and frown at the woodland, as if she knew she was being watched.

What Alice had been saying was that she felt uneasy after the food, and that she hoped she was not sickening for anything. William did not respond, but silently hoped that it meant she was with child.

Deirdre took a new path, away from the fair. She wondered down it for a few minutes, and then coming to a clearing, began scanning the trees for any signs of birds. How much did she hate that woman? There was something awful about her.

There was nothing in this clearing. There was probably nothing in any clearing, her mistress would be the only one to send a servant into the woods to hunt for a bird. All of Christendom in the way of birds could be in this wood! How was she to know where it was?

She was walking down another path, about half a mile away from the fair; too far to hear it, anyhow.   This path led to a large clearing. There was a stream running through it. Trees were set well back, with a lot of moss covering every stone. She didn't like this place, so deep in the woods like this. And then she saw it.

Near the stream, about ten feet up, there was a nest, with the knife sticking out of it. She stared at it for a moment. There seemed to be no easy way for her to reach it. Instead she was going to have to get over to the other side of the stream, climb up the tree, get the knife down, and then back over the stream. She thought of returning to her mistress without it, and felt the marks from her last disappointment still sting on her back. She swallowed, and began to make her way over.

There was a tree fallen over the stream, which provided an excellent makeshift bridge. She managed to make her way across it easily enough and walked to the tree. The bird had returned to it while she was crossing the bridge, but seeing her so close by, merely tilted its tail once or twice and flew off. Deirdre stood at the bottom. There was one branch about five feet up from the ground, and another above that at about two feet higher up. The nest was higher up again, just above the second branch. She rolled up her sleeves and tied back her skirt as much as possible, after making sure there really was no one around. Reaching up to the first branch, she managed to get a foothold there and start climbing up. She easily made it to the second branch, and there in front of her was the nest. She picked up the knife and hid it in her tunic. She had it!

She began making her way down the tree. Half way down, she realised she was going to have to jump. She braced herself and let go. She landed with the most awful thump on the ground. She rose to her feet and brushed herself down. The knife was still there, safe and well. She brushed back her hair, and made herself presentable. She began to gingerly cross over the river again.

From behind Deirdre, at ear level as if the bird was right behind her, came a huge cry from the bird. Startled, she stood still for a moment, and then kept going, not turning around. Eventually she reached the other side, and hopping down from the tree, fell badly on her left ankle. She looked back and there was the bird, black and white, as brazen as anything, looking straight at her. It tilted its head, getting a good look. And for a moment, Deirdre was afraid.

She moved quickly enough, but as she walked the pain in her ankle was sharp and sore. She did her best to ignore it, and just keep walking, but it soon became clear that the ankle was actually quite badly hurt. After a while she knew she would need some help. She managed to pick up a stick and kept on walking.

The day was getting late when she came back, and there were already some families leaving. Lady Alice and William were still sitting there as well.

"Finally!" said Alice, seeing her hobble out of the wood. "What on earth took you so long?"

"The bird's nest was quite some way away, my lady," answered Deirdre, producing the knife and holding it out to her.

Alice looked at it. Deirdre's hand was filthy. So was the knife. She looked at the nervous girl, and felt the same need to hit her she always felt. Why were they always so cringing? She opened her mouth to Deirdre.

"So you thought I would want it now, after a bird has had it in its filthy nest and it gets warmed by the worms of a filthy maid? So you brought it back and thought I would just accept it! Get it washed the minute we get back!"

The girl nodded.

And so they began to make their way back, with William and Alice in the carriage as before, and Deirdre and Philip, the houseman, tagging along behind. The weather was beginning to get cold, and a few drops of rain were falling. Deirdre had left her stick behind her and so the party started off.

For Alice it had been a short journey in her carriage, when in fact it was close to three miles. Deirdre was in trouble immediately, hopping along. But she was clumsy, and nearly fell under the wheels of a carriage.

"Be careful!" growled the houseman. "They won't stop for stragglers!"

They continued on. Nightfall came along, with clouds that hung threateningly over the city. Rain fell, and the path turned muddy. Soon everything she wore was soaked, and she was shivering. She was falling behind too. She was crying in horror at all of this, seeing the carriage blithely go on without her, when she slipped again.

The driver behind her did indeed see her, but merely yelled at her. She was too tired and cold to move fast, and the carriage ran straight over her.

The houseman rushed, but it was already too late. The tiny little thing of a girl was dying, rain falling down her face as if she had been pulled up from a river. She did not seem to see either of them but instead reached for the knife tucked into her tunic. She seemed to press it into Philip's hands, or try to throw it away, he wasn't sure.

Philip saw this and called to their own driver to stop. William put his head outside the window.

"What is it?"

Philip went to the window to explain.

"The maid, my Lord, I think she's hurt."

William didn't hesitate.

"See to her then join us at home at once."

The houseman looked at him and then nodded slowly in the rain, and the carriage set off.

By the time he got to her he could see it was too late. He held the young girl's forearms as her eyes glazed over. He blindly wondered would she be missed, was there anyone to tell to see to it. He looked up and saw the carriage go through the gates into the city.

A few shocked locals had gathered around. They were the local peasants, those people who for one reason or another did not live within the city gates. A woman leaned forward to him.

"Is she dead Sir? We have an alchemist if you think it is needed?" she asked, concern and worry real in her voice.

Philip looked back at her, at this poor woman he had never met and who was offering him help. This was help offered to him by a stranger. He remembered the sight of the carriage going through the city gates,

He raised his voice to be heard over the rain.

"I fear it is too late for her, but you are very compassionate to ask. I will need to get a Holy Father. May I ask you to find one and bring him here?"

The woman nodded and was gone. The others crowded around the man and the girl, gawking, staring. Philip looked at them for a moment, and then turned his attention back to Deirdre. She was lying in the rain, the ground beneath her turning to mud. Very slowly he reached down and closed her eyes, and folded her arms on her chest. The skin on her hands was as cold as a stone, and he found himself thinking that she must be so cold. He looked up. Was there no home that would do as a temporary refuge? The rain seemed to pelt down harder as the question occurred to him, and he marvelled that they all continued to stand there staring.

The woman was back, running and panting, but alone.

"Sir, I have asked for the priest to attend us, and he will be along shortly, he must merely complete a matter at his home and find us then."

"Did he say what the matter was?"

"No, only that he must complete a letter to his Holiness and would be along shortly."

Philip stared at her for a moment and then nodded, looking back at Deirdre dead in the mud. A dead child on the road, and a letter to complete.

Philip looked up again.

"Is there somewhere we might bring her away from the rain?"

"We might bring her to my home."

Philip tried to lift Deirdre, but discovered that there are few things less easy to move than a cooling body. He and another man lifted her onto a rough carriage, and made the short distance to the woman's home.

She lifted the door latch and let them in ahead of her, Philip holding Deirdre's torso and the other man holding the legs. Philip found himself in a hovel, albeit a clean one. It was a rough lean-to made of wood, with a fireplace in the east wall that would have done nothing to block drafts. The table was bare of food, and the smell was minimal. For what it could have been, it was clean.

She put a cloth over the table, probably the only one she had, and the two men slowly lowered the dead girl. Once there, the other man merely turned and walked outside the house, saying no word, and leaving the three of them alone. The dead creature was soaked, water dripping from every limb and streaming from her hair, which had flecks of mud in it. The woman moved quickly about the place, stirring up the fire, lighting a candle or two. Philip had a better look about the room, and saw that it was as comfortable as possible. No animals inside, and there were some signs of finery – cushions, a tapestry. A very strange house.

He looked again at the dead girl. She was so young. She did not need to be dead. Since when was death ever necessary? Regret had not saved his mother, or his friend at ten years of age. Why would it have saved a young girl who had hardly felt the wind in her face?

The woman was watching him. He looked up at her and gave a small smile, as if he had been caught out. She returned the small smile.

She gestured to the fire.

"The priest will be here shortly. A cup of beer?"

She sat down on a stool, her back tall and straight. He slowly joined her, sitting down on the other side of the hearth.

The silence stretched around the three of them, with only the snap of the fire to break it. He looked at Deirdre, at the firelight playing on the dead girl's face. Still forever, now. He watched it closely, trying to see if it was in fact moving, but nothing. Instead, he seemed to see the shadows grow in her eyes, her chin, her neck. He felt the woman shift on her stool and he turned to look at her.   She was looking at him with something like alarm, holding out the cup of beer. He took it, bashful.

She spoke in quiet tones.

"I saw my father die one summer's day while attending to his Lordship and I to my Lady, a terrible death that made him drop his tray and spit and cry as he left us. And I nursed my mother here in this house, each day seeing her weaker and weaker, before she was in God's hands. I know death." She smiled for a moment, and then her voice hardened slightly. "But it's best not to look at them for too long. It does no good to see what you don't need to see."

He smiled slightly, and took a swig of beer, glad of the cold liquid, then looked around for something to say.

"So you live alone in this house?"

"Since my mother died, two months ago. I had been attached to the manor house in Waterford, as had my father as houseman there and my mother as lady's maid before she had me in wedlock. But when my mother was near death, I asked to join her here so that I might nurse her proper, as a daughter should. I couldn't think of leaving her, that was no way to be."

She looked away from him, looked back at the fire for a moment.

"So, you left the manor then?"

"Yes, I did, but they would not let me leave and come back. They said that they had no need for a lady's maid that would not stick to her duties and retain a place that would be welcome and wanted by others."

She looked at him, and smiled.

"So I left and came back here. Mother was near death and prey to every thief in the area. Just as I arrived, I found her at the mercy of those who insisted she owed them money, when she could not have left the house. I locked the door to them and put Mother to rest. She didn't live beyond two weeks of my arrival, but at least I could say right was done by her."

She refilled their cups. The fire played on her face, and for a moment she looked weary and sad. But then she composed herself again, and he found that she looked no more than 18. How old was she?

"And what of this child? How is it we have another visitor here in this house who will soon leave us? Not that she is not welcome, mind, but she has a story to tell as well, no doubt."

35

"Her name is Deirdre. Maid to Dame Alice Kyteler. She was clumsy and fell under the wheel of a carriage, and no good came to her." He said, harsher than he had intended, and took a swig.

"Good or no, she was a young lass, and such can be prone to mistakes. She has a kind face, was she kind? She looks kind."

"She was a girl," he said, as if that answered it. Then, after a moment, "She liked to sing. She would sing when putting the items out in the morning, and she had a nice voice. She would sing in the morning, and she seemed... cheerful enough."

The woman nodded.

The silence came over them again, the mood too sombre for talk. They sat and looked at the fire. Light played around them, as did their thoughts. It was warm and dark. Outside, somewhere, a dog barked.

The door opened. In stepped the priest, a soiled looking character with little teeth and a wide smile. Still, he smelled cleaner than most.

He shut the door after him, and seeing the beer, smiled wider. The woman moved to give him a cup, and he addressed himself to Philip.

"How now my good fellow, I see a calamity has come to this poor girl. What happened?"

"She was struck by a carriage on the road outside," answered Philip. "It was sudden."

The priest looked at the young girl dead on the table. He was not struck by how young she was, that was nothing new to him. Ah, me the poor souls, he thought. So many and so young. The poor things. The poor, poor things.

He lifted the cup to his mouth and drank it down.

"My thanks, my good woman," he said, in French.

"You are more than welcome," she answered. Philip stared at her, surprised. She speaks French as well, she's clearly been around nobility, the idea in his head before he knew of it.

The priest lit some more candles and knelt at the head of the dead girl. She was truly past now, her head lolling to one side and her jaw open.

The priest gave the signal to the other two, and all three of them were kneeling now, their heads lowered and their eyes closed.

36

There was no sound except that of the woman's skirts as she knelt and then that of the priest's sibilance as the Latin flowed from him. Just like the water from the girl, thought Philip, his head tired. The priest conducted the ritual, anointing with oil and holy water, and giving the last rites. Soon, very soon, it was over, and the matter was done. It seemed a very quick solution to what they were always told was a lifetime of sin, and meant as much as a tale told in haste.

The priest stood and then the other two followed.

He smiled and looked at Philip. After a moment, the other man looked into his pockets and produced some coins for him.

"She will need burial," said the woman.

The priest seemed surprised she spoke, and yet after a moment nodded.

"I can ask the graveyard Chaplin to bring her to the grounds and we can conduct a small service for a small charge," he said, and looked at Philip again. Philip looked back for just a moment, and then opened his pockets and gave the man all that he had, leaving just enough to make it through the city gates and walk back like a peasant to his home.

The priest was not happy with the amount that he got, but there was nothing else for it. He nodded sadly as he put the money away; a gesture no one assumed was due to grief for the girl.

"I will ask him to come directly," he said to the woman, taking his leave. The woman nodded, accepting that for a while she and the girl would be company. The door shut behind the priest quietly.

Philip knew it was time for him to go, too, but he found himself hesitating.

"I should depart also. You have done a great good here."

She shook her head silently.

"Will you be all right here on your own with her?"

"I'll be fine, with such a young girl, what harm could she do me?"

"You have done a great good here today."

The last thought that occurred to him was one he felt he should have asked already.

"May I be so rude as to ask your name?" he said, turning in the doorway.

She looked at him for a moment, her black hair curling around her neck.

"It's Petronella de Meath."

An hour later, Philip stood to attention in the hall of the Kyteler house before the chair of William. He had a pain in his back and his feet were wet from the long walk home, but he stood still and straight and gave no sign. There was no real anger on the part of his Lordship, merely a desire to get details from the younger man.

The hall was a room used for most if not all of the functions of the house. It bore many of the features of Petra's home but was vastly greater. There was the fireplace, the table (unusual in that it was dormant and freestanding, not a lean to put up as it was needed) and long seats. There were also several seats at one end of the room, at various heights. The highest was reserved for William and Alice, both being occupied at the moment. Alice looked like she had the potential to grow furious, but then she always did. She was no longer in her floral gown, but had returned to her more usual dark tunic and headband. She sat and looked at Philip like she could have him run though.

"Go on," said William.

"I saw that she had passed away almost immediately. I asked a local woman to get a priest, and when she returned she said that one was on the way. While we were waiting, we moved the girl's body to a house and there the last rites were given. The priest arranged to have the burial at small expense this night in the Churchyard outside the gates. I gave him a small recompense for his trouble and made my way back here." He was finished.

"Very well," said William. "Did she have any family?"

"I was not aware of any, my lord," said Philip. She may well have had people depending upon her for every penny, but no one knew anything of it if that was the case, and they would have a hard lot of it from now on no matter what.

"I see. That seems to be the end of it," said William.

"Not quite, I am afraid," said Alice. "There is the matter of the knife."

Philip stared back blankly.

"Was there any sign of the knife she was carrying? It was quite an expensive item and one that should not be lost, if possible."

Philip recalled the shocking sight of the dying girl pressing the item into his hand. He hid his remembered shock, and pulled out the knife from his tunic. It lay in his hand, heavy.

"Please excuse me, my lady, my lord, but I had not recalled this item. She pressed this into my hand as she lay dying, and unable to give words to what importance it may have, I did not give it thought, but instead put it safe away from my sight and therefore my mind. Please excuse me."

There was a heavy silence, intended to cause him shame.

"At least it is properly returned," said William. "See that it is cleaned and returned to use."

Philip recognised his dismissal.

"Very good my Lord."

Then he remembered about Petra, but decided that now was not the time. .

He put the knife back into the pile of the others, and left strict instructions for it to be cleaned to the highest standard. The kitchen boy, standing there slack jawed, had not said anything, but merely nodded. Philip had looked at him for a moment, fighting the urge to hit him.

The house was in darkness when Philip's duties were done. He went to his bed knowing his thoughts would whisper to him.

Once again he was on the dirt track, the girl stumbling beside him.

Once again he was nearest to her as he heard the bones break under the wood, the snap sharp and high.

And once again, he looked up for help; he saw the carriage move through the gates.

They left her! His mind roared in the dark silence. They moved away, bored in the cold and the rain, heading for their home with no more thought for her than to a dog on the street. The two figures in their coach, their torsos as cold as the body he had held. Cold hearts, untouched by fellowship. More dead than Deirdre. Lady Alice and her knife! The concern over his delay! Such high views for one so high born!

His anger was making him nervous; he didn't want to grow hot with the heat of it. Keep calm. He remembered Petra. He saw her leaning forward from the crowd, concern on her face. He saw her sitting in the grate, firelight playing on her face and hair, soft tones all about her. He saw her compassionate when none were compassionate beside her, and he was calmer.

Cooler, Philip saw what they had done to Deirdre. She was chattel, as was he, and their betters granted them no soul. The dark was beginning to claim him to sleep. This is the same dark Petra sleeps under, he thought. But the last thought he had before he fell asleep was the stark "They will never keep us safe. We must keep ourselves safe." And thus, his eyes closed.

Alice lay in the same dark as Philip. The colour of the darkness about her was brown, a wood-wet colour that stayed near her nostrils no matter how she shifted. She swallowed, sober. Her hands stayed deliberately away from her midriff.

She might be pregnant. She might be in the process of growing a thing inside. In the warm dark of her there was something else. It equally might not be, she could be imagining it. What if it was? What if its face growing inside her, as it slowly took over her organs, taking from her? It might hurt her; it might kill her, as she had killed her own mother in childbirth. Alice didn't believe she herself could be that weak, however; she considered herself made of different stuff. She mentally rushed a prayer out for her mother in Heaven, hoping the woman would leave her in peace.

She might be having a baby. The Nurse could raise it. She would need clothes, and the advice of the Nurse, aged as she was. She would need the carriage even more now and could not ride out. The child would be born in January, and the house would need warming for the winter. Food and fuel. There was also the business to be considered – she and William had planned a large dinner in their home for all the towns' merchants, to sweeten and smooth the channels of business. They still did not know if the Nobility, who very well might view it as an attempt to usurp their authority in some way, would approve of such a gesture.

A child. A son. William would be pleased. She must not lose it, on his behalf; she must ensure its safety. She must stay away from old straw, and drafts, and all that the nurse would advise her. She felt her eyes grow heavy, and she slept.

And across the town, men who did not know her name lifted the body of the Maid Deirdre. Carrying it with only the occasional grunt of effort, they came to a grave. Her body was thrown back into the dark soil as a puny fish is thrown back to sea. There were a few words, and less thought. And only Petra stood beside the priest and watched her go, sad for the loss of a life so young. By the morning, all was if it had never been.

Chapter Four

The Year 1317

Alexander Bicknor, Archbishop of Dublin and Royal Appointee, entered the large hallway of his home and greeted firstly his houseman, his dogs and then his secretary. The thin man stood beside the door, waiting to be noticed.

"Ah, Carpenter. How fares it with you?"

The small man nodded, grateful for the friendly welcome. He held an envelope in his hands.

"I have, Your Grace, details of the synod in Kilkenny."

His Grace paused, one glove on and one glove off.

"Ah, he sent the letter! Please, do not open it, but bring it into the office."

"Very good Your Grace."

Alexander finished handing over his cloak and gloves to the manservant, and then headed into the office. From the beginning, Le Drede appeared to be a disaster waiting to happen. He had thought it very foolish to appoint to the Irish Sea an English Franciscan from the Papal court. He therefore arranged for a full report from one of the attendees of the synod.

He thought the synod a perfectly sound idea. It was the best way to assert authority and ensure that everyone knew the sound of your voice.

He went into his office. The letter was sitting there waiting for him as instructed, unopened. He turned it over and broke the wax seal.

My Grace, it began.

I write to you from the diocese of Kilkenny, as instructed. As you are aware, Richard Le Drede, Bishop of Ossory issued a summons to all clerics, priests and members of the Holy Church to attend St Canice's Cathedral Church, Kilkenny. At this synod, he has deplored publicly the state of the diocese of Ossory, determining to those there gathered that it is 'lewd, sinful and gravely wrong' in its conduct and management.

He has become most condemning of all his priests, citing them for behaviour shocking and sinful. He also has raised a grave concern for heresy in the congregation.

Finally, the collection of taxes by the Crown is commonly cited as the reason that tithes cannot be collected for the Church, especially as we know that the recent shortages have left so many of the faithful without means for food and shelter.

In seeing the man that has here been speaking for some hours to us, I am called upon by you to exercise my humble judgement with regard to his character and nature. I do not do so lightly, and will do my very best to exercise full understanding of him.

He is decided and confirmed in his faith. He believes he is humble, in his own mind, but demands glory for the Church, and fears greatly any possible demotion of the Church.

He will seek victory not by means subtle or politic, but instead by warring with words and by reliance on Public Worship of the authority of the Church.

He will not plan but will act rashly and inopportunely. He does not guard for mistakes, or believe he will make them, but instead, will merely take on the mantle of warfare without thought. Therefore, he does not enjoy surprises or expect them.

He will not change his opinion or his belief in either his rightness or his methods.

He will not make friends for either the comfort of personal affiliation or for the sake of benefiting the Church. He dislikes music and stories, but will daydream. He is not unintelligent, but is lacking in the sensibility to see the result of his own actions on others.

This man will gain no backers other than those already supporting his goal. Therefore, both the English Crown and the Papacy support him, but the local authorities will defy him at every turn.

I supply a list of the Constitutions of Ossory, as decided upon on the 6th October 1317. As the extant list is quite extended in parts, what follows now is a summary.

1. *If any person is aware of any person preaching heresy in the diocese, they are to give that information to the Church in one month.*
2. *All undedicated clerical property to be dedicated within six months from last Michaelmas.*

3. Persons who cure souls and not being priests are within one year to obtain promotion to Holy Orders.
4. No one is to gain a vicarage unless he is a priest.
5. If someone is leaving a benefice, they shall nominate a replacement.
6. All concubines are to be put away from priests within a month, on threat of suspended and lose a third part of his salary. This comes on foot of several such commands, which have been ignored.
7. It is forbidden for laymen to farm on Church lands, starting immediately, on pain of the greater excommunication.
8. No priest may farm on Church lands except on the grounds of urgent necessity and with the Bishop's licence, and then for not more than five years.
9. No priest may collect tithes for their own benefit.
10. Laypeople may not debt collect from priests.
11. Those laypeople who seize those who seek the sanctuary of the Church are to receive the Greater Excommunication.
12. There are to be no more clandestine marriages, celebrated without posting the banns.
13. Any malicious defamation of a cleric is punishable by greater excommunication.
14. These charges have been raised with the consent of the clergy of the diocese.

My Grace, many of these charges arise from specific incidents of disobedience and lack of discipline from the clergy. While it is certainly the case that Le Drede seeks to impose discipline, it is far from certain that he will be able to impose it.

He is, as I have already stated, a man unwilling to negotiate. I therefore am of the opinion, that he will violate any and all good wishes of the men he leads before long.

I remain your humble servant.

Friar John Clyn

Alexander was immensely grateful to John. He had, as usual, been extremely useful to him in the provision of information. Alexander read the letter three times, and then sat back and thought. Le Drede seems to have made enemies all around him, he thought.

There was little or no telling what the groundless ambition of the man might bring about. If he could have his way Le Drede would be on the next boat back to France, but he was powerless to act. No, they had been visited by this penance. Who knew what would happen before it was over?

Chapter Five

The Year 1292

William got out of the carriage and ran into the house.

"Where is my wife?" he called to Petra, who gestured to the counting room.

Alice lifted her head from the desk when she heard him come in.

"Well?"

"We are close, very close."

"Where do you meet to talk?"

"In his private chambers."

"And who attends his Lordship while you are there?"

"His clerk, usually. There's also a second man, who appears to guard the door."

"The terms are finalised?"

"I have had several conversations with the clerk on this, and the terms so far have not been clearly stated. There are matters regarding the date of repayment that are not clear at all."

William looked away in the distance, seeing again the brief hurried conversation he had had with the clerk in the hallway before the door into the Lordship's chamber. His contribution consisted of the word 'Yes' several times, like a child. Half way through, he had become conscious of his own foolishness, and, shame of shame, felt his cheeks burn like a bride on her wedding day. The clerk, seeing this, felt bold enough to let his smile widen, briefly nodded good day, and was gone. William had left with his throat dry and angry.

Alice thought again for a moment. She dearly wanted to be there, but obviously could not go. William would need to bring terms with him. He would need to have in his hand details of the deal that they wanted (as well as the deal they could most realistically provide). It was therefore the only option left to them. She called to the maid for mead for William, and told her to bring the clerk. He would need his writing materials.

Petra looked at Philip.

"It's all right, he didn't see anything."

He cupped her face in his hands again.

Later that night, at a tavern bench near the city walls, the clerk was drunk in his cups.

"That woman would have the balls back from a bishop," he cried to the assembled mass, and hiccupped.

"She rules him, like a rider rules a horse!"

"And she looks the type to be ridden!"

"I'm serious!" The clerk was trying to make a point. "She's picking and poking and fusing about, she's like a bird, what's that bird, that likes shiny things...."

"A magpie! She's like a magpie, all eager and hungry and vicious for carrion!"

"She's a magpie!"

And the cheer went up again.

When William was next in his Lordship's chamber, he brought with him two things; one, a clerk, and two, the terms the House of Kyteler felt would be most advantageous. The Lordship and the merchant looked at each other, both seeing the change.

Then, after a moment, his Lordship smiled broadly.

Alice was waiting for them when they arrived.

"Well?" she asked.

"We have agreed most of the arrangements for the loan."

"Good! Oh, but what is left? Was there a delay?"

"Her Ladyship entered the room before we could conclude the matter," answered William, uncomfortable in a way he could not explain. "The discussion will have to be concluded at another time."

Her Ladyship! She would never intrude on her husband at his duties, especially when not expressly invited to enter. And with a slump, Alice saw that that was exactly what had happened. The negotiations had been going well with no clear escape for his Lordship, so an interruption had been quickly arranged. Or not. Either way it did not well for them.

No, that was an exaggeration. They had confirmed a great deal, really, there was only one sticking point – the date of the final payment of the loan. This would decide the calculation of the interest, and the dates of the payments they would be received, and therefore meant the body of the loan itself had yet to be scheduled. So it would still be early days before they could breathe easy.

Alice looked at her husband, standing with a shaky stance and with an air of hidden shame about him. His face was slightly pale. His composure is put out by this, she thought to herself.

She looked away, thinking.

The last negotiations took place in the Castle at the end of the summer. Alice had bid William good luck as he left, that night, with the details of their terms and the clerk Galrussyn beside him. The order to come at night had been a surprise. Those called to the Castle at night were usually criminals or scoundrels.

William took the carriage again, conscious of his wife's expectations of him. He watched the gates of the Castle open and close behind him. For a moment when the carriage stopped he waited. Suddenly he remembered Alice's father, the thin Dutchman's lowered eyelids looking at him as he watched William from a chair. Damn their unreadable eyes. He stepped out from the carriage.

Instead of being brought directly to the Lordship's chamber, William was first greeted by his Lordship's clerk.

"Good evening to you, Sir William. His Lordship has asked me to escort you to him."

William merely gave a terse nod.

The entourage did not go to his Lordship's chamber. Instead they wound their way downstairs, to the dungeon below. William felt his back straighten as his fear grew with each step. Down here it was dark and foul and wet, with air that seemed surely sickly and contagious. Down here there were men crying, and wailing, and somewhere deep down in the faraway darkness was a scream that would not stop. It was a child. William felt his eyes grow wide and tried to hide it.   His Lordship stood, posed, reading a long piece of parchment that seemed to contain a list. His eye merely travelled up and down the list, when he lifted his head and exclaimed.

"Why, Sir William! Why have you been brought down here?"

His Lordship gave no time for an answer. Instead, he moved quickly away from the dungeon, and led the way back up to the chamber.

William and the clerk stood before his high chair, while they outlined the terms once more. William was conscious of his voice sounding different.

"And so we feel we may best serve your Lordship by extending funds up to and including May seven years hence, with the final date of payment to be on the first day of May."

His Lordship gave a benevolent smile, and nodded.

"Certainly – seven years hence, final payment on the last day of May."

William didn't think.

"Oh no, please excuse me your Lordship, I must have misspoken. The first day in May."

The tone was too strong, far too strong. There was a pause, as the men waited to see what would happen next. The man on the high chair looked at William. William looked back, not blinking, and then, after a moment, lowered his head in a bow.

A dry cough, and then his Lordship spoke.

"The first day of May accords well with me." He gestured a hand to his Clerk. "So be it."

After William had returned home, after he had eaten and told Alice what had happened, after he had kissed the head of his son (so tall already!) and lay down in the dark with his wife, he lay for a long time remembering the moment down in the dungeon. He remembered the smell and the dark and the fear. He remembered the crying, and remembered the sight of his Lordship looking at the parchment. Lying in the dark, he almost pitied his Lordship. Instead of instilling fear in the Merchant Banker, as he had hoped, the only response he had created was one of anger, an anger that had no fear. It was that anger that had led William to insist on his terms in such a bald faced fashion. Were it not for the poor attempt at bullying, he could have called his own terms, William thought. He'll have his return for what we did, though.

49

Chapter Six

The Year 1301

William stood at the top of the hill overlooking the town and tried to avoid the panic. He watched as Alice, her maid Petra and their son William proceeded down the hill before him, their backs turned to him in their cheerful chatter, the lad following Petra, hanging on her every word as the child did. No, not a child. Practically a man now.

He stood there with the pain of it waving over him with each breath, and saw them walk further and further away from him. He did not know what was wrong, only that the pain had come upon him as they had come upon the hill and had grown with each step. The pain was not new to him. But the suddenness and the severity were.

William's father was still living; if that was what it could be called. He lay during the day in a bed beside a dying fire silent and white with the aches and pains of life. At night the house would see him wheezing in his bed, the death rattle on him, weak, weak and weaker. William had seen him in his bed five years ago, and had said the prayers that a good death would have seen said. But the haggard remorseless decay of the man before his eyes meant William wished him dead years ago. In his mind was a sincere horror of the helplessness of his father. The inability to protect himself, as well as the failure to mind his own ways, was disgusting to him. His father was a child in all ways that mattered.

Petra was singing beneath him. The sunlight streamed as they walked on and on, her voice raised in a hymn. Alice wore blue and white. Petra was in red. The light caught their clothes and seemed to make them glitter in the sunlight. They are going from me.

The pain was not new to him. No man lived to his age without knowing pain. But this was one that made breath impossible, that took the light from his eyes and that made his skin seem numb and dead already. No, he though, not death. My son will grow without knowing me. My wife will be alone in the world, with no protection. He saw his son, walking after Petra, the wind blowing his hair in the cold. He will be loose to the elements of this world, he thought. He will be without me.

The pain growing too much, William fell to his knees and let the ground hold him, for he could not hold himself.

Alice suddenly was above him, frantic. He could see the clouds above her as his breath left him slowly. He was going, he knew, going from them into that he had never wondered at before. He said the words he had heard that morning at mass, said the Latin that had been taught to him. The clouds on the windy day blew on and on behind Alice, and he found it easier to watch them than to see the look of panic on her face. My son, he thought, and let that one go too. Alice's face was fading from him, her voice lost to him, her smell, body, face, all lost to him. All that was left was the clouds in the sky, and the sound of the wind around him as he went.

That night, eyes wide like a trapped animal and kept safe behind closed doors, Alice had one thought that she remembered. That she had had a loved one die, a loved one like the old woman in the cave had promised, and that she had survived. She had lost her husband as she had been promised, and she had lost him to the Lord God Almighty, instead of losing him to the world such as to a woman or to his own indifference

Her son did not understand how it could have happened. A part of her did not understand it herself. She had raised herself that morning as a wife, and thought so by those around her. Now she was to lay down that night as a widow. She sat on the side of the bed, her hands clasped in her lap.

Petra stood behind her, silent. Mead and food sat on the table. She was waiting, not saying anything, not doing anything, her eyes on the woman before her, on the back curved slightly as it rocked a little back and forth. She knew the woman would not need her to do anything, merely to provide a sense of presence. Philip had pressed her hair in support before she came up, pressed her hand to show her he would be thinking of her-

Alice, sitting on the small bed she had shared with William, sat rocking slightly. She was in a very unusual position for her, one she didn't know how to admit to herself. She was unsure. Indecision was utterly new to her and she already despised it. What on earth to do? William had failed her, had left her alone and without succour. She shook her head silently, and she heard Petra move somewhat behind her. She would need advice of some sort. She would have to send a missive to someone to come and give her advice. She looked to the door, where she could call for a scribe and have them come to write her words and send them. But send them where? She did not yet know which destination should receive her words, nor did she think she could compose herself enough yet.

He was a good man, she thought. He was tall, and strong, and had a laugh that was a relief to hear. He was planted in her memory from a day they had spent in the woods in or around the time she had discovered she was pregnant. They were on the way back and he had turned from looking outside the carriage at one point to smile at her. She had that image of him smiling at her in front of her now, and she tried to escape it. She needed it gone so she could see her way clearly. The image would not leave her; it stood clearly in her way. She shook her head slightly to remove it but it stayed where it was. Other details came to her, his smell and warm weight next to her, the scent of them after tupping. She shook her head harder against it all. His hand on top of hers as they walked, his voice in her ear "Alice, my Alice"-

She stood up. Violently, she stood, staring for a moment at the blank wall, then she started walking back and forth in the room, to the wall, to the bed, eager and desperate and running from all she had seen. She greeted Petra in a voice made loud by bravado.

"What now, Petra!" she said, rolling up her sleeves.

"What now, my lady?"

"What do you say to this, huh? This a fine day we find ourselves in now. No man of the house and the women left to fend for themselves. William too young to take the reins of the house and I too womanly to hold them. What we are to do?"

She kept walking back and forth.

"What do you think we should do, Madam?"

"What should we do? We should have chosen more wisely, that's what we should have done. The faults and flaws of one man may greatly outweigh the flaws of another. Such is humanity thus graded and credited, in the eyes of God. William was a flawed man, a weak man. A man who let those who depended upon him down when they needed him most, a man who let the innocent and the helpless be defenceless when they could least afford it! Such was the man himself, and such was the state he has left us in. A state! If this is a state, a place of more ill forsaken runts cannot be found. What say you?"

She was dry faced, her eyes glinting dangerously. She looked at Petra.

"The flaws of one man may not be the flaws of another. You may find you could receive good advice and guidance from another man, a friend of William, perhaps, or his brother in Dublin."

Alice stopped walking back and forth and instead made for the food waiting for her on the tray. She picked up the bread and bit into it whole.

"We will need sustenance for the days ahead."

"Should you think it wise, Madam, a letter may be sent to the Viceroy or some other trusted confidant, who may give you the direction you seek."

Alice kept chewing for a moment. Another man, get advice and direction from another man. But advice would still need to be carried out, and she would have to do it. She would still be vulnerable and unsafe, out of doors from protection. Advice could be obtained from another man, but it would not be as good as another man. Why get the advice when the man in question was the thing needed? Get another man, no need for fear or indecision.

The fierce, angry energy of Alice bounded and fixed upon that idea with all its great and untapped might, and never doubted it again. She swallowed the mouthful of food with determination.

A husband to get. She rubbed the spot between her eyebrows in exasperation as she considered her job. What was the decent mourning period, two years? The time was far too long; she would never be able to stick to it; a year at most. And while the English families would be scandalised, the Norman ones would not notice the lack of black on her after six months. Nor would they care, or at least show they did in her presence. And if she were already married they would not dare raise an eyebrow in her presence. So be it, she thought again, her eyes wide with the decision. She would get a husband.

Alice, thinking this, did not think with desire of another man in her bed, or a companion, or a soul to care for, or even of other children, or of any of the concrete realities that a new husband would mean. She thought of not being vulnerable any more, of not being afraid. She thought of the end of her indecision. Once this period was made to end, then they would be safe. They would have nothing more to fear, and all would be well.

Chapter Seven

The Year 1302

There was no subtlety in her choice. Plenty in her execution, oh yes, she was cautious as any diplomat. But her choice was made as a brute rude thing, and it was a thing that she grew inside her for days before acting, or indeed even telling anyone.

She was kept in the house in confinement, silent and dark, and she was glad of the solitude. She needed to plan and to rest and to gather her composure, to simply live with no concern for other than the future and for the day itself. Petra was to organise the great house to receive guests (they did not come to see Alice, of course, nor would it have been proper for her to see them. But they were to be granted food and drink in a suitable style when they called, and that fell to her and to the Houseman, Philip.) The house was to tick over as usual while Alice was removed. William would need care and concern. All was to be as usual.

The businesses were a more difficult matter, but eventually a temporary solution was found. The clerk would deal with the financial matters, taking in and recording the funds, distributing them, and the control of the bailiffs when it was not taken in sufficiently. Nothing was to be left to chance, and while it was out of the question for Alice to grant an interview to the man, he could leave daily reports of a written nature to be reviewed at a later date. Philip and the other workmen that were around the place could look to the taverns, the bailiff work and the other matters of various natures. Such it would continue, the oiled machine that had been built up, and so she let it fend for itself for a while, as she slipped back into the darkness of her thoughts.

She gave herself, realistically, a week to withdraw. She saw that she would not contend with the roughness of life at all for a while, but decided that the most that was necessary was a week. She would not give cause for scandal and appear before her allotted time (certainly not before six months). For a week, therefore, she did not leave her room. Food was brought to her. She did not dress or wash, but sat, and thought, and cried, and thought, and planned. She gave herself a week in which to mourn and miss the man she had shared a bed with and a life with and who she thought surely he would outlive her because of the children she would bear, but who instead was now the reason she was a widow. So let the house and the life go on without her for a week. She would slide into the blackness of her loss for a while and let it win.

She would wake at night, when the house was utterly without noise or light. Lying awake in the room, nothing would reach her to prevent her feeling of loss. The silence was her grief. It was heavy and real and unwieldy, and it would not bend to her will at all, but instead forced like a physical weight the reality of her loss. He is gone, Alice. Gone, and he is never coming back.

Like this she would wait the dawn.

Once it came, she would slowly sit up and gather the sheets around her, and make her body as comfortable as it could be. There, in that position, she would ask herself how he could have left her. What was so cruel about the world that he could go, so bitterly, and leave her be like this? Was she at the mercy of something unholy? Was she evil? Was the world so cold? Her thoughts went around like this, helplessness gathering within her until she felt her very limbs go heavy and her eyes unable to look up.

On the fourth day of this, she found she was watching this process of her spirits lowering with an air of detachment that had not been there before. She was watching her thoughts go lower and lower without interruption with a kind of cold curiousness. The sensation was new. She saw she was recovering. She asked for more food that day. Now she could plan.

On that morning she still made herself comfortable in her bed, but now she had a task to carry out. She would be a wife again, and she needed to reflect. She would need to find a man to be a husband, and she doubted very much she would have little trouble in that regard. She was too well connected. But she needed to choose, and she trusted herself alone to do that one wisely.

He would need to be young. Alice, a few years over 30, counted herself nearly old, but it was different for women. Men could be said to be in their prime much longer than a woman. She wanted someone who would be young, then, no more than 35 if possible. He would need to live nearby, in this county or the next, though that did not preclude a second estate if it existed. But he would need to have his business here. He would need to be well connected, obviously, as well connected as her, if not more so. He would need to be a businessman, one on a par with the Kyteler family and the Outlaw family. He should be pleasing in manner and appearance, but did not have to be fancy in his looks. She did not like vain men, in conversation or in appearance. And he would need to be rich. Rich beyond fear, if that was possible.

Alice thought that the wedding day would need to be in the Cathedral, but perhaps in a small side chapel rather than at the main alter. It would have to be discreet. She let a small sigh escape her, allowing herself to recollect the smallest detail of her own wedding day there, when the wind had been so cold and loud. Then she merely turned her face away and looked at the wall and made herself think of other things. The side altar, surely. They could not deny her that.

She was still sitting up in bed as the night fell. She sat through the night, making herself say good-bye to the image of herself as William's wife. As Alice, Dame Kyteler, married to William Outlaw. She was to be someone else's now. She was no longer his. She was to give herself to another. And she would do all she could to be a good wife to him.

And when morning broke that day, she looked at it with dry eyes, and was ready.

Alice sat straight backed and serene in her chamber. She sat alone, looking towards the door. Her hair was dressed modestly, and she had taken care over her clothes. She sat with her hands in her lap, waiting.

After a moment the door was opened by Petra, who let in William, his teenage years disappearing, and the clerk, Johannes Galrussyn.

Petra shut the door behind them. William sat; Galrussyn stood, and remained standing throughout the interview.

"Good day to you Mother."

"Good day to you my son. I am gladdened in my heart to see you so well. You are your father's son, and your well being would have matched his hopes in all things."

The young man nodded, grateful for the compliment extended to him.

"Mother, I thank you. Please, do but bid to me your wish or fancy that I may grant for your comfort and I will do all I can to provide it."

"My son, glad I am to see how kind and gentlemanly you have been raised. You are a credit to the household of your father and you make me proud, even though our Holy Father would have it is a sin. Yet I do not think it can be so when it grows so warmly and strongly in a mother's heart."

Alice smiled at him, and he smiled back, waiting to know the reason he had been called here.

"My son, you are, as we know, without a father. A son should according to the rights of nature have a father to guide and protect him as he grows towards manhood. It is a point of further grievance to me at this sad time that you are unprotected. This loss has been brought to this house as a result of my losing my husband. Therefore we have no husband, no husbandry to guide us in our travails. A house without husbandry is unprotected against the vulgarities and vicissitudes of society, and of the world at large. I have asked you here today, to gain your counsel and to hear what it is we are to do in this time."

The young man heard all this with slightly widening eyes. With a gasp the truth of it came to him.

She means to marry again!

He lowered his eyes slightly so as to hide the knowledge of it from her, knowing as he did so that she must guess. But he was unable to hide his action from her; he required a moment to grant himself his thoughts and to accustom his mind to the idea.

She will marry again! He had supposed it to be so. The servants, especially Petra, had attempted to warn him, saying that she would need marriage to preserve the lands, and that she would soon need a man to protect the estate of his father; to expand it, even. But they had spoken of the matter in terms of much longer a time, not right now. His father had fallen to the hillside very recently,

58

and the soil he lay under was yet still wet. A needle of anger reached him. It was improper. It was unseemly, and rushed. She moved too soon.

He lifted his eyes again, and looked at his mother. She, still speaking, saw the look of hardening defiance in her son's eyes, and glanced at the clerk.

William was somewhat aghast to hear then the clerk speak, but suffered it in his mother's chamber.

"If I may greatly leap the requirements of manners and class, and give my small service in this matter, Dame Kyteler. We are as it is so commonly known in a very dangerous time. The matter of the wars in England and France daily cause concern to all in this country. These matters require, if only to some extent, the expansion of protection over the estate of Sir William. However, there is another matter that may also further your decision. We are, as you know, kindly offering terms to the Lord Marshall, and to other personages of great esteem. While it is not possible to believe that such personages will do anything so low as to renege on these terms, these are indeed difficult times. We cannot foresee what difficulties may come our way and we are indeed wise if we take the surest course."

He cleared his throat, and got on with it.

"The terms of the agreements were extended to several parties, but were all offered by William Outlaw of the House of Kyteler. It is to be said without doubt that the loss of the Offerer is a loss that places us in a most perilous position. Were unfortunate difficulties to arise on the part of those persons who have received our money, we would be in a less than secure position to obtain that, which is rightfully yours, Master William. However, were we able to call another master of the household, we would be looked on most favourably by the Courts."

William sat up.

"I could do it. I could be master of the household and be a petitioner in court."

Alice looked at him for a moment.

"No," was all she said. Her voice was soft only in tone.

The voice of the clerk continued on, but William was not listening. She had drawn a line under his husbandry, and at some level, he would collude.

59

"What, therefore, is the next step, Mother?" he asked, all pretence at discussion removed from him.

"I intend to ask the Clerk to draft a letter of request to Bishop Fitzjohn, so that he may tend his thoughts and prayers towards our cause. We may await his reply and then act on it as is necessary."

A marriage proposal. One made by the Bishop who would act as a marriage maker for the correct sum. William's jaw hardened momentarily at the idea of so quick a union being made. Who would it be? A friend of his father's? Some old man they had snickered at only weeks before?

Alice, seeing his jaw harden, suddenly saw William her husband back again. Ah, me!

So be it. She will have her day of days once again. He stood and bowed deeply to her.

"My lady, I remain your servant," he said, thinking to himself, please God it may not be for long, and left the room.

My most gracious and noble Bishop of The Lord Almighty, Lord Bishop Fitzjohn, Bishop of the Diocese of Ossory. May the Lord bless and keep you well and grant success to all your endeavours.

Sadly we write to display our sorrow and loss to you at the sad news of our Lord Master's demise, and of our great sorrow at this sad passing. Master Outlaw was but a man still young in word and deed, but in every way was a figure noble and great. He gave support both in his heart and in his words and deeds to the great efforts being undertaken in the Holy Land and was a man whom temperance and patience had taken a hold of early in life and who never released their hold on him. His passing is marked with daily prayers so that the safe return of his soul to the Heavenly paradise is assured.

This sad event is more further saddening for she who is most affected by it, meaning Dame Alice Kyteler, the noble and gentle wife of Master Outlaw and who is mother to his son William. She grieves greatly for the loss of her lord and master and daily feels the weight of sorrow that has befallen her. In these greatly uncertain times she fears greatly the possible fate that may fall on her.

Thus she comes to you in her hour of need, greatly in need of your assistance that only you may provide for her at this time.

Bishop FitzJohn received the letter into his hands at approximately midday four days after it was written. He reviewed the letter on several grounds. One, with a review of the poor but understandable Latin used; Two, to ensure that the writer paid him the correct respect and honorific terms as was appropriate; Three, with a keen self interest that has guided him well so far; and fourth, with a sniggering sense of Alice's need for a man in her bed.

He looked up from his seat in his interview room, which was his general office and workroom. To his right was his Clerk, who was looking over the pile of correspondence for His Grace still to review. The sunlight spoke of mid afternoon through the windows, and the Bishop wanted to be rid of work for a while, knowing he could not.

"The Dame is seeking a husband,' he said to the Clerk's back. The younger man turned to him.

"I understood her husband is only briefly passed away."

"Indeed," agreed the Bishop, who reread the letter.

"The request is written from the hand of her son. No doubt at her request."

"No doubt," said the Clerk, waiting for His Grace's instructions.

Ireland had two masters, at this time. The Normans, who had their army to support them, took decisions over Governance and matters of State. However, there was also the Church and Canonical Law. There was no clear concept in anyone's mind of a Government for the People, so the arrangement was accepted to all intents and purposes. However, the division was not an easy one to maintain, and both camps did their best to gain points and power. This was the matrix that ran through the mind of the Bishop reading the letter.

Yes, it was too early to gain a husband, and she did break the norm in that regard. But a wedding arranged for a member of the Kyteler household was a sign of strength and power, and the fees would be nicely generous as well. Let her rush up the altar in her hasty lust. The flaw would be on her, not the Church. He gave a nod of decision. He had just the man for her.

The pair met in an open meadow near the walls of the city. His estate was a good ten miles from Alice's home, near the town land of Callan, and so the compromise had been reached that the first

61

meeting would be half way between them, at the border of his lands. It was agreed that they would meet on a date in May, in the morning. Alice had driven with her entourage of Petra, a maid, her Clerk and her son. He had come with his adult daughter, his son-in-law, and a manservant. The pair had arrived in their carriages at the appointed time. His decorated carriage was waiting with its blinds drawn when Alice's had pulled up parallel, approximately 50 yards away. The pair of carriages had sat there silently for a few moments.

"There's no sign," said Petra, sneaking a look outside the blind.

It was still very early, but already the day was promising to be wonderfully warm. The green grass was brightening to iridescence, and the heat was beginning to rouse the butterflies and birds. Alice sat in her carriage, thinking, and then she too sneaked a look. Behind her lay Kilkenny. The meadow lay before her; a gentle slope rose to her left for about a hundred yards or so, and curved towards a tree with a hedgerow. The carriage of Adam Le Blund was directly in front of her. Suddenly one of its doors opened, and she dropped the blind. Distant sounds could be heard, which were coming closer. Eventually there was a tapping on the door.
The clerk opened it slightly, to see Adam's manservant standing outside.

'The Noble Adam Le Blund would be most honoured if the excellent Dame Alice Kyteler would condescend to join him in conversation at a point or location of her choosing in the meadow."

The Clerk looked at Alice, who inclined her head in agreement.

"The excellent Dame Kyteler acknowledges the kind invitation of the Noble Le Blund, and wishes to inform him that she accepts this invitation with all humility and gratitude."

The two men nodded at each other, then the other bowed and departed.

Alice looked at Petra, who gave her a nod. Petra then nodded to the Clerk, who stepped out of the carriage and left the door open. Alice stepped out, and then Petra, keeping two steps behind. A similar dismounting was happening at Le Blund's carriage. The two parties, thus safely put on God's earth, began to ceremoniously make their way to each other in the middle of the field. Thus did Alice first cast her eyes on her next husband.

Adam Le Blund was not William Outlaw. William was a creature open in his way, with a heart that was cheerful and astute. He had taken a bride and made a wife of her. He was cheerful, canny, hard working, and, as much as the times would allow it, big hearted. He would not have been ambitious but for Alice. And he was ultimately not given to ideas of a grand scale. Alice's father had chosen him firstly and mainly for the extensive business William's family had owned. He had also chosen him because he rightly believed William was straightforward if not sophisticated, hard working if not clever, and pleasant if not charming. But Alice's father was dead, and she had chosen Adam solely from the point of view of wealth, nothing more. She did not know him at all. And a decision rushed is rarely founded on rational thought.

Adam Le Blund walked slowly and with confidence on the grass, focusing on a point in the distance. His eyes narrowed slightly in the breeze, his dark hair briefly touching his fringe. Adam was shorter than William, and of slimmer build. He carried a touch of the Roman in him, and it was said his House had threads abroad. His hair was a straight dark black. His eyes were dark brown, with a faint sense of overhanging lids. His nose was aquiline, a hooked thing that bore his ancestry clearly. His mouth had thin lips that pursed often. He had a slim waist and hips, and was dressed in a clean pale yellow silk tunic that was well crafted. It was flattering. He regarded the approaching figure of Alice with a sense of intensity that was strangely disconnected. Alice was, for him, an opportunity and an expression of greed. Her feelings and her needs were, an excellent method of manipulation. He let a small smile reach his lips as she came closer.

Alice, for her part, regarded him with a growing sense of bemusement. She had not in her short life yet met a man who looked like he did, who bore such exotic looks and who was dressed with the art of a courtier, not a merchant. She found the idea of being an object of attention a matter of silent amusement. She felt her lips smile slightly.

She's experienced, thought Adam, noting the serious mien of Alice. She's aware of men and of me. Good. He despised virgins as a breathtaking waste of time. He focused on maintaining eye contact with her.

Adam was a man with not one outlook on life, but many. Like Alice he had a manipulative perspective, depending on what was best for him, but he had taken it to an extreme she had not. He was not tied to any one place or principle that outlasted his self-interest, and his understanding of human affection had been so far remarkably short lived. He was cold to the normal human demands of warmth and love, while giving himself enormous rights over the loves of others. He regarded himself as immensely attractive to women and both dangerous and influential to men. He reproached himself for nothing but foolishness, and even then forgave himself.

William Outlaw, watching his mother walk to her new husband, snorted to himself at the foolishness of the woman. She goes about with too much speed, he thought again. She shows too much haste. His eye fell on the entourage of Adam. There stood his daughter, married judging by the clothes she wore, with her husband beside her. She had the look of her father, he thought. She was not unattractive, but she had the same coldness in her looks that Le Blund bore, and she was not fair for it. William nodded respectfully. The pair broke into laughter, and William felt his face blush.

Alice finally came to a stop a few feet from the middle of the field. Adam stood at a point approximately five feet from her. He smiled at her slightly as he frankly took in her figure and face. And what did he think? He thought that she was pretty, but not too much. A little severe for his taste. He liked her hair, and she had beautiful eyes. But she had a slightly cold and judging air about her, especially as she looked at him. This was in fact her intelligence, which he was unable to see. She liked him, he thought. She should have felicitations on her good taste, but she seemed already enamoured of him. If there was no chase, he knew, he very quickly became bored.

Alice curtsied deeply in front of Adam, glad of the opportunity to lower her face from his eyes. He was beautiful, she thought, but so far she had no indication as to his character or principles. She became unconsciously aware of a clean scented aroma from him that was utterly unique. He returned her gesture with a deep bow.

She rose again and stood there in front of him, not lifting her eyes, waiting for him to speak. She knew that her role in this was not the advancer, but that she could instead await his comments without prompting.

Adam inclined his head to her.

"It is a great honour you carry to us today, in your visit to my lands. We are greatly appreciative of the honour you provide us," he said, starting negotiations.

Alice was thinking quickly, he is honouring and submissive, yes, a good start, I'll give him that.

"The provision of your kind gesture in carrying to meet me this fair morn does me more honour than I surely deserve, Sire." She let herself meet his eyes for one brief moment, lowering them almost immediately. There, she told herself, I have hinted that I am bold. I will show my colours soon enough to him.

She raises her eyes! She is already loose to the demands of her place! She should show more character, he thought to himself, but reminded himself just as quickly that a loose character can quickly be made taut.

"In truth, my fair lady," said Adam, allowing himself a little freedom in salutation, "I am greatly in esteem of both you and your noble house. While we are far from the eye of greatness here in our little world, we are occasionally visited with news of those nobles near us. We are aware of your nobility in comparison to us."

The statement of nobility was a kindness to Alice, and one she was aware of. To be called noble was a straightforward flattery, but she granted him that one with no rancour. The flattery came with the words 'fair lady', which gave too quickly to familiarity. What was his personage, whom were his parents? Was such a man so without inherent standards that he was a familiar to all?

Petra, watching him, saw that he said nothing about his lands, property, household management, finances or commercial concerns. She had not expected him to, this was not such a day for this. The estates would be compared and combined by the lawyers and there would be little or no overt discussion between the couple regarding them. But the absence of any real conversation from Adam made her wish to frown slightly in front of him, boldly. She didn't, of course. But she saw in front of her a man that she was to give little credence to.

Adam believed Alice was sweet on him, and sensed very faintly the disdain of her handmaid. He gave a very deep bow, and then very slowly withdrew from his sleeve a flower. This, he thought to himself, will settle her.

Petra blinked twice and said nothing.

William, still standing at the carriage, rolled his eyes.

And Alice, seeing the gesture, knew she would be master. She would indeed agree to be his wife. She smiled her first real smile, for reasons he could not have guessed.

Chapter Eight

The Year 1324

Bishop Le Drede read the letter again, trying not to overreact.

In the year of our Lord 1302, it would appear that Dame Alice had another husband, one by the name of Adam Le Blund. This honourable gentleman had a large estate in Callan, and had been apparently been known and respected by many men. However, in 1309 he had given his stepson all his property, and then been taken from this earth. Richard had not the father's instinct. But he could not imagine any man having the desire to help William Outlaw. The letter went on to complain about the cruel manner of his death and the likelihood of wrong doing by Alice and her son.

Le Drede could see that they were trying. The evidence was right in front of them, but they were simple and did not see.

"Show her in," he said.

The manservant opened the door and in stepped Adam le Blund's daughter, her beauty still strong.

The woman immediately rushed towards the Bishop and kneeled, kissing his ring with great reverence. She was dressed extremely well, with pearls about her person, and she had a dark eyed beauty that was highly exotic. She reminded him of the beauties about the Papal Court.

"Holy Father, thank you for seeing me."

"Please be seated my child. Your letter caused me grave concern upon my reading it. Can I ask you to outline the events to me, in your own words?"

"My father was married to the Dame Kyteler in 1302. The match seemed an equitable one. Dame Alice had recently lost a husband, William Outlaw, and their estates were of a size," said Helen Le Blund. She paused, and taking a small handkerchief, dotted her eyes.

The Bishop inclined his head with sympathy.

"I was married myself at that stage, and lived with my husband and children in our estate in Suffolk. I received initially numerous pieces of correspondence from my father, who wrote that he was well and happy. However, these letters soon ended after the year 1307. I was to write again, and again, but my letters were never answered. It was in 1309 that I informed of his death!"

She was overcome.

"My dear child, may I get you some wine?"

"Please," and a draft was put in front of her. She dotted her dark eyes again and made a great effort to compose herself. Eventually she was ready to go on.

"I was informed that my father's estate was to be taken over in its entirety by the Kyteler son, William! Imagine my surprise at such news! My father, failing to make provision for his young grandson, in these difficult times! I do not believe that I would be ignored, or my son ignored, if my father had been allowed to carry out his wishes. I was greatly troubled by this. I was soon to learn that my father had died most grievously, in a manner most unnatural. He did not die an easy death, my Grace."

She leaned closer.

"I believe my father was forced to give his estate away, and then had his life untimely ended. My husband and I have commenced a suit against the Dame, but we find that we are blocked at every turn. Can we commence a case in the ecclesiastical Courts, and thereby undo a great injustice?"

The Bishop paused, then spoke.

"My dear child, you are an innocent, and mercifully have not become exposed to the terrible realities of the unholy one. Be prepared, it is almost certain that Dame Kyteler did not kill your father by normal means. Instead, she has become aligned in a most unholy association with the Dark Arts. I am also informed by the adult son of her next husband and victim, Richard de Valle, that he also suffered an untimely death while married to Alice."

"You mean?"

"Yes, it is true. I am of the honest and wholehearted belief that we have no ordinary mischief here. Instead, I know now the truth. Your step mother is no ordinary woman, you see."   "Dame Alice Kyteler is a witch."

When she left his office, Helen was all gratitude. However, once in the carriage, she lifted her hands to her eyes and rubbed them with weariness.

A matter that has been delayed in the courts for years, she thought to herself. And now that I have played my last card with the Bishop, he speaks of witches and demons, rather than homicide and theft. We will never see the money back. We will never have justice for his death.

No doubt her father brought it upon himself in some way. She knew exactly what he was capable of, especially in a darkened room with a weak victim. But he was her father, and they money was theirs. She must seek justice for him. She must seek, as well, that which was rightfully hers. She lifted her cane to the roof of the carriage and gave a thump.

"Drive on," she called, and closed her eyes as the carriage moved off.

Chapter Nine

The Year 1302

Alice's second wedding day was on a very different scale, obviously. Firstly it suited both the bride and groom to show off. Adam had no intention of keeping his status small and unknown to those of the town.

The second reason was publicity, at least on the part of Alice. The business would soon be able to expand further to Dublin and the surrounding counties. They were making enormous amounts of money, in large-scale loans to the monarchy that were seeing £5,000 being the norm. Keeping and meeting such funds would mean making as many contacts as possible with merchants in Dublin. It meant ensuring that these men would want to come down to the wedding, to receive the largess that the Kyteler family would provide. Hence there would be a week of festivities, and there was a long roll call of nobles attending. Arnold Le Poer, Merchant. William Doucemann, who had enormous trade going on in Dublin and who held 5,000 acres there. She personally had always enjoyed his company and that of his wife, Brasila. Richard and Thomas de Valle, of Tipperary. Even Edward, the Earl of Carrick and son-in-law of the Earl of Ulster.

Alice had business dealings with all of them. She knew, for example, that Richard de Valle would be trying very hard to ensure that the legal contract he had with the port in England would be carried out, and that it depended upon his solicitation of the daughter of the mayor of that town. Alice also knew that William Doucemann was trying hard to gain the role of mayor of Dublin, if only to access the enormous wealth that came through its ports every day. And she knew that Edward was visiting her on her wedding day so as to investigate his long awaited desire, the invasion of Ireland. Good for them. Good for all of them.

She lifted her head again and reviewed her face. It was a passable thing. Its features were neat and did the job as demanded. She did not wish for more. Her face was properly coloured as the style expected, and her headdress was excellently jewelled. She was well after thirty and cared not a jot. She didn't need to be pretty. She was rich. She lifted her pearls, imported especially for this occasion, to her neck.

There was a brief knock behind her. She smiled to herself, making him wait, and then lifted her voice.

"Come in."

William her son entered. So like his father she thought. In fact, she could see a little of her own father in him. He was older these days, and he was no longer a child.

"Good evening William."

He bowed his head with respect.

"Gracious tidings to you Mother on this day. How do I find you?"

"You find me well, my son. Come sit with me." She gestured behind her to the upholstered couch near the fire, where wine was waiting.

He sat down with her, not speaking.

"You are aware, no doubt, that I am soon to be married again."

He nodded, patient.

"You may not be aware that while it is necessary for the preservation of our house, it is the only requirement by law we are asked to make. I need make no place for my new husband in our business ventures other than that which I choose."

He looked at her saying nothing at this news. She must know I'm surprised at this, he thought. So why is she marrying him?

"It is therefore my intention to have both my husband, and my son, carry out the business along with me. I seek your assistance in the business my son, and would like your assurance that you will give me every aid you would give to your father."

William sat back into his chair, attempting to think through what the offer meant. She watched, the firelight on her face.

He blinked a few times.

"Of course Mother, I will do all I am able."

"Good," she said, giving him one of her brief smiles. "Then it is my pleasure to offer you a gift on this day to mark your new status in our eyes. I have made provision for you to obtain and receive the full and complete title to a house, for your own use and enjoyment exclusively. Here are the details."

She reached out her hand to him and in it were documents for him to read. He let his eye run over them as quickly as he could and as far as he could tell, his legal education of several years behind him, the documents appeared correctly drafted and notified. He looked up, momentarily startled at the largess.

"I cannot say more than my esteemed gratitude to you and my new father for this honour that I do not deserve."

Alice waved away the platitude, not interested.

"It is no more than your father, William would have intended for you to receive when you reached your age. However, we do have an obligation to place upon you." She paused to take some wine. Of course there would be something. There always was.

"Your father and I wish to have permanent storage rights of the warehouse at the back of the estate. It is a small matter, it is really no more than a shed, and as such is not worth much thought by you." She glanced at him to see his expression.

"I am pleased that I may serve you in even this small way," he answered quickly, trying hard to keep his tone level.

"Good," she replied. Good. Now the rest of it could go ahead. She rubbed her hands briefly, attempting to find something else to say to him.

"Your studies are going well?" she asked him.

"Very well, I am to be made attorney in a few months and will therefore be able to assist you even further once that is done."

"Oh I don't doubt it. However, you are still quite young, and a young mind deserves more than education. At least your mind does. What say you to a year or two abroad, perhaps? Maybe in England?"

It was a new thought for William, and he took a moment to answer.

"I cannot say I had contemplated it before now," he said, honestly.

Alice nodded gently. You really should, however, my son, as you are now faced with it, she thought.

"However, I am again led by you and my new father, Mother. I shall enquire as to possible postings immediately."

Alice coughed slightly.

"I have taken the liberty of enquiring as to a possible posting with the Earl of Gloucestershire, who tells me he is eager for you to join him there. He and his court are embarking on ambitious reforms, and would be interested in your council on them."

"Indeed! Forgive my surprise, but I do indeed feel the suddenness of this move!"

He moved his fingers over the clasped paperwork, which suddenly seemed to come with a price, and then looked into her face. A year or so away would be most welcome, he thought. Her eyes, seeing the consent in his, glinted in satisfaction. Most welcome, he thought, and swallowed.

The house of William, once he saw it, made him sad to leave. It was to the east of the city, facing the midday sun, with rooms made honey sweet by being away from the smell and near the calm of the river. From the top windows he could see the trees of his woodlands nearby, and from the front door the main pathway to Carlow. The house was excellently placed, but was also excellently furnished, with many pieces of polished wood and glass being used to decorate the place.

William saw it one autumn day. He rode out the few miles to the great gate and trotted up the pathway. The façade curved perfectly to meet him as he came around the last turn, and he stopped the horse. It really was wonderful, he marvelled. Why did this come to him now?

He stirred the horse on, and up to the front door. It was opened by a housemaid who, seeing him, told him that the master of the house had not yet arrived, and could she send the Steward to him? William decided not to say who he was yet, but instead said he would merely rest his horse for a while before embarking on the way back.

She merely nodded and shut the door again, leaving William with nothing more to do but to go around the back of the house.

I hope she lets me bring Philip with me, he thought, taking off his gloves and strolling. He found there all the usual, unknown implements of farming carefully stored and hidden in sheds, and left them where they were. Instead he headed off across the fields, listening to the sounds of the birds greeting their new master as he took in the trees, the grass, all that was now his. Most of his peers would consider this terribly small, and in truth so did he. But he considered it a beginning, and his first estate. He would have more, and larger.

William continued his stroll, contented. In two months, he thought, I will be away, at my new role as Attorney. I have to my name a first estate, with more almost certain. I almost have too much, he thought.

"Hallo!" came a cry behind him.

He turned and saw a man striding towards him across the fields. The man was about two inches shorter than him, and a great deal wider. He had a very red face, with a bulbous nose. The neck of the tunic seemed tight around his neck, and he moved with a slightly wobbly stride on the grass.

"Hallo," he said again. "I saw you coming across the fields and thought to myself, that man is the owner. He looks too content to be anything else. Allow me to introduce myself, neighbour. I am Arnold Le Poer, owner of your neighbouring property, and well known of these parts. How'd ya do?" he said, holding out his hand.

William smiled, despise himself.

"How do you do? William Kyteler, owner of this vast estate, and contented indeed, Neighbour. How does this day find you?"

"How does this day find me? How does this day find any man, when they are living in the best country in the world, except for the God forsaken Clerics insisting on their Canon law, and the English Crown to back them! What's more, it's been five hours since first matins, and a man could earn a soul and a half with the hunger I have on me at the moment! I have not yet seen you about these parts. Are you new here, brother Kyteler?"

"I am Sire, for my sins. I come today to review the new estates my family in their goodness have seen fit to give me, and to discover for myself all that needs to be done."

"A noble intent, indeed. Would company make the road quicker for you, Master Kyteler, or do you seek to travel the road alone?" asked Arnold.

William looked at the robust little man, his face red with vices, his eyes merry and friendly. The man was the definition of unceremonious, with his informal tongue and his intrusions. William found him different, and a pleasure.

"Indeed, a person could indeed do worse than to seek company on such a fine day. Your company is more welcome, brother Arnold," said the younger man. Arnold gave a grin of delight, and the two men began to walk together.

"Kyteler," mused Arnold, "that isn't a local name I warrant you. Not that it isn't noble for all that. But I dare say you or your kin are not from around these parts?" asked Arnold.

William looked at him surprised.

"Surely you must have heard of the family Kyteler, in Kilkenny city? My father and mother were well known as merchants there. We entertained the bishop, and are known by blood to the chancellor of Ireland. We are known to many, Master Arnold."

"Indeed, it seems I may indeed have heard of you as well. Come, let us enjoy this fine morning and this excellent walk together, so that we may become better acquainted."

The two men walked on together. William was comparing the behaviour of Arnold, loud and quick to jibe, with those of the clerics and masters with whom he had studied for so long. These men never criticised his mother or family. They did not speak to him in any other fashion other than to instruct and to inform. William could see one in his mind's eye now, a tall, thin man, as pale as the parchment he handled, thin under his grey robes, blinking in the morning sun. A small shiver of revulsion came to him with the memory.

The day was beginning to grow gently warm. The sun lit upon the short grass as was its custom, and the birds sang and danced in the air. Arnold, sensing the change in his companion's mood, quickly forgot his own misgivings. Besides, the Kytelers were rich, everyone knew that. And being rich meant being forgiven.

The two men arrived at an embankment on the land, and looked down to find a river, wide and strong, running through it.

"I didn't know this was there," remarked William, who so far had seen the Nore, the river that ran through Kilkenny, as merely a non-stationary lake. He gave it no further thought than that, and so was surprised to find that it existed outside the city walls.

"This is the main method of travel for some folk around here. If you so wish, it can also be a nice earner, in that you may charge folk a fare for safe passage through your lands. However," he said, hitching his pants, "my advice would be to let folk be and give them free passage."

"Why?" asked William.

"A good landowner asks for only that which can be given fairly and easily," replied Arnold, his voice confident. After a moment, William nodded.

The truth is, thought Arnold, as like as not, you and yours will one day be lords and masters over all here, and there is no sense in seeking to anger those who you will need to win heart and soul over. Lord knows, we all know this, William. Did that mother of yours, viper that she is, teach you nothing at all?

Chapter Ten

The Year 1302

Life had begun, in her memory, with her father knocking on the kitchen door. One of the staff opened it. Her father was thin, dying. There was a wild look in his eyes built by months of hunger. After a few muttered words Philip was brought. He looked hard at the man.

"She does not take much, Sir, and she will work hard."

The bundle was opened. Rose slid down until her feet were on the ground, looking up at Philip. After a few moments he had nodded and pulled her inside. The door closed behind her and her life began.

She'd been a member of the Kyteler household for a long time now, and in that time had learnt a lot. She had learnt to keep her tongue silent when working. She learnt how to lose her awareness in her work, of forgetting herself when she was sweeping the floor or scrubbing the clothes. She knew that she must have an eye to her hair and to her hands that they would be clean every day, but that to take to water was to invite certain sickness and death to herself, and to those around her.

She had, most importantly, learnt the skill of being there but not there. She could be in a room with the Mistress and the Master, and could see and anticipate all that was needed. But she would not hear or see or think anything. She was gifted in that way.

Sometimes the others called her silly or a dreamer, and at times in Church she could feel herself drift with the chanting, watching the priests make the holy mass to the Lord. She would imagine herself floating, drifting higher and higher with the sacred words, until she reached Heaven itself, where the blessed Mother would be waiting to love and forgive her. The robes the Mother wore would be a white softness, and her eyes would be large with the love and compassion she would offer Rose. Rose would gasp at the idea, and then would have to hold her tongue, or be discovered in her daydreaming by those around her.

Rose knew she was very lucky to be able to go to Church, as a member of the household she was now permitted to do so. Mostly the poor were barred from entry, to ensure law and order was maintained. The poor were mostly like her father, she knew, and reminded herself again of the truth of her life; she was Very Lucky. She could have died or taken on a worse fate, that which had been the lot of those who had fallen on a bad lot. But the Holy Father had saved her from such a fate, that she knew. She must be humble and honest and Good to show her gratitude. At this she was quite skilled. She thought not of greed or of lust or of money. She thought, in a worse way, of safety, born of a genuine fear, and a necessary cowardice. She was now about 13, she thought.

Rose grew tall that year. She still smiled quickly when put to task, and still honestly believed in the goodness of those around her. She honestly believed in the goodness of High Rank persons, such as Alice and Adam. If they said something was a certain way, then for Rose it was so. It made up the order of her world. It was the order in her world. She could not, like Philip, be a certain way in front of the Mistress, and then be, as quick as quicksilver, turn to another way once they were gone. She has seen him once, at the end of a long banquet dinner, return to the kitchen for a moment and pause, exhausted, every muscle flagging in strength, his lip curled in hatred of those he served. However, Philip must have a reason for it, perhaps, and so she would not think too much of it. She seemed to be obliged to not think about a lot of things in her day. It was in fact for this reason that she was quickly becoming a glad sight for Petra, who liked the growing child with the innocence that was far from ignorance. She and Philip would never be able to have their own child safely and remain in service. Petra imagined she could see in the child potential.

In the dark blackness of night, there is no way to be sure if you are safe. The two men approaching William's house in the country were breathless with fear. They were William le Kiteler, Sheriff of Kilkenny, and Fulk of le Freyne, Seneschal of Kilkenny. The two men had ridden on their horses out of the city gates and across country the few miles to William's house. Le Kiteler, who had searched for it earlier that week, was the surest rider, and dismounted first. It was very late and very dark. When one stumbled over a stone, the other cursed.

"Gods wounds would you keep quiet!"

The pair slowly and quietly made their way up the lane that led to the house. They left their horses at the front so that no one would hear.

At the main door to the house, they paused. Le Kiteler looked at it. Made of strong oak. Safe as anything. He gave it an investigative push, and found that the way was barred. He would have done the same.

Le Kiteler was a distant relative of Alice and her brood, and he had been born in Ireland to a mother of Irish origin and a father from Holland. He had not had the riches of Alice, however, and so found that his way in life was much less smooth. He had seen his mother die from pneumonia. His father had gone to fight the wars in Scotland and had not returned. And his sister had no dowry to keep, and so had joined the Abbey in Dublin, not to be seen again. He had managed, by way of joining a gang, to fight to the role of sheriff, a role that had more to do with collecting scum for the Court's justice.

He had become aware of Fulk earlier that year. He was an English man who despised the Norman scum that raped their soil. They had plotted together to get that which was deserved for them, that which was their right. They were no Irish savages, made to take refuge in the god-forsaken sea soaked west. They were high born, and they aimed now to live like it. Both of them had seen the rise of Alice on the back of those less fortunate than herself, and her unholy status was immodest for one so common. She had a carriage and fine clothes. She did not go about on the streets but withheld herself from the gaze of all but the most high-born. She was too high. And so was her foul bastard son, who assisted his mother in all her foul endeavours. The lad had a home for himself at an improper age, insulting all those around him and his God. William needed, as much as his mother, to learn that the town would not stand for such an insult. What did they think would happen? Did they really think such behaviour would not be marked and punished?

Fulk looked a question at him.

"We'll try the side of the house," he said, and stepped back into the black.

At the side of the house was a large gated well, which was kept locked to prevent contamination. Le Kiteler and Fulk were walking around the side when they saw the warehouse; the one Alice and her husband had sought for their own exclusive use.

Mother's heart, the size of it. It was easily as tall as the house, and almost as secure. There was a large wooden bolt over it, made so big that one man could not lift it. We have out thought you, thought Le Kiteler; we have come as a pair. Therefore you will not –

"Do you think it could be in the warehouse?" whispered Fulk. Le Kiteler took a moment, and answered.

"I am of the same mind as you. Let us investigate."

The two men went across the yard and towards the warehouse. William went to one end of the beam and Fulk to the other. Together they lifted it, panting in the dark. They opened the door.

Inside the house, William was suddenly awake. Something had disturbed him, but what? His room was calm. He got up and, taking up a cudgel that rested under the bed, walked slowly around the house. He saw nothing, not until he got to the kitchen at the back of the house.

The warehouse door was open.

Since he had taken up residence in the house he had not dishonoured his promise to his mother, he had not entered the warehouse. So when he saw the door open, for a moment he wondered if Alice was here. But she would never work by night when she was free to go there during the day. Intruders. He very silently let himself out of the kitchen and began to make his way across the back yard.

Le Kiteler and Fulk had entered the warehouse, unsure of what they would find. But when they entered, they saw nothing. The warehouse was empty.

"He lied to us!" hissed Fulk.

"Wait! He said it was here, it's here."

They went deeper in. Their steps were terribly loud. With no torch or light to guide them, the blackness was scary. Le Kiteler had a terrible sense that there was someone else in there with them, waiting for them, waiting until they got just a little closer, just close enough so that he could reach out his hands to them, until -

"Wait!" said Fulk.

"What!"

"It's here! I can feel it under my feet!"

Le Kiteler put his foot over Fulk's, who then withdrew his own. Under Le Kiteler's shoe was a curved iron bar, attached to a stone flag. He swallowed away his fear and knelt on the ground. He took one side of the bar, while Fulk took the other.

Together, they pulled.

Slowly the flag moved, revealing a small hole. Le Kiteler put his hand in and drew out two bags. He stuffed one into his own tunic and gave the other to Fulk. They began to find their way back to the door.

William was standing outside with the cudgel.

The first to come out was Le Kiteler. William got him on the windpipe. He groaned and fell to his knees. Fulk came running out and hit William in the stomach.

William reeled but came back, giving Fulk a blow to the head. Lights were beginning to show in the windows. Fulk gave a hissed "come on!!" to Le Kiteler, dragged him up. William gasped when he saw the Sheriff. The other man did not hesitate. He gave William a vicious blow to the jaw, knocking him off his feet, and gave the two men enough time to run off.

William, dragging himself up, made his way around to the front of the house, in time to see both of them escape on their horses. The front door was open, and the houseman was running out, with a torch, yelling.

"What ho! What goes on! Sir!" he cried, seeing William, "What goes on? Are you hurt?"

"I am not hurt, Basil," said William, "But I don't think I'm done hurting yet."

He turned to the older man as he walked back in the front door.

"Wake the house. Saddle a horse for me and prepare my clothes. I am to my mother's house."

Throughout the dark night, William rode to the city. He pondered the events that had just happened, the two men entering his land, opening the warehouse, finding something there and laying

81

hands on him before they left. He fumed at his mother's lack of words to him, how she had given no warning of any sort to indicate that caution would be necessary. And it would have been necessary, he was the person obliged to keep the items, he owned the land, the risk fell squarely on him. Not on his mother or her husband. On him.

And it had been the Sheriff! William had met the man many times, they all had. He had often been charged with carrying out the rulings of the court with regard to bad debts, and such. But William had at least once met him in his mother's house, in entertaining the personages who had hand or part in their business. The man had always seemed cordial enough to William at the time.

By the time he had reached Kilkenny, it was nearing dawn. He paused at the gate to ask the gatekeeper a question.

"Have any men been here since Matins?" he asked, meaning since before the pre dawn hours.

"None other than the usual my Lord," answered the gatekeeper, which gave no information at all.

The reaction to him on the streets was strange. Everyone was afraid of him, as though he was notorious. They snatched children back from his gaze. They kept their own gaze low and away from his eyes, stayed in doorways, hid down lanes. Why did they fear him so?

He arrived at his mother's house. He dismounted and went to the main door, which was wide open in the blue light of dawn. He stood for a moment at the threshold, looking at the swinging door in trepidation. Finally he entered.

The main entrance area was deserted.

"What ho!" he called.

A noise could be heard somewhere. At the sound of his voice it stilled and was quiet.

William called again.

"What ho! It is William son of Dame Alice!"

A face appeared from behind a canvas. It belonged to an old serving maid the house had kept, and upon seeing William she rushed into the room. She fell on her knees in the centre of the room, and began tearfully moaning and crying.

"What on earth is this? Get up and explain this, immediately!"

She got a hold of herself somehow, and got up.

82

"Oh sire, thank goodness you've come. How did you get here so soon?"

"So soon?" he said, frowning. "What do you mean?"

"Sire, they have come this morning and taken your mother and father! They are to face a charge of murder!"

At this the woman broke down again, crying with all her might. William stared. This was the reason for the change in the townspeople he noticed. Why had no warning been leaked to them before the charge was levied-

Suddenly William understood. The Sheriff normally carried out the charge. This Sheriff, hearing of the charge, or perhaps even being responsible for it, used the opportunity to seize what funds he could in the chaos. That was why they had received no leak from authorities. Money was coming to them another way. William needed an hour to think upon a plan of action. He looked at the woman again.

"Come, calm yourself, old mother. Do not be alarmed, all will be well. Attend to the matter at hand, the house, and bring me food for breakfast. We will soon see your Mistress home again."

Soon seated at the fire, William finally gave himself proper thought as to how to remove this accusation from the record. There would be no easy path in this case.

At dawn, Alice had been writing in her room. Since her fortieth birthday some months before, she found she woke earlier. And, rather than merely lie there, she would read papers at her desk and make notes for correspondence for the clerks to draft. And accounts, always accounts, which she made a point of reading often. The sums for the wheat that had been paid for and stored were lower than she had expected, she would have to see to it that she got an explanation for it-

Suddenly there was a sound downstairs, a loud one. It had sounded like someone had dropped something heavy on the wooden floor. There was nothing further. She turned her attention back to the accounts.

The handle on her door moved. She saw it and, not making any sound, stood up at her desk. She couldn't move to the bed to hide, as she would cross in front of whoever was opening the door. Instead, she took up a sharp knife she kept. She held it tightly in her right hand. Where the hell were her staff? She tightened her grip on the knife. She would not go easy-

It was Adam. Alice gasped as he came into the room and shut the door behind her. He looked like a desperate man.

"There are men come for us, downstairs. They claim that we are responsible for a death."

Alice looked at his face, stunned.
What on earth was this?
She looked at him.

"No!" he hissed at her. "I am not responsible for any such thing!"

"Then we must answer these charges with all possible vigour at once! I'll dress and address these men and see if they will stand up to the charges they make!"
She made to move across the room, and he suddenly grabbed her and held her tightly to him. He held an arm around her neck, and another around her waist, and she could feel his hot breath gasp.

"You mustn't make any such claim! If we anger or displease these men all that I have worked for is lost, and I am done for! You must come with me now and we will go with these men, and we will soon be free!"

"What? You think I will so soon allow myself to be-"

"Please Alice! I ask this of you with all mercy and fear, please do not condemn me! We must carry out what they do so as to ensure we are safe! Please!"

Going with these men? To the gossip of the town? The loss of status for her and her son would be huge. And what would she possibly have to gain for it? What would be the reward? Adam's peace of mind? Not good enough! She broke free of his hold and turned, furious, to face him.

"Adam, no! You ask too much! I will not go! You wrong me to ask it of me! Why should I do such a thing! Why?" she said, not caring if her voice carried.

"Because my wife, these men carry evidence, false evidence, of my crime. They believe because they have such trumped up foolishness to placate those around them, that they will gain access to our hold on William's land."

Alice gasped at the idea, and her hand covered her mouth.

"Because they have done this, because they have the evidence that does not exist against me, we must answer their charges quietly, and wait for our chance to seize back what is ours."

Alice stared at Adam and finally understood. He did murder someone! He is lying, and been found out! But not who they say, someone else, someone he does not want anyone to know about. Perhaps he has been paying these men money for months! His foulness and idiocy now threatens all of us, independent of our innocence!

That was when the marriage ended.

Alice looked at Adam and saw a man who put in danger all she and her father and William her husband had worked for. She saw a man who could take away her status, her respect and her wealth. She saw a threat, not a husband. She saw a fool. He had cost her money and security, and that was unforgivable.

She turned away from him, and began to think. So, we must answer the charges, or at least go with these men to do so. We have more than enough in sureties to cover ourselves, and we will ensure that others will come to our rescue as well. We will send out word before we do this of our plight, and will ask those we can truly trust to lend us support at this time. She stood tall and sure again, and turned to face her husband.

"Go dress. Prepare yourself for what is ahead. When I am ready I will send for you."

He looked at her.

"What will you do?"

"What I must. It is no concern of yours. Leave me," she said.

He looked into her face and saw. Without a word, he stepped back, bowed, and was gone.

Alice stood alone for a moment. She shook herself slightly, and sat at her desk. She pulled some paper to her, and then breathed out her fury to all.

The letters were sent out before Alice and Adam left the house with the men, before William arrived. When Alice came downstairs, dressed and ready, she was dry eyed and imperious. She left Petra in charge, and took Rose, the maid, with her. Her last words to Petra;

"Send for William. I trust only both you and he."

Petra nodded. She bowed formally to Adam, who stood behind his wife. You are a guest in this house, sir. He swallowed once, gave a brief nod, and escorted his wife out of her house.

Petra pressed herself into Philip's arms once the house was silent. "What to do?" she cried.

Philip held her face and smiled at her.

"We will do the right thing. We always do."

Petra received word immediately when William arrived. She found him beside the fire taking his first bite of food. He did not formally acknowledge her presence, but merely gestured to the other chair and continued eating. Petra took the chair without a word, privately noting to herself that William was treating her like another male. She must not be too insulted.

"How now, Petra, how was my mother when she left?"

"Excellent well, my lord. She had sent out much correspondence to those who should support our cause before she left. They should stand beside us at this time."

William lifted his eyes to her.

"To whom did she address correspondence to?"

Petra handed out a piece of paper to him.

"These are the names she addressed them to, Sir."

William read it quickly. He would have chosen all except the Viceroy, but in hindsight could see why she had done so. The more who knew of this the better. As usual she was showing the way.

He looked up at Petra, who was watching him. She seemed calm enough.

"How are you? When did the men come?"

"I am passing well, my Lord, such as can be expected. The men came well before dawn. They did not make their presence known, but instead entered without knocking, assaulting Philip in the hall. They sent word to Master Le Blund regarding the warrant, and merely waited for the house to wake afterwards."

"Philip? How is he now?"

"He is well Sir. He has a bad bruise on his back, but I have treated it and he will be well within a day."

William nodded, understanding. Good.

He sat back in his chair, thinking. This was passing odd! Men that sneak into a house, then merely stand and wait for those they have come for!

Then he saw it. They had hoped to raid the house of its wealth, by coming in under stealth. Once discovered, they had no option but to remain where they were and wait the pleasure of those they had come to take. William's jaw hardened at the idea of this filth taking their possessions from them. That was what had happened at his property. They knew what was there and how to find it. He looked at Petra again.

"How was Master le Blund?" he asked her quietly.

She looked at him, testing her answer in her mind. He could see her balance the desire for honesty with the need for temperance. Eventually she spoke just one word, but it was enough.

"Compliant."

William wasn't sure when Alice sent the letters, but they must have been as soon as she heard the news. A messenger thumped on the door with a reply before Sext. The messenger came in, panting. He had clearly pushed his horse to the limit in getting there, and stood before William, his shoulders heaving.

William looked at the wet, tired face of the older man, and gave him a moment to breathe.

"Well?" asked Petra, looking up at the messenger.

In response, he pulled out a scrolled piece of parchment, and handed it with a bow to William.

It was very good quality. He may have to increase his own expenditure on such things. He opened it and began to read aloud.

"My dearest Dame Alice, felicitations and best wishes to you. Please note that news of your unfortunate circumstances were delivered to us early this morning and caused us great distress. We send this messenger to state that we are making haste to you and that we are due to arrive before nightfall at your residence in the city. We intend to make our way with all haste to you in your current difficulty and will give every assistance we can at this stage. May God bless you and keep you in this difficult time and grant you the succour you need to overcome all that has befallen you. Le Poer." He looked up at Petra.

"See to him, give him something to eat," he said, nodding towards the messenger. Petra nodded, showed the man out. William looked at the fire in contemplation.

This was the first letter they had received, but it would not be the last. All the sureties would be met almost immediately, and his mother would be home soon. To have calming letters from the family of Le Poer was an enormous boost. He decided he would leave Petra here to receive them and go give his company to his mother immediately. He did not know in what way he would find them.

The jail house was located in the centre of the town, at the crossroads. Alice, Adam and Rose had been led there in the carriage of the Sheriff, and mercifully the streets had still been somewhat empty. Alice sat straight-backed beside Rose, and had kept her eyes at a point somewhere above Adam's head. Adam didn't notice.

Who had he killed? Did he have it arranged, or had he done it himself? Was it a man or a woman? Did he do it for gain or for revenge, or for some unlikely good?

The carriage rocked suddenly on the uneven road, and the child beside her whimpered in fear.

"Do not fear, child," said Alice. "We will soon be home."

Rose nodded assenting, but did not lift her eyes. I should not have brought her, thought Alice. She is too young to be useful to me.

The carriage brought them to the jail house proper, and stopped. Alice sat looking at it with contempt in her eyes. The door to the carriage opened.

"All right me lady, lets' be having ya!" cried a voice outside. Alice lifted her head to its highest, and promised herself that she would never forgive Adam for the injury he had done her today.

William was furious, and not hiding it. For too long had they delayed him at the gate, like some thief's wife hoping to see her

88

husband. He gave a cold stare to the jail house keeper from inside the carriage, and then nodded, handing over the small bag of coins.

The keeper immediately opened the door behind him, and bowing as much as his girt would allow him, permitted William Kyteler entry into the jail house.

The smell, like everywhere else, was what assailed you first. The dreadful smell of the sick, the dying, and the insane. All were here, in the dark, giving out their corpulent stink of shit, sick, and all the rest. William held a handkerchief to his face in an effort to avoid the illness that must surely be prevalent here. He turned as the jailer locked the door behind them, and then made his way down the jail. William had to force himself to take one step after another, as the darkness of the jail curled around her.

To his left he could hear the men groaning in the dark. Sad small sobs escaped one of them. They were separated from the walkway by small barred doors. On the right were the women, who seemed little better. Creatures made out of rags rose and stood as the two men walked by, their eyes the only things that indicated they were of the same race as man. William noticed that the same barred doors here as well. He reasoned that there would be a huge fear of illness from touching such a creature.

His mother was at the last cell in the corridor. William, his cloth still over his mouth, gestured to the jailer to open the door. There was but one candle in there, and it was hard to see. The jailer unlocked the barred door, and let him in.

It took his eyes a moment to make out figures in the gloom. He peered about him.

"Dame Alice?" he called.

"William, I am here," she replied. Her voice was strong and very much in charge.

He stepped forward until he found her, sitting beside the small slit in the stone that passed as a window. Rose sat beside her, very small. The walls behind them were filthy and coated with goodness knows what. The smell was dreadful beyond compare. There seemed to be no sign of Adam that William could see, and he did not ask for him.

"Mother," he greeted her, and sat down beside the two women.

"I have the first letter from the Le Poers, giving assurances that they are on the way, and that they will all assistance, be it financial or otherwise, that they can give." He pulled from his tunic the letter that he had received from the messenger and handed it to his mother.

She scanned it with a great speed, and then handed it back to him. "Good," she replied. "They will need to send sureties to the jailer to provide for our release. See that they receive the best in the house and all we have to give, but ensure that they give the surety with all speed."

William did not interrupt, but merely nodded as she spoke. She went on.

"Ensure that we receive details of the charge and all that is listed against us as evidence. So far all that I have been able to ascertain is that the charge is one of homicide. But surely they must have more against us, details and the such."

William thought for a moment, and then asked a hard question.

"Have we received any further details from Master Le Blund?"

Alice's lips thinned, and she looked away for a moment. When she looked back, her head was high.

"No. We are depending upon you, William. I know I will not be disappointed."

William had never heard such words from his mother. But he did not pause. He stood up, and bowed to them both.

"I shall return once we have secured your release and have more information," he said. Then, bowing once deeply to them both, he left the cell.

On the way out, he spoke to the jailer.

"Where is Adam le Blund?" he said.

The jailer coughed once.

"He asked to be given his own cell, which, once he had paid the right amount, was accorded to him as was right and proper."

William nodded, respectful.

"Very shortly a lawyer for Dame Kyteler will be arriving. Please arrange for the details of the charge to be ready for perusal."

The jailer duly nodded, ready for the request.

"And finally, what surety is required for immediate release?"

90

The jailer was also ready for this query, in that he had paper in his hand ready. The script in it was workman-like but good.

William looked at the piece of paper for a long time, and then lifted his head to the jailer.

"Surely this is incorrect?"

"I have been told it is in fact the correct amount, Sire. My apologies."

William merely nodded, and walked out of the jail in a dream. It was over, it was lost. Surely they would never get such a sum in their hands! He made his way out to the carriage, but paused before giving the order to move on. A thought had struck him, and he sat and thought for a moment. Then he was out of the carriage again, and banging on the door of the jail. The jailer looked out, puzzled.

"I want to speak to Adam Le Blund!"

Adam's cell was no better than Alice's. He also sat as close as possible to the window, his lace cloth little protection. William did not greet him, but merely entered the cell once the door was opened. He waited until it was barred behind him again.

"Tell me all, please, for your own sake if not for the sake of your wife."

Adam lifted his head, in true despair. He was sitting on the stone flags, his eyes red from the stench. William might have felt pity for him. He said nothing.

He stood in front of him, and held the piece of paper that the jailer had given before Adam's eyes.

"I have been told that this amount is the surety for both you and my mother. Not less than twelve hours ago, a raid was made on my property."

Adam gasped in horror at William, his faced a picture of fear.

"Then all is lost! We are doomed, for they have taken it all!" he cried, his voice breaking. He lowered his head again and sobbed.

"Control yourself, you are not lost yet!"

He squatted in front of him.

"Tell me, what did those men take from my warehouse?"

Adam lifted his head.

"They took the sum of money that your mother and I intended to provide to the Earl of Ulster."

William looked at the piece of paper, at the unimaginably large amount of money that was written there.

"And was the amount of money you had hidden this amount?" he asked.

"Yes!"

William stood again above him.

"You had three thousand pounds hidden on my property and saw fit to tell no one of the fact? To not tell me of the fact?"

"I felt it the most safe course of action! If no one knows of it, then it cannot be stolen! No one knew of this, especially you!"

William looked at him. Now he knew exactly what to do.

The details were discovered, in that there were almost no details. Fulk and Le Kiteler were the main witnesses in the accusation of homicide, in that they held they had seen Adam Le Blund 'most crelly and foully cause the carriage to run over a childe with no thought or concern for its safety'.

"A child?" asked Alice, disbelieving. "They say they saw him run over a child? Where is this dead child, then, where is the dead thing, the crying mother, the stoical father? Who cares about such a thing, if only the witnesses come forward?" She snorted to herself once more before reading on.

William let her read. He had dispatched a letter of complaint to Edward, the King of England to bring the suit to his attention. As well as that, the Le Poers had supported the Kytelers in the counter-suit they had launched against the accusers. But the matter could go on for months, possibly.

The surety matched that which had been snatched from his property, as well as £100 he had given to the business from his own coffers. The idea seemed to be that the two men would steal the money in the dead of night, and then by morning oblige the family to agree to their keeping it. All above board. William found himself mentally storing away the idea for later, if necessary.

What he intended to do was to allow them to have their moment of glory and thereby to be placated. But he would not allow it to be left so. He could not afford it, first of all, as he and his mother's neck would be wrung if they could not ultimately provide those funds for the Earl. But as well as that, he had no intention of allowing such an act to be carried out against his family. He looked out of the cell window. The door of the cell behind him opened.

"Youse is all free to go, me lady, you have met your surety."

Alice, hearing this, stood as tall as her tiny frame would let her, and brushed down her gown.

"Come, Rose. We are going."

Alice bowed her head in prayer along with the rest of the congregation, feeling the white unfocused feeling of religion flow over and through her. They would have you dead on the ground while they would search you for coins, she thought to herself, and closed her eyes to give an appearance of humility. Always believe you are being watched.

William sat beside her, waiting for her to answer his question. She did not lift her head, but merely whispered slowly to him.

"Do you wish me to give up these funds so that I unable to make the request of the Earl?"

"Do you wish me to believe that my arrest and imprisonment were but humble assaults upon my status and security and that in all manners and ways I should perhaps exercise forgiveness? Do you ask me to ignore that which has been done and may yet be done again? Should I give the money away, perhaps to the poor?"

William did not immediately speak. She needed a moment to compose herself. Eventually he slowly leaned forward until he could whisper into her ear.

"Mother, I seek only the safe return of the funds and an absence of guilt being associated with our house in doing so. We must move with caution if that is to be the case. A delay will allow this to be so. They are being watched, nothing further can happen." He paused while the priest intoned the Latin somewhere ahead of them.

A few minutes passed, while they were alone with their thoughts. William remembered again that morning when he had heard that Fulk's body had been found in the river. He had been stabbed, twice, once in the hand and once in the heart. The suit and counter suit would soon falter to nothing if they lost any more witnesses.

Money divides, he thought. All money is. It is a force of nature. It cleaves nations, separates family, creates and wins wars. Money of that amount is like a wild animal that one can only steer, but never tame. And it should always be kept at arms length, or otherwise see your neighbour, your friend, yourself change. He listened to the songs of the singers for a moment. They sing to Heaven, and their voices carry to the Lord above. But they themselves must still remain below, with their concerns, cares, aches and pains. We must all remain below. He could see one of the monks singing with the rest at the apse, who had feet so blue with the cold it was a wonder how he sang. The back of the man was twisted with a hump, that made him obliged to twist his torso every time he wanted to look to the left or right.

William looked at his mother again, her back still straight, her veil so white and pure, falling on the cloth of her spotless dress. Her hands, clear of all dirt, rested together in penitent prayer.

He thought over the plan again, and felt it was the safest way. His mother looked at him out of the corner of her eye, trying to judge his face.

"And it will be all of it?"

"It will be all of it."

The mother and son sat, in great humility, for the rest of the mass.

Payments made out of the Surplus of Richard De Bereford's account, Treasurer of Ireland,

Adam Le Blund and Alice his wife, repayment of loan:

Adam Le Blund of Callan and Alice his wife, in payment of £214 8s. 3d. Owing to them in the surplus of Bereford's account, for a loan which they made to the treasurer and chamberlains of the Dublin exchequer, for the king's use,... to pay wages to those going from Ireland to Scotland for the   expedition of the king's war there, paid to them by their letters of acquittance, and the king's writ patent of the said loan was taken from them:

£214 8s. 3d.

The granting of the enormous surety had had a miraculous effect upon the case, in that it seemed to have stalled and could not be progressed any further. Alice, Rose and Adam had been released, and had therefore had a banquet to thank those who had answered the letters of Alice. All was well again, it appeared.

William Le Kiteler tightened the rope around the carriage, and ensured that the last bundle was tied securely. He gave thanks, once again, for the good fortune that had come to him and his family, and called one last time for his son to join them outside the house.

"Henry! You delay your mothers and your sisters one more moment, we will away without you!" he cried, his heart full of good humour. A moment a small boy appeared, panting from running.

"There you are!" cried Le Kiteler, and scooped the five year old up in his arms. "Now, you sit with your sister and be as quiet as you can, you hear?"

The boy merely nodded, snuggling into the figure of his older sister. William looked at them, at his two girls, his only son, and his young wife, who raised an eyebrow at his sentimental mien.

"Now, sir," she said, "let us be off before the light is gone and we are done for!"

He nodded, smiling, and took his place at the top of the carriage. Before long they were at the edge of the town, and, after paying the toll, they were on their way.

"And where are we off to again?" he asked them, now free to talk once out of the city limits.

"We go, Father, to Dublin, for a new life," replied the eldest, Elsa.

The carriage quickly made its way out to the countryside, the air clearing of the smell of the city. Before long the children were asleep, and their mother looked at them.

"They will like Dublin, I think," she remarked.

"With the money that we have now for a few hours work, we will be able to like anywhere," replied her husband. And it had been a few hours work. Fulk was now nowhere to be found, as Le Kiteler had intended. A small matter to ensure that the man took a slip on something small and sharp, and went to meet his Maker. Now

William and his family were free to enjoy what was rightly theirs anyway. He looked around him at the expanding countryside that was spread around them. Good men always rise, he thought. You can't keep a good one down.

The motion of the carriage was soothing, making the journey seem quick. It wasn't long before they saw an excellent camp-site for the night. This was a comfort for William. He did not fear being outside the city gates in the wilderness, when what was most dangerous was being within the city with the rest of the wolves. He drove into the woods where he could not be seen from the beaten track, and made camp with his wife. They made a small fire for their last meal of the day, and after eating, put the children to bed. Finally William and his wife lay beside the fire, looking at the heavens through the trees. William, looking up, wondered at the turn of events. How could things change so quickly?

He heard the twig break so loudly it seemed almost at his ear. He looked up and received a strong blow for his trouble. He could hear his wife and daughters screaming from somewhere behind him, and he tried his hardest to turn his head. A voice sounded in his ear.

"Turn your head my lad and those girls will die faster than you can breathe. Shut up!" it called out, and his wife and children were quietened. William tried very hard to remain calm, and failed miserably. His will hardened that they would get out of this alive. They would survive.

"Now, you are going to do two things. You are going to tell me where you have hidden that which doesn't belong to you, and then you are going to be on your way. Do I make myself clear?"

The point of a knife stung the skin under his chin. William found himself nodding automatically. The voice in his ear spoke again.

"So, where is it?" it asked.

"Under the carriage boards, near the back wheel on the right," he muttered. A command was called out and someone made their way into the carriage. At least, that was what it sounded like to William, who could not move his head to check.

For a long time nothing happened. William tried to move his head away from the knife. Whoever held it immediately saw what he was doing and gave him a small gash for his trouble.

"No getting away from this one, my lad."

After a while, a shout went up. They had found the bag. He closed his eyes in sorrow at the life that he and his family would now never have. Somewhere nearby him a bird sang.

Behind him he began to hear the sounds of the men leaving. There was one jumping out of the carriage, the bag and its heavy load ringing in his hands. There was another, moving over the children. Suddenly he could hear a scream, and then another, as his children began to cry out.

Henry! He thought, and tried to move against the knife. But it was too late for him, too late for them all, as the blade slashed against their necks right down to the bone of their spine, again and again, until each one of them was dead.

The men left them, left them with their dying fireside, as the lights went out around the children and their parents. Each of them tried to live on, and each of them died. All they had now were the cold unblinking stares of the stars, who looked on unmoved as the family bled out onto the cold soil.

Chapter Eleven

The Year 1303

William lifted an eyebrow in surprise and took a bite of pigeon, finding it excellent. He took a swig of wine and thought about his answer. Beside him, Arnold did the same, knowing enough not to egg the younger man on.

"For all that my opinion is worth," said John Le Poer, "I believe it is an idea with merit. Otherwise I would not have permitted Arnold to have put it to you."

And how would you have stopped me?" asked Arnold, snorting in derision.

"By reason, Cousin, and by quoting the authorities."

"Aye, that would work!" laughed Arnold, taking a bite of food. William laughed with him, his heart at ease.

Ye Gods, thought Adam. How did this idea come about? Now, where is Rose?

The four men were sat at table, resting after an excellent day's hunting. It was summer, 1303; one year after the money had been stolen and regained by William. The ties the two of them had with the local nobility had, if anything, become stronger as a result. William frequently took hunting parties out to the local countryside, returning to either his house or his mother's house to entertain and feed his guests. He had become a firm associate of John Le Poer, who had been an excellent friend to them during their last difficulty. William found his advice well thought out, and a much-needed counter to Arnold's hot headed beliefs. He leaned forward and gestured to Rose to fill John's cup. The older man protested.

"Now, William, you will make me intemperate, and that is not a good thing for an older man such as myself."

"Older man!" exclaimed Arnold. "If you are an older man, then may the good Lord bestow his kindness upon me, because you are only a few years older than myself!"

"That may be, Arnold. But you wear your years more loosely than I do, and I also feel the effects of wine more cruelly than you. It is my nature." He looked at William.

"We're told that experience is not the best teacher, that the leaning upon authorities who may give us clear examples is the best way to take on wisdom. But I have my experience, such as it is, to guide me, and it says not to drink too much wine!" he laughed.

William laughed with him, liking the man greatly.

"Do not ignore experience, poor handmaiden as she is to wisdom. Instead, let us be a good set of friends to you and not press that upon you which would do you no good."

He turned to Adam, smiling.

"What say you, more wine Adam?" he offered.

"I will partake, thank you William," said Adam. The man's tone told all the men around the table that they were not friends. The air emanating from Adam stilled William's good humour somewhat, but he granted Adam his opinion for the moment and let it be. Rose moved further down the table to fill Adam's cup.

William was about to turn away, when he saw Adam's hand rest on Rose's while she poured him his wine. Rose blinked furiously several times at the gesture, while Adam stared into the child's face, daring her to meet his intruding gaze. Aw, God's wounds, thought William.

"So what say you to our enterprise?" asked Arnold.

William looked into his lap for a moment and then lifted his smiling face to Arnold once again.

"What are the merits of it, Arnold? What would I gain that I have not already gained?"

He knew right well the answer, but wanted to hear their views.

"What to gain!" exclaimed Arnold. "Why there is a wealth to be gained! For one thing, your house will be responsible for the retaining of tax for those friends of ours in Dublin."

"Why is that of benefit? We Kytelers are already able to gather funds owning to us. We're much slighted for the skill as it is. What other point do you have that would be of assistance to us?"

"Well, those in authority, such as you would be, most often are friends to those others who are in authority. Such is their class, as is assigned to them at birth by the blessings of our Holy Father. Where you to achieve such a role, you would gain the friendship of many men of authority." This response came from the thoughtful John Le Poer, who said all this while looking at a distant point on the far wall.

"I already count among my friends such great and noble persons such as yourselves, my good friends."

Arnold snorted. "Lord help you if I could be called great and noble!" he laughed. William continued.

"Is it not also the case that men of authority cannot be sure which of those friends among them are there due to the goodness of their hearts and the kindness of their natures, and those others who are there solely to gain from the authority that is held? It is surely wiser to adhere to that which is known, rather than cling, uncertain, to that which is not."

"My God!" exclaimed Arnold, banging his pewter cup down on the table in amazement, "he is a word smith with his arguments. We are undone by him and his twisting ways!"

There was general amusement across the table.

"I do not know what else would convince me," said William. "I am still unconvinced. Is there no further argument on the matter to be heard?"

Adam leaned forward, and cleared his throat.

"We do not know what is coming to us William, not from King, God or our neighbour. We cannot guess, either, or make plans to prevent hardship. If we do not prepare properly, we may be damaged, in ways we cannot foresee. If you are not mayor, then someone else must be. In this way, we cannot prepare. Be mayor. You are clever and able, and you will be a good one. In this one way at least, we will be prepared a little more for that which is to come."

Silence followed the long speech. Then, after a moment, Arnold banged his cup on the table in agreement, and John slowly nodded at the reasoning. William looked at his father in law.

"It is a very good way of seeing the matter," said John. "I believe I concur with the reasoning."

"Ye Gods, so do I!" yelled Arnold.

William continued looking at his father in law.

"What say you, William?" asked John.

After a long moment, William nodded, his agreement clear. He would be mayor, or at least would indicate to the Viceroy that if the post were offered he would not refuse it. The city fathers would stand behind him and the position would be his shortly, within a year or two. He would be responsible for the tax on imports on the river, and would be obliged to keep and arm the defences of the town for its own protection. So, where in all that did a benefit fall to Adam, as he would not have suggested it otherwise?

"Good," said John. It was done.

William as Mayor, thought Adam. Whatever next, Arnold as Seneschal?

Later that night, Adam left his bed in the house of William, and quietly stood at the bedroom door. He could hear nothing; there was no one outside. He quietly lifted the door latch and stepped out.

All was still.

He stood beside his door for a good five minutes, not making any sound at all.

There was no movement from anywhere else in the house. He stepped away from the door and moved down the corridor. He knew exactly which way to go with the minimum of noise. He made his way down the stairs and into her quarters, where she slept having cried herself to sleep. Or some such nonsense.

Adam came quietly in, and sat on her bed. She did not waken, or at least gave the appearance of being asleep. He brushed back the hair on her face.

The time of his infatuation with her dated from shortly after his incarceration with Alice. Their release had brought about Alice's utter rejection of him in all things bar social, where she seemed to suffer him for the sake of the appearance of their marriage. He did not expect her refusal of him to wound his ego so much, but it did. He felt as though he had been found wanting in some way, and the idea niggled him no matter what he would do. He spent more careful time on his land, or on his business, or with his own family. Still, the rejection of the Dame Kyteler seemed to negate his own person in some small, unknown way, and he could find no peace of mind.

Then, one Sunday while returning in the carriage after Mass with the Dame, Petra and Rose, he had felt the frosty air coming from both of the older women. Only Rose had granted him a bashful smile, and he had instantly seen in a moment how he could turn the child as a weapon against Alice. This had not been what he had told himself. Instead he said to himself that the smile of the girl had greatly gladdened his heart, and had lifted his sorrowful soul somewhat.

The idea had rested with him for a while, quiet and black somewhere within him. He had been waiting for time to past so that the act would not look too much like revenge upon Alice for her actions to him. Instead, he had waited through the winter, begun slowly in the spring, and now was actively pursuing the girl in the summer, always with an eye to the damage he must eventually cause at the end.

It occurred to Adam, sitting on the end of the bed, that when he found himself thinking lustful thoughts about Rose, at least he gave himself no credit. He knew what he was doing was wrong. This was because to him, Rose was in fact hardly human. He was of the opinion that her pleasant curves and her smiling face impressed his lower nature. He did not think that he liked her, or loved her, or wanted her. He thought that his desire for her was akin to bestiality, roundly condemned by all right thinking people and a thing to be hidden at all costs. She was a serving girl, ignorant of all but the lowest thoughts of life, and merely instructed or educated enough to carry out simple tasks. She could not know beauty in the true sense, but instead was a thing, and he had made himself a thing for wanting her. He considered this belief of his a sign of his good character, and classical education. He did wrong, but at least he knew it was wrong.

He brushed back her hair again, and she stirred slightly in her sleep. He pulled back the sheets on her, and examined her. She was but a thing, he reminded himself, but she did indeed stir him. Her skin was smooth and untouched by children. She did not bear weight like his wife but was young and clean of the touch of man. Her breasts were small and young, and he freely cupped them in his hand, feeling himself rise. Ah, to feel alive again, young again, that was the joy.

Her belly was small, her hips curved pleasantly. He took his hands off those lovely breasts to pull down the sheets further to see her legs. They were slim and tapered, and he began to lift the shift that she wore so that he could touch her. She stirred in her sleep. He put his hands between her legs, touching her sex, and now she was immediately awake. She jerked suddenly, trying to get away from him, and he clasped his hand over her mouth as hard as he could. With the other hand he shook a finger at her.

"Now don't be bold. Behave yourself. Be quiet, be quiet."

His manner was of a dog owner quieting a pet. He stopped shaking his finger at her and began to lift his hand from her mouth.

"Now," he said quietly, "If you are bold, you will be punished. You know this. You know also that if you displease me, you will also be punished. I don't intend to explain myself to you, nor should you expect such a thing. Do you understand?"

Rose made no movement, but instead merely stared at him.

"You will be very quiet, and you will not make noise."

He pulled down the rest of the sheets from the small bed, and pulled her shift up until it reached her armpits. She closed her eyes.

He put his hand out and touched her ankle. Ah, the soft skin around the strong bones. For a while he merely let the warmth of her skin warm his hand, but the sight of her moved him on. He let his palm slowly travel up the soft skin to her knee, curving gently around the bone there, letting it touch his fingers. And then up her thigh. He imagined the soft folds of her skirt brushing against her thighs all day long as she worked, as she lifted, carried things, as she looked at him, leaned over to serve him. Sometimes the skirts must get caught between her legs, get trapped in the warm hollows of her. He allowed his own hands to get caught there, to touch the soft hair he found curled there. So precious, and delightful to the touch. And then around the buttocks, letting his fingers curl around the wonderful curves there.

Her eyes flew open in pain and alarm and she struggled hard to get away from him. He merely grabbed her by the neck and turned her on her stomach, shoving her face into the bed. He shoved his fingers even harder into her, a playful smile on his face. His fingers jerked again and again into her, but he very soon found that boring. He pulled her up into a sitting position on the bed, ignoring her cries of pain, and took time to wipe his fingers on her skin. Rose, for her part, was terrified. A part of her was saying to the rest of her soul that this must surely end. This would soon end. His hand still on the girl's neck, he shook her until she opened her eyes to look at him.

He looked at her, and with his hand around her neck, hit her hard across the face several times. He had only intended to hit her once, but he found that the violence within him was more than he expected. She soon had a red streak across her mouth from his blows.

He pulled her off the bed and onto a kneeing position on the cold flags. He shook her again, as hard as he could without letting go of her, his teeth grinding together as he did so.

The door behind them flew open, and William rushed in towards them. Adam immediately let her go, and she flung herself away from him. William didn't even wait to let him speak but merely dragged him away from the girl and out of the room. He marched the man along back up the stairs and into the room Adam had woken up in. Adam turned to face the man, furious at the presumption he had shown. William didn't hesitate; he hit him squarely in the stomach. The older man bent double, he then hit him again in the face.

William leaned over and whispered into Adam's ear.

"A man that forces those weaker than him, is a man foul through and through, Blund. Do you understand?" he whispered, his fury making spittle come from his mouth.

Adam, grasping through the pain, merely nodded. William turned and walked out of the room.

Adam's eyes blazed with utter rage. To be so humiliated! To be discovered, and recognised, by William! Over a serving girl, no less! God help you, William Kyteler. I will see you destroyed.

Alice read the letter through once again, not sure she could trust her eyes. Petra and Rose were walking across the green pasture, the two women's backs facing her as they walked. She sat on a fallen tree, reading the letter that William had sent to her with Rose, who was so changed after one week helping William at his estate.

Alice read again the sentence that disturbed her most. 'On that night a most grievous mischief was attempted on her, from one close to our home.'

Alice sat back. Damn him. Damn him again. She must have been cursed on the day she thought she would take him. She had liked his tunic, she remembered, and had thought he would be pliable! Ye gods, was any woman so foolish!

She looked at Rose and Petra again, the two women so different. How dare that man harm any of her House? How dare he, so worthless as to be dangerous and unwanted, to cause them already so much difficulty, be so blind as to think he could carry on as usual? A serving girl may not have the same refinement as herself, but to abuse her in such a fashion! Alice knew the blow was aimed for her alone.

William would be mayor, as she had hoped. John Le Poer was indeed proving a very good friend to the family, in that once again he had steered them correctly. Until then, she could not act. But once William was safely Mayor, once that was done, she would and could be able to act against her husband properly. Adam will feel justice. He will not hurt us all in this way and not feel our anger. We will strike back.

She folded the letter carefully.

Petra and Philip lay silently together in the pale afternoon light. A tear moved from her eye into the dark richness of her hair.

Philip knew why she cried but could not make it better. He held her silently.

"That child! Oh Philip, that poor child!"

Chapter Twelve

The Year 1307

William, safely Mayor, looked over the river Nore and frowned.

"It's not good enough, though."

It should be a simple thing. They needed a port, a proper harbour that would allow the quick loading and unloading of goods from boats, and then move them onto the city proper. The river was allowing a market to start down by the docks, and the Kyteler house was excellently placed to take advantage of that. Instead, the riverside had become poorly constructed and run down, and there were weekly accidents and deaths.

William looked again at the plans laid out in front of him. What he was seeing was a small deck approximately wide enough for one man to walk along, and nothing more. That was hopelessly unmotivated. Instead what was needed was a proper port, made out of stone instead of wood so that it would last longer, and with a crane to lift the heavier goods safely on board.

William pondered the problem of the harbour for a few more minutes. The town coffers would not permit any more than what was laid out in front of him, which was not good enough. If the town were to get the port it needed, then it would have to find the money. He sent instructions for the builder of this port to come see him the next morning, and departed the town hall for the day.

It was late already, almost ten when he departed. The work of the town hall consumed William, and would for the next few years. The city of Kilkenny was seeing the economic expansion that had spread across Europe since the year 1000, and had caused much in the way of innovation in urban areas. William, sitting wearily into his carriage, looked at the changing landscape of the city he moved through. There was so much to be done. They had to move every year to ensure that there was no further flooding in the town, and every year they failed, with the subsequent damage done to property and goods. There was common disorder on the streets, particularly in the

106

part of the town frequented by the Irish, and getting men in to deal with it was always a hardship.

The neighbouring towns in the county were constantly seeking assistance with law and order, putting their already poor resources to the limit. The Irish were always causing problems as well, he had forwarded money to some Peter Bermingham for subduing the O'Connors and beheading their captains. As well as that, he was receiving more and more messages from abroad that worried him. The foulness of the corruption in Rome had, in 1303 seen the Italian noblemen lay hands on the Pope, who in his shock had died soon after. Not that Boniface hadn't deserved it. He had argued and abused most of the kings in Europe, even going so far to have two swords at his ordination, to show his command of temporal as well as spiritual power. William knew little of who came after him, only that the man was having difficulties with the Romans. They're all mad over there, though.

William was finally home. He descended from the carriage and made his way wearily inside. The plan for the evening was to eat a late supper, read through some papers, and then make his way to bed. He sat beside the fire and called for more lights so that he could read more clearly. The light seemed to escape his eyes more these days.

Philip served him his supper, some hot meat with lots of seasoning, and some bread or other. William didn't look up when it was served to him, but instead merely muttered thank you to Philip and kept on reading the letter. He really must talk to the scribe, were the harvests going to be collected at that time or not?

It took him a moment to realise that Philip was still standing in front of him. He looked up with a small smile on his face.

"Yes Philip?"

Philip was in a lot of discomfort. William immediately gave him his full attention and waited for what the man had to say.

"I have a matter of some sensitivity nature to discuss with you, Sir."

William nodded, sat up in his chair, ready to listen. Was someone stealing from them again? He would have to give Philip more of his way in choosing staff.

"Master Adam has been tupping young Billy, Sir."

For a long time there was silence.

"Do you know what you are saying, Philip?"

"I do, Sir."

"Are you absolutely sure? Beyond all doubt?"

Philip remembered his opening the bedroom door, his hands laden with some errand or other. In front of him, splayed on the bed, was the figure of 13-year-old Billy, his leggings pulled down to his ankles, his face tearful and grimacing with the pain, with Master Adam behind him swearing with excitement.

Philip immediately shut the door and stood for a moment, trying to breathe. A few seconds later the door opened, and young Billy came out, crying, still pulling up his leggings. Philip had taken care of the lad, tried to clean him up as best he could, but honestly, was wordless as to how to placate him. It had occurred to him that it explained why they never seemed to stay for long these days. There had been a few others, who had never given a clear reason, but had been gone before they had needed to.

William swallowed once, and decided that now was the time for action.

"Who else knows about this?"

"Only yourself Sire, no one else."

"Can you vouch for the boy?"

"Only while he remains here Sir, not after."

"And will he remain here?"

"That will depend, Sir."

"On what?"

Philip was silent. On what action I decide to take, thought William. He turned and looked into the fire once again. Adam, you sodomite. You assumed because we did not act before you were somehow safe. But you did not think we were waiting. And now we will wait no more.

Of course, the man must die. But the question was, what was the best way for that to happen?

Fate was kind in this regard. One day later, a letter arrived for Adam at his estate in Callan. His clerk duly forwarded it for his attention. He received the information the next day after breakfast, and stared aghast at the news.

"What? How much?"

"We have been asked to provide a considerable tithe of the estate to the King, Sire. It is calculated as a percentage of what is held by us. Therefore we will need to quit the estate in England, Sire."

"Quit my estate? Are you mad, man?" said Adam, aghast. "Do you think that I am a fool, man? I will NOT give away my estate. You," he said, pointing his finger at the clerk, "You DO something to change this! I will not be giving away my estate!"

Adam slammed the door behind him in his fury, all thought of gallantry gone.

Alone in his office that night, the clerk had a visitor in the guise of Philip. He looked up, smiling at the Houseman whom he liked, in his way.

"I have become aware of your Master's recent difficulty," began Philip.

"Difficulty?" asked the clerk, all innocence.

"The demands of the Crown on his estate. Do I understand correctly?"

"Yours is an accurate picture, it's true," said the Clerk.

"I may be able to suggest a solution to you that your Master may find beneficial."

"Indeed?" wondered the clerk. He was trying very hard not to be rude now, but what could Philip know about such things? Of course. This idea would be coming from the Kytelers, not from a mere Houseman.

"Do please go on, Philip."

"Were the estate of Master Le Blund be quit-claimed to Dame Alice, then the estate in England would be held by his wife, not by Master Le Blund. Hence the claim on the estate would be null and void."

The clerk sat back in the chair at the brazenness of it. Philip, you must have been forced into this, you do not act in such a way, he thought.

Philip looked at him, asking a question.

"And what will be my part to play?" asked the Clerk.

Philip looked at him.

"If this suggestion is put to him, it will be, by necessity, in the guise of advice, of recommendation. I must ask you, what is the benefit accruing to me for putting this to him?"

Philip blinked at the man. William had told him that this might happen, but had not believed it. Yet here it was, as sure as anything. He slowly drew out a small bag from his tunic.

"This is an advance payment on the advice you will hopefully will see fit to give. Were the advice to be found suitable by Master Adam, a gracious commission shall be arranged for you."

The man measured the bag, thinking.

"I believe we do indeed have an agreement."

The next morning, the clerk asked to see Adam. He found him in the grounds, practising archery. He made certain to stand well behind the man while speaking, so as to avoid any injury, accidental or otherwise.

"My lord, I believe I may have come upon a solution to the problem raised yesterday."

Adam raised the bow and took aim.

"Oh yes?" he asked, releasing the arrow. It hit close to the bullseye on the target.

"Yes, I think there may be a way where in we can show you don't owe the property involved."

Adam turned on the spot, staring at the man with the long, black cloak.

"What? How?" he said.

"We create what is called a quit-claim, my Lord, where in you sign over your property to Dame Alice, so that she, rather than you, holds it in perpetuity. Therefore the Crown cannot make claim upon that which you do not hold...is something the matter, Sire?" he said. Adam was staring at him in the most peculiar manner.

"You suggest I should provide that all I own should be in the name of Dame Alice?"

"My lord, not at all. I would never suggest such a thing."

The clerk looked around to ensure no one was listening.

"What I propose, my lord, is nothing more than a document instructing that all such property is in the hands of Dame Alice from here on in. It should be signed by Dame Alice, and by a witness on your side, perhaps your daughter. This matter may be done by a matter of say, lack of involvement by the parties named. We may never need to properly involve them in the first place."

Adam frowned, and stood closer so that no one could hear his voice but the clerk.

"You mean, falsely indicate their names?"

"Exactly, sir. Firstly, this will allow us security to ensure that we are not endangering the estates abroad, and also were the documents to be relied on by parties unknown in the future, we would be able to point to the fact of their being forgeries to deny execution."

Adam was silent for a moment while he thought about it.

"What are the negatives? Where are the potential risks?"

"We must ensure utter secrecy in the matter at all times, Sire. I might request that the matter remain something between us. Were we to involve any other party, the risk is that such a document may become useful to them."

Adam bit his lip, and after a moment spoke.

"Let me think on it," he said, dismissing the clerk and turning back to the target.

"Very good, sir," said the Clerk. And if that is the only target you hit today, I will not be surprised, he thought, walking away.

Later that night, again alone in his study, the clerk looked up to see Adam enter. He immediately rose to his feet.

"Let us carry it out, then," said Adam.

"But let us not put it in Alice's name, but instead that of William's. He had none of his mother's evil ways and is a safer option to receive it."

The clerk nodded, making notes.

"You will be able to make an accurate representation of his mark?"

"I shall endeavour to do so, Sire."

"Very well. And I shall ask my brother, rather than my daughter, to witness the document. My daughter would refuse to carry out this, for fear for her own interests. My brother will be of more assistance."

"Certainly, Sir."

111

Adam looked at him.

" You do think you will be able to do this, won't you?"

"I am confident I will be able to be of assistance, Sire."

Adam looked at him intently for a moment, and then merely nodded.

"Bring them to me when they are ready."

"Aye, Sire," said the clerk, who was already speaking to an empty room. He waited for several moments, and then sat down again. He sat back in his chair, and then took a small sip of wine from the glass in front of him.

"That should please you Philip."

After a moment, a door behind him opened, and Philip came out.

"It doesn't matter whether I am pleased or not, as you well know," said Philip, giving himself a small glass of wine from the jug as well. He sat down and looked at the clerk.

"What matters is that our masters are happy. We do not have our own desires to fulfil, as you know. Instead we are obliged, as our Maker would wish us, to fulfil the desires of those born above us."

"We have no desires?" asked the clerk, laughing. "Philip, while I know you as a man of good sense, I marvel at you now. Do you mean to tell me that you do not have a human heart, with human needs and wants, along with a soul to be grateful for the salvation offered to it? Did I hear you correctly?"

"You did," replied the Houseman.

"And what would prompt you to say such a thing? Do you count yourself with no soul, old friend?"

Philip merely looked sadly at the clerk, and then at his wine. What he wanted to say was, today I helped bring a man closer to death. Today I arranged for lies to be told, for misconceptions to exist, for deception to occur. I know and you know that when he signs that document, for all the falsity it may contain, he is surely signing his death sentence. And I arranged all that; saw to it that it is done. I am not blind. I am glad he will die, for he is a danger to us all here. Yes, I am one of us here. I am truly the servant of my Master. But Lord help me, Lord help us all, for I fear my Master is the Devil.

112

Alice was in her room, looking at her glass. I am older, she told herself, but she did not feel it. What age was she now, forty-five? Forty-three? She wasn't too clear. But she knew she was still an able Mistress for her house, and she considered that enough. She lifted a hair back from her face, tucking it into her headdress. That reminded her, she wanted to go to the warehouse tomorrow with Petra and Philip, to review the storage methods for the cloth they were going to be importing later that month. If the rains came before it was properly insulated, then they would be without the linens from Italy for weeks-

There was a knock on her door. She frowned slightly. Petra would normally just knock and enter. No one else would be knocking on her door this late.

"Come in," she called.

William opened the door.

"William! I thought you in the country tonight! Come in by the fire."

She drew her sewing off the chair and gestured to him to sit. He sat down slowly, hesitant to begin speaking. Instead, he found himself remarking to himself that his mother seemed to have changed. She is softer, more welcoming, he thought to himself. How will this change her?

"Now, what brings you to me?" she said, smiling.

He looked down at his shoes for a moment, and then told himself he was being a coward.

"Mother, I have information I must tell you. I warn you, it will be most unwelcome."

She looked at him, her face changing.

"Please go on."

"It is time to respond to Adam."

This she had not been expecting. She leaned forward to him, her eyes staring at him.

"Why now?"

"Because Philip has become aware Adam is forcing our staff."

She leaned slowly back from him.

"Both boys and maidens, it would seem."

She swung away from him, hiding her face from him, forgetting that her glass showed her.

113

She sat with her eyes closed for just a moment. Then she opened them, and turned back to William.

"Then it is time, indeed. What are your plans?"

"There is a way we can do this, and can access to his estate."

"How?"

"I am in the process of obtaining from Adam a document signed by him quit claiming all his property to me. Once we have this, we will have not only justice but revenge."

"William, how have you done this?"

"I along with his staff invented a claim from the English Crown to obtain a tithe of his estate. In order to avoid it he is creating a fictional quitclaim to me of all his lands, so as to claim that another holds the ownership. I will get this document."

"And then you will control his estate."

"Then I will own his estate."

"And once you own his estate-"

"We are free to move in any way we see fit."

Alice stood up, moved to the other side of the room while she thought. From her window she could see Adam in the courtyard, getting down off his horse, and shuddered.

I did not enjoy my time in prison, she thought. I will not go back there.

But this is no mere family of beggars and their brood that easily dispatched and forgotten about. No one ever even said their names to me, did they? But he is different. He is close to me, near to me. An accident in the woods would be far less likely to succeed this time. We must find another way.

She turned once more, walking towards the bed as she thought. A gradual, slow process, she thought, wherein he is seen to get sick before the eyes of all. He retires to his bed, he falls weaker. A doctor is called for, who administers medicine, to no effect. He dies in his sleep at night, peacefully. The document is produced, giving his estate to William. Then all is well again, and the House of Kyteler is safe. I will need to be quiet, and circumspect, for days, maybe even weeks. I must be kind and friendly and gentle with him as he dies. And I will need to be exact about the poison as well. Only we can see that. But the rest of the world must know of it and see it happening.

114

William, for his part, was watching Alice thinking, with patience. She is removing him, step by step. She looks like she has him. I think we have him.

Downstairs they could hear him, greeting Philip as he entered the house.

The next time a plate of food was put in front of Adam, he was watched with a morbid fascination. He took up his fork and dipped it into the stew. He slowly lifted a mouthful out and brought it to his lips. Alice, sitting beside him, was obliged to lower her eyes. He took a bite out of it, and chewed.

"So how was the day for you, husband?"

"Passing well. The rains have finally arrived, and the fields are grateful for it. I hear about the town that the Viceroy has remarried."

William let the gossip flow over him. This is going to be difficult, he realised. I may need to spend more time at the country house while this is going on. Then he realised he couldn't. He would have to be seen to stay near the house here, just like he always had in the past. Only during the summer months did he spend most of his time in the country.

Alice went on conversing with Adam, if anything charming him with her chatter. She is flattering him, thought William. She is placating him, cheering him. She may need to be the best wife she can be for the near future. I do hope he enjoys it while he lasts.

One week later, in a week which had been like all the others, Adam stood at his glass in his room. There was a strange cast to his features that he had never seen before. There seemed to be a drooping in his face, a sagging around the eyes that did not look familiar. And his skin was greyer than he could recall. Winter, it seemed, was not being kind to him.

Alice heard Adam coughing in the next room. She stayed where she was for the next five minutes, but then rose from her bed. She dressed as quickly as she could in the cold blackness, her breath showing.

She slipped out of her room, and walked to his door. Knocking quickly, she opened it and entered.

"I heard you coughing. Are you unwell, Adam?"

He looked up at her from his bed. Alice blinked slightly as she saw the change in his face. His eyes seemed to droop more and more these days, and the skin on his face was so thin and pale. His hair was thinning too, and she could see a clump of it on his pillow.

She rushed to him, allowing her alarm to work to her advantage.

"My husband, are you all right?"

His voice was frail and weak, and he took a long time to get the words out.

"I am most well, Alice. You are so good to me to help me. I do feel a little weak, however."

"You have caught a cold, I fear."

"I think I have. I may need to stay in bed awhile tomorrow."

He lay back on his pillow, exhausted.

"Can I get you anything? Some wine, perhaps?"

"A draft would be most pleasant, thank you."

Alice went to the jug on the table by the door, and poured him a cup. Bringing it to him, she lifted it to his lips and raised his head so that he might drink more easily. When he was done, she gently lowered his head and made sure that the glass was close to hand should he need it. She brushed the hair back from his face, and bent to kiss his forehead, hiding the clump of hair that came out in her hand as she did so.

"I am next door should you require anything, Adam," she said. "Do not hesitate to call upon me."

He looked up, surprised by her kindness.

"Thank you Alice."

She smiled gently at him, and then left the room.

Back in her own room, she threw the clump of hair in the fireplace, watching as it smouldered and burned. That's the first of him, she thought. Getting back into bed, she listened to the sound of his coughing.

Alice climbed into the saddle, watched by Petra, who was

116

helped up next. She could feel Adam's eyes on her from his bedroom, as he watched the two women prepare to leave the house for the day. Alice stirred her horse on. How much longer will he live, she wondered? This would be the last time she would be able to leave the house while he was still alive. She stirred the horse on, making it gallop. She would have to make this day count – from here on in, she would have no chance to compose or relieve her feelings until he died.

Petra finally caught up with her after a few minutes.

"Our Master is unwell," she commented.

"I have hopes it will improve shortly," answered Alice. "He will of course get the best care I have to offer until then."

Petra was silent for a beat.

"Master William has some paperwork for you to review this evening."

"Good. Good. So be it."

The piece of parchment was sitting on the clerk's table, a quill and ink ready beside it. Alice stood at the desk, looking at it.

"I am ready to read it, should it prove necessary," said the clerk.

William blinked at the man's stupidity. Alice merely smiled.

"I am not in requirement of assistance at this time, thank you," she said, smiling.

Alice went back to reading the Latin on the parchment.

"*Adam le Blund has for ever granted to William Utlawe and his heirs all goods and chattels which William at any time had of Adam. Also all chattels moveable or immoveable, jewels, gold and silver and other goods, debts owed to Adam which he has had or ought to have. Furthermore he renounces any previous will and all remedy of law which might obstruct William.*"

Alice read it through twice, seeing nothing there to alarm her. She was no lawyer but was relatively familiar with the quitclaim process, due to the money-lending side of the business.

Beneath it was space for William's signature, Adam's and a third as witness. Alice looked up to the two men.

"This seems fine. Will you sign it?" she said to William. He moved away from the fireplace towards the desk.

Alice looked at the clerk.

"What will you do for the witness signature?" she asked.

"His brother's mark will be placed there, after he himself has signed it."

"And when will that be?" she asked.

"I believe he is expecting to sign it this evening," he replied.

"Good. Excellent. Well, I will be away or I will miss Vespers. Good evening," she said, slipping out of the room.

William followed her, saying over his shoulder, "Let me know when you have that signed."

The clerk merely bowed slightly, picked up the piece of paper, and blew on it to dry the ink.

Adam was aware of little, but it seemed to him that there was a knocking on the door of his room. He blinked, like a slow dog, and then cleared his painfully dry throat.

"Come in," he called.

The door opened and it was the clerk.

"My lord," he said, holding a papers folder in his hand.

"I have an item here for your review and signature, Sire."

Adam frowned, trying to think.

"Oh yes? I'm not sure I remember."

"We recently discussed a claim that had been placed on your property by the English crown, my Lord. A solution had been discovered, however, and I am now bringing it to you for signature."

"A solution? Ah yes, I think I recall," he said, his mind only recalling that it seemed to need his brother's signature. The clerk opened his folder and found the parchment. He put it in front of Adam for review.

Adam remembered the rest of the details as it was being put in front of him, mainly that it was a false quit-claim to William of his estate. He pulled himself into a sitting position as he did so, holding the folder and parchment in front of him against his knees. He looked it over, examining it from start to finish. He read it several times, ignoring the clerk. Occasionally he gave brief coughs, as his lungs fought for more air. Then he turned his attention to William's signature. The imprint made really was excellent. He could not fault it at all.

He looked up at the clerk.

"Master Outlaw's signature is excellent," he said aloud.

"Thank you my Lord."

"No, in truth, I had not expected it to be so well put together. You are a dangerous fellow to cross, if you are so well versed in the art of forgery," he said, coughing at the end of the sentence.

The clerk waited politely for him to be done coughing before speaking.

"I am but a humble clerk, my lord, lucky in my way to be gifted with some skills."

"Some skills indeed," replied Adam. "Lucky for me you are using them in my favour or we would have a bad way about us indeed."

The clerk bowed again, and brought forward the quill and ink for Adam to use.

Adam lifted the quill to the paper, and paused. He lifted his eyes to the clerk to see his reaction. The man's face was utterly still.

"You are sure no one else has seen this," he asked him.

"I am, my Lord," said the Clerk.

Adam sat looking at him for a long moment. The clerk did not react in any way.

Eventually he looked again at the parchment. Good thing he works for me, he thought.

He signed it.

He looked at it.

He handed it back to the clerk.

"Very good, my Lord," said the Clerk.

"If there is nothing else," said Adam, "I will thank you for now."

"Indeed not, my Lord, thank you my Lord," said the Clerk, who put the paper carefully in the folder, and, bowing, was gone from the room.

Adam, lying in the silence, looked at the closed door, and only then was gripped with a sense of caution. He had no way to ensure that the man was honest, not now. He looked at the door with a growing sense of unease, which was broken by another fit of coughing.

Alice came out of Adam's room, exhausted. It was late at night, and her husband had now been sick for over a month. His end was terribly slow, as needs be. She was so tired herself, she knew, but somehow she would keep going on. She thought of her father, his pale blue eyes regarding her as though her thought of stopping made him raise his eyebrows. She pushed herself away from the door and made to move into her own.

There, she dropped her filthy bundle onto the floor and washed her face with the basin that was there. She was so tired, she had asked one of the maids to sit with him while he slept, while she took two hours before dawn. She didn't undress, but merely lay down with her clothes still on her back.

Adam's condition was horrible. He was without any figure at all; in that he was so thin it was terrible. His hair on his body was all gone, and his skull shown though the skin on his head with a terrible translucency. His eyes had dropped horribly, showing the red eyelids underneath his eyes, and almost hiding his pupils. Tan coloured spots had appeared on his hands, and their hideous craw-like aspect would rise to greet her every time she entered the room. And he was thirsty, always thirsty, his throat demanding fluid as much as possible. None of the staff wanted to be in the same room as him, but Alice had insisted this time. She desperately needed sleep and was afraid she would fall down unless she took rest. And she would need to be able to focus in the morning. The final dose for the man would be given in his jug today. He should be gone by today.

She was on the bed, trying to rest her over tired mind, when she thought she heard something. She listened again, unsure. It was a bird, outside her window. She didn't think she was sure if she was awake or not. A bird, rattling its cry outside her window. She wasn't able to keep her eyes open. A bird, victorious and proud. She was asleep.

They let Alice sleep for four hours, not two. She was too exhausted to wake the first time they came for her. When she finally did wake, it was with a start, alone. She suddenly opened her eyes on her bed, feeling as if she had not slept at all. Without moving, she looked up to the light that came in the window. It was late, much later than she wanted. He might already be gone, which would not be good. She would need to be there. She lifted herself up from the bed, feeling stiff in her joints. She pulled herself to a standing position at the side of the bed, barely able to stand upright. I must keep going, she thought, and straightened up. She pulled her clothes into some kind of order, fixed her headdress. She thought for a moment, and then called out.

"Petra. Petra!"

After a moment, there was a knock on the door and Petra entered.

"Help me dress. I'm about to go to him," she said.

Petra moved into the room and began to help her. Silently the two women stood together in the room, lit with morning sunlight, working on the buttons and cloths on her back, not a word passing between them.

"How is the Dame," asked Petra.

Alice was silent for a moment.

"I am, Petra. Nothing more," she said. She was too tired to have a conversation.

Petra could see it. She assisted the woman to change, and did so as quietly and gently as possible. Once done, she stood back. Alice looked down, checking once more that all was in order, finally lifting a hand to her headdress. All ready. She didn't look at Petra, but merely walked to the door and stepped out alone.

Alice walked quietly into Adam's room, empty of all but the dying man. She sat down beside the bed and looked at him.

The man she had married was gone, and in his place was a ghoul. His face had dropped completely. His dark eyes were red rimmed and covered with a white sheen. His hair, so smooth and glossy, as dark as a blackbird's wing, was all gone, leaving a small few wisps on his head. His torso seemed to have collapsed, leaving a scrawny, thin, man. She could see his neck bobbing up and down with his rasping breaths. She could see the bones sticking up sharply out of the skin on his hands, the dark spots all over him. He wore a shirt of thin material that fluttered each time he breathed out.

121

Alice, sitting down beside him, saw with a clear eye what she had done. Lord, let it be soon, she thought. She rose and went back to the door, calling for Petra. The older woman came and stood near her.

"It's time. Please arrange for a priest now," she said.

"Of course Mistress," said Petra, nodding.

Alice turned away and shut the door. She went back to her seat and then settled into the final stretch. She coughed slightly.

His eyes fluttered briefly at the noise, and then after a few minutes, opened. She saw him peering into the room, finally seeing her sitting beside him.

"Alice, my wife," he muttered softly. "You have always been so faithful to me in my illness."

"It is no more than you deserve, my husband," she replied, equally soft-spoken. "And if I served you, it has only been in the small humble way of mine."

He smiled briefly, shaking his head at her disclaimer.

Minutes passed, while he slept again. Alice was letting her attention drift off, when she heard him speak again.

"I recall the first time we met, so long ago," he said. She turned sharply to him, and found him smiling, nostalgic.

"Seven years," she said.

"It seems at this remove another life time."

She merely smiled.

"I can still see you, walking across the grass of that field towards me, your face so serious and dour. I thought that you were afraid of me."

"I remember," she said. "I thought you dapper and well dressed."

"We have had a good run, my wife," he said, trying to hold out his hands. She will be crying soon, he thought. I should comfort her, she will be distressed.

"We have, my husband," she said, smiling softly.

So brave, he thought. So strong! He smiled back.

"You are not like my Annabelle," he said.

Alice's smile froze.

"Who is Annabelle?"

122

"She was my first wife, and she bore me a daughter, and a son. Our Charles lived but a year, he was lost to the winters that year." He coughed weakly, trying to speak.

Alice gave him no aid or word, merely sat there watching him.

"She was so shy! She wore her modestly so close to her, even before she died," he whispered. He could see the young girl his first wife was before him now, her eyes lowered to the ground as the dress fell to the floor, the blush high on her face. And the curve of her made her so perfect. He paused, saddened again by the loss of her. Never did his soul sing so high as when it had her love. When she was gone he was nearly unmanned with the grief. Losing Charles had hurt her terribly; she had never been joyous after that. One bad fall and she was gone to him.

Suddenly he remembered how she had found him with some girl together, how she had stepped back suddenly from the room, and how the tower stairs had tripped her up. Her on the bed, her head fallen back, the breath gradually removed from her like wind moving on. He had cried tears over her body, had said he would never marry, but go to a monastery. He had, but for only a month, and had come back, hunting for something ever since.

He shifted uneasily in the bed, his mind hunting for something to remove the guilt from him. He did not even register what he had just remembered, just that his mind gave him no peace.

"My wife," he whispered, "tell me, what does it look like outside that window? I am here so long I grow restless," he said.

Alice rose quietly, and moved to the small window. Looking outside, she said, "It's a bright day. The sun is clear in a blue sky. There is a smell of winter, though, and there is frost on the stones. There is a maid coming towards the house, carrying some kind of bundle in her hands. A dog is barking somewhere nearby. And there is a carriage stuck in a mud hole, and a man is swearing to himself trying to get it out."

She took a step back from the window, irritated at being put to work by him. She had done enough for him over the last few weeks; she did not intend to do any more. Let me be, old man, let me be.

"Which maid is it?"

"Which maid?" she replied. She had not recognised the maid, they all looked alike at this stage.

"I think it is Rose," she said, looking at him for a reaction, any reaction.

"Ah, Rose?" he said. I think I remember which one was Rose, he said to himself.

"She's a nice girl."

A pause.

"Did you ever want a daughter, Alice?"

"A girl?" she replied, startled. Why would she seek more children? A daughter was something she had never thought of. She had enough concern ensuring William was successful.

"No, I have never thought of a girl," she said, truthful.

"I had had thoughts that we may have children when we married," he said. "You were, I thought, still young enough. But it was not to be, it seems."

Alice looked at him, wishing him to die as soon as possible. She could remember the first night they were together, his face so close to hers as he kissed her, his hands over her, exploring her. She had been briefly titillated, but she had soon felt her desire die within her. He had been blind to the fact, and his desire had only grown stronger, and by his end she was dry and thinking of other things. He had not pressed his suit against her for much longer, and she assumed that that had been that. His speaking of children now she took as a lie or as a fancy. His tone seemed to be judging her, and she noticed it.

She slowly retook her seat, watching him breath.

"Still, I was able to assist the wealth of your house," he said. She said nothing.

"When I came it was only the boy and the clerk managing things, a recipe for certain neglect. However, once a proper manager was installed, it moved smoothly until William was of an age to take over. He is so like his father!" Adam marvelled. "And so good at business."

Alice said nothing.

"I am, at least, glad I was able to assist in that regard."

Alice still said nothing, and he seemed to move into a deeper sleep. She heard his breath rasp in and out for what seemed a long time. She developed a pain in her side by slouching on the stool for so long, but ignored it.

Then, for no clear reason, she heard the breath stop. She had not been paying attention, she had been daydreaming, but she looked at him suddenly when she realised the difference. He was prone in the bed, his chin pointed to the ceiling, his mouth open and empty. His hands had gripped the blankets to him, and he seemed to have just stopped. The rasping merely ceased, went silent, and she held her own breath in surprise at it. Seconds went by. Then a minute. Finally she breathed out.

He was dead. Adam was dead. She was a widow. Again.

For a long time she did nothing. She did not move from the stool, but instead merely looked at the cooling body of her husband. His eyes were finally closed she thought, then made her turn her attention away from him as she found that thought morbid.

His estates were hers. She had released them all from a great threat, one that had endangered then internally and externally. She flicked her eyes to him and away. She had been the one to invite the threat into the house in the first place, though. She had wanted a husband and had not cared whether or not he was clever or sensible. She felt she would need one for safety. Now she was faced with the result of that need, its mouth gaping open in the bed beside her, the hands that had held her slack and cold. She had done this, because she had done that. This must never happen again, she thought.

There would be much to be done. There would need to be a funeral and the reading of the will and the extending of William's claim on the estate. There would need to be a show of grief and mourning, and the demands of society to ensure all was above board. They would be kept busy on this theme for months to come. She should get started.

She stood up from her stood and looked at the dead man.

"At least I got the best of you," she said, and left the room, empty as it was to anything worth her concern.

Rose was in the downstairs reception room when she heard the news. Petra approached her while she was cleaning out the fire.

"Rose, pretty, come here for a moment," she said. Her voice was soft and kind, her manner gentle. Rose stood, looking up at the taller woman.

"You know how the master is very ill?" she asked.

Rose nodded silently, eyes wide.

"The Lord has seen fit to take him this morning," she said.

Rose gasped, took a step back.

"Now don't be upset, Rose. He was very ill for a very long time, and his passing into God's care was something that means an end to his pain."

Rose's eyes began to fill with tears.

"We must be very strong and brave for our Mistress, and we must be very quiet for her, as she is very weary after taking care of him for so long."

At this Rose nodded intently. Petra looked at her for a moment, wishing she could give her more direct comfort. There was nothing for it. She had too much to do to prepare for the next few days, as indeed would Rose. She left her.

Rose stood alone in the empty room, her thoughts consuming her. He was not a good man, but he was deserving of God's forgiveness, as we all were. And now that opportunity is gone, forever. She recalled how, when she returned home to Dame Alice's house with her shame still high about her, Petra and she had walked across the pasture one morning. Petra had said nothing for a long time, but before they had turned to make their way back, had said a strange thing. She had said it under her breath.

"Rose. You will be protected."

That was it, that was all. Rose had blushed furiously, shamed again by her knowledge. But later, alone, she had wondered on it. Surely there could be no safety for her. They could never remove the master of the house.

And now she stood alone beside a half empty grate, wondering at what had happened. She heard a voice asking something in the next room, and made herself move. The grate was cleared, and she moved with the hot ashes into the yard. Philip, looking up from his work, saw the withdrawn look on her face, and paused, pitying. There was nothing that could be done for her on this day of days.

126

Rose removed the ashes, throwing them down the outside drain. She could hear voices from the room behind her. She made a quick decision.

She put down the bucket and shovel, and moved back into the room. She quietly moved passed Philip, who didn't notice her, and made her way quietly to the upstairs of the house. She didn't make a sound, nor did she need to, there was no one there at that time. Alice was speaking with Petra downstairs about the arrangements and so her way was not barred.

The Master's room was not locked. She quietly opened the door, and stood there, the handle in her hand. The door was only slightly ajar, her fear coming over her. She could see the jug on the table. She had seen so many dead bodies in her time, everyone had. But she could not face the sight of him dead. She shut the door again, having seen nothing.

She stood there for a moment, looking at the smooth wood of the door. Then she turned her glance at the mistress's door.

Petra's voice came back to her.

"Rose. You will be protected."

Why did she say that?

She didn't know. She didn't want to know. She turned away from that. She was on her way to forgetting it. She made herself take one step back, then another. She slowly made her way downstairs, unnoticed by anyone.

Down in the kitchen there was plenty to keep her busy. She quickly took up all the tasks assigned to her and found the day passing her by with speed. Occasionally she would remember the shock of the day, and then swallow, horrified. Once she found herself remembering the event itself, and nearly dropped what she was holding. Lord, help me to be strong, and to bear what you have put on my shoulders, she prayed. She had her hands covered with flour making bread that afternoon, when Petra walked through the room carrying the jug that had been in the Master's bedroom. Rose watched as she walked into the back yard and emptied it in one long stream down the drain. The look on Petra's face was of a silent triumph. Petra could feel someone staring at her. She looked up, alarmed.

Rose stared at her, shock and horror on her face.

Chapter Thirteen

The Years 1310 – 1316

In 1310 William began to take on more and more work for Gilbert de Clare, Earl of Gloucester. William had gone, once, to visit him on his estate in Wales. The two men had spoken together over the course of a week. He had greeted William when he came in.

"Master Kyteler! Come in and join us. See how we are already preparing for the spoils of war." De Clare indicated the map spread out on the table.

William looked at it as de Clare spoke.

"See how we plan to pitch our men here, at the ascent of the field. And how we will strike at the heart of their advancing forces, thus cutting them off and choking them. Do you think it a good plan?" he asked.

The room seemed to pause to hear his reply. William had glanced at the plans, seeing in them a variant of the battle method of Caesar against the Gauls. If de Clare built his fortresses properly he would succeed. If not, then they would fail, and have nowhere to run if the opposing force fell on them.

"It's good if you win," he said, a shorthand for his thoughts, but a terrible assault of the protocol that the conversation demanded. Never once, for example, had his own clerk spoken to him in such a way.

The silence that fell was a slap on his face. William, realising what he had done, looked up with alarm. After a frozen second, Gilbert had merely spoken again.

"And have we done enough to do that?"

William pointed to various sections on the map.

"A moat here will prevent incursions into your area. And if you mount hidden sections here and here," he pointed, "you'll deny your attackers the option of circling around and attacking you from behind your flanks."

He looked at the older man again, who merely marked where William had pointed to on the map with a quill, and then led him out of the room.

"So," he said, as they went into a private room with further maps on the walls, "What of my interests in Ireland?"

"Well Sire," began William, "I am very pleased with the rents received from your estate in Kilkenny."

The report William then gave was concise, complete and left out nothing. William had been trained well.

Gilbert nodded, then asked a question.

"You married, William?"

The question took William by surprise, but only for a moment.

"I, Sir? No, Sir, I am not married."

"Why not?"

William thought for a moment.

"I already have a mother, I could not cope with a wife," he said.

Gilbert laughed out loud, and then spoke again.

"Good for you. Nothing but trouble, I can assure you. If I were a cruel man I would wed you to one of my daughters. Three of them, and not one married yet. Their mother wants them to wait, says they're still children. We'll have time enough yet, I suppose."

A beat of silence from William who let the topic fall past them.

"We do still have the small concern of the case we wish to send to Edward's court," said William.

The Church and King Edward always wanted to try their own cases. The Church still had enormous authority to try certain matters in its courts. As a result, therefore, matters concerning Wills, patronage, sacrilege, heresy, perjury and certain sexual offences were Church matters. When these matters, especially those of Wills, were heard in the Common Law courts of the King, fury arose. Gilbert sighed at William's words.

"I dread the ire that will arise from this matter," he said. The case was nothing contentious, at least, not in the usual way. A matter of Patronage had been reneged upon and was to be brought before the Common Law courts. The hornet's nest that would alight upon the Earl would be unpleasant. And it would alight on William's head as part of the duties he held. So be it.

129

The matter de Clare brought before the court was, in fact, to be quickly resolved. However, the question over who could decide legal questions remained highly disputed. The Church was in most of Europe the sole method of administration. It alone recorded the major events of a person's life; their birth, baptism, marriage and death, and it was for many the ultimate authority. However, temporal power would and did struggle with the Church for dominance, and Gilbert de Clare was not the only member of the nobility to sigh deeply over the Church's views. By 1311 the Council of Vienne had complained against King Edward's blending of royal and ecclesiastical jurisdictions.

The reply of King Edward is not recorded.

My son,

The weather is passing good since we travelled here, and the days are not too cold. I had found the roads to Tipperary not smooth, but we made a journey of good time and arrived comfortably. The manor house of Mr Richard De Valle is very large and well set into the landscape, and I understand it is one of six that he owns in this area. Since he and his kind sister have made their invitation to us to come stay, we have been treated most well and respectfully.

I have been informed that Mr De Valle will request to present his suit to me to you. I am as yet undecided. I feel it may be too early to allow me to think of such matters at this stage. Also, I have not yet seen the remainder of his estate so cannot yet make up my mind. I will however write and send a message once I have done so. His behaviour towards me has been excellent and exceeds all expectations, and his wealth is schedule to increase over two years with the completion of two more estates.

How are the discussions with regard to this year's rent increase being completed? Have you succeed in this endeavour? Please be sure to include details of the next round of negotiations in your next letter. We will have twenty five tenants instead of twenty, due to the birth of several offspring in the household; be sure to include this in your calculations.

Note that you must now write to de Clare as promised, for it is now June.

With best prayers for your health and success,
Your Mother,
Alice.

By 1313, William's good faith with Gilbert saw him appointed his attorney in Ireland for five years. Gilbert had included a brief note in the letter confirming William's appointment, written at the bottom of some brief list concerning supplies.

"I am away, William, and I will be placing in your hands decisions concerning my estates in Kilkenny and elsewhere. Use sense and safety rather than greed, and have all ready for me when I call for you. I wish you and that mother of yours all that you may want. God's speed. De Clare."

William, reading the informal French, grinned silently to himself over the common touch the older man used. He could see the man's skill at leadership even as it worked on him. William hoped he would see him again. He liked him.

It was not to be. In 1314, news reached William, and quite a few others, that Gilbert de Clare had died on the battlefield of Bannockburn. The three daughters that de Clare had decried were all unmarried at the time of his death. Thus, in the absence of any Will or Testament to do with the man's huge estates, they were all married off quickly. The eldest, Eleanor, was married to Hugh Despenser, 15 years younger than her, and a man wild for all he could get. The second, Elizabeth, married Roger Dammory, and the third married Hugh Audley.

The immediate aim of Despenser was to absorb, as quickly as possible, the vast estates of his new, sober, saintly wife, no doubt in an effort to cheer her grief. To do this, he launched himself in warfare against the husbands of her sisters. The Crown, seeing the matter develop so quickly, froze the inheritance of the estate until things were on a more even keel. That included the lands, of which there were several, in Ireland. And as they were under control of the Crown, William was expected to give details to the Treasurer, Walter Islip. Islip, stationed as he was in Dublin, sent word to his executive in Kilkenny to meet with William there to determine the wealth and management of the estate. William thereby was told to expect, on a certain date, a visit to the main Kyteler house in Kilkenny by the Crown's man. He arrived there one morning with the accounts and matters legal ready for review. He and the clerk were reviewing them when there was a knock on the door.

"The Crown's man to see you, Sire," said Philip.

"Thank you Philip," said William, who, seeing who it was, started to laugh out loud.

"How now," said Arnold Le Poer. "Any wine to hand, or do you run a tavern here at all?"

"What is this?" asked William. "Are you the king's man, Arnold?"

Arnold gave a rye grin.

"I am, for my troubles, William. If it keeps those men over there and our sort over here, than I am happy to assist in any way I can!"

William took a moment to take it in.

"When we spoke for the first time, you seemed so black in your view of those who come from England. Surely I thought, you must be against the Crown in that regard."

"And indeed I am. I am against them in their way of deciding what is best for us, when any man who lives here with money in his pocket is the best man to decide what is the best for him. In truth, the decisions made by them pertain solely to taxes and land, and as we are the ones who need the benefit of it we are the ones who should decide the paying of it! I am a man of practicalities, you see."

"Forgive me Arnold, please be seated."

"Now," said Arnold, "to business. You have your master here and I have mine. Neither of us are men who take money from our Masters and then refuse to work. So, if you please, I will be reviewing the details you have available on the estate."

William immediately presented the information he had regarding the houses and lands that were held by de Clare. He looked at Arnold reviewing them, and noticed that the older man gave them intense attention. The attitude of a buffoon was gone from him completely, and for a while he reminded William of John Le Poer, Arnold's cousin. They are more alike than the common view would believe, thought William.

"All this must make you miss being mayor," said Arnold, still peering at the first of several ledgers.

"I do not regret the work," said William. "But I do not miss the people I was obliged to deal with, as I am sure you well know."

"Indeed I do, every court date seems to bring less and less credit worthy cases to my court."

He put up the first ledger. William gave some general comment to what was in front of him, but found that Arnold was ignoring him.

Arnold did not speak for a very long time, merely going through all the books of accounts for the various homes in the town. He paused for a very long time over the house near the river, which had suffered water damage due to a recent flood and which had a matter of disputed rent over it. But he made no comment on it.

Soon all the ledgers were read and there was no comment by Arnold on any of them. William looked at him.

"Are you happy with them, Arnold?" he asked him.

Arnold sat back, sighed and looked pointedly at the clerk. The clerk looked at William and receiving a nod, quietly slipped from the room.

"I'm happy to Heavens with them, as would any sane man be. William Kyteler, looking after the estates? It is a dream, no doubt. But one question stays in my mind, good friend, and it does not concern these estates."

"Indeed," said William. "And what would that be?"

Arnold leaned forward across the desk.

"What will you do during the Invasion?"

William looked calmly at the older man, not letting his features move.

"She and I will extend welcome to all who visit our shores, you know that Arnold."

Arnold snorted at the diplomatic answer.

"You know and I know that we must be more than that. There is great support for this matter from all around us. I hear even Donal O'Neill will be giving his welcome to them. We must ensure our way of life will stand."

This surprised William. He and his kind had almost no dealings with the Irish per say, and he partly believed Donal O'Neill to be a savage who might well drink the blood of his young. The sheer lack of cohesiveness of the Irish Clans made getting any clear ideas about them next to impossible. The clans were each of them different, each of them out for themselves. None of them had ever bandied together to make themselves a full fighting force. But hearing that Donal O'Neill supported the force that was now posed to invade gave an added reason to move with extra caution.

"Is that true?"

"Yes, it is true."

William thought for a moment. The English will never invade here; they are too concerned about the French. The King will need to investigate his own Queen first of all, that mad French wench. No, this invasion will fail, and fail greatly. There will be a need, however, to appease both sides. The unpleasantness between them both cannot last for long. He looked at Arnold. Work to do.

Dear William,

Many thanks for your last letter. Please note that I have decided to accept the proposal of Mr De Valle. He has shown me great favour and daily holds banquets and other events in my honour. I have confirmed the value and size of his estates and am greatly pleased with them.

Please see enclosed some material for Carpenter or Galrussyn to review.

I intend to remain here for the moment, and it is likely that the ceremony will take place in this region in the near future. It would please me greatly were your father and I to see you during the wedding day. Please ensure that you have ample time to stay a while with us. This estate has many pretty fancies to enjoy about it that I feel you would be pleased with.

I would be most pleased if you could let us know the standard of the harvest for this coming season. I am told that the rains have been very poor this year and that the grain is of a poor quality for it. Do we have full yield from all estates or are we to suffer this year? Are there any measures we can take to prevent losses and are you taking them? Signal this point to me quickly.

Also, word has reached me here that the women in the town have now taken to choosing damask silk for their headdresses. Can you confirm if this is so? I will be able to quickly order some material which can then be purchased by them before next month.

We also hear of the likelihood of troops from Scotland. Send word quickly to Roger Outlaw in Dublin, so that the right ears may hear of our support. Ensure that we maintain a port holding in Waterford, as the Dublin ports may soon be out of our hands. Also, give Point of Attorney to our agent

So it was in 1315 that Edward, Earl of Carrik, son-in-law of the Earl of Ulster, and brother of Robert the Bruce King of Scotland invaded Ireland. Word came to the Kyteler household one morning that there was a battalion stationed on the outskirts of town, but otherwise all appeared to be normal in the town. The mayor, thankfully someone else this time thought William, went outside the city gates to pay the ransom required to ensure the town was not sacked, and to grant safe passage to the men. William watched along with a few others from within the city walls. No women were there, and it would have been shocking if they had been.

They saw, from the distance they were stationed at, the interchange between the two men. William saw the diplomatic gestures, the friendly smiles, and could almost believe it. As they watched, the rain began to pour down, and all abandoned the attempt at diplomacy there and then for another time. William made his way back to the house, putting the horse out for the stable boy to take off, then making his way into the house proper.

Rose silently, with one of her gentle smiles, brought him something hot to eat. Petra, seeing him by the fireside on her way to complete an errand, stopped to converse.

"How did it go? Does he appear a great king?" she asked, smiling.

William smiled at the question.

"He appears a king, both by intent and merit, which is all any man can ask. He'll not be a king for long though, his enemies will see his head buried far from his body. "

Petra frowned, looking at him.

"You're soaked through! Were you out in it long?"

"No! It came down with great force, and with almost no warning."

135

Petra turned from him, to finish her errand.

"Well, I hope it stops soon. Rain like this will ruin any crops still waiting in the fields."

The rain didn't stop. It continued, along with winters of vicious and unpreventable cold. The harvest was not saved that year of 1315, and the people suffered terribly. Prices for food rose, and the army at the city gates grew more and more impatient with the city that could provide coin aplenty, but no food for their men.

At least the men were warm to some degree in their barracks. The rest of the population saw neither warmth nor food for a long time, starved as they were. The rains were to continue until 1318, and by that time there was terrible pillaging by the invading army, who found not any resistance, merely a terrible absence.

William,

I am passing well, though the signs of hunger are beginning to reach the estate here. We have been having difficulties with management of the estate and while no good comes of sitting in judgement, we are left daily with more and more deprivations in both our food and in other materials in life.

Your father has spent time in the second estate in an attempt to husband some success out of the current landscape. However, success is unlikely at this stage, despite many kind sentiments of advice. He has sent me many letters and been most solicitous to me. These times have been trying on all of us.

Ensure, please, that you receive the shipment of the cargo before the second week of September. Write in very good time, giving them clear terms, with no possible chance for them to dispute our instructions. It is very common for poor weather to be used as an excuse to delay the supplies and thus increase the cost, so this must be avoided. However, if you make a purchase for it now this tactic on their part can be prevented.

It is likely that I will be able to spend some time with you in our home in Kilkenny. I will write further to you closer to the date.

Your mother,
Alice

William and Philip were travelling back to the house in the carriage. A matter of business had Philip in the carriage with him, answering questions. William suddenly saw a child, no more than eight, lying on the muddy verge in the rain, green foam coming from its mouth.

"What has happened to it?" he wondered, causing Philip to look outside.

When he saw the child, he fell very quiet. Sitting back into his seat, he looked at William sadly.

"The child has taken to eating grass in its hunger," he said. "The green foam or juice is the sap from their mouths."

William looked at Philip.

"How do you know this Philip?" he asked.

"It happens around these parts," said Philip. William did not ask any more questions.

That night, William was woken by the sounds of crying coming from the back of the house. He heard a member of staff roundly abuse the man, telling him to be off. William then turned over and got some sleep, if such a thing was possible with the constant sound of rain all about them.

William
It is with sadness that I write to tell you of the death of your father Richard De Valle. He had been travelling from our home to the second manor house at an hour most late and unsafe. I would have wished him stay but would not see him made ill tempered by causing obstacles to his choice.

His carriage was therefore on a road in the dark late at night, when the rains we have been having caused the banks of the local river to burst. The carriage overturned with great violence and his injuries were so severe as to cause his death. Two horses of great value were also lost.

I was unable to travel with him that night due to illness.

I will be travelling back to you shortly, once the proper formalities have been introduced. I would be most grateful if you could ensure that my room is ready for my arrival. While I may soon attend social events, I would like to remain indoors for at least two months once I return. I will also be providing materials that confirm my right to the widow's dowry of two of the six manor houses.

We will be speaking to the envoy with regard to his offer later this year, but remember that the terms must be raised to a five percentage for the matter to be accepted. This should be signalled to them in some capacity now, but do not give them full details of the offer until they request it, as to do otherwise would be rude.

I look forward daily to seeing you and to our home soon. Please offer a prayer to the memory of your father in the Cathedral.

God's blessings,

Alice.

Chapter Fourteen

The Years 1317 – 1324

Alice examined the envoy's offer.

"Fair, but not fair enough," she said to the Clerk. "There is nothing else for it, we will have to meet them again. Please send them a letter requesting a meeting."

She handed the papers back to him and looked up at William, who had just entered the room.

"How now William. What news?" she asked.

"Edward still trying to change the terms?" he asked, seeing the letter in the Clerk's hands.

"He is, indeed. But we'll give him a good fight before we give in to them," she smiled. The Clerk looked up at her words and gave her a smile back.

William picked up the papers and began to review them.

"News from town," he said, while he read.

"Oh yes?" she asked.

"Yes, seems we will have a new bishop before the year is out," he said, still reading. "Three months, are they genuinely suggesting – oh hold now," he said.

"Oh! I'm sorry to hear that! I thought Bishop Fitzjohn was most popular."

Bishop Fitzjohn had been at one time the Treasurer of Ireland, and had been bishop of Ossory for some time by Royal Appointee. He was now being appointed to another diocese in Tipperary, where he would serve until his death.

"Do we know who will be our next Bishop?" she asked him.

William scanned the next page of the envoy's letter.

"Not yet, but it's unusual..."

"In what way?"

"Well, apparently the man is a Papal Appointee. I've never heard of that happening before."

"Neither have I, I didn't know that he could."

139

"It is a new power, Mistress, the Pope assigned himself earlier this year in cases where there was a transition of the original appointee."

"How generous of him," remarked Alice, getting to her feet. "I am to supper, otherwise I will have Petra complaining in my ear, and that I seek to avoid. Are you coming, William?"

Over that same dinner, William looked at his mother.

"How goes your suit, Mother?"

"Very well, we are still at the early stages. However, I'm confident that we'll see the correct allocation being made before too long."

Alice's stepson, the son of de Valle, had refused her the widow's dowry she was entitled to, namely, one third of those six manors. The matter was now before the courts, but it was straight forward enough. William hoped it would be finalised before too long. In his experience often all that was needed was the matter being brought before the Courts for a respondent to be ready to settle.

"I have a suggestion for you, Mother,"

"Do you, my son. Well, speak, and I can but promise an open ear to hear it."

He looked at her, catching her mood of cheerfulness.

"That is all a son can ask of a mother."

"That is all this son can ask of this mother."

"I have news of a suit made towards you."

"A suit against me, or a suitor against me?"

William smiled at the pun.

"A suitor to you."

Alice handed the plate to the maid for some more serving of the roasted chicken that was in front of them.

"I am to gain another suitor, am I? Who had come enquiring?"

A beat, and then he spoke.

"John Le Poer."

Alice looked at him, surprised.

"John?" she said, the name sounding familiar in her mouth. She looked away for a moment, her eyes blinking as she thought about it.

"Yes, he wrote to me specifically to raise the matter. You know him so well I would have thought it perfectly acceptable if he had written to you, but you know how he is, he would want to do things proper."

"John le Poer wants to marry me?" she said, still surprised. A pleased look was coming over her face as well. She laughed a little, clearly delighted.

"Mother, you're pleased!"

"I am not, you're terrible to tease your mother, you know it's far too soon for a marriage and they will all be talking, I simply did not read his character correctly."

"I don't understand you," he said, but she didn't go into it. She wasn't exactly blushing; Alice Kyteler never blushed. But she did look a little flushed, for some reason.

"Very well! Please write back and tell him, we would be happy to consider his suit."

He looked at her. She must have looked like this when she was young, he thought. Laughing, he nodded.

"Very well! I will go and write to him, and tell him you accept."

Alice's surprise was genuine. She did not harbour foolish notions about Le Poer being the most handsome or romantic man. She did not love him. But she did respect him. She respected his intelligent calm mien. She respected his thoughtful nature towards her and other people. She had seen how he had avoided hurting others less strong than him. She had seen his attention to detail, his avoidance of the common or course, and his unfailing good manners. And she had believed he saw nothing similar in her.

Alice was not a person who had poor self-esteem. But she had acted in the world, and had presented herself to the world as a woman of action. She did not give herself notions that this granted her respect in a world where women were not meant to speak. And hearing of his suit to her was a genuine surprise. She had not expected it, or looked for it, or hoped for it. She told herself severely that it was a meeting of estates as much as anything, that the man had compared their wealth and considered it an equal match on that basis. She must always regard him as an excellent companion and not expect true affiliation from him; Lord knows the world had told her not to expect more from a man than that. But wasn't it great fortune, at her approaching age, that he had still chosen her!

The wedding was quiet, and very small. They were married in a chapel on his estate by his local priest, and William, Petra by necessity, a married niece of John's, and a few villagers attended the service. It was by far the smallest of Alice's weddings. The small Church was lit by candlelight and decorated with wild flowers. Alice found it rather touching, really, despite herself. Once the service was over, she stood outside with her new husband and accepted her son's congratulations.

"Good tidings to you Mother."

"Indeed my son, thank you."

"I must away to the City on business this evening."

Alice nodded.

"I should be joining you," she said, "but it would never do on this day of days."

He nodded, feeling that she was in fact ignoring her duty. Still, it would have been churlish to argue with her here. He gave her a nod, and shook the hand of yet another stepfather. John Le Poer shook his hand solidly, and smiled at him.

"I will do my very best to take care of her, William," he said, smiling.

She has always done remarkable well in taking care of herself, he thought, but again, just gave a nod.

On his way into town, the wedding party taking place behind him, he had for the first time a feeling that he wasn't needed. He considered himself ridiculous for the reaction, but the criticism did nothing to remove it.

Alice stared across the fields and realised she had married a fool.

"You're a fool John Le Poer, and I'm a bigger one for marrying you."

"Ah, my wife," he said immediately, "One woman's fool is another woman's joyful lot." His face was completely sombre and serious, and she burst out laughing.

"What, laughter from my wife so soon after we are married! I am struck dumb with grief. What is a man to do?" he said.

She recovered herself, and looked at him with affection.

"We are in a hard place, however; How are we to get in the harvest with so few?"

She gestured to the wheat filled fields that they stood beside. The long stalks stirred gently in the breeze, and it made a wonderful picture to see. A bee buzzed heavily among the flowers in the hedgerow. Alice held her husband's hand, happy.

She had not been expecting this. They had had their quiet wedding, and she had been grateful for the compliment he had paid her. She had made no provision to move out of her home. She had planned to remain Alice Kyteler, as always. She still had to conclude the suit against Richard de Valle's son, and Adam Le Blund's daughter was heard to make complaining noises. She felt that this, as well as the usual business of her life, would be what would occupy her. She had readied herself to return to her home.

However, the next day, she had come into the house after a horse ride with Petra, and was told by a maid that Master John awaited her in the main hall. She had taken off her cloak, and, still with her gloves on, walked in.

What she saw made her stand dead still. There stood Master John, standing beside a table set for two people, the glasses gleaming, the plates shining, candles lit all about them. He stood beside the table, looking nervous. Looking at though he was waiting for her.

"Ah," said Alice, not remotely prepared for the scene.

"Come, my wife," said John, smiling. "Come sit and tell me of your day."

He gestured to a seat, and Alice simply stood there, surprised. She was a year from her sixtieth birthday, and while she had eaten a meal with each of her husbands, naturally, it had always been in the course of a day. It was always if they had arrived home at the Kyteler house, and had called for food. It was always for the sake of eating. Never had she walked into a room and found that her husband was waiting for her so as to have a meal, or share a meal. She was still standing there when John gently pulled out the chair and gestured to it again.

It occurred to him for the first time that she might say no.

It occurred to her for the first time that he might actually want her for a wife. She rejected that idea immediately. No, he did not want her for a wife. Instead he merely sought a dinner companion for the evening. Instead, he would give her conversation and charm and nothing more and in the morning, instead, she would return to the house in Kilkenny and he would stay on here. She would not let herself think of how false he had been, so that she could greet him with warmth the next time she had seen him. She would never ask herself who he would be having dinner with the next night.

She took a step forward, and then another, and then before she could question the wisdom of it, sat down. John smiled, the smile of a delighted boy.

"I hope you like it, I had to look quite a while before I found it," he said, lifting the cover on the food.

She put her hands, palms down, flat on the table. He looked with concern at her face.

Don't you like it?" he asked with alarm.

"This is rabbit," she said, her voice sounding very strange to him.

"Yes."

"Did you know that rabbit is my favourite dish?"

"Yes, of course, that's why I had it made," he said smiling, very puzzled at her.

She was silent for a very long moment.

"Why?"

That night, after dinner, it had been too late to travel back to the city. Petra had joined the other servants in the kitchen for dinner, and Alice was shown to a bedroom upstairs for the night. Petra has assisted her into her bedclothes, and then, wishing her a good night, had left her to sleep.

For a while Alice had just lain there, thinking. It had been pleasant to sit with her husband, conversing over the course of the day. She had enjoyed his manner, as always, but as well as that, she had found in him none of the usual ways she detected in other men. Alice was not expected to hide her opinions. She had not been condemned for them either. A most peculiar evening.

She heard the door open and looked up from the bed, alarmed. John Le Poer came in and shut the door behind him. Ah no, she thought, so that was the reason for his understanding nature and

144

his good ways towards her tonight. She must indicate herself quickly to prevent misunderstanding.

She held up a hand to him, and he paused, as he was about to take off a boot.

"Before you make any other gesture," she told him, "I wish you to know I have no interest in matters carnal, nor can I provide them to you. I do not expect fidelity from you in this matter, but tell you now I cannot be a wife to you in this way. I am most sorry if this offends you, but I, ah.. I...." She trailed off, noticing that she was seeing a smile break out on his face.

"What, please, is so funny?"

He pulled his boot back on, and stood.

"Do you mind if I sit," he said, gesturing to the bed.

She shook her head. He sat and paused for a moment, not sure where to begin.

"Alice, I have never been married before. I have known the company of no brothers or sisters in my life, and my position in these parts has meant that for much of the year I am without known associates of any description to speak to."

She looked at him. What was his point?

He gave her a look that seemed to ask for her understanding.

"I do not seek a carnal marriage bed. I am 70 years of age, and do not demand of others what I cannot provide myself."

She smiled for a moment at his words. He looked down at his hands when he spoke next.

"But I do seek a companionable one. I am a man made under the sun God provided, with a heart as frail as any other. I seek a companion, one who matches me in thought and intent, and who complements me where they do not match me." He looked up from his hands to her.

"I am lonely Alice, and I will continue to be lonely if you will have it. But let us share a marriage bed, if not a carnal one, and I'll not be lonely."

Alice looked away from him for a moment, trying to decide what to do. He's lonely, she thought. She drew back the sheets for him to join her.

So for the first time in as many years as she could recall, Alice Kyteler was hugged and kept warm as she fell asleep. What did she feel as she began to drift away from the world, held as she was by another? Did she resent the demand put upon her? Did she wonder at what had befallen her? Was she frightened at what she herself may have found herself feeling? Like so much, it is not known.

Alice stayed the next night as well, cradled by John Le Poer. She fell asleep with him beside her, in arms she hadn't known she'd missed. When she woke up the next morning, she felt a lightness to herself. She woke beside him and felt him next to her. She moved slightly beside him, and it was enough to have him reach out and pull her to him. She shuddered with real, pure joy at the feel of another beside her, who cradled her with no threat or demand. She was almost afraid to recognise what she had found. Lord, she prayed, please, please, please, do not let me be without the kind comfort that I have found in my husband.

"Woman, your feet are *freezing*," he muttered, and then looked with surprise when Alice burst out laughing.

So she stayed on his large, comfortable farm all through the summer. She sat with him and went through the accounts with him, and gave him great assistance with the management of the large estate. And always they touched, with their hands and their feet, their heads close together as they looked over some book. In the late evenings, she would sew while he would read aloud from some tale or other, usually an Arthurian legend of some sort. Sometimes they did not speak for hours instead merely smiling to each other now and again as he read and she sewed. Alice did not know by what alchemy she should find herself in this situation, and she maintained a sort of watchful balance that would not let her plan for tomorrow, nor seek to decide that today was wrong.

So it was that when the harvest came, the watchful pair of the Dame and the Knight was surprised. Alice, standing at the large field full of wheat, almost had a wish not to cut it. It seemed to her to mark the perfect summer that she had had, and that to move away from it, to enter into the discordant autumn with its grey palate of colours, was to risk change and loss.

"Shame we have to harvest it at all, it seems so lovely as it is."

"Oh, so we have now a soft hearted woman who wishes for harvests never to come in, suns not to set, and tides not to change. It will be a different story, my sweet, when you have no bread to eat, and who will you blame then, but none other than your hen pecked husband, that's who."

All this was said as he moved an arm around her waist, and moved her so as to face him.

"So be it, I am a soft hearted woman. However, we still need to get this harvest in, and we will need more men than we have to gather it. What do you propose, oh wise husband?"

"What do I propose? Well, we should start to harvest it in soon, before the next full moon. And to do that we will need hands, so I will send to the next few farms round about to gain assistance from their men. We will need to be vigilant to ensure that these men and women only go about their work while they are here. It will be a lot of work my wife, and I will need your help."

"Mine!" she said alarmed, "You want me to work in the fields!"

He laughed for a moment,

"No, not at all! Goodness, Dame Kyteler in the fields, goodness, no. What a thought. We will need to supervise the men and women who we ask to work for us, particularly at the further fields; otherwise we may never get it in in time. Will you help me?"

She looked at him, unsure.

"Of course."

"Good. I've sent word already to three farms about, we should see them come tomorrow morning."

Alice nodded, hiding her alarm. She almost never had worked with peasants directly, she didn't know what to expect.

With the moon still high, the pair of them rose the next morning. They came downstairs in the dark and found down there nearly a hundred people waiting for them in the blue night.

Sir John didn't speak directly to them either; he merely just let the foreman hand out scythes to the men and bags and rushes to the women. No one spoke or chatted amongst themselves as the group walked out into the dark fields. They were all too tired for that. Instead, they all worked to develop a quiet rhythm amongst them. The men, bent at the waist, cut the wheat as close to the soil as they could. The women, equally bent at the waist, would walk behind them and quickly and nimbly twist a few strands around a cluster of wheat to ensure that the bundle would hold.

147

There was no other sound. There was no bird singing at that hour. There was no dog to bark or any other animal. There was no chatter or conversation from either the men or the women. Instead, there was merely the faint ting from the scythes as they met each strand of wheat, again and again, in the same old rhythm, and the faint crunch of shoes as they stood on each sheared wheat stalk. The skirts of the women billowed out as they sat, quickly, gathering up another bundle and tying it up with the thread they had in their bags. Then they would fall back into place as they stood up and followed the men again.

Alice, looking at all this, wondered at how strange it all was; the blue blades in the night making their sounds, the bundles standing up straight, being lifted up towards Heaven, the light of the moon shining on the backs of the peasants as they worked. Where would she be, if she weren't here? In Kilkenny at her home, maybe, worrying over some problem or other? She was glad, now, of where her fate had brought her.

Occasionally one of them would call for water, and the foreman, Sir John, or Alice would give them a drink from the cans of water they carried. Alice stayed near the women, Sir John and the foreman near the men. No one really called for water until hours had passed. They were all seasoned farm hands; they knew not to drink until the third time they had gotten thirsty.

The sunrise came, and the sun rose high, and still they worked. At some point in the morning, the foreman called for a break. Without a word, each one of them dropped tools immediately and began to congregate. As before, the men stayed together, and the women stayed together. Sir John and the foreman began to talk amongst themselves as to how much was done and as to how much was left to do. Alice was about to join them when a woman called to her.

"Sorry my lady, may I have some water please?" she asked.

Alice produced the water for her. The women had sat beside a large bundle of wheat in an effort to hide from the sun. Together they had made a roundabout circle. Alice, looking over the shoulder of the woman drinking, saw that one of the women had brought a small child with her. She waited until the woman was finished and then approached the women.

"Would your child like some water?" she asked. The young woman merely nodded, very grateful, and let the child have a sup. As Alice was giving the child some liquid, one of the other women suddenly gave a yelp and covered her face with the bag she carried. An older woman, presumably her sister, ribbed her gently.

"What is it?" asked Alice, perplexed.

The woman whose child was drinking looked around, and then grinned.

"She hopes one of the men there will be her sweetheart," she said.

"Really? Which one?" asked Alice, and had the young lad pointed out to her.

"He seems a fine fellow," she said, and smiled at the younger woman, who blushed all over again.

Before long it was time to get back to work. Alice couldn't help but notice that the young woman was trying to collect the bundles of the young man that had taken her fancy. She smiled to herself at the spectacle of it all. They had all seemed so quiet earlier on, she thought, but now here it was, all hearts passions being played out before her.

Someone started the singing, she wasn't sure whom, but they all took it up with a rousing air. It seemed to keep them all in time with each other, and the cutting scythes kept perfect time with the singers' voices. It was some song Alice couldn't distinguish the words of, but it made the time go by.

The day passed, and the field was harvested. As the moon came up again and as the sun set, the last few strands were bundled up and each man stood and did not have to bend any more. Alice could see the exhaustion in their faces and wandered over to Sir John.

"Well my husband," she said.

"Well my wife," he replied. "Did we not do well?"

"We did! What remains to be done now?"

"Now? Now we thank our men and woman for coming so far to work for us," he said, pointing to the jugs of wines and beer that were being put out for the men and women. The last of the bundles was being loaded onto a horse drawn cart, which would then be led into the warehouse so that the wheat would be stored, dried, and either prepared for market or for milling.

149

The men took long, deep drafts of the beer, passing it amongst themselves. The women took more delicate sips of the wine, but still drank deeply.

"And then they return to their own homesteads for another year," said Sir John. The men and women were leaving the field, bringing the scythes with them to put on the ground in a bundle, and to get back on the carts that had brought them here, and would return them to which ever farm they normally worked on. Alice noticed, as the crowd of them strolled towards the field entrance, the farmhand handed a garland of wheat to the woman who had hoped to be his sweetheart. She accepted it with a blush and a smile.

Alice gave a big, contented sigh, and looked out over the field of shorn wheat. God is good, she thought.

The Cathedral was filled with nobility and merchants, all eager to have a look at the new Bishop. His mass on Easter Sunday had gathered many to the Church, including those who normally attended service in their own parish. The officials and highest nobility were all in the first few pews, including Alice, William, and Sir John, as well as Petra in attendance. William saw and acknowledged Arnold, now Baron Le Poer, and Seneschal of Kilkenny, Carlow and Waterford. Sir John led Alice up the aisle by the hand.

"Look at this!" remarked one of the ladies attending. "Young love under an old roof!"

The woman next to her nodded. "I've heard say it's first time she's both walked up and down the aisle happy!"

They smiled at each other. Then, after a pause, the first woman looked at Sir John wistfully. I'd be happy too, she thought, and sighed.

The Bishop appeared, in his best vestments. It was so far the closest Alice had got to the man. He does not appear so very threatening, she thought. A firm slap and he'd be cowering. She listened to the mass and to the homily with a good understanding of the Latin. He's educated; I'll give him that, she thought. She sniffed once and rejected him. He is but a man, like them all, she thought. Why would I give care of my soul to him?

The singers in the choir began their chants. Ah yes, I remember hearing about these, thought Alice. Didn't he find fault with the 'bawdy' songs they were singing, and so sat down and wrote sixty of his own? Modest, I'll give him that. And they appear to be of limited capacity, at least in terms of tone. Ah, they're done, thank Goodness. Yes, I think we are drawing to a close here.

The service was in fact drawing to a close. The Bishop, on this day of days, was there to meet them at the door, now newly vacant of any and all beggars. Guards had been posted at the gates to ensure that there was no one allowed into the grounds that was not the right type. Sir John paused beside Le Drede, and lowering his head, received the blessing. Alice did the same, meaning it and not meaning it, as she had been obliged to do so all her life.

They heard the brief muttered intonation in Latin, and then Sir John had taken her by the hand again. Alice and Sir John had lifted their heads in preparation to move on, and had seen the look in Le Drede's eyes.

He stared at both of them with eyes of such obvious dislike, that instinctively the pair moved to get away. Alice was startled by what she had seen, and Sir John was very disturbed too. For a moment they did not speak, merely stepped out of the dark entrance, into the light. Alice composed herself, breathing deeply.

She would not permit harm to Sir John. She was able to defend herself, capable as she was and able to take to action. She was also able to recover from the damages that such battles could inflict. But she would not permit John to suffer when she was the cause. No, that she would not allow, not when she was able. She gave him a glance, and found that he was frowning, alone in his thoughts. She gave his hand a gentle squeeze, which, after a moment, he returned.

"I think we should return to the homestead tomorrow," she said. He looked at her, and nodded.

"That is a good idea, my wife," he said, smiling.

Chapter Fifteen

The Year 1324

After Adam Le Blund's daughter left, the Bishop felt himself feel with a gleeful, bubbling anger. She was a witch, full of heresy, a terrible thing, and she and her cohorts would not be safe from the wrath of God. He looked again at the list of the names that Helen had provided;

Alice Kyteler
William Kyteler
Robert of Bristol, the Cleric
Johannes Galrussyn, cleric
Petronilla of Meath
William Payn de Boyd
Alice, wife of Henry Carpenter,
Annota Lange,
Elena Galrussyn
Syssok Galrussyn
Eva de Brounstounh

Some of the names were very well known to him. The first five names were members of the Kyteler house, and presumably Galrussyn had a wife and child. The rest, however, he did not know, and he intended to find out.

I will to carry out a visitation to the parish again, to ensure all is in order and to commence enquiries. I will need to be very, very secret as this is a matter of heresy and to ensure that the culprits do not fly from my judgement. I will need all of God's help to hunt them down and punish them. I will need to be careful, very, very careful.

Alice sat beside Sir John's bed. She watched him sleeping peacefully, his chest rising and falling with ease. She was finally able to relax. He had been ill for quite some time, with a terribly rasping cough that shook him again and again. She stared at him. He was well over the age of 70. His eyes were failing him, and he did at times seem terribly confused. He didn't seem to recognise which home he was in, and could be prone to strong emotions overcoming him. Thankfully, however, he always seemed to recognise her. She looked at him smiling. Still so handsome, even at his advanced age. And at hers.

He shifted uneasy in his sleep, his head turning as if in a bad dream. Alice, concerned, leaned forward and put her hand on his face. With a start, he awoke. He recognised her with a great sign of relief.

"Alice!" he sighed. "You're here, thank you."

"Where else would I be, my John."

They smiled at each other.

"You should be getting some sun, you are too pale," he said.

"And you should rest and not worry about your old wife," she said. "I have some food for you, and I insist you have a bite or two."

He looked at her, and smiled.

"I would like that very much, thank you," he said. She turned to the fireplace, getting the rich stew ready for him. He took a few forkfuls from her, licking his lips.

"It's very good, I might be able to finish it," he said.

I do hope so, she thought, you are too thin by far my love.

"Aye, you were always a man of intemperate appetites," she sighed.

He gave her a small smile at her gently ribbing. He took her wrist in his hand.

"When I am too sick, you will know," he said.

"Nonsense," she replied, deeply shaken. "You will outlive me, John Le Poer."

"Will I?" he asked.

"Yes. I insist upon it," she said, in her firmest voice.

For a long time there was no conversation between them, merely Sir John taking another mouthful of food.

He looked at her with eyes of the uppermost kindness.

"Very well," he said, and let it rest there.

In early March 1324, Le Drede held an inquest open to all. Dressed in his full regalia, he stood beside five knights of the locality

153

at the top of a table in the Castle, and attempted to discover the truths of these dark times.

He was able to ascertain who the rest of the names were. William Payn de Boyd was a Norman merchant who had a very large dealing with William Kyteler when he was Mayor (and by what dark arts did he come to have that post, wondered Richard) and the man had a small partnership or agency of Kyteler in Calais. The rest of the unknown names were associates of Petra; Alice Carpenter, Annota Lange and Eva de Brouhnstounh were friends of the maid, who were seen very often spending evenings there when the Dame was not at home. Cohorts in the Devilish plans to corrupt the rightful authority of the Church, he thought, listening to the crowds. No doubt a coven.

There were many objections to overcome. Amazingly, it seemed that there was a very great concern to the bringing of charges against the Kytelers. They were a very great family, the concerns went, so they should not be treated with the full vigour of the law. They had the support of the authorities. They should be able to be spit in the face of the Church.

Then, it would seem that the existence of the two cases in the Common Law courts, that of the children of Le Blund and De Valle, meant that the ecclesiastical courts would probably find their own cases blocked. Richard found this idea ridiculous, even if it was true. For was it not the case that the higher court was the ecclesiastical court? If it was not, then it was a grave and serious wrong and one that he intended to put right. He felt himself stirred on, eager to fight for his Church.

The inquisition was able to come up with many details concerning the Dame Kyteler. For one, the public rumours about her were terrible; that there was a most unholy and evil coven of witches in the town, involved in terribly heresy and black arts; that they had got all they had by means of sorcery and black arts; that they would deny the Church and all that it believed in; that Alice slept with an incubus (this one had come from a reliable source, who spoke in a most…passionate tone about the carnality of these encounters), and all manner of appalling events and beliefs being demonstrated about the town by these women.

All that remained now was to issue a letter to the Royal Chancellor, to get a writ issued for the coven's arrest. It was the law that any Bishop could seek and order the sheriff to imprison persons for Heresy. He knew that usually it was for those who had been excommunicated for more than forty days, but this was a different case. This was terribly serious, at least in his mind, and he could not believe that they would ignore such goings on as he had discovered. He sat at home that night and dictated a letter as quickly as he could, trying to impress upon the Chancellor the necessity of moving quickly.

William's eyes narrowed with anger as he heard of what was going around about him and his mother, but he was surprised when he learnt of the details concerning the writ.

"He seeks a writ against us? From the Lord Chancellor himself?" he asked Arnold, incredulous.

Arnold nodded, grave.

"The man believes he has evidence against you and your mother, as well as others, for the crime of Heresy, and for the crime of Sorcery. He seeks to have a writ to arrest all of you, so that he can carry out an Inquisition into the matter and try the lot of you."

William stared at Arnold, but only for a moment.

"An inquisition? Here? We are not at the Papal Court, Sir Arnold, such things do not happen here!"

"Indeed. However, we must still move quickly to block him. He is a Bishop and has powers granted to him by law that may very quickly cause us all a great deal of harm."

"What do you suggest?"

"I will write on your behalf, informing this English man of my disapproval of his actions and of my request that he adjourn or delay the case indefinitely. The matter overlaps with the cases ongoing against you in the Courts by De Valle and Le Blund's children, and that is not permitted. I'll copy what I sent to the Chancellor as well. We may seek out other supporters to help us, while we are about it. You and your mother are held in high affection by many in high places, we will see whom we will get to speak on your behalf."

"Will that be enough?" asked William.

"What do you think? The man wants glory for himself and pain for you; this will not be enough. But we may have another way forward."

He paused while William looked at him.

"It is obligatory in such matters to have suspects undergo a public prosecution and to have been excommunicated for forty days, before such a writ is issued. What the law intends is that the ecclesiastical courts should carry out the investigation, and that the crown should carry out the punishment. He's ignoring due process in how he's going about this. The Chancellor can simply ignore the request and tell him to go about his business."

William looked at Arnold, slowly nodding. It may work. But he didn't think it would.

The two letters were hand delivered to the Palace very soon afterwards. Le Drede reviewed the letter from Sir Arnold first. He had been told that the man had an excellent faith.

It is, wrote Sir Arnold, a matter of common knowledge of the high nobility and excellent manners granted to Dame Alice and her son. Their natures were pure and excellent, and they were honest and hard-working, and pure of faith. Le Drede read all this shaking his head in sadness. Sir Arnold must have been persuaded by the pretty coins of the Kyteler household, to have so perjured himself in this manner. He was lost to the right cause, thought Richard, and had been corrupted by the evilness in that house. He read with saddened resignation of the plea by Lord Arnold for Richard to forget the request for a writ, or to allow the matter to be adjourned indefinitely. You do not, wrote Lord Arnold, know or can gather fully to you a true understanding of the House of Kyteler, and thus I humbly and honestly make my plea.

Richard put it to one side, intending to pray for the man so that he may see the errors of his ways and come back to the true heart of the Church. He turned to the second one.

It was from an unexpected source, Roger Outlaw, or rather Brother Roger Outlaw from the Order of the Hospitallers of St John, in Kilmainham in Dublin, and Chancellor of Ireland. This was a very noble position, Le Drede saw, and one vested in the full sanctity of the Church. The tone taken by Outlaw was different from Lord Arnold. The man wrote with an intelligent, thoughtful air, and Le Drede, reading it, had the sense that he would have liked him.

My nephew William is a man in all ways like his father, in that his soul is pure of all malevolence and mischief against the Mother Church. We are blessed to count him amongst our faithful, Brother Richard, and should put to one side all thoughts of his being in league with the unholy One.

Richard read it with a gathering sense of loneliness, with the sadness of one who must stand alone. Corrupted, he thought, the sight of the gold of that family has corrupted them all. They have sold their souls like Judas; they are lost to the Church! Presented with undeniable evidence, they plead mercy!

He sat up straighter in his chair. He alone would preserve the honour and sanctity of his Mother Church. He called in the clerk to him, and began to dictate a letter.

Arnold was laughing as he entered into the office area of William's house in Kilkenny. He put down in front of William the letter from the Bishop. Lord, thought William, looking up from the document he was reading with the clerk, what is it to be concerning now?

The letter was brief, to the point of rudeness.

Lord Arnold,

Were I to avoid the clamour that such crimes raise up to Heaven, I would be gravely remiss in my duty to our Lord Father and his Church. Please note that I bring to your attention the fact under no circumstances could complicated cases such as this one, involving the faith and the Church be so handled. I therefore am unable to grant your request that I allow the matter to be adjourned indefinitely.

Your Bishop

Richard Le Drede

Diocese of Ossory

William, reading this, recognised finally what was happening. This was not some once off writ that the lawyers would take over and remove from his attention, letting him get on with the more important matter of his business. Le Drede was on his doorstep. Le Drede wanted to ruin them. And he would not let them go.

Hence, the next step would be to write to the Chancellor. The difference in legal procedure would need to be pointed out. William thought with envy of the solution he had put into place with William le Kiteler and his brood, still sitting alone and undiscovered in the woods. It may come to that, he thought. But not yet.

Le Drede read the letter from the Chancellor.

I am prevented by the laws of the land and the duties of my office in granting this writ.

At the moment it is the case that no public prosecution has been held and the suspects in this case have not been excommunicated from the Church for forty days.

This verdict from the Chancellor was entirely in accordance with the Common Law of the land. Section 39 of the *Magna Carta* demanded that the procedure of the law be followed.

This was in direct and undeniable conflict with the legal basis of Le Drede's actions. The Papal Bull *Ut Inquisitionis,* issued by Boniface VIII in 1298, called for the immediate detention of suspected heretics. Le Drede, reading the letter of the Chancellor, saw this, and felt certain that he could convince the Chancellor of the wisdom of his request. A gentle reminder should be given that there was a need to act quickly against such heretics, and that such a need was absolutely necessary.

The letter to the Chancellor was sent almost immediately – they joked that the horses were not yet cool when it was sent;

My experience in this matter and in other matters of faith is great, due to my time at the right hand of the Holy Father in Avignon. I have witnessed there the great deception that is possible from such people in such circumstances. Therefore, heretics must be handled differently from other excommunicates, for otherwise, once they know the Church intends to take proceedings against them, they can straight away flee to another region, thus causing a great scandal and damaging the faith.

A day passed. Then two. This was stretched to a week. There was no reply from the Chancellor. There was, thought Le Drede, alone in his study one evening, not going to be one. The evilness would be permitted to go about the land. There would be no protection of the faith. There would be no assistance offered to him in this matter.

So be it. So be it! He had declared himself the protector of the Faith. Far be it from him to cry womanish tears of fear when it was finally clear to him his position. He sniffed a little, and then was strong.

He would act alone. But act he would.

The Citation, which was indeed issued according to the law of the land, was that Alice Kyteler was to appear before a court of the ecclesiastical authority, namely the Bishop, to answer the charges as named against her. Word came via the clerks involved that it would be acted on in the next 36 hours. What would happen would be that two enforcers, probably sheriffs' men, would be sent to Alice's house along with a company of priests. Then Alice would be seized and brought to jail, eventually being charged and then found guilty and punished. Once Alice was charged, Le Drede knew, any other concerns regarding the other lower, poorer ladies, would be forgotten, and matters could continue apace.

William didn't even wait to speak to Alice, but sent a quickly drafted copy to Roger Outlaw in Kilmainham, the Chancellor Le Drede had implored, and William Kyteler's uncle. We require your assistance with all speed, he wrote. Please send your legal advisors to appear in our place, giving any and all legal arguments you may compile. We are close to being at the mercy of this man, who so far has rejected all proper legal recourse as decided by the Magna Carta.

The messenger took off immediately, the ink still wet.

William sat at his desk. Two things would need to be done. His mother would need to be gone, now, today, this moment, without delay. The second thing to be done was that the money that they needed to free themselves from the illness of Le Drede's attacks, would need to be removed from the house. Soon they would be obliged to have the Sheriff's men all about them, and William wanted their wealth protected.

"Petra," he called out. "Petra!"

The woman came into the room, and he suddenly saw how old she was. Over fifty? Doing well, he thought. No time to complement her on it, no time for anything anymore. We are all made savages by that man, he thought.

"Where is my mother?"

"Sir John is near death."

"What? I thought he was improving?"

"It was not to be. The cough has turned to a fever, and the fever has not broken. He is to be taken from us very shortly."

William looked at her, distressed.

"We are very shortly to have the Sheriff's men in this house. They will come for my mother, so that she may answer the Bishop's charge of Witchcraft. I must answer it. So must you," he said, to which she stared at him, shocked and frightened.

"We must take you and my mother away from here, see her safely away in Dublin for the moment while all this is going on. I need you to see that she is prepared for her journey and that she has all she needs."

"She will not go!" .

"Petra."

"She will not go! She will not leave him, not in his final few hours with her. She will have to go as soon as it is possible for her to go, but it won't be now."

William stood.

"I will go to her."

"I'll start preparations for her journey, there is much to be done," said Petra, walking from the room. Then she stopped.

"My Lord, how long will your mother and I be gone for?"

William looked at her and lied.

"Not long. Go now. See to my mother."

Alice was upstairs in Sir John's room, the room that had been Adam's, and then Richard's, and now his. She sat beside him, smiling, and ensured that his brow was mopped carefully. The light was kept low, so as to ensure his rest. She was conscious of something she hadn't known before beginning to break through her chest, but she stalwartly kept it at bay. Her eyes shone with the effort, though. He opened his eyes and saw it in her.

"My wife," he whispered, his voice so gentle and kind. Oh, how she would miss him!

"My husband!" she whispered back to him.

"Why do you cry?" he asked.

"Because it is your fault I am sad, and I cannot blame you."

"I have finally won the argument," he said, "I did not know it would be so easy in the end."

She tried to smile, but instead found herself overcome with tears. She lowered her head on the bed and sobbed.

"So sad, my Alice, so sad," he said. "I did not think I could have made you so sad."

"Well, you did," she said. His hands reached out to her over the blanket, and gripped hers with all the love he had for her.

"My wife, I want to see you happy. I believe I did, didn't I?"

Oh yes, you did, you did so very much!"

"Good. Then I have done some good in this world, and I will be welcome into Heaven."

"Oh, John, don't leave me! No one will ever be as happy to see me as you were!" She lowered her head again, feeling the terrible loneliness of her earlier life come out to touch her heart, as if John had never happened.

"Don't cry, don't cry, my Alice. Listen to me."

"Please stay, please stay," she pleaded, "Don't go!"

"I must, I cannot stay," he whispered, his own voice tearful.

She cried as though her heart would break.

"Listen to me Alice, listen."

She lifted her head, and made an effort to compose herself.

"So many people never have a companion in their lives. To be without one from birth to death is the common lot. You and I have had a bond known to so few; we must be joyful at what has been given to us. You know this, don't you?"

Tearful, she nodded.

"So be glad we had this. Do not be sad we are now without it. Be strong, and happy, and know you are loved, my Alice. You have been a good wife to me, and have made me very happy."

"You have made me very happy too, my husband."

"I love you greatly, my Alice," he said, his hands losing their grip on hers.

"I love you too, my husband," she said, leaning over him.

"John," she whispered urgently.

His hand went slack.

"John," she whispered again, not believing it.

He was gone. Alice gripped his cooling hands, and lowered her head on the bed. He was gone from her, and she was alone again. She cried and cried as if her heart would break. After a while, after a long while, she lifted her head from the bed, and pulled the blankets around him to ensure that the cold could not touch him. Then she bent down and tenderly kissed his forehead.

"I will love you forever," she said to him. The tears came again, and nearly undid her, but she fought them back. She would need to do things, he had had the last rites an hour ago, but he would need to be prepared for the funeral and such matters readied. She stood up.

There was a brief knock on the door. Alice, standing there, found that staring at the body of Sir John could not but bring tears to her face, so she had to turn her back to him to keep her composure.

It was William. He stared with shock at the scene in front of him. He knelt in front of Dame Alice, one hand on his heart.

"Mother, my sincere heartfelt sympathies."

His mother's voice sounded so strange.

"Thank you William."

He stood and looked into her face. It is grief stricken, he thought, and then he thought, I have not seen that since my own father died.

"You must away," he said, no time to pander to her grief. "Le Drede and his men come for you this night."

"What?" she gasped. "I am newly a widow, surely he will grant a dispensation to me in my state!" She leaned back, touching the bed board with her hand. "I must stay with my husband, now most of all, to do my duty for him." She looked at William, as if he could change the way of the world.

"I cannot help you Mother, I only know that you must be gone now, tonight, within the hour."

"No!" she whispered.

"Yes," he said.

She nodded, resigned. "Very well."

162

"Petra is preparing your things as we speak. I will ask her to go with you to serve you."

"No," said Alice, "I'll take Rose. I want Petra to stay with Sir John and see to it he is buried properly."

William looked at her tear-streaked face.

"She is mentioned in the writ as well. She is in danger."

"As are you. You will not allow any damage to come to you or to her."

He looked at her again.

"Very well," he said.

"I will be here. Send word to me when it is time," she said, and sat back down beside her husband.

William, looking at her, saw her holding the hand of her husband with a straight back. She cannot bury him, so she will sit with him, right until the end, he thought, understanding. He left without another word.

Alice sat beside Sir John, and let the tears fall silently. If you had been near her, in that room on that day of days, you would have only heard her say one thing.

"What great fortune I had to find you. What great fortune," she marvelled. And then all was silence.

It was nearly dawn when they heard the pounding on the door. Philip, who had not slept that night, nor had anyone else, opened it immediately. A scroll of parchment was shoved into his face.

"Stand back," came an order.

The men, twelve in total, marched into the foyer with a military air. They were dressed with no military finesse, however, and each of them carried a variety of farming tools as weapons.

"What is the meaning of this?" asked William who had appeared in the foyer.

The parchment was thrust into his hands, and he looked at it while the Enforcer intoned the Latin. It demanded by authority of the Bishop that Dame Alice be seized and presented at the Episcopal Court on the next available sitting.

"This is no hour for such a call," said William.

"His Grace feels differently," said the priest. "Where is your mother?"

"She is not here. She is in Dublin."

The priest's eyes widened at the news.

"Search the house!" he called, and the men separated and began the search.

"Where is she?" he whispered to William, so like his father in his way.

"She has escaped you. She is in Dublin," he said quietly.

The priest promptly spat on the floor in fury.

A call came out from somewhere upstairs.

"No sign, Sire, but Sir John Le Poer is here dead!"

"What?" said the priest, turning an accusing eye on William.

"He died of natural causes, as the priest who gave the last rites can attest."

"Aye, a likely story!" exclaimed the priest. The men reassembled down in the foyer.

"Come on," said the priest, "we're leaving."

The men began to file out.

"Good day to you, Master William," said the priest.

William nodded to Philip to lock the door.

In his Palace, Le Drede plotted. He had just returned from the ecclesiastical court he had set up to try Alice. She had not appeared of course, he had not expected the brazen harlot to do so. But he had not expected to see the clerics of the Chancellor of Ireland appear as the advocate of that witch. They had had the brazenness to appear before a court of God and suggest that she did not have to appear in person, but to merely send a proctor for her. Le Drede had stared at them for minutes while hearing them drone on, until finally the Lord Almighty parted the clouds of his confusion and gave him the answer. Let the trial go ahead, let Alice and all the rest of the vipers be dealt with according to the Law of this foul and godless land. The Witch was now fully excommunicated, as demanded, and would be so for forty days; thus was it so written in Lucius III's decree, and as that was issued jointly with the Roman Emperor put it far above the mere common law practised in these parts.

No, Alice was gone from him, at least physically. But he was not completely without ideas at this stage, he did still have the Lord on his side. He would be made resourceful.

"If we cannot have the mother," he said to the waiting sheriff, "we cannot have the mother. But we are not undone yet. Instead, we will hold fast, and still work to remove this den of vipers in our midst."

"What would you like us to do, your Grace?" asked the man.

"We will appeal to the local authorities. We have had no success with those in Dublin, where her money has reached. But we will appeal before the local men of this area, and ask their assistance in this matter."

He looked at the young man standing beside him.

"Please take a message to the court. I believe it is sitting on the first Monday, twenty-third of April, is that right?" he asked, to which the other men in the room nodded.

"Then please take this message. I come to you to seek the help of the secular arm from the seneschal and the ministers of state. I send these two men, members of the Dominican order, as well as the warden of the Franciscans in Kilkenny, to ask the Seneschal, that I be allowed in a case of the faith to speak before him and the nobles, people and my own parishioners."

He looked at the cleric who was noting all this down.

"That should be enough."

The men in the large room roared laughing, and each of them stared transfixed at Arnold, who held the paper in his hands. They were in his house, each of them drunk in their cups, and listening to him read the letter again.

"Thus," began Arnold, "I do humbly request and respect to meet the Seneschal on the first Monday after the Octave of Easter in 1324!"

The men roared once more.

"How about it lads! A bishop humbly requests a Seneschal! I don't think I've been this lucky since I tupped the maid in the hay barn at Yuletide!"

The men roared again, mostly at the foolishness of Le Drede rather than anything else. Le Drede asking for Arnold's help was similar to asking an enemy to kill himself on the battlefield for you. Arnold stood before them in his great hall, and felt himself invincible.

"What say you men? Will we show him what we think of his humble request?"

A roar of consent went up.

Arnold, thus confirmed, went to the cleric standing at the side of the room, who was by now well terrified of the unpredictable Arnold.

"Give yourself to writing this reply to your master. Tell him, that the bishop would enter the seneschal's court of justice at his own peril."

The cleric's eyes opened wide at the words.

"What!" snorted Arnold. "Do I speak too rough and plain for his Grace? Well then, maybe he will be so kind as to see sense and not seek sanctuary outside of his Mother Church's skirts."

He spun the cleric around so that the younger man faced the door, and gave him a boot in the backside. The men behind him cheered.

"Away with you! Get you back to your master."

He spun back to the men, and looked at them.

"Who is for more wine!" he called, and the men cheered again.

The messenger returned to Le Drede the night before the first Monday after the Octave. He stood, shamefaced, before the bishop, and offered the piece of paper to him with a sense of the terrible thing he was doing. Le Drede looked at the face of the cleric before he took the paper. Before he looked at it, he laid it face down on the table that he sat at. He needed to prepare himself.

Surely they had said yes? Surely it was so done, even in these parts? The ways of the Church, of civilisation and of the salvation of souls were not so far gone that they were lost here as well? He looked at the cleric. The fear and shame of the man told a different story. They told of a refusal that was grave and ultimate. But perhaps it was not that black a situation. Perhaps it was not that bad.

166

Le Drede turned over the paper and read it.

The cleric saw him turn white, and saw his eyes bulge. He saw the bishop stare at the page for minutes, not lifting his eyes or making any comments. He saw the Bishop close his eyes in horror, but then open them again immediately. And then stare at the paper again. The young priest, a mere fifteen years of age, was frightened at the injury he had done to the Bishop, and feared greatly that the man was out of his wits.

The Bishop eventually pushed the paper away from him. He lifted his head to the young priest and nodded at him.

"You should away to Nones, brother. I would not have you kept late for the Abbot."

The young priest merely nodded, and backed away.

Le Drede's own secretary looked at the Bishop. Le Drede felt the look and glanced at the man.

"Oh, I am not frightened, Brother Matthew," he said. "Never let it be said that I should fear that man or his punishments." He stood up in the reception room, a decision made.

"I will present myself to the Court tomorrow, in the vestments and apparel of my office apparent to all in the Court. Let them, then, deny me my rightful authority before them all." He paused for a moment, and then spoke on.

"They are but peasants and unholy sinners in the eyes of the Church, Matthew. Be not afraid. We will show them the way."

The following day, approximately twenty men stood before the entrance to the Court. Situated in the centre of the town, it was busy with clerks and messengers going in and out, as well as the usual petitioners ready to plead their cases to the court.

At the top of the room sat Arnold with the court clerk. To his left was the usual audience of nobles, knights, and freeholders around about the location. These men would hear the pleas and notices and would decide situation. As Arnold sat there, a messenger rushed ahead of Le Drede and whispered to him of what was coming.

True to his word, Richard Le Drede was dressed in the full vestments, carrying the host in its decorated gilt vessel, and at the head of a procession of over twenty men, who carried candles and chanted hymns.

The room folded over into silence. There was also a slight sense of sinking back into their chairs to avoid the man's gaze. How was Arnold going to handle this?

The Bishop arrived at the centre of the room in front of the men. The smell in here was simply terrible, he thought, as indeed it was. The stench, however, would have to be borne.

"Lord Arnold," he said, his high pitched tone filling the room, "I call upon you, as Seneschal of this Court and land, to swear to us and to the Church of God, to attend carefully and seriously the constitutions promulgated through my diocese and to denounce and persecute any heretics, their followers, aiders and abettors, and any who should protect them."

A silence followed, more tense than a lyre string at its tightest. Arnold sat looking at the man, who had appeared before him in full regalia of the Church. He was being forced to choose, in open court, between the authority he had sworn to uphold and the one that he was now being asked to protect. There was no way he could offer a satisfactory solution to the Bishop, nor should he do so. He was on the side of the Law as laid down in the Magna Carta. He could not say yes.

"My Grace, I cannot do that. I have sworn an oath to protect the law of the land as laid down by the Crown. I cannot say yes to you."

To Le Drede, he was hearing an overt refusal of obedience as rude as any slur. His eyes opened in rage at the action.

"You cannot refuse me! I come before this Court dressed in the vestments of the Holy Mother Church, with Christ Himself before you!" Le Drede lifted up the gilt vessel above his head.

"Knee before me, you heretic!" he cried, his voice crying in his rage.

Arnold had had enough. He stood from his chair, gesturing aggressively at Le Drede.

"Oh, you ignorant, lowborn tramp from England, do you think that your authority is so high here you do go before the law?"

Le Drede, for his part, drew back in exaggerated fear of the Seneschal.

"You *dare* come before this court, my court, and command me?" He looked around in amazement before the knights and nobles to his right.

"If some tramp from England or somewhere has obtained his bull or privilege in the Pope's court, we don't have to obey that bull unless it has been enjoined on us by the king's seal. Is this not so? Is it not?" he asked the men, who gave a general mummer of assent.

"In fact, is it not the case, that heretics have never yet been found in Ireland. It has always been called the "Island of the Saints", and while some might doubt that now, we are still a holy people. Now this foreigner comes from England, and says we're all heretics and excommunicates, on the ground of some papal constitutions that we've never even heard of. Defamation of this country affects everyone of us, so we must all unite against this man!"

A larger, more heated cheer went up, and a few of the men rose to their feet. Arnold, confident of their backing, turned back to the Bishop. Le Drede was gazing in horror at the turn of events.

"So get someone else to help you from the King's court, or from somewhere else. In this business your authority from that court will never win any support from us."

Le Drede stood, staring at Arnold, who seeing him still standing there, rushed over and manhandled the man towards the door of the room. Followed by the rest of the knights and nobles, it soon became an unequal skirmish, and the priests were soon thrust out of the court.

"By God, lads, maybe we have convinced him to take the next boat back home!" he cried, and grinned when he received their cheers.

The door to the Palace slammed open, and the entourage of the Bishop came in. Le Drede was insane with rage, a wild, coursing revengeful rage that did not bid of reason or rationality, but sought instead to cause pain immediately and to see offence everywhere.

He went into his study and began to strip his vestments off, and saw that the clerk was not there.

" Where is my clerk? Where is he! I want him to appear before me immediately! Immediately! Do not deter me gentlemen, get him in here immediately! I will not be held off! You, you there, you help me out of this immediately! And you, you get me my robe at once! DO NOT PAUSE! Hurry! Finally, Brother Matthew, you appear! You do poor service as usual to me your master, you stupid man! Note my words, every and each one, and do not fail or falter in any sense of them. Note this, this is to be a new point in my constitution. Do not hesitate, man!"

"We excommunicate all those who maliciously harass, molest and defraud the rights and liberties of this Church of St. Canice, or who unjustly through secular power strive to prevent the observance of warrants and detain abbots publicly or secretly, together with any who offer them help, counsel, assistance and favour in these matters, let all these be cursed by God, the blessed Virgin Mary, all the saints of God and by us; let them be cursed within and without, on the roads, in field and city, at home and abroad, going out and returning, eating drinking, sleeping while awake, standing and sitting, making war or in peace. Let them be struck from the book of the living, let them not be written down with the just, let their dwelling places become deserts, empty of dwellers, let their eyes not see, let their backs be bent. Put out upon them, O Lord, your anger," said Le Drede, gripping his hands into fists and his jaw clenched in rage, "let the fury of your rage embrace them, pile iniquity upon iniquity for them and do not admit them to your justice; let their livelihood become for them a knot of retribution and scandal; let the usurer ransack all their substance, let outsiders plunder their labours; since they love cursing, let them be the victims of cursing; they do not want blessing and they will not get it; let their sons be orphans and their wives barren; let God grind down their teeth and may their tongues never utter wisdom, may Dathan and Abiron be of their faction and company, Saphira and Anania, Judas and Pilate, Simon and Nero; as their lights go out so let the brightness of the vision of God's light be extinguished from them; so let the souls of those who do evil deeds of this kind or plan to do them in the future, plummet down to Hell with the Devil and his ministers, unless they return to their senses from their evil-doing and make proper amends. Let all this happen. Let all this happen. Amen."

He looked at the clerk, and smiled. He was filled with a perfect calm that soothed his nerves wonderfully. He looked quite insane.

"It is very simple. Where we cannot have the mother, then we will have her son."

He handed the writs, all of them, to the Sheriff.

"See that these are put on every Church door, every market place, all where it may be seen by the populace. We will get our justice yet."

Chapter Sixteen

William was furious. Not just angry, but truly beside himself with the frustration born of helplessness. News of the writs had reached him before they were on the door. He had snarled at the idea of that little man daring to think he could touch the House of Kyteler. But his attitude of true rage was instead due to the news that Rose had returned. He was completely confused as to why his mother would have returned her.

Rose stood before him in the main lobby, her attitude the same apologetic silence as before. He read again the letter his mother had drafted for him to read.

"She misses home, William. I have many to serve me here at your good uncle's house. And she will be of assistance to Petra in servicing the business in my absence."

The reasoning was weak, he fumed. And she was, frankly, one more annoyance to a man already stretched to his limit. He sighed, and merely gestured her away, his attitude one of true irritation.

In 20 days he and the others would be expected to be before the court that Le Drede had created, there to answer charges of Witchcraft. Witchcraft! He was supposedly a master of Black Arts! If he was, Le Drede would not be alive to come out with such a charge of nonsense. He sat and thought, angrily, fuming, his mind churning through the options. He would not have to sit before a court that was without Le Drede. The man was untouchable, however. Any damage coming to him now would point immediately to them.

The writs appeared as ordered. There was, during morning celebration of mass a great thumping on the door, which made the singers pause over their music and made the celebrant look fearfully over his shoulder at the entrance. When they did finally go out, at the end, they crowded around the door, amazed. The writ sought the presentation of now not Alice, but instead William, Petra, and all the others. In 19 days. The matter was well known at this stage, due to Le Drede's constant harping on the subject, not to mention his well known expulsion from Arnold's court. But this was yet another assault upon the Kyteler house, and one that came upon news of Alice fleeing the town. The matter was growing more serious.

Many in the locality saw them for themselves, but those who did not got the details from others. William was to be arrested, as was Petra, and all the others on the list. There was to be a trial. There was to be a conviction, according to the rules of the Church, not the Crown. And that meant a trial by inquisitorial standards.

The reaction was mixed. To many, it seemed a shocking thing to do to one so high born, and would mean a terrible fall for the Church to fail. He is the nephew of the Chancellor, snorted one person. Such a fate will never fall to him! Another felt that the poorer or lesser known on the list would be affected, but not William, nor any member of his house.

Others were not so sure. He is a Bishop appointed by the Pope himself. He has the backing of the English Crown, he can do what he wishes. And will he be stopped? By the Chancellor, or by anyone else? No, it bodes poorly for them all.

And some were silent, and thoughtful. The Kytelers own much, and are owed much by me. If I can be rid of them, I will do so. At the right time.

And so it went. The town crier went through the city all that day and several days afterwards, calling upon the populace to be aware of the matter. They would stand, dumb and exhausted with work, bundles on their back, listening to the call of the crier giving the news of the writ. It seemed to at least one of them strange that those in charge should argue amongst themselves; the idea that there could be debate among those who made the rules had never occurred to them.

Rose was in the front of the house when she heard the crier. She was lifting a table so as to put it away, when she heard the Latin intonation from outside. They are talking about us, she thought. She stood, fixed on the spot, not breathing, as she listened. There was to be a trial, and all were to be made aware. She was hearing this, she thought, but they had had no writ hammered on their door like before. At least, not yet. She put the table down and was about to go to William, when he came into the room of his own accord. She immediately indicated to him to listen. The man stood, silent, his eye focusing on the stone over the door as he made out the words. Nineteen days. They had nineteen days. He would go to Arnold.

173

Arnold himself already knew of it. He had retired to the tavern after court with some of the men he had attended with. He was brooding, plotting, over the foul Bishop and his meddling ways. Arnold was dealing with an expanding sense of unease over the scene that had happened. He was conscious that he had acted in a hot-headed manner, that he was rash and unthinking in his conduct. He told himself that he had been placed in an impossible position. The Bishop would not have listened to reason. But the others in the room would have, he argued back. They would have had sense to listen to the words he would have said, thus insuring even less support for the Bishop. Plus, the laying of hands on a holder of high office in the Church would be looked on poorly by many. He had missed an opportunity to increase his influence, and his conscience stung him over and over about it. He took another drink.

The crier came into the tavern, singing the intonation of the writ against William and the others. Arnold sat staring in horror at the matter. Dear God, not since Jesus and Mary was a son and his mother so inflicted and persecuted! Arnold let the man finish his chant, and then stood up. He would have to get to William's house, soon. They may have only a little time to act.

He moved through the streets on his horse with a barely contained sense of urgency. He was careful to remove all show of it in front of the populace, however; he kept his back straight and his mien calm in front of them all. He wondered, internally, where his face could not be seen, how he could be rid of the illness that Le Drede had become. The pestilence of the man simply would not end. He moved his horse down to the Kyteler house and dismounted.

Inside, he merely moved though the house until he found William, in the audience room (the room where, so long ago, Philip had been forced to account for a silver knife). William was sitting with his back to the door, leaning back in his chair with the writ in his hand. Arnold could not see his face. Will sat up upon hearing someone come in and looked around.

"Lord Arnold, God save you."

"Indeed, William, you deserve and need His intercession more than I at this moment."

"You are aware of this, no doubt?" he said, offering the writ to him.

174

"I am- the man's a fool."

"Fool or no, we must find a way to deal with him. A fool can have the ear of a King and make all manner of comments and suggestions to rule and decide a people. This is one such fool."

"You should not be afraid of him."

"I am not afraid of him, but I am not unconscious of the man's power over this city and over this house. My mother has fled out of necessity to avoid him. What else will he do?"

Arnold moved to the chair beside him.

"What we must do is find a way to convince the Bishop of the error of his ways. We have always in the past managed, in both of our lives, to gain favour and understanding of those around us. Let us try to do so now."

William looked at him.

"Do you mean bribery?" he asked.

"I mean bribery, coercion, persuasion, wit, tenacity and sheer hard headedness. These things may be the things that are needed to convince a Bishop of the necessity of giving us peace."

"And how do you propose to do this?"

Arnold ran a hand over his face, wishing he had not had so much wine so that his head might be cool.

"The Bishop is currently on a visitation of his parish, as you know. He is on the outskirts of Kells tonight, and will be tomorrow. We should go there tonight, and passionately speak our case to the man as best we can. And as best as our money and position can."

Arnold looked at William, the meaning strong between them. They were silent for a moment. Then William spoke again.

"And if neither of these things is enough to silence the man?"

"Then I will silence him. I will arrange for the Bishop to be brought to the Castle and interned there until the date issued on that writ. We have the right to do so, due to the meddling of that man in our affairs for so long. We also have the authority to do so, as I am Seneschal. I can ensure that the men who do this can be trusted and that they will carry out my orders. We can see that the writ is not carried out, one way or another."

"So if he refuses, we will see him in prison?" asked William, incredulous.

"We will, by my faith. Let us slow him, or his resolve."

175

This rocked William. He sat back in his chair, amazed. They might put the Bishop in jail, where he and his foul power might be removed from public sight. His voice would not be heard, nor his face be under the light. The man might be removed from doing them all harm. Instead, what might happen would be that the constant unpleasant influence of Le Drede would stop. Be quiet. Be silenced once and for all. And once the time had passed, and the writ made useless, Le Drede would know once and for all that the might of the Kytelers would not allow his flights of fancy to take effect. Let the man piss in a pot made foul by years of madmen and then see how quickly he removed himself.

He looked at Arnold, who sat there waiting for them to move.

"Let it be so."

Arnold smiled.

"But before we go to meet this man, I will write to my mother and uncle in Dublin. We will outline to them our request for support to us with all speed."

And in a short while it was done. The two men, with their entourage, rode from the town gates and into the dark of the night, their number many, their purpose clear. To stop the Bishop. To stop him, by one means or by many.

And Philip, standing at the door watching them go, looked once again at the folded, sealed parchment in his hand. This letter, he thought, enlists help from the Mistress in Dublin. She will frown and narrow her eyes and she will exert her force again. She will turn a Bishop now, and deny him his will in an effort to gain her way.

He shut the door behind him as he realised the nature of his thoughts. The letter he held made the entire situation known to all outside the town. It would grant them peace and safety and ensure once more that they would have their way. They would harm a Bishop to have it, but they would have it. Philip blinked rapidly as the horror and gall of it became apparent to him. They were scandalous. They were fearless in their resistance. They were devilish. That was it, they had a pride most unnatural that would allow them to act in such a way. Where was their modesty? Where did their hearts reside that they could plot and plan in such a way?

For a moment he saw himself again in the study with the Clerk, the same man now listed in the writ. Philip knew he was at least a good

176

man. But none of the others seemed to see the real nature of their acts. They were without hearts that could see mercy, or God's purity. None of them knew what they were doing. But he knew what he was doing. He knew it now.

He leaned over and was about to put the letter on the fire. The white parchment held over the flames for a moment, as he hesitated. And hesitated. He breathed in and out, he blinked. The heat of the flames reached the back of his hands, burning the hairs down.

He pulled it back from the flames, and merely stuffed it under his tunic. He would hold off from sending the messenger today. He would decide on it tomorrow. And if not then, the day after. There would be time. He would need time to temper his thoughts. Time.

The room of Le Drede was on the second floor of the small wooden building. It appeared grubby to him, but he was assured by the parish priest that it was the best premises in the small town of Kells. The fire was at least well lit and the room warm, with the windows securely fastened to ensure no dirt could come in on the air.

He sat on the chair at the desk, the papers spread in front of him. He was a man who was given over to the written word, finding in its subtle invocations a much more gentle and kinder interpretation than that which existed in reality. He recalled in his mind an incident from childhood; once a dog had lain dying outside his house. It was a small, innocent thing, and its eye had followed him as he stood above it. The ribs of the animal stuck out as it breathed, and for a moment Richard the boy felt a terrible, urgent pang of empathy. The death of the dog would be a terrible, mournful thing, would scar him forever, he had felt. It would be a tragedy. He had gathered the animal up in his arms and it had whimpered in fear at the touch of him. He didn't want it subjected to every stone an urchin might throw at it. In adulthood, he had to reach back in his mind to recall what had happened to it. Ah yes, when he had been released again from his studies, he had gone back to where he had left the dog and found it dead. He hadn't been so sad, though. The feel of it in his arms had at least aided the pain of his empathy. He looked upon his work as the same effort, he thought. He was bridging the gap of his isolation when he gave himself in effort to it. Otherwise, he would have had only his father's scornful glances to decide him, and he would never have survived that.

He wondered tonight at his mood. So many years since he had thought about that animal, and how important it had been! How many animals had been born, lived and died, in whatever circumstances since then, and he gave his thoughts solely to this one! Such were the capricious, selfish ways of man. The only world that mattered was this one, not the one to come. It had been demonstrated to him during the day. The Constitutions he had written had been taken on board by the Priest, who had removed the concubines of his parish, prevented any farmers using Church lands, and halted bawdy songs in mass. Still the man sought to increase the alms gathered, solely for his own use. Le Drede had lectured him soundly on the necessity of the vow of poverty, and warned the man to look to himself.

Maybe that was what was missing from the soul of William Kyteler. Maybe he believed that he was not in danger of losing his soul, that somehow he was safe. Such complacency was foolish, to say the least. Especially if the man did indeed conduct himself as the rumours did say. Le Drede shifted in his chair somewhat and farted with relief. Dinner had been large tonight, and he had felt the need to pass wind for some time. He briefly crossed himself to undo the ill, and read on. Foolish or no, the aims of Kyteler could not be permitted to touch the authority of the Church. He would be no champion if he did permit it to be so.

There was a knock at the door. Le Drede frowned in surprise at the noise, it was well after midnight and there should be no good reason to call on him at this time. What was wrong?

"Come," he called, and the door opened.

The door opened, and in stepped Arnold Le Poer and William Kyteler.

Le Drede was amazed to see them there, in his room so late at night. He felt a gathering alarm at the very idea of their being in his quarters. He waited, eyes widening to see if either of them had evil intentions.

Arnold saw this and was amused; William saw this and was alarmed, their efforts could be for nothing before they even started.

178

He paused before Le Drede, a good five feet from him, and lowered his head in proper respect.

Le Drede noting this warily with a small inclination of his head, never taking his eyes off the pair of them. He looked at Arnold, who slowly followed William's nod and did the same. The three men looked at each other.

Le Drede was the first to speak.

"It is late, gentlemen, and your presence is unbidden. May I ask the reason for your visitation upon me?"

The tone was arrogant and commanding, and Arnold felt his shackles rise. William did not react, but was calm in the face of it. He spoke.

"We come, your Grace, to bid you to halt all manner of persecution of our House, and to ask you to adhere to the law and letter of the Law of this land, for all our sakes." He made to go on, but was interrupted by Le Drede.

"Such a request is both bold and wrong, William, you must have awareness of that. To lower the Church to follow the shackles set on her by any and all lands she finds herself in, would be to do her a terrible wrong. She would be subject to all, handmaiden of all lands, when in fact she should be Mistress without question." Le Drede's tone was earnest, heartfelt, and William responded to that. He took a few steps forward to Le Drede, and stood before him.

"But to state that the Church must never adhere to the laws of her lands, is to risk carrying out grave injustices in her name. She must be concerned that justice is done as well as righteousness. She seeks to educate as well as rule, so that sinners may find their right and proper way to salvation. So she must guide by reason as well as by faith. She must ensure that she conducts herself with justice as by the law of the land. Otherwise she has no law to guide her priests and bishops in their conduct, and they might make mistakes towards the brethren."

The look on William's face made it clear that he felt such a mistake had occurred with regard to him.

Le Drede regarded the younger man with an almost kind look, and looked away for a moment to marshal his material. William took the liberty to sit down beside him while he did so.

"William, from the very introduction of worship of the Divine, priests have been held in honour by the peoples of the world. We can see this by Melchisedeck and Aaron, for example. Even pagans, gentiles and Saracens in their own sects are accustomed to worship and honour priests and pontiffs, as is clear in the Koran and their other books. For example, even Alexander, that magnificent ruler of the world, seeing Saddas the priest running towards him and bearing the name of God on his forehead, fell forward onto the ground and worshipped him and furnished him with many kinds of gifts. Even the emperor Constantine in full general council allowed a lesser priest distinguished with full pontifical dignity to precede himself, and likewise said that bishops were to be preferred to all other mortals as judges of souls."

The talk of honouring bishops reminded Le Drede of his recent disgrace in Arnold's court. He felt once again the burning rage of that day and reminded himself that his argument with Arnold was not yet over. He went on.

"It was Jesus Christ Himself who designated bishops as the successors of the apostles and entrusted to them the keys of the Church, the power of binding and loosing and the administering of the sacraments. To carry this out without ecclesiastical jurisdiction, is not possible. Therefore it is necessary beyond any and all argument to rely on ecclesiastical jurisdiction."

Le Drede threw a spiteful glance at William, and then glared at Arnold, the rage high in him now. Arnold, seeing the smaller man's spiteful face, gave out a bark of laughter. William stood so as to block the two men, but the bishop was standing, yelling at Arnold.

"This pestiferous new outgrowth in this region, in contrast with all other faiths of the earth, full of the spirit of the unholy one, cutting itself off from the persuasion of all worshippers of God, more cruel than gentiles and Jews, harass! Yes, harass! The bishops by despoiling the patrimony of the Christ in this diocese."

His voice had become raised in rage at seeing Arnold's reaction, which was to laugh harder and harder in his face. Arnold could not take the little man seriously in any sense of the word; to him the little bishop resembled nothing so much as a barking dog.

Richard was beside himself. He was yelling with no concern for the dignity of the Church and was horrified at his lack of propriety. He stood back from Arnold and faced William.

"Take your foul presence out from my sight William Outlaw, I will not hear you anymore."

William did not object at all, but merely pulled the still laughing Arnold away from the spot, and away from the little man who would not listen. Just before the door closed behind them, Arnold called out to him.

"What, we don't get to offer you money?"

Le Drede turned and stared at them in horror.

Once the door was closed, Richard was left with a bitter sense of impotence that he could not shift, no matter how he tried to settle his mind. A curse on those nest of vipers!

William merely walked out of the house to where their horses were waiting. It was a wasted opportunity to have it end the way it did, he thought. Arnold had not assisted. There may be other opportunities to speak to the man, but William did not think so.

Especially now he was going to jail.

Chapter Seventeen

It was morning, the day after the Bishop had conversed with the Seneschal, and all had come to nought. The Bishop rose, saying prayers as he washed his face and hands, and as he dried them. The two priests aided him in his dressing, ensuring that the vestments he wore were correctly and properly fitted. There was a moment, when the sunlight came through the window at the two figures gathered around the one, that he was reminded of a window in one of the Churches in Avignon. But here they did not have the blue. Once dressed, he was ready to leave the tavern and make his way to the next town on his list. He and the priests were making their way down the rickety stairs, where they met the owner of the tavern.

Le Drede gave a little sigh to himself. The owner had been very much about the place when they arrived last night, utterly beside himself to have a bishop stay under his roof. Le Drede had no interest in hearing of the greatness of his gesture once more. He turned his head over his shoulder and muttered to his priests to pay the man, then brushed past him once down the stairs and out the door. Le Drede heard him cry out behind him, "No, Your Grace, wait!" and only then saw why.

Twenty-five men were assembled outside the tavern, in a military formation. They each of them carried weapons of a good quality, and each of them wore the livery of Arnold Le Poer, Seneschal.

And each of them was looking at him.

Richard Le Drede blinked rapidly in the silence, and said nothing. A magpie heckled somewhere about them. What was this? Why were these men here? Was it for him? He looked at the face of the simpleton at the head of the charge. Why was this man looking at him? Richard felt the realisation lean on his consciousness, but refused to allow it entry. These men were nothing to do with him. Nothing.

One of the men broke formation from the line and moved towards his priests. The two men spoke briefly together, the priest speaking but a few words, the sheriff's man most wordy. The priest moved back from the other man, and placed himself behind the Bishop. Richard did not want to hear what he had to say.

"Your Grace."

No.

"Your Grace," he said again.

He looked again at the face of the simpleton at the head of the line, the man who was charged with the responsibility of arresting the Bishop. Did he dare to meet his Bishop's eyes, charged as he was with such a task?

Indeed he did.

The man looked at the bishop and spoke loud, for all to hear.

"My name is Stephen Le Poer, bailiff of this land."

Le Drede stared at him, open mouthed with surprise at the audacity the man was showing.

"I am bid by law of My Lord, Arnold Le Poer, and by the rights and duties of my Office, to arrest and attach you, Richard Le Drede, Bishop of Ossory, and to convey you to prison in the castle of Kilkenny." The man did not move, but instead said in a low voice, "Come away with me now, please."

Le Drede stood, rooted. The new tactic of Kyteler was completely unexpected by him, and his mind scrambled to grasp all the implications. William was to put him in prison. He would go to that dungeon that he had inspected

Surely not

where the mad woman roared, and be subject to the laws of this foul land, and they would all be winning the battle around him while he was lost to them all. There would be no victory march, there would be no conquering of sinners, he had failed and they would come for him, come like the solders for Christ

Agony in the garden

who were there to test him, to deny him his kingdom so that he may appear greater to those around him, greater by his submission to the tyranny, to the evilness, and then the later visible victory

Christ Victorious

and by surrender he was made greater in front of them all.

Le Drede was suddenly clear what he had to do, clear with the hysterical vigour of the desperate. He looked away from the man, looked away from all of them, to hide his face while he made himself realise what was going to happen. He would be obliged to go with him, to obey, to comply, and therefore fail in his first attempt against the Kytelers. He would be in prison with criminals, madmen and murderers, and he would be there for at least seventeen days. He must bear this, smile through this, no matter what was given to him, and he must give signs of compassion and of forgiveness to his brethren, in each and every circumstance. He must be God to them.

He turned back.

"Very well, Sir. I am in your custody."

A gasp rose somewhere from within the waiting men, and Richard knew he had chosen the right path.

"Please. Lead on."

The trip to the Castle took the best part of the day. There were delays – some of Richard's entourage complained both in anger and grief at what had befallen their Bishop. Richard insisted on seeing and then keeping the warrant on him, which led to further delays in starting out. However, eventually they were on their way. And eventually they reached their destination.

Richard had thought about the procession to the castle. He had faltered in his resolve at the thought, and had fervently prayed that the streets would be made empty and the town's nobility would not see him in his moment of disgrace. But he saw that the town's people were all present and ready to see him being led. He heard the name Kyteler being whispered by the crowds, and knew that they were all concluding that the battle was over, that the war had been lost. Still, he prayed to God to keep his head up high through his difficulties. He prayed and then, he knew, he just knew, he would be victorious.

The townspeople watched the figure of the Bishop move past them, from the city gates, into the market place and to the Castle. Le Drede moved into the fortress proper, and he looked at the high walls above him. He had a sense of seeing them for the first time, that they were new to him, and indeed they were. Richard was for a moment almost afraid.

At the door was the Sentry, and he had a face cold as the walls about him.

"Richard Le Drede," he called to the Bishop as the other man approached, his entourage behind him. "I am the keeper of this prison and I will speak to you," he said.

Le Drede walked in the same pace to the man and did not let his face change. The man waited patiently for him to approach and then spoke to him in a low voice.

"I am the keeper of this prison. I will be your keeper throughout this time."

"You will be treated well here. You will be respected here, and all high stature be accorded to you as is appropriate. But you will be a prisoner here, and you will be in my keep. Do we understand each other in this matter?"

"My son, I am in your mercy. I will comply with you and your men and all your commands with all my power. If I can ease this difficult task for you in any way please do not fail to call upon me; you will not find me wanting."

An understanding passed between them, and they nodded. The keeper stood to one side, and Richard and the other men entered.

Richard had a sense as he lowered his head in entry, that what he was doing was going to make his name known for centuries. He felt himself in the same mode as Thomas Beckett, and blessed God for the grace that was being bestowed upon him. He looked around him at the men who watched him, and felt utterly calm. Richards' entourage consisted of only two chaplains and two others of his Palace, all of whom had journeyed with him to Kells.

The men made their way down the steps to the dungeon. It was exactly as it had been when Le Drede first arrived in Kilkenny – if anything, the more frequent imprisonments meant it was worse than before.

That it stank was a given. What was unexpected was the sheer blood that ran on the walls; blood new and fresh, the violent splatters still clear on the stones; blood aged and ageing, its palette one of browns and blacks, telling a story of years of open veins and hearts. One might even fancy that here was the inner heart of the land, its blood rich walls deeply hidden from its façade. Richard glanced

185

neither right nor left at the castle's walls as he descended. Instead he recalled to himself the story of Christ's decent into Hell just before his moment of greatest victory. This would be nothing to him. He would see to it.

The body of men reached the bottom of the steps. Richard kept his back straight as the keeper turned to him and his men.

"This way, Your Grace," he said.

The next morning, Le Drede could make out sounds about him before fully awake. He thought, in his sleepy state, that he was back in the Friary during his training. The air would be blowing white cold through the barred window and the temperature would painful and sharp all day. He came to realise, however, that he could not hear the birdsong that he had come to expect each morning, nor were the bells announcing Matins.

He opened his eyes, and found himself in his cell at the Castle. An effort had been made to make it hospitable, but it was still far from a proper standard. The straw was matted and foul, and the walls were blackened with the soot of the fireplace contained in the corner. This was in fact the assistant keeper's room. Otherwise there would be no fire and no beds. Le Drede, waking, intoned to the black ceiling above him.

"Oh Blessed is He who Grants me His Favour."
He heard the murmured 'Amen' of the men around him. He pulled himself up and saw the three of them lying in their own beds about him. Le Drede wiped the tiredness from his eyes.

"Brothers, let us pray."

Slowly the men made their way up from their rough blankets, and they readjusted their cassocks after their night's sleep. Le Drede rose and faced the small window, and then knelt. Soon all the men in the small cell were kneeling. He began the psalm as he had began it the day before, and the day before that.

My soul is waiting for the Lord.
I count on God's word.
My soul is longing for the Lord more than those who watch for
daybreak.
(Let the watchers count on daybreak
And Israel on the Lord.)

As he spoke the words of Psalm 129, his mind flew over the coming days. He would be here a total of seventeen days, until the warrant was done. He must give strong thought to how best use the situation from the point of view of the power of the Church. How would this look to those men and women whose hearts he must impress? Richard gave his voice over to the intonation as his mind began to work.

What did it look like, to the men he sought to impress? The Bishop was imprisoned, on the authority of a merchant and his friend. The Bishop was not just some humble cleric, terrified out of his wits of the debts he had created and the loans that must now be paid off; He was the Bishop of this diocese, the Papal Appointee, and the voice of God to all men. He *was* the Church, and he was in prison. He was the Church, and the Church was in jail. Therefore the jail should be used to hold the Church.

His voice rose as his plan developed. Yes, let the townspeople see that their faith, their hope and their salvation could be taken from them by the whim of those in power. Let them see what happened when the authority of the Church was questioned! There would be NO mass said, not just in the Cathedral, but anywhere in the diocese! No funeral mass, no wedding, no daily communion, nothing. If the body of the Bishop was not free then neither would the Church be free to act. And as his body and blood were looked up here, he would bring the body and blood of the Risen Lord Jesus Christ to this place, to this very room, so that the body of the Saviour might also suffer, with its Bishop, the indignities planned by William Kyteler.

Le Drede was ready to call over one of the clerics to give his instructions, when he saw a movement out of the corner of his eye. Tucked under his bed, barely visible but there, was a large rat, almost sleeping in the darkness, glaring out at him in the black shadow. You watch and wait. I will not be beaten by you.

Chapter Eighteen

"He had done WHAT?"

Arnold stood in the main hall of his house on his estate, in the early dawn. It was the second day of Le Drede's imprisonment. He was speaking to the messenger sent by William to his house, who had woken him with urgent details.

"He has declared that there will be no mass said throughout the entire diocese; none at all, no wedding, no funeral, no christening, nothing. It means no last rites!"

Arnold gasped as the words reached him, but there was more, he could tell.

"Also, my Lord, he has insisted that the Host be brought to him from the Cathedral! He is to have it by his side at all times during his imprisonment!"

Arnold said nothing while the fact made itself known to him. He looked at the weedy face of the man in front of him, tired and weary from the long trek.

Le Drede would have both the faith and face of the Church by his side at all times. He would have the walls of the Church built around him, ensuring his safety and his authority without question. The man would have to be stopped.

Arnold looked again at the man.

"Go to the Kitchen and eat. I will dress and make ready and go to town. Be close by to come with my departure."

"Aye my Lord," replied the servant, but Arnold was already moving to his private quarters. Alone in his room, Arnold marvelled at the Bishop's audacity while he was dressed.

The man was insatiable for trouble, for conflict and strife. Stuck in a prison he was nominally in charge of, dumped in the deepest dungeon the city could provide, he still fought back from the blackness. Le Poer had dearly hoped to remove the Bishop once and for all. Well, why not? The man was hated by all in authority, both by the Church and the Royal Standards, and the ease by which such a slip of the knife could be done was sorely tempting! Now all that would be for nothing! The eyes of the city were on the Bishop, God curse the foul Englishman.

Arnold had to admit that the tactics of the Bishop were excellent. They both raised the profile of the Bishop, thus ensuring his situation was well known to all, but created enormous tension throughout the diocese. No last rites! For anyone! That would strike deadly fear into any man's hearts, making an entry into Hell almost certain. Arnold felt the exact same fear himself. He feared for himself as much as any of them. That foul English bastard. That bastard.

He made his way to William Kyteler as quickly as possible, not wanting to tire the horse in case it was needed later, but still travelling at a fast trot. There were a lot of peasants making their way along the roads, travelling the same way as he. He gave them no thought at first, thinking only of the journey ahead. They walked in twos and threes, some alone, some whole families. They weren't joyous or singing, they merely walked alone towards the city. Only when he reached the city gates did he grasp the numbers were higher than usual. There was a cluster of them trying to get into the gate, complaining to the guards about the hold up. Le Poer merely gave the tariff and moved on, wondering at what could be so interesting.

He had entered at the west gate. He made his way slowly up towards the Kyteler house, seeing the figures alongside him travelling with him. The ones that walked alone seemed the most out of place. They seemed to have a feverish eye. They glanced at him with a wild look.

He had reached the Kyteler house, with its ornate door and excellent stone work over the windows. The flowers were beginning to grow, still tended by Petra. He lifted his fist to pound on the door, which was opened by Philip.

"Is your lord and Master at home?"

"Indeed Sir, he is not. It is my belief that he is about the Castle, seeing the sights there."

"The Castle, you say? What sights are there to see there?"

Philip stared at him, and Arnold had the sense that he had said something very foolish.

"Sir Arnold, there is daily more and more pilgrims, who come to see the Bishop. Sir William is surveying the crowd now."

Arnold said nothing, merely moved swiftly away from the door and up the street. Behind him he heard the door lock behind him.

Remounting his horse, he moved quickly up towards the Castle, not caring if the damn crowd were in his way or not. As he reached the turn where the Castle came into view, he knocked down in his speed a peasant or two, which he did not mark, nor did he need to.

Coiled in a long line, that eventually lost its form and became a grand mass, were at least two thousand people gathered around the Castle. There was some queuing to enter the dungeon, no doubt to see the Bishop. These people carried animals, children and documents, the usual flotsam that such a man is obliged to review. But there were others who made no move to the entrance. These people had made camp. Small fires burned where food was being prepared. Lean-tos were made up so as to be giving some kind of temporary shelter. Children ran from hovel to hovel, playing. A group of dogs ate something being thrown to it by an old woman. And there was the tell tale smell of shit and piss, that indicated these people had been there for days.

Arnold moved his horse up closer. To the side of the prison entrance, a much less grand entrance than that of the Castle proper, were two guards. They stood with their lances beside them, utterly accustomed to the sights before them.

Where in the fuck was the Gaoler? Why were these people permitted to loiter in this place with such freedom? Why were they permitted to be here *at all?* Arnold felt his temper rise. These were not visitors proper, not folk that had any business here. Instead what was here were the scum of the countryside, those people that both State and Church made a point of staying away from as much as possible. These were the unwanted and the despised, and rightly so. They should be moved or removed or both.

Suddenly someone whispered his name.

Arnold, startled and very much unsettled, looked around wildly. He searched the faces he could see about him for some kind of recognisable element, some form of symbol that would be for him an indication of similarity. Nothing, he thought wildly, there's nothing! He dragged a hand through his hair and for a moment felt a man lost.

Then his name sounded again, and he could see William standing near the trees with his back to the wall, his horse uneasy in the crowds. Arnold moved quickly to him and stood beside him.

For a long time the two men said nothing, merely viewed the spectacle in front of them. Arnold strove to regain his equilibrium, silencing his beating heart with all its fears. Why had fear bestrode him so? He could not say. He only knew that he was afraid, and that made him angry.

He threw a glance to William. The younger man seemed to have aged, taking on a harder line to his jaw. The boy Arnold had met all those years ago could not be seen now in any shape. He must be nearly four score at this time, thought Arnold.

William seemed to be reviewing the scene in front of him like a soldier reviewing a battle scene.

"Enough!" William said suddenly, and pulled his horse about.

Arnold followed him. The two men were duly avoided as was to be expected. But the looks of fear and hate and yes, gloating, were new for them both to see.

The door to the Kyteler household opened before them and Philip showed them in. By the fire was a table with food and wine. William took a swig as he thought.

"You know this contravenes the conditions of the warrant, don't you, where he was said to be held in privacy against the populace. He's flaunting his illegality in front of us!"

Arnold took a bite of meat and then spoke with his mouth full.

"He's created a shrine for himself there, so that all may see that the Church is active while being held in the prison. He's making a living martyr of himself – He's preaching from the tomb."

William's lip curled.

"Then let us step on his clever intention, and ensure that the light of worship he craves so much is denied to him. Let the Warden there insist that day and night he keeps to himself. Let luxuries be denied to him, and servants too. Let his court be removed from him and see what might become of his preaching then."

Arnold saw in William a new found anger. The young man grows bitter, he thought to himself. He has good cause. An angry man is very often a reckless one. Arnold should know best of all, the temper he had.

William looked at his friend.

"What say you, Arnold?" he asked. "Do you think the next step is to prevent this outrage? Or should it be ignored like so much of the man's musings and nonsense?"

"We would do ourselves wrong to allow him to be held up to greatness. Let the warden, as you say, hear our thoughts on the matter. Before long we will see Le Drede's smile turn to frowns."

The two men ignored Philip as they had always done. Philip, so tired and so old now, heard everything that they said. He had even refilled their cups as they had spoken but they had not looked up at him. He still carried with him the letter of William to Alice to send aid. He was never more glad that he had not acted on it. He heard their thoughts regarding their Bishop, when they sought to block and bar the heart's love of God and to insist that the sacraments be refused to them! Philip wondered at the perversity of these men, that they might block the sun of natural love of God to those who sought it. Would men die and live in torment because of the unstoppable ambition of the Kyteler house? Would the sin sting and burn on them because William's fight with the Bishop went on? Ah no. Surely no.

Philip replaced the wine jug on the table and smoothed down his tunic once more.

William and Arnold were soon finished their scribbles over the crumb covered table. William looked up at Philip.

"Philip, sir, please see that this letter is delivered to the Chief Constable at the Castle. Tell them to await a response."

Philip said nothing, merely nodded and left the room. He could hear the two men speaking behind him as he left. He called to one of the kitchen boys.

"Here you, take this and bring it to the Castle. Ensure the Chief Constable receives it, do you hear? The Chief Constable. And ensure you get an answer, don't leave without one. Go on now," he said, gesturing the boy away.

For a moment he suddenly remembered young Billy, Le Blund's favourite, and winced in horror at the memory.

What was wrong with him? He seemed, at this late stage of his life, to see in ways he had never seen before. He had a heavy head, closing his eyes in silent pain.

In the room behind him, William and Arnold were still talking.

"Is there any word from your mother?" asked Arnold.

"No, she has not responded to my letter."

"Hopefully with this new strategy of the Bishop in goal she may not need to," said Arnold.

"We will need to wait and see," replied William.

It was soon after that same day when the instructions from Sir Arnold reached the Chief Constable in the Castle. The last meal had been served and cleared away. The candles had long been lit to dispel the dark that came so quickly down here below.

The messenger reached the Chief Constable in the lowest part of the prison. The man was standing, along with a few others, watching the Bishop take part in the mass that was just one aspect of his stay there. The Bishop's imprisonment had altered the atmosphere enormously. Before, it was a place of filth and torture. It was now a place of overt shows of piety. A large amount of tension came over all who went there. They saw the Bishop in his finest magnificence, behind bars and apparently a victim of a vicious evil regime. And they saw him go willingly, innocent and accepting like Christ.

The boy reached into his satchel and pulled out the message, panting, only to be immediately quietened by the Constable.

"Sssh! Quiet boy, can't you see his Grace is celebrating?"

The boy nodded, subservient. For a moment the two looked into the small cell at the men there. All knelt in the candlelight, intoning the Latin chant as was their way. The scene, as seen in the corridor, was one of utter peace.

The boy, after a while, leaned forward to whisper to the Chief Constable.

"But sir, it is from the Seneschal, Sir Arnold. He requests an urgent response."

The Chief Constable looked at him, and at the piece of paper in his hand, then kept looking at the Bishop. After a moment, his eye still on the bishop, his hand came up slowly and took the piece of paper from the boy.

The Bishop's voice still drifting over them, they retired to a cell off the main corridor. The man lit a candle, and leaned over a table. Slowly, he opened the instructions from Sir Arnold. His eyes slowly made out the stiff instructions, his lips slowly moving as he travelled across the paper.

With the movements of a puzzled man, he stood upright. Frowning, he looked outside the window, trying to marshal his thoughts. He heard the voice of the boy behind him.

"What is it Sir? Is the bishop to be released?"

The Chief Constable took a moment before answering.

"No lad. No, not just yet…"

He turned back and looked at the boy for a moment, and then he stepped out of the cell and stood looking at the Bishop in his cell. Stillness was his cloak. Patience was his gift. The Chief Constable returned to the small cell again.

He merely turned over the original instruction and, drawing a quill and ink near, slowly began to write.

Master,

It is novel, and unheard of in Ireland, to imprison a Bishop and we know not what will be the result or end of this matter, nor am I the sort of man to dare imprison so great a prelate in this matter. I had rather renounce my office and emolument for ever than that he should be thus guarded, or even detained by me."

The Chief Constable stood and refolded the paper. He handed the paper back to the started boy.

"Take that back to your master. See to it he knows exactly where it came from."

William and Arnold were still at the same table when the messenger returned. He entered quickly by the back door and placed it into Philip's hands. Philip looked at the boy, whose demeanour still looked startled.

"What did you see there, lad?" he said, wanting to give the child a chance to compose himself.

"Terrible things, Sir, terrible things. The Bishop is surrounded by the faithful on all sides, and each day prays with great sanctity in his cell with the other priests. But he is still in the prison Sir, and to see him when he is so strong and so good, is a terrible thing! A wrong thing!"

Philip looked at the child. He blinked for a moment, trying not to form a lump in his throat.

"I will take this to the Master."

He turned to the boy and made his way slowly from the kitchen area to where the two men were sitting.

At the halfway point, where he could not been seen, he paused and wiped his tired eyes. Oh, that he might rest and not weary his heart in such a way, he thought, not sure of what he meant. But he continued on, entering the room where William and Arnold sat talking.

194

The two men sat with their heads close together, their voices low. There is a surprise, thought Philip, but straightened his features as he stood before them.

William noticed him first.

"Well, what news Philip? Do we hear back from the Castle?"

Philip offered to him the piece of paper the boy had returned. The other man took it from him, but continued looking at Philip.

"You look tired, Philip. You shall go to rest early tonight."

Philip merely smiled slightly and nodded.

Then did William lower his head to read the response of the Chief Constable. He looked at the piece of paper in his hand and realised that he was seeing his original letter. He then turned it over and saw the response. His head lowered, Philip saw the top of his head, where there was a small gap of hair showing the scalp. He was struck by how vulnerable William was, with Philip above and he below. He could lift his hand and with a blow make them equal, remove William's power over them all.

William lifted his eyes, all ablaze.

"What is this? Is this the response received by you, Philip? Nothing further given to us in reply?"

The spell was broken. Philip was a houseman again, William his lord. He gave no hint of his thoughts when he spoke.

"Nothing further, my Lord."

William merely swore aloud and handed it to Arnold, who scanned it quickly and stared. Philip knew that look on Lord Arnold's face, it meant that he had met something that he would move, remove, or kill.

"What means he by this?"

"He means by this to reject completely the authority both you and I have here. He means to say that he is afraid and cowardly and will not serve us!" William pounded the table in frustration.

"But that is an abomination!" cried Arnold, horrified at the thought. " In face it is more than that, it is the end! If we are not to be heeded we cannot save ourselves at all!"

William was holding up his hand, calling for calm.

"No, wait, wait, Sir Arnold. We call the play too quickly and therefore loose our game plan. We must think on this thing, think hard and quickly with all cool heads, and come to a decision on what to do. Let victory be our guides, not anger."

Arnold let out a blast of air in disagreement.

"William, we are not to be outdone! The man is an evil menace to us both, creating a risk of loss of all that we have accomplished! Why do you hesitate in the face of this one man! I will not!"

Arnold stood, and took up his cloak.

"Where do you go now?"

"I will to the Castle! Tonight, when darkness falls! I can still gain entry there, as Seneschal. I can do to him what I have done to others, and rid the town of the rat from England. You will hear from me when the moment is passed! Good night!"

Arnold stomped from the house, slamming the door behind him. He thumped his feet on the path as he walked up the street, towards the Castle, ignoring all that passed him; in truth he was so angry he could not have seen them. He turned from Kiernan's street and right towards the Castle. The crowds grew thicker here, and Arnold found his progress slowed. He planned to enter the castle grounds and remain there until night fall, then demand entry and dispatch the Bishop in a private audience. He would tell them that the Bishop attacked and he defended himself. He did not care what he told them! They would accept his words and that would be that. Like a drunk in an alley, Arnold rewrote the truth to suit himself and continued on. He would kill that man! The strength of the impulse was enough to convince him. The crowd was too thick to walk now, and Arnold for the first time looked around him.

Thousands now filled the large square before the Castle. Thousands now stood, respectful, as a small caravan of priests moved from the main street onto the square, to the Castle and their Bishop, waiting inside for them. The crowd was humming in excitement at some element of it that Arnold could not see. He frowned, confused. Why did they gaze in such awe?

The men made their way onto the square proper, which rose towards the Castle at an angle. As they did so, one of them raised his arms.

The priest held the Host, the consecrated body of Christ, in a gold chalice of some kind. The Host was the very body and spirit of

Christ, it was His authority and His majesty. It was being removed from its proper place in the Cathedral and brought here to the opposite side of the city, in view of all, to the Bishop.

Most of the poorest people of the city had never yet seen the Host, they not being allowed into the Churches. Arnold looked around him, to his left and to his right, and found that the men and women were utterly transfixed.

When the priest lifted the Host, a great cry lifted from the crowd in amazement. Those nearest the Host knelt as it passed, followed by all in the square. The thousands that had gathered, that had waited, all knelt before the Host in adoration and in silence. Without a word, or a child's cry, or a cough, they knelt, heads lowered as the men walked by. They knelt and prayed and meant the words, as the men walked by.

And Arnold, seeing the wave of people kneeling, must kneel also, in supplication to the Host, and keep his tongue silent. The sight of it buckles his stomach and makes his mind finally stop. He finally thinks.

The eyes of the city watched the Host move past them, eyes full of worship and reverence. Silence was the only noise. Once the Host moved to the entrance of the Castle, and then down the steps to the dungeon and the Bishop waiting there, the crowd relaxed. The people got to their feet, and the voices that had been silenced were free to speak again.

Arnold turned and walked back.

Chapter Nineteen

The Bishop had been in prison for seventeen days. By the end of his stay, the crowds had grown every day. Each new day brought more and more crazy sights to behold, such as women weeping at the injustice done to their Bishop, screaming, gashing of teeth, foaming at the mouth.

The point of the prison stay had passed, in that the day the Bishop had cited William Outlaw to be arrested and tried had come and gone. The writ William had had issued against him did not allow for any more time. William did all he could to extend the period, but Sir Arnold doubted the likelihood of success. The Chief Constable stood at the gate of the bishop's cell, in symbolic readiness to open it at the first sign of the mandate to liberate the prison. The bishop was dressed and ready, the cell emptied of his possessions. He leaned on his crozier, waiting.

The mandate arrived in the early afternoon. The Chief Constable opened it, and after giving it the smallest glance, opened the gate of the cell.

"Your highness, you are now released and free to go."

The Bishop stood as tall as the small figure could. He cleared his thought and spoke.

"It is not becoming a Bishop to go forth from prison as a thief or a homicide. Bring our pontificals to us, for this day the Church of God begins to triumph over its enemies, and it is just and laudable, therefore, that we should give thanks to God, with due solemnity and joy of heart."

The Bishop moved to the gate of the cell, which was held open for him by the Chief Constable. He moved slowly and solemnly through the jail, and as he walked, the clergy that had visited him daily, and had waited for this day, joined behind him. First one man, then two. Then there were five, moving slowly, with certainty, up through the jail.

He made his way up, and up, his heart lifting with each step. They will see! They will be saved!

They were now at the entrance to the jail, and about ten men were behind him. Most were clergy, but some were the more noble of the merchants of the town. Le Drede stood for a long moment, blinking in the light.

"Your Grace?"

"A moment to gather my strength. Now, my child, onwards!"

He set off, and after a moment, was on the perimeter of the castle. For a moment he stood, startled, at the scene which greeted him.

A thousand people were waiting for him. The starving, the sick, the sinful and fallen, had travelled for miles to see him released. Set-to dwellings had been constructed, with fires burning for food. Le Drede blinked again. The smell was simply repellent, a filth bore solely of their sins. Oh, how they needed the salvation only their Lord could offer!

A young boy saw him first, and gave up a shout.

Le Drede had his ears filled with the roars of the crowd, cheering, screaming, yelling with delight at the release of their hero. All the voices in heaven, he thought to himself, could not sound so rejoicing.

After a few minutes, the Bishop lifted his hands. At this signal, the crowd quietened itself, and listened.

"My children, long have we suffered under the yoke of the unholy one that has spread his foul influence throughout this holy land!"

The crowd gave out a murmur of consent.

"I, your Bishop, hereby give my word to you, my people, that I will do all in my power to release this land from the unholy yoke of those sworn to serve Mammon!"

The crowd gave a cheer.

"I and my pontificals go from this jail today to celebrate in our cathedral, for this day the Church of God begins to triumph, once and for all, over its enemies!"

The crowd roared its approval. For a few minutes there was nothing but the wall of sound rising high over the town. Then, when there was some semblance of calmness among them, the bishop stepped down into the crowd, followed by the laity.

The crowd was truly silent as the Bishop approached. They immediately parted, giving him and the other men passage throughout the crowd. One or two hands drifted out, taking a brief touch of the cloth of his cloak as he passed by.

The bishop gave no indication of feeling anything. If anything, the only expression on his face was one of pious serenity. He moved through the crowd and slowly made his way down the Parade. The crowd watched the group of men pass them, and then slowly, began to follow them. First a hundred, then half the crowd, then the entirety followed as the bishop made his way down the wide street. The Chief Constable watched from the main gate.

"May God forgive me for jailing him in the first place." He left the main gate and joined the crowd.

The large contingent had no loud bells announcing it. It had no cheering men, no dancing women. Instead, it silently, solemnly, made its way through the narrow streets of Kilkenny, moving from the Castle gates and down to the main thoroughfare.

As it moved, it silenced the town as surely as an accusation. People going about their business stood in utter amazement at the sight of the Bishop, moving at the head of a thousand people in utter silence. All knew of the Bishop's campaign, of the inquisition and the attempt to arrest the Kytelers, and of the imprisonment of the bishop.

"Mama!" cried a small child in delight from a side street. The child was hushed by its mother, who dragged it into the crowd without delay.

This show of power on his behalf froze the town. It's townspeople saw immediately which way the wind was going. Fat merchants and their grasping wives scrambled to join the silent procession, noblemen and knights rode at speed to make up the crowd. Through the main street, past the Thoshel or town hall, down through the town.

By the time the procession had reached the Cathedral gates, the majority of the town was indeed present and following the bishop.

The startled gate keeper stumbled in his haste to open the west door so as to allow the group entry, and they came quietly and solemnly into the Cathedral. He stood there, letting each one enter. The priests lit the candles, and prepared the altar for mass as they went, so all was ready for the Bishop. He watched as the Bishop made his slow and steady way up to the lectern, turned the page on the Holy Bible, and, resting his hands on the lectern, prepared to speak. The Bishop noticed the gate keeper holding open the great oak door.

"Brother Michael," he called to the gate keeper, "close the door. We have returned. And we have much to do."

And slowly, very slowly, the Cathedral door closed behind them.

The men that assist such things were waiting a long time for it to come about. Impatient men, restless men, who sharpened their tools and who gazed in the distance, waiting. Or they would joke amongst each other how they would show justice to those that had it coming to them, when justice never seemed to come to them at all. They had sensed, like those who lived by their senses, that the time for them was coming soon, and they were straining at their leashes to do that which they did best.

The Bishop, newly returned to his palace (a welcome sight that was, after the dungeon! He never thought that that day would come!) wasted no more time. He called for his scribe and his clerk and duly gave forth his commands. The house would be raided. The household would be emptied of all that were there, innocent or no, mentioned on the writ or unknown to them. All the ladies were to be taken, all the clerks and their wives. Everyone was now to come to his attention, to the majesty and jurisdiction of the Church, and everyone would be at his mercy. They had no more support. They were his.

The men, straining at the leash no more, had their commands. The leader snatched the signed parchment and stuffed it into his tunic. Le Drede looked at him blankly.

"You will not wait for copies?" he asked him.

"No need Your Grace," replied the man. "We can put them up later for those that want to read to read. Until then, I'll act as I'm ordered."

Le Drede nodded.

The men were waiting for him outside, and with a nod from him they all headed off. They were young and they were old. They had all seen good times in their way, and all of them had been bent and twisted by the bad times. All were battle scarred. Some were hardly men any more. To the Kyteler house they travelled, in formation, their weapons open in their hands, their chain mail flashing in the light, for it was nearly summer now.

Deep inside the Kyteler house, there was a dark silence. All the members of the household that were there were silent and fearful. In the kitchen down below, the cook opened the back door into the yard.

"Go now," she whispered to the girl and lad that helped. "Go, quickly, and say nothing."

Without a sound, the two youngsters moved out the door and into the yard, from there out into the street and away. The cook stepped out herself and turned to close the door. She saw Rose begin to enter the room, but quietly closed and locked the back door behind her so they could not be stopped. Rose only looked up when she heard the sound of the key turning. She stood in confusion for a moment and then understood. She did nothing. Upstairs she heard a pounding.

201

William was in the study, scene of so much of his life. He lifted one letter draft after another, trying to decide which one gave the correct and accurate information, which one made the best case to his mother and therefore the rest of the world. Why had she not answered him? The corridors were too quiet without her imperious step making her skirts swirl about her. The absence of her commanding voice made the air too silent. He bent himself to re-examine the papers. He would have to ensure that this went as soon as possible. If Philip's methods had become unreliable, then they would have to find another route. Philip had seemed too quiet these days, the ordeal was taking its toll on the older man. Though it was taking its toll on all of them. Philip's face didn't reveal anything anymore, though. William then heard the pounding.

Philip was seated near the second stair, sitting on the chair that had been placed there. He was feeling tired and weary after only one flight of stairs, and he had found himself unable to go on. He sat, breathing heavy, patting his face with a cloth to rest himself. He glanced to his left and saw the stairs beside him, waiting for him to try. It was only six more steps. What was ailing him was the despair that lined his heart now, and made six steps far too much to ask. He would just rest for a moment more, and then he would continue on. Just a moment. Philip heard the pounding.

Petra was sitting in the hall, near the fire, with the sewing on her lap. Not since she had to prepare for the last wedding had she seen so much to be done, you would think the house had never seen linen. Maybe her eyes were failing her, making her make more mistakes these days, but she tested her thread each time to ensure the work would endure. Petra lifted the cloth up near the sunbeam and squinted. No, no she was wrong, this work was suitable. She settled it back into her lap again and made the material taut. She heard the pounding.

Rose began to leave the kitchen to see if she was needed.

William half rose in his chair, knowing as he did so that the pounding came from the Bishop's men and that the house was about to be raided.

Philip thought the same, stood up and began to run down the stairs.

Petra stood up and began to move towards the door.

Rose made her way up the first flight of stairs and onto the second.

William raced up the main stairs with all the speed he could.

Philip made it down three flights but had to pause for breath.

Petra had reached the door and began to lift the latch.

William burst into the room and began to yell a 'NO!' to Petra. She, hearing him, began to turn her head in surprise.

The door burst open like a bubble on boiling water. Petra was thrown back into the room and fell back onto the floor. William rushed to block the door and had a blow to his face by the handle of a pick axe for his trouble. Yelling filled the room, especially at the sight of Petra, for they thought she was Dame Alice.

"How now witch!" cried one, but they didn't come to taunt. Petra received a blow to her face of such severity that it broke her nose, all in the room heard the crack of the bone. She fell back once again on the floor, blood coming her face in gushes and streams. She put her hands to her face in an effort to cup it.

William was thrown by the blow he received but it was soon followed by others. He was hauled to the side of the room and received further blows on the back of his legs. His roars travelled beyond the room.

Philip, hearing the sounds below him, hesitated, hesitated. Petra. William. Another cry. Another thump. How could he save them? How could he save them there? He stared hard at the door.

Rose stared up at the small door separating her from Petra and William. She heard the blows, and the pleas for mercy. She tried to make herself go up the steps but she could not. Instead she took one step back. And then another. A vicious blow was landed on Petra, and she screamed in pain. Rose jumped down two steps. And then turned and quickly made her way down the stairs.

Philip knew the house, better than William. He slid and slipped and scurried away down to the back door, the same one that Rose had fled out of just seconds before. The letter. He still had the letter. He would make amends, he would send it straight away and he would solve the dilemma once and for all. He would not see the house ruined, they always stood against everything that attacked them. It would be all right, it would be all right.

Rose was on the street, looking for a long moment at the façade of the house. The windows on the main street let the urgent movement of the men be seen. A roar could be heard somewhere outside. Rose, looking over her shoulder the entire time, began to slowly walk away. Philip, at that moment, came around the corner. The two looked at each other as they passed, not saying anything. For a moment Rose thought that Philip was to pass her, let her go her own way on her own with not a word of comfort or solace, but after a moment he turned and walked back to her on the street.

"Go quickly to the Mayor's house. Tell them everything that has happened and wait there. I will arrive for you shortly. Go now, quickly, why there is still time."

Rose said nothing, just merely nodded and began to run.

Philip watched her go and then pulled out of his tunic the letter he had been asked to send all those days ago. There must be time, there surely must be time, still.

The house surely could not fall. Surely not. What would he do if it was? Where would he go, what would he do to survive? He would be left to fend for himself, take up some position in a tavern making the best he could. Fear gripped him at the thought. After years of believing silently the house must fall, Philip suddenly just as firmly believed that the continuing existence of the house was the only path to his own survival. So the letter in his hand became his only method to safety and security.

So what to do with it? Who could give him succour at this moment when he had no one and nowhere to go? He took a few steps in the direction of the Castle, not knowing where to go or what to do. He needed time to think, he thought. He needed time to clear his head and to understand what he should do.

Behind him, the door of the house burst open and the yelling of the men could be heard. Petra and William appeared, pulled and dragged towards a cart. William looked bloody and beaten. Petra's dress was half off her, and she tried as best she could to preserve her modesty as well as care for her broken nose. Philip stood horrified in the street. They were pulled up onto the cart and given more blows for their troubles to keep them down in the cart. He realised, finally and physically, the sheer danger that had surrounded them for years. In the street, out in the dirt, Philip had brought home to him the very savagery of the threat around them. And he saw what his delay had brought about.

Richard Le Drede, Bishop of Ossory, felt a grin begin on his face but was enough in control of himself to hide it. He sat in his reception room, in the large chair that befitted a bishop receiving official visits. He inclined his head in a respectful manner to the speaker and listened on.

"They are fully arrested in the power of the law, Your Grace. Both William Kyteler and the maid Petra of Meath are now in the custody of the King on authority of yourself, and are in the Castle dungeon. We await your further instructions."

The Warden, the man who had been responsible for Le Drede's own imprisonment, stood before him. The man carried the same stoical face and bearing as he had for Le Drede's stay in his care. Indeed, the man had uncommon skills of serenity, particularly for a position such as his, which one would imagine would encourage the crueller humours. Le Drede regarded him for a moment. He is not afraid of me either, he thought, then put the distraction away from him.

"I see. The prisoners are to be visited daily by those members of the Inquisition that have been extended rights of investigation. I will give them letters bearing my name and ring which will grant them permission to the prisoners. Is this authority sufficient for you?"

The Warden considered this.

"They should be limited in their hours, Your Grace, to permit the rest of the Prison to continue to run smoothly. We have, as you know, our own staff who will be coming and going as usual."

The Bishop nodded at what he saw as a mere matter of logistics.

"Absolutely. We would also be most grateful if you could extend facilities to these men, such as a private room, with a fire, and water to hand."

The Warden looked at the Bishop. The Bishop looked blandly back. A long moment of silence, of understanding, stood between the two men, even though nothing was said.

The men being sent were torturers, who were there to wreck havoc on the bodies of those now held by the Bishop. The Warden

205

was being asked to permit these men their way and to grant them facilities to do what they did best.

After the moment had passed, the Warden blinked, and then spoke.

"Very good, Your Grace."

Chapter Twenty

Petra spent the night alone in the cell. She had no helper and no servant, unlike Le Drede and Alice before him. She was thrown in by the same men who had brought her here, and she had fallen hard on her head, but mercifully not on her nose, which was terribly broken. She lay for a long time merely trying to gain some calm, but then for comfort's sake moved herself to the bed. She could feel her nose swell as she lay there with her eyes closed.

She thought fretfully of the state of her clothes. The fabric of her dress had ripped when they had pulled her up from the floor, but the brutes that they were had ignored her pleas for mercy, for a chance to cover her indignity. She thought for a moment of the agony of her trip to the Castle in view of all, but then put it to one side. It could not be helped and would not calm her. She opened her eyes and looked at the cot she was lying on. The bedding was not bedding, it was merely some wood that was stripped of all comfort. She could see marks and stains on it, and something else that looked suspiciously like mouse and rat droppings. She closed her eyes again.

Where was Alice? She had been written to a very long time ago, to send help in the form of the Law and to counteract the vengeance of the Bishop. Alice must have heard what had happened and would help. The house would not be left by her to fall. William was the very thing that the house stood on, the stone that Alice had built all she had. She could not desert William now, could she? She would not desert Petra, not now...

There was a sound outside. Petra was lying with her back to the gate and could only see what was occurring if she had stood up and put her face to it. She was too weary to do that, so merely listened to the sounds.

The footsteps approached the gate, apparently burdened with something in their hands. There was a brief pause, then the sound of keys dangling, along with a muttered swear. The gate was opened and the footsteps came into the cell.

"Your food," it muttered. Alice turned her head and looked at the speaker.

It was a man, about 20 years of age, who had a long scar down his scalp, he must have seen battle. He wore clothes of a type she hadn't seen before; they weren't like any she had seen in the city. He gave her a glance that was almost frightened as he put the bowl down on the floor. She didn't move until she could see him step back towards the gate. Then she lifted the bowl of gruel to her, trying not to let her fear and her hunger make her a savage. After she ate she lay down again, distressed. Somehow the fact of they're giving her food made her feel even more melancholy. She was to be here a while. She slept.

During the night, she woke suddenly, awareness reaching her in her dreams. All around her was blackness, the dark of night seeming to reach behind her eyes down here. She remembered immediately where she was. She listened in the dark for some sign, some signal that would give her strength in the middle of the night. All she could hear was men's voices, muttered, not clear, speaking in their turns. She felt she was being decided as they did so.

She slowly, silently, lifted herself off the wooden cot. Scurrying sounds in the dark made her glad she could not see. She went as close to the gate as she could, and then tilted her head to listen.

The men's voices were to her left, further down the corridor. It wasn't clear, they were keeping their voices low. As she stood there, she had a sudden visual image of where she was; she saw herself down a deep dark dungeon, in an impenetrable castle, alone from all help in a city that had condemned her. She felt utterly alone.

Petra took a step back from the gate in despair, as the feeling washed over her. She could not be seen by these men, not when she was so alone and frail. She wanted to hide, to hide away, to not be seen. She was afraid.

It was morning. It was morning because she could see more light behind her eyes. She was on the cot, her eyes closed shut, trying to hide from it all. She needed to urinate. She needed to eat. She didn't want to open her eyes.

There was more activity around her, she sensed. She could hear the chink of metal on metal somewhere, sensed people walking past her cell. She knew it was nearly mid day, some time, she could hear the bells ringing in town. The bells. Last week she had had heard them as she walked back to the house from the market, her arms laden with materials for dinner. She had smelt the beginnings of summer in the air, the day was warmer. Now she was here, a week later, cut off from the light and the air and all the hope in the world. No, there was still hope. She was to be saved by Alice. Alice herself had been in prison and had gotten safely out, and the Bishop as well. She did not have to give up hope yet.

The noise outside the cell seemed to reach a peak and then fall away again. Natural curiosity made her open her eyes for a moment, and then shut them. The cell in daylight was a hideous affair, made more real by the sunlight. The walls were covered in stains of various hues. The straw contained shit and urine and blood and rags and things that scurried. The air was dank and foul. She wished so much not to be there!

The noise appeared again. The need to urinate was there again. She opened her eyes. Oh, this terrible place! She wanted so very much to be home! She braced herself, she was being silly. It was not going to be helped by being like a little girl. She looked and saw a pot that clearly was what she was looking for. Oh, dear Lord. She would have to steal herself to use it, or otherwise foul herself, which would be much worse.

She slowly pulled herself up from the cot, and gingerly, trying to avoid the worst of the straw, began to make her way across the small cell. She reached the pot and then slowly, self consciously, began to lift her skirts. The need was now terrible, and she tried hard not to pant in the stench.

Petra finally relieved herself, gathering her skirts around her in a way to ensure the least possible staining. She closed her eyes against the image she was seeing and instead lifted her chin up and to the right, facing the gate. After a moment she opened her eyes.

There were three men, gathered with their backs to her, gathered around something, she couldn't see what at first. There was one man on each side of whatever object they held, and a third. Each of them held up whatever it was they held, which didn't move. Petra frowned slightly, trying to make out what she was seeing.

The object they held convulsed, buckling a little and sliding towards the floor.

"Hold him!" cried one of the men, and all three renewed their efforts to hang on to the man, for it was a man that they held. One secured his arms around him and hoisted him up. The man's head fell back, and Petra could see that his face was terribly hurt and bruised.

She was finished. She immediately moved away from the gate, and rushed back to her cot, trying not to hear. But fate was cruel to her; now she could make out the shadows of the three men and their charge on the wall in front of her. She listened with the fear of a hunted animal to the sounds that she could make out, blinking in fear as she did so.

The men called out instructions to each other, trying to keep the fourth on his feet. There seemed to be a discussion going on between themselves, as they didn't seem to know what to do. Whatever the man they held had said, it didn't seem to have been enough.

Petra then heard something that didn't make sense to her, some bang jangle of metal on metal. One was fiddling with something, while the other two muttered, grunted, and swore at their burden.

"Is he awake?" asked one of them. There was some investigation by the other two as they tried to find out. One of them grunted something, Petra couldn't make it out. The other two responded in the same way, grunts she couldn't properly hear.

The shadows on the wall showed all three of them straighten themselves up, tensing for what was to come. Petra's eyes winced as she did the same.

The scream that came out of the slumbering man jolted her eyes wide, as he fought desperately to be out of their clutches and whatever they were doing to him. The men yelled to each other again, insisting that the other hold him tighter, lean into him. Then they went silent again and tensed, and another scream reached up and out and battered the walls and all their skin with the pain that he was then.

Petra closed her eyes and held her hands over her ears, trying hard to turn her face and her mind away, free, gone from all of it. She wanted to cry but the adrenaline within her kept her from it. The man's scream lowered in pitch to a moan and then a whimper.

The men and their shadows seemed to relax, seemed to have finished. The man they held was completely collapsed between them, no movement to him at all. Petra heard one of them say the word "cell", and she saw the shadows shift themselves around. She dared to lift her head and peer down the length of her, at the gate and the men as they passed.

She saw two men dressed as English soldiers, carrying a third among them. He was blond, his head slumped forward. The two men who carried him has as much blood over them as he did, the three of them were stories of pain being inflicted. As they went past the gate, the man's feet came into view. They were so bloody and beaten, that one of them had been split in two like a magpie's beak. The foot was being dragged into the dirt and filth of the floor.

After a moment, a rat scurried after them, squeaking in the blood.

Petra shuddered a great big tremor of revulsion, tears very close now. Oh God, she thought, and Sacred Mother, who looks down on us with eternal love and compassion, please please please give me courage in this terrible place! Grant me freedom from here, so that I can be free of this awful place! Please! Please!

She turned her head away from the gate, closed her eyes and tried very hard to find some good image to succour her. But all she could think of was of her mother, who died a quiet death in her bed, with the Rites having been said and the daughter who loved her nearby. She had kissed her mother on the face as she died, the prayers strongly whispered about them in the room as she had done so. She had felt no sadness, just devotion to her mother, who had been such a good woman. Petra wondered why such an image had come to mind in that place.

The sounds coming down the corridor were fading somehow. Petra could hear the man being carried to his cell, the men coming out again and the gate being closed. They were speaking between themselves for a moment now, their voices low and normal. Petra shuddered again, and had to wonder why. They were normal, she decided, that was the evilness about it. They were men, with men's voices, and stances, and smells. They were her neighbours and townsmen. They might bow respectfully to her were they to meet her on the street.

They always had been though, that was the innocence she was losing now. They were always among her, walking the same streets and breathing the same air. She had merely seen the sky with its sun and the day with its colours and been unafraid. But now she had seen a rat running after a man for its food and she was afraid.

They could think of doing the same to her. The idea came to her all of a sudden. They might think of the same punishment being afflicted on her. But no, Dame Alice would never allow it. She was of the house of Kyteler, such an insult would never be permitted. No. No! William her son would not permit it. He may be in jail now but he would get out and get her released. She would leave this cell and be free, and would take Philip and Rose and run from this city somewhere into the country, where William had his house, or to one of the Manor Houses held by Dame Alice in Tipperary. They would hear the bells on the lake and be silent in their calm.

Petra stared at the gate between her feet as if it held the way to sanity. No one came to open it. Its hinges and its metal bars did not move. All of a sudden she saw the images of the torture she would go through be played in her mind, in a flash, all pouring out like the guts of a pig before she could stop it.

Petra ground her teeth together and blinked twice, keeping her eyes wide. Eventually she was calmer, in a way. A tear ran down her face. She was afraid to close her eyes. She was afraid to move. She suddenly felt so tired she was overcome with it. She had closed her eyes before a few minutes had passed.

When she woke up she wasn't startled. She looked around her with resignation, remembering that this was where she was now. It was the resignation that startled her. She had already become used to this. Surely she had not always been in this cell? She tried hard to remember another time when she had not been bound in these walls, when this had not been the limit of her universe. There were other pictures in her mind, certainly. But she could not remember living anywhere than here. Would she always be here? She didn't think so.

Petra looked down to the gate. There was no real sign of sunlight, it must be night. She wished she could keep on sleeping, she hated the idea of being awake here. She should close her eyes again and sleep. Instead, Petra kept her eyes open, watching the gate. Somehow she felt there was a stirring in the air somewhere. She felt that the attentions of those nearby were beginning to be focused on her, and that they were getting closer.

Closer. She could imagine them preparing their knives for her, making them sharp and hot to hurt her. She saw them crawling silently towards her cell, creeping and planning her torture, while she lay here helpless and unable to do anything! Petra remembered her prayers and clung onto them as hard as she could do, trying to recall the sanctity and peace she had felt in her heart by them. God the Father would make her safe, if she had but faith, if she could but trust in God the Father, the Son and the Holy Spirit...

Still, in her mind's eye the presence seemed to come ever closer, and closer. A random draft or breeze blown from God knew where made the gate rattle on its hinges. She lay with eyes wide, head tilted to have a look at the gate, frozen with the fear and the terror. Her heart was pounding and she felt a depth of fear she had not known since she was a child.

The two men were at the gate! Petra begin to whimper in fear, holding her hands to her mouth. She lay there staring in horror at the men, not believing what she was seeing. They were the same men as before. They opened up the gate, not looking at her. Petra crouched back into the wall, trying to avoid them. They walked into the cell and walked towards her, not talking. Their faces were still, calm as they reached out to her. She could not go quietly, she pulled back from them even as they lifted her up from the cot. She made herself pull back, which was when one of them put his hand behind her head and pulled her by her hair.

Petra's fear gave her a voice.

"No...no, no, no!" she said, pleading with her voice. They didn't listen to her or look at her in any way, they merely pulled her along with them, between them. She was struggling in earnest now, despite the pain to her hair, trying so hard to get away from them, to get their hands off her. They pulled her wordlessly from the cell, she pleading with them to release her. Out the door of the cell, her heart pounding and her breath panting with the fear, not believing this was happening. Turning right, down the dark corridor, cells to her left and right with figures of people in them, crying, moaning, silent. At the

213

bottom of the corridor is a turn, to the right, and on the left is a cell. She looks in as she is dragged past and sees the man with the split foot unconscious on the floor. She is dragged into the larger room. It is empty of all but the guards and the metal. In the middle of the room is a large chimney shoot, with a fire built up in the middle. She is brought to a stop, made to lift her arms. She now pleads again, but she knows that there is nothing to stop it now. She is in the centre of the room, her hands tied above her head. She is on her toes to try and give herself some slack in her muscles. She cannot see the men. There is a sound of metal near the fire. She listens, her eyes wide, crying a little. Then there is a shove behind her, on her, and she feels the fabric of her dress being torn down her back. Her back is now shown to the room, the skin white and thin and fragile. She tries to swing herself around, so that she might see, but she cannot, they have tied her too tight, they knew what they were doing. What now? What now?

She hears the snap of the leather behind her. She sees now, in a corner of the room a man sitting at a small table, a piece of paper and a quill in front of him. He regards her with a controlled air of excitement, he is here to do a job, but is a great man for it. He looks Petra in the eye, the only one in that room to do so.

"Petronella de Meath," he intones, "You are imprisoned upon suspicion of this Inquisition of having demonic intimates, of being guilty of the charge of heresy, of consorting with the devil and with demonic entities, and of having conspired with Dame Alice Kyteler, William Kyteler and with various other members of your coven to commit acts of heresy. Be aware that this inquisition will seek out the truth from you in all manner of ways. We seek from you a confession."

The man was shortening his speech, hurrying through it, all the time his eyes darting behind her. He was hurrying up, he was being told to do so. The men wanted to start the torture. Petra tried to speak but what could she say? She made some words come.

"I am innocent!" she cried, her voice stronger than she had expected. The first lash came down.

The pain was a side of her she had not known before, it was at first a merely brute thump, a mere sensation on the skin, but then it hit her muscles and she opened her mouth and released a silent cry

214

of pain. She could hear the man's voice again and had to try to concentrate to make it out.

"Be aware that the Inquisition is wary and knowing in the ways of the Unholy One. We advise you, Petronella, to confess freely to your ways. You will be chastised for your evil nature if your silence continues."

Petra opened her mouth to speak again which was when the second lash came down. This time the skin was ready for the burning pain and so gave no protection. Petra was unable to prevent a cry coming out, and despite her squirming on the rope was unable to turn in any real way.

"I AM INNOCENT!"

The torturer began to lash in earnest, to raise his arm and seek out the paler white flesh near the ribs. Petra screamed a scream of terror and of fear. The burning went on and on, and she found she could only keep her sanity by closing her eyes tight and allowing only the pain to reach her. She could hear the voice of the Questioner somewhere within the sound of the whip and the pain that it caused, and the words were clear, despite herself.

"Did you have congress with the Devil? Did you reject the Eucharist? Did you deny your faith and the faith of the Church? Did you accept the favours of the Devil, so that your mistress might succeed? Did you accept the favours? Did you?"

The lashes were at the fastest the torturer could make them. If he could just let her breath between strokes! But each time he did she caught her breath in a knife sharp pain of ribs, and then he continued on again.

She could not think, she could not do anything. The pain was a black, ringed thing that ran itself down her back and would not leave her. Oh my God, the pain! She could hear the questions of the Questioner again sounding somewhere in the room and found herself giving an automatic grunt.

The man held up his hands and the torturer stopped. The pain stopped. Petra found herself taking enormous gulps of breath, trying to feed her starved lungs. The man was speaking again.

"Do you have something to say?" he asked.

Petra stared at the man, his blank face looking back at her. She could see his eyes drooped slightly as he stared at her, looking a little like a tired sheep. Those drooping eyes reminded her of something, she had seen something like them somewhere before.

She rocked a little on the spot, her arms hanging over her head, as she looked away from him trying to think. Le Blund. She had not thought of him for years, yet here he was coming to mind in this place. He had been Alice's husband. They had removed him. They had tailored the wine and removed his life day by day, creating a monster that stared from the bed before his dying. They must have done wrong. They must have been evil to do that or the man would not be here before her now in her eyes, in the eyes of the man staring at her.

Petra looked at him again.

The man lifted his hand again.

The torture started again. There was no pause for fifteen minutes this time.

Petra was hurled into her cell and the gate closed behind her. She sank to the floor with her arms on the cot. Her body was in shock. There was more to it, however.

She was another woman now. The abuse on her body made her mind vastly different to the one that had existed a few hours before. Then, the one before had been formed on lines of some kind of civilisation; it believed in and expected goodness from those around it, up to a point. Now the person in the cell was a creature fighting for survival, an animal in the woods. It knew there was no one to protect it and that the danger to it was very real. It wanted very much for the pain to stop.

Petra remembered, with no feeling, her recollection of her mother's dying, and did not have presence of mind to wonder why she had thought of that. Still, because she had thought of peace while in Hell, tears came to her a little. They did not last, however, her survival instinct would not permit them.

Petra in the cell, on the floor that was caked in shit and piss and blood, some of it now her own, sat with her back bloody and exposed and found in herself a fierce will to survive. She must arrive at a strategy to live, to play a bargain and to succeed. What would Alice do if she were here. Petra thought of her, of that woman who could stand in front of you and reveal not a thing. Of that woman

216

whose will was a thing, like a wall or a stone or a fact of nature that would not move under any circumstances; she would be like Alice. She was to sell the truth. She would do so, but in a way that would not give them the truth. Le Blund will still have a peaceful death, no one would doubt that. But she would give them witchcraft, and potions, and spells, and all the nonsense every child believed, and then grew up and only half believed. Petra tried hard to breathe, a gust was coming through the gates and the exposes nerves wanted to shudder, which would only wound her more. The moment passed. Petra fixed her eyes on the wall opposite. There was nothing composed about her mind, but there was purpose, intent to survive, and this gave the sense of focus. Within her mind, the story began.

Le Drede was interviewing the man who had spoken to Petra during her first torture session. They were in the audience room.

Trying not to appear urgent took a great deal of effort on Le Drede's part but he managed it, mostly.

"Describe the session."

"The woman was brought into the main foyer and immediately began to call for her master. She raised her voice and gave way to her passions."

"In what way?"

"She screamed and fainted. Upon recovery of her senses, she abused all there with dire warnings of the fate that would befall them if they put harm to her body."

"Did the men loose heart?"

"They did not, your Grace, though they were sorely worried at the curses and screams she did let loose."

"I see. Go on."

"She was pinned up, Sire, and the cloth modestly removed from her back. It was possible to discern many marks and symbols on the heretic's skin that revealed her corporally perverse nature. She fought throughout the procedure, showing great and inhuman strength."

"Did she answer questions?"

"My Grace, she was without reason or understanding for the duration of the session. We attempted to correct her senses by the application of the whip. While this abated somewhat the demon's strength over Petra, it did not loosen its hold enough to release her to rational thought."

"How long did the flogging go on for?"

"Just over two hours, Sire."

"Is she grievously injured?"

"Much blood was shed, Your Grace. The witch did not lose consciousness, however, and stood at the end of the flogging."

"And at the end there was nothing said by her?"

"No, Your Grace."

Le Drede looked away, thinking. A witch in league with the unholy one. She seemed to have inhuman strength to avoid a confession at this stage. She must know secrets that would blacken any heart, he thought, shuddering. What had happened to the innocent Petra, the child that at one point was held in a state of grace? What road had her heart taken that she should be, at this stage, so lost to salvation? He felt genuine grief at her moral state.

He looked back at the man. They did not yet have a confession, and that they would have to have. He swallowed his emotion, made his intent his will. No doubt that the evil in her soul had been there for her always, inherent to her nature from the beginning. She had had amble opportunities to repent before she had come to their attention. She would have to take care of her own soul now.

"Go back to her tomorrow. Try water."

The man bowed, nodded.

"Very good, your Grace."

Petra's body was subjected to enormous stresses and strains over the next five days. She was to have her limbs and torso whipped continuously for hours. She was doused with cold water, scalded with boiling water. She had no sleep, no food and no conversation with any other human being other than the man charged with drafting her confession. Of course she talked, she talked and chanted the words she hoped they had wanted to hear from the beginning. The very severity of the punishments indicated their intentions that Petra was to be the instrument that broke the House of Kyteler.

Petra's consciousness was already smashed and ruined by her ordeal. Nothing in her experience or her life gave her any basis to survive this assault on her. She was no longer the maid of Alice, or the competent housekeeper of the House of Kyteler. She was no longer the woman who had teased William as a child, made love to Philip or who had exerted protection over Rose. She was instead a thing in pain, in constant fear, maddened by agony, all understanding reduced to the next blow, the next cut, the next pain she would have to endure. She thought only of ending this. End this.

So she worked her cunning and her understanding to see clearly what it was they wanted her to say. She watched with eyes made sharp with fear each word as it reached the ear of the Confession Taker. A nod meant she went on, a frown meant that she should rethink, try something else. Each session, with her arms tied up above her, her wounds reopened and made larger, she thought harder than she ever had in her life. Only once did she forget her plan.

It was the third day of her ordeal. The torturer was in front of her, placing something hot onto her now shaved scalp. It may have been tar, it may have been boiling water with salt in it, to scald her wounds. She let out a silent yell, then closed her eyes and her mouth as tightly as she could to prevent any of the foul liquid to reach her.

In the darkness off her eyelids she suddenly saw just for a moment the figure of her mother, some unlikely moment, when she was able to see her well and young, with dignity and joy, holding out her hands to her daughter, Petra, smiling to her. Just a moment. Petra wished with all her heart that she could join her, that the sweetness of the woman could fill Petra's world the way it had when she was alive.

For a moment, Petra had sweet, unexpected relief, with no voice to goad her nor any further wounds to hurt her. She was free of it and the fear of it.

Then she opened her eyes.

The torturer had his face to hers, his eyes looking directly into hers. His eyes had a terrible insane glint in them, gleeful at the terrible pain he was about to inflict.

He lowered the poker onto her scalp.

Petra was unable to remove herself from the room, unable to help her panic in any way. She started to scream, scream and scream, for Alice, for William, for her mother and father, for God to save her. God, save her, save her from all the pain.

"Petra, you seek salvation from God and He hears your prayers. Answer the question as put," said the scribe.

"Your mother is in Hell, witch, and you will be with her soon! No escape from God's vengeance!" said the Torturer, pressing the poker in.

His face was too close, his breath on her cheek. She was getting madder and madder with each second, the fragile spirit she had for survival getting more and thin. Petra tried hard to hold on but all she could see was this room and that man's face so close to her. All she could feel was the pain of her body, over and over and over again, telling her there had never been a time before pain, never had she lived free from it and she always would. Petra saw that all was for naught. She moved into the final stage of her despair.

And became blissfully, distantly mad.

By the authority of the holiest Father in Christ, Lord John XXII and by the Justiciar and Council of the land of Ireland belonging to Lord Edward, and so that the religion and the Faith of the Holy Church may be permitted to grow and shine, his Grace Bishop Le Drede, after due convening of the Inquisition, hereby makes the following charges against Dame Alice Kyteler, William Outlaw her son, Petronella de Meath and other persons;

First; that the sorceresses hereby named below would deny faith in Christ and the Church for a whole month or for a year, according to the extent of what they wished to obtain from the sorcery. During that time they would believe in nothing that the Church believed, they would not worship the body of Christ in any way, they would not go into a Church, they would not hear mass, they would not eat the holy bread or drink the holy water.

Secondly, it was claimed that they were in the habit of making sacrifices to demons with living animals which they would cut into pieces and scatter around the crossroads as offerings to a certain demon who called himself the son of Art, from the lesser levels of the underworld.

Thirdly, that by means of their sorceries the witches would seek advice and answers from demons.

Fourthly, that the witches were usurping the authority and the keys of the Church when they held their nocturnal meetings because by the light of waxen candles they would hurl the sentence of excommunication even at their own husbands, calling out one by one the names of each and every part of their body from the soles of their feet to the top of their head, and then at the end the witches would blow out the candles and say "fi:fi:amen".

Fifthly, that in a skull from the head of a decapitated robber over a fire of oak wood, they would boil up the intestines and internal organs of the cocks which, as mentioned above, had been sacrificed to demons. They would mix in some horrible worms, add various herbs and countless other vile ingredients such as nails cut from dead bodies, hair from the buttocks, and frequently also clothes from boys who had died before being baptised. From this they would concoct various powders, ointments and lotions; they would even make candles from the fat left in the cooking pot; chanting different chants, they would incite people to love and to hate, to kill as well as to afflict the bodies of faithful Christians, and to do countless other things which they wanted.

Sixth, that the sons and daughters of the said lady's four husbands where publicly instituting litigation before the bishop, seeking remedy and assistance against the lady. Openly and in front of the people, they alleged that she had used sorceries of this kind to murder some of their fathers and to infatuate others, reducing their senses to such stupidity that they gave all their possessions to her and her own son, thus impoverishing forever their sons and heirs. Moreover the lady's present husband, the knight Sir John Le Poer, had reached such a state through powders and lotions of this kind as well as through sorceries, that his whole body was emaciated, his nails were torn out and all hair removed from his body. This knight, however, with the help of one of the lady's servants, had forcibly grabbed from her hands the keys to the lady's chests. These he opened and found there a sack full of vile and horrible ingredients *which he sent with all else that he had found to the Bishop in the hands of two trustworthy priests.*

Seventh, that the said lady had a certain demon as incubus by whom she permitted herself to be known carnally, and that the demon called himself Son of Art, or else Robin, son of Art. Sometimes, it was claimed, he appeared to her in the shape of a cat, sometimes in the shape of a shaggy black dog, sometimes as a black man with two companions bigger and taller than himself, one of whom carried an iron rod in his hands. It was claimed that the lady entrusted herself and all her possessions to this demon from whom she admitted that she received her wealth and whatever she owned.

We make these charges in the year of Our Lord 1324, in Kilkenny, in the land of Ireland.

The day they finished getting the confession out of her, Petra was slumped on the ground in the main chamber. She had most of her hair gone, and her broken nose had a terrible bruise on it. It had swelled up awfully, so that her face bore a very different aspect to the quiet, clever woman she had been. Instead she looked thuggish, brutal, a woman of viciousness.

Petra's dress was soiled, with her blood and faeces. She had several broken toes from their hammers, and only two fingernails left. She had a bare back of lashes, which had healed and reopened and been joined by new ones. She had not eaten for four days, no food of any sort, and only a little water. She was not the maid of Alice any more, nor a residence of the city. She had become a non thing, a bruised thing, that seemed to only exist for the impact of others' blows. She did not feel, or have emotions, or loss, or pain. She was instead a blank page.

The men were nearby, in the room, picking up their tools, wrapping the whips to put them away. Petra had sung like any bird before her, she had emptied her voice of words until her throat ached with the speed of them from her. She did not know words any more, she was leaving them to others. She had her head resting on her hands, which were resting on the floor, facing the wall. At this angle she could just about see the dim light the two inches window permitted.

She heard a noise. She had not heard it for quite some time. She opened her eyes and looked.

Outside, starlings fluttered around the green space that somehow grew there, hopping from spot to spot. Their coats flashed royal blue and emerald green, and they moved with energy and speed. Petra blinked, looking at them. This was a beautiful thing. They flew in packs, in great unison, and were marvellous together. She watched carefully, trying not to let the men see she had something to see. The sight of the birds were awaking something in her.

Suddenly the birds were joined by another, a larger bird; a magpie. The magpie had something in its beak. Petra blinked several times, her eyes not understanding. The magpie had in its beak a baby bird, a starling, stolen brazenly from its nest. The other birds' frantic motion was not the paced calm swoop of night fall, it was the frantic, panic-stricken attempts to somehow stop the brute, to remove its danger, to stop this blatant attack.

The magpie took no notice, but instead settled itself directly in front of the small window, dropping its load as it did so. Petra stared at it, and she saw the magpie lift its eyes to the barred grate. The birds around it fluttered terribly, their song not a song but a scream of distress at this act, at this eating of their young. They did not attack, they merely watched and called out their pain.

Petra slowly moved her hand to the grate, and tried to flick her hand at the bird, that the young one might be spared. But instead, behind her, she heard the men cry out in vicious glee, their heavy boots thumping across the floor, their hands out to catch her again. She moved her hands as quickly as she could, trying to get quick in her weakness. But she merely flayed uselessly, as the men caught her, dragged her back, and the magpie took off with the young starling caught forever in its mouth.

Chapter Twenty-One

The Trial

The man walked calmly and with poise through the streets, the letter tucked safely into his tunic. He walked smoothly around the cart stuck in the mud, skirted past the two women chatting in the middle of the street, and avoided the herd of sheep being brought to the abattoir by the Shepard. The man avoided all of it, his eyes alert and sharp, his movements all controlled and calmness. At one point two knights nearly collided with him as they came around the corner.

"Here, you cur!" came from one of them, but he paid them no mind and kept going. The task given to him gave him leave to ignore the normal civilities. He kept on walking. The letter was too important.

The Castle was before him now, once he had managed to avoid the milling crowds that congregated in front of it. The line of people trying to gain entry was long; and who could blame them? The spectacle about to unfold was a special treat. The guards at the entrance had their instructions, however, and those instructions were clear. To allow no-one entry unless they had specific business on this day of days.

The man did not even consider queuing, to do so would have been to waste valuable time. He held up a gloved hand as a barrier.

"Halt; stop. No one is granted entry unless permitted."

"I have an urgent letter to be delivered into the hands of the Bishop, to do with today's events."

The guard sniffed. He reached into his tunic and pulled out the letter he had guarded so carefully.

The guard looked at the writing on the front of the letter, thinking nothing much of it. Then he turned it over, and saw the wax seal imprint on the back of the paper. Surely not... he paused at the seal, bringing it closer to his face to see it better.

"You'll need to bring this straight in, with all speed, they're about to start."

The guard moved pass to grant him access, indicating to him that he was to go on through.

The man went through the grand arc, and then found himself in the open courtyard of the Castle. Here, there were more guards. Some were dotted at strategic points along the walls. There were also, however, the military nobility, invited specifically by the Bishop for the occasion. They were milling around the vacant space before the battlements, sharing news and gossip.

He walked quickly to the inner castle entrance, and knocked on the door.

The guard who opened it looked at him with a curious eye. "Yes?"

"I come to deliver a letter," said the man, pulling out the letter again from his tunic.

The procedure was the same as at the grand entrance. The guard reviewed the letter until he saw the seal. Then all attention, he permitted entry.

The foyer of the Castle was decorated with the insignia of the Franciscans, a clear indication of the Bishop.   The air of intent was increasing.

He made his way into the hall, with the Italian marble, and up the grand staircase.

He was halted again at the ante room. The man in question was brought before a large table, where papers were arranged in strict order.

The messenger was made to wait, before the table, silence reigning all around him. He stood, patient.

The figure at the other side of the table was examining a parchment in front of him, which was absorbing all his attention, apparently. Eventually he finished reading, carefully rolled up the parchment and put it back into the pile, along with all the others. He sighed, and slowly rubbed his eyes. Only then did he look up.

"Yes?"

"I come to deliver a letter," he said, and then pulled out the letter from his tunic.

The other man did not move.

"Many come here to deliver letters, what is so special with regards to this one?"

"The sender is one that makes it important."

While the clerk was not so common as to raise an eyebrow in disbelief, his face did take on a slightly more alert air. He reached out and took the letter.

The messenger again stood waiting patiently. The clerk, like the others, reviewed the face of the letter, and then turned it over. He took a deep, quiet inhalation of breath as he saw the seal, then gave him a few moments to compose himself. Then he raised his face to the other man, who had the grace not to smile.

"Take this and bring it up to the next room."

Again the messenger merely nodded, and taking back the letter, turned and walked out of the room and back onto the grand staircase.

There were more and more figures, each of them apparently blessed with earnest purpose. None of them made eye contact with each other beyond a quick nod, and then moving on. An eager nervousness hung in the air. The messenger moved through all of them, untouched by it. He knew to not let such an atmosphere affect his concentration.

Walking up the steps, sidestepping the two black clad clerks who were in whispered conversation beside the door, he entered the great chamber. He walked past the ante-room and into the large chamber proper.

The messenger surveyed the room. He was looking for someone in particular, and he wanted to be sure he had the right person. The room he was in was larger, about forty feet by twenty-five. Around him were the parties interested in the day's proceedings, which had yet to start; the lawyers, clerks, proctors, and notaries.

They seemed to be hummed to silence by the room, and so whispered quietly amongst themselves. Pews had been placed in rows going up the length of the room, and each of them were filled with the great and the good of the city. While Inquisitions were as a rule held in camera and were not open to the public, the Bishop had huge discretion in how it was conducted. And here, for a small donation to the Church, anyone could be granted access.

Thus, the pews held the Great of the City and beyond. These men sat with their attendants and pages in a type of silent expectation. The best way to describe them would be silently alarmed. They looked neither right nor left, and engaged in no conversation. None of them anticipated that they would be here to see the day. Certainly, none of them expected it for the house of Kyteler.

The messenger took in all this, the anticipation, the small level of fear. He looked to the top of the room. There a podium of sorts had been set up. A table, filled with scrolls was placed to the right of the podium, with a clerk seated at it. Behind him sat an empty table. There were no papers on this desk, which was covered with a simple linen cloth. No one was seated at it.

The messenger strode up to the clerk.

"I come with a letter for His Grace."

The clerk had looked up, surprised, but did not react unduly. Nor did he say anything. He merely nodded, after a moment, and then rose from the desk.

"Wait here," he said, and stepped away into an adjoining room. The messenger glanced at the audience. They went to great pains not to appear interested. In a moment, the Clerk had returned.

"Come this way, please," he said, and the messenger followed the clerk into the adjoining room

It was a small chamber, used by the Bishop to prepare before appearing in the Inquisition. Two candles burned by the window. Glass hung on the wall to allow a reflection be seen. And a crucifixion hung on the plain wall, to allow spiritual succour.

The Bishop himself stood with a priest behind him, his arm outstretched for the vestments. The priest walked around him, correcting a line or two.

"Thank you, Brother Thomas," said Bishop Le Drede quietly, and then turned his attention to the visitor.

"I understand you have a letter for me?"

The messenger nodded.

The Bishop held out his hand.

The messenger knelt solemnly in front of him, and quietly touched his lips to the ring offered. Only then did he stand and place the letter into his hands.

The bishop looked at it for a moment, and then turned it over.

The messenger found it necessary to speak at this moment.

"It was received last night and was given to me this morning. I set out at dawn to bring it to your Grace at the first opportunity."

The Bishop's lips went so far as to thin as he purveyed the seal in front of him. The news of the letter must have already spread throughout the city, he knew, and he found he wanted a moment to compose himself before he reviewed the options.

It was from the Pope. Richard did not think to hear from him at all for months, and then only some missive dispatched by a minion from an office deep within the Holy See at Avignon. But this was a missive with the seal of the Papacy displayed prominently on it, for all to see. Richard knew the words inside would have been highly considered.

He paused before opening it. What reason would they have to correspond with him now? Were they seeking his renouncing of this trial, like the authorities in Dublin and London had done, to his disgust? If they were, Richard knew the impulse came from the terrible desire to placate and make friends where the Church should make enemies. He blinked as he reviewed the unopened letter in his hand, unaware of the tension of those around him. If news of criticism from the Pope reached anyone else on this country, then this trial would fail. The Secular arm would not obey him, instead following an expedient course towards the Pope. If he were being censured in this letter, the news would be very hard to keep quiet.

But the inverse may be true. The Holy Father may be seeking to encourage and praise him, thereby raising Richard's status once again both in his own eyes and in the eyes of those around him. He would find doors opening to him again, the trial and its consequences easier for him to carry out.

But then he remembered that they were different here. Those things that were sensible to him and those he knew in Avignon were unknown to those here. The Pope's authority was frowned on, denied, feared and rejected here. They seemed to have a greater regard for their own sinful law, savages that they were here. An attempt to press this law on them, to expect their admiration for it, was not likely to succeed. They would sneer, as they had always sneered, as Arnold Le Poer had sneered all those days ago when Richard had come before the court. Richard swallowed as he remembered that humiliation again. They would not listen. None of them would ever listen to reason or right authority.

So if the letter criticised him, he would be damned. If it was affirming of his efforts, then he would still face further obstacles. He looked at it. He would burn it, but not here, and not before reading it properly when he was alone. He put the letter into the hands of Brother Thomas.

"Keep this safe for me to carefully read it when I get home."

The Brother, alarmed and startled at this unexpected decision, merely took the letter, eyes wide.

Richard Le Drede looked at the Messenger.

"We have not been introduced."

The messenger lowered his head in a bow at the words.

"I am Sir Richard Gile, sent by the Archbishop in Dublin."

Le Drede did not allow himself to frown.

"Sent? To what purpose? You do not strike me as a mere attendant, Sir Gile."

"I am his Grace's servant, it is true. But I am sent to act as Notary for His Grace in this matter, in the way authorised by his licence."

A notary in an Inquisition was highly valued. Every word in an inquisition was noted down and retained by the Notary. The role was given to highly educated men, who worked under licence. For one to be appointed by the Archbishop was an outrageous affront. Richard, again, did not react.

"Please explain yourself."

"His Grace has no intention of reserving the right of Notary for himself. However, in this matter, which has stretched over several years, and which has sorely tried your Grace with many insults and injuries, the Archbishop seeks to show his support to you in any and every way possible. To that end, I am bid to provide you with legal expertise and with notary skills to the best of my humble ability."

A spy, thought Richard.

"Very well," he said, his tone calm, his eyes wide. "I am pleased by the gesture and am grateful for your presence. We will be commencing the trial in a short period, the prisoner is still being prepared. Also, we are expecting representations from the House of Kyteler to be part of the proceedings, but as yet have not yet received

229

the names of those attending on their behalf. That may also delay matters."

Sir Gile inclined his head, indicating his assent. The calm practised manner of the man was an irritant to Richard, who was himself highly agitated on this day of days. But he was practised enough in the ways of the Papal Court to give no indication of it. He continued to give Sir Gile his gaze.

"We are as yet still in consultation with our counsel. We will join you and the rest of the Court shortly."

Sir Gile was being dismissed. He gave no sign of upset, but inclined his head once more, and then turned and left the small room. Richard watched him go. Another viper to concern himself with. He seemed to be facing danger wherever he turned. But no matter what happened today, he reminded himself, he must give his full attention to the matter of Petra and her fate. She must not repent, under any circumstances.

The rules of an Inquisition dictated that a specific priest, independent of his order, could conduct the trial without record to the laws and statues, or to the very principles of justice that at that time existed. While the Catholic Church had encouraged such principles of justice throughout Europe (especially when it accorded in its favour), it disregarded them with vigour when dealing with Heresy. The reason for this, at least in ecclesiastical terms, was that heresy concerned the body of the laity of the Church. To find corruption within it meant that it must be rooted out, lanced, amputated with all speed, so as to save and preserve the souls of those innocent of such crimes. Another very important reason was money. The estates of those found guilty but unrepentant of Heresy, could and would be seized by the Church. This penalty was to the second generation, meaning that the sins of a Grandfather could result in the estates of a Grandchild being removed without appeal.

It was for this reason that Le Drede faced a real and delicate task. His role was not just to convince those assisting judgement today of Petra's guilt. Such an outcome was already the case. But he must ensure that Petra gave the Court a plea of guilty but unrepentant, that she agreed with their finds but did not plead for her life. She must not ask for mercy or insist she was sorry. If she did so, all would be lost for Le Drede. The money of the Kyteler household (it should be a simple matter to attach guilt from Petra to them) would be lost to him. And Petra would not die in the fire he wanted to show the world. She would go unpunished. He could not let that be. For it was the case that the Church could not give sentence or carry out punishments on those that came before it. It was decreed that it could only create penance, not punishment, and only for those that sought to repent. If a person declared themselves guilty, but unrepentant, then the Church had therefore no authority to give sentence. That was the role of the Secular authorities, which almost always burnt those so guilty. So if Petra was to say she was sorry for her sins, if she was to ask for forgiveness and agree to come back into the folds of the Church, Le Drede would be foiled.

The silence around him grew, as he stood considering how he should conduct himself. The men around him knew better than to interrupt. Occasionally a sound, such as a cough, would be heard from without the other room, but otherwise all was silent concentration for them.

Richard thought about the woman he had seen in the cells. Petra had only seen him once, but he had been there on the majority of occasions. He had seen a woman strong in her beliefs, and in his opinion sure of her place in her Lady's house. She had been initially hesitant to voice the words they had eventually driven from her. She had been of the belief that she had a source of protection in the House that she served. She had been wrong, he knew, and he felt she had learnt that in the third day of her ordeal. She had spoken only the word 'No', for a long period. This, he has slowly come to realise, was not in response to the questions being put to her, but to the painful realisation on her part of her wrong doing, and the wrong doing of those she had served. She had eventually, as the blood dripped down, blinked in the darkness and began to signal her assent to the questions, and of course from there it had all flowed.

But she no longer trusted the Dame. Did she trust him? It might well be so. She had no one to trust at the moment. She had been permitted no visitors, no Counsel had appeared on her behalf. She had had no advice to make things clear for her. There would be no one assist her today either, the concern would be for her House, not for her. Could he utilise this? Could she be made to provide the answer he needed? The old Petra would have refused any such

231

attempts. The tall, slightly cautious woman she had been would have prevented anything of that sort. But she was not that woman. She was very different now, in outlook and spirit. He may well have yet hit upon the thing needed to make him victor.

He looked at the other man and made a gesture with his hands.

"We are ready."

The door to the Court was opened and he exited the room.

The coughing, murmurs and mutterings silenced as soon as he joined the larger court. The two knights of the Judgement were already seated at the top table waiting for him. The assembled personages were all waiting and expectant. The sense of his own importance, which he struggled to avoid, grew until it filled him, despite himself. He brought himself to his seat with solemn ceremony.

Sir Gile took a seat, with respectful air, beside the appointed notary. Le Drede saw it and did not let it reach his calm air.

He raised his voice to those present.

"On behalf of his Lord the most High Jesus Christ, and His Holiness the Pope, I Richard Le Drede, Bishop of the Diocese of Ossory, hereby call all those here present to witness the trial of Dame Alice Kyteler, William Outlaw, and other personages known to this Court."

He looked to the guard at the door.

"Give orders for the prisoner to be brought forth."

The guard quietly left to carry out his order.

Le Drede spoke on for a few minutes setting out the details of the case as he saw it, from the initial report from the children of Alice's husbands, the seizing of potions in the house, the torture and confession of her Maid. All this was merely redundant filling of information. He was free to conduct the trial in any way he pleased, and it pleased him to set before those present the correctness, and appropriateness of his actions against those aligned against him. Plus there may well be some lingering belief that the Magna Carta had jurisdiction here, doubtful as it might be. He let himself hold strong on the points he favoured, ignoring the passage of time. Then the guard returned and silently indicated that the prisoner was ready to be brought in.

"Bring forth the prisoner," he commanded.

The doors opened. All those in the room turned in their seats to see her enter, as they would for a bride in a Church. One by one they took in shocked gasps of air, horrified at what they saw.

To each of them, Petra was not an individual as such, but a member of a House in their proximity and circle. She was a sign and signal of the prosperity and standing of one of their peers. Every assault upon her person was an insult to the House of Kyteler. And a most grievous assault had been done here.

Petra walked slowly, stooped by the chain attaching her two ankles together. She had no hair, only a blood soaked scalp. One of her eyes was black and closed, and she peered pitifully out of the other, trying to see ahead of her. Her broken nose was huge and vile, and dark with internal damage. She had bloody scars on all visible parts of her body, on her neck, her collarbone, her hands and legs and feet, where they had gouged out her skin. A robe of some filth coloured cloth covered her somewhat. She had a broken toe on her right foot. But the eyes that peered out of that shrunken skull; She was a thing destroyed.

Everyone in that room had seen her before the imprisonment. They remembered the tall dark haired woman with the narrow nose who had been so respectfully quiet, with a sense of humour behind the eyes, the dignity that existed there. They all compared what she was with what she was now. And they saw each blow, each injury as a threat to their own Houses, their own loved ones, to themselves. More than one turned his eyes away from her in horror, to give her some dignity. And they turned their angry eyes on Le Drede. This was going too far. This, and he, must not be allowed to stand. This must not be allowed to continue. Kill this one, if you must. You will not get another.

And Sir Gile saw the damage done to this woman. He saw the mood of the room turn to appalled horror, and saw that this was an insult new to all of them, dreadful and profound. Le Drede has overstepped himself terribly here, he thought. He has signalled the end of his power with these people.

To the surprise of all, they heard Le Drede speak with a voice made gentle and kind, following his plan of gaining her trust.

"Petra, my child, come forth to us," he said, gesturing to a spot in front of his table. The offer was a cruel one, being as it was the length of the room for her to travel. She seemed to hear him, however, as she slowly painfully made her way towards him. People frowned in distress at the sight of her, limping her way towards Le Drede.

She reached the point he had pointed to. Le Drede remained seated at the table, while she stood before them in pain.

Le Drede gave the nod to the notary, to his own appointed man. At this signal the man nodded, swallowed and rose to his feet. The charges were read out again, slowly. The man seemed to feel the strength of the case as he read, his voice grew in intensity as he made his way through them. Le Drede rose again when he was finished.

"I now call for the Confession of Petronella De Meath, maid of Dame Alice Kyteler, to be read," he intoned, and sat down again.

The confession, identical to the charges, was read out to the Court. Sir Gile found his eyes trailing back again and again to Petra, who stood swaying before Le Drede. She seemed to stand solely because she was too thin to fall in any one direction. Was she aware of her surroundings? It seemed doubtful.

Le Drede nodded as the end of the Confession was reached. He then turned to Petra.

"How now Petra? What say you?"

She said nothing for a moment. Then her voice, too frail to be clear, spoke for a moment. Le Drede responded.

"To the confession you have signed. Do you repent, child? Do you ask for Mercy from your God and your Church?"

Silence. And then the same indistinct murmur. Le Drede frowned.

"You do not? You are not repentant?"

Another mutter. Sir Gile like the rest of the room, leaning forward in his chair, trying to hear. The room was utterly quiet, all concentrating on her. But she was unclear to all but Le Drede. Hearing her last statement, he sat back, eyes full of grief.

"Petra, if you do this, you will be removed from the authority of this Court. Do you seek this?"

She nodded, a distinct nod.

"Very well. It is the finding of this properly appointed Court, that Petra has declared herself unrepentant. She is therefore removed from the authority of this ecclesiastical court and placed into the hands of the Secular Authorities for punishment. May God have mercy on your soul."

Guards came forward and moved Petra away from the sight of them all. As they did so, Le Drede's voice rose again.

"We now turn to the charges concerning William Outlaw."

There a general murmur arose. Would William appear to defend himself? Would Alice?

A figure rose to his feet.

"Your Grace, I humbly appear before you on behalf of Dame Alice Kyteler. With your permission may I come forward?"

Le Drede was furious at seeing that a mere advocate was before him. He had wanted very much to have Alice appear in supplication and tears, begging for forgiveness and crying out her wrongs. But he saw now that this was not to be. He nodded.

"Your Grace, I come charged with missives from Dame Alice Kyteler, as well as letters of Instruction from the Viceroy of Ireland and other personages of great renown. These noble people bid me to speak to you and all the other members of this Court, which is rightly set up to carry out its most proper work."

Cunning. They were all so cunning. The man was giving little or no indication of whom it was, exactly, he represented. All smoke and daggers. As well as that, there was the most distinctive reminder that this was not an Inquisition, not on technical terms, but a court constructed by Le Drede. The fact itself was not threatening, but Le Drede was today sensitive to all possible threats that might be in existence. He touched a section of his vestments in an abstract manner, not realising he was revealing his worry.

The advocate continued.

"While Dame Kyteler is fully aware of the charges laid down by the court, and give full respect to the authority of His Grace and that of the Papal Court, it is not possible for her to appear before this court today. As such, it is my instruction to appear on her behalf."

Le Drede leaned forward.

"Does she not take the charges as laid down by this Court with due seriousness?"

"She does indeed Your Grace."

"Does she therefore seek to create the displeasure of this Court by avoiding the charges and not attending to answer them?" he said, conscious that his voice was rising.

"She does not, Your Grace. However, recent events, both within the City Walls and without them, have made clear that the safety and well being of Dame Alice Kyteler is threatened, and cannot be guaranteed. These events create the strong impression that a fair trial, to be witnessed as such, cannot be assured or guaranteed at this time, nor can the physical safety of Dame Alice be granted."

Le Drede listened with growing incredulity to the man. Was he serious? To come before him in this place of authority and to state clearly that the physical safety of that woman was in question? Of course it was! The point of the thing was to incur punishment upon her for her insolence, to inflict the punishment that the Church in its wisdom saw fit to present! Yet she declared herself too precious to allow the authority of the Church to be carried out.

He allowed himself a blink, nothing more.

"Therefore it is my humble duty to present myself here on behalf of this personage, and to state that I am fully versed with and instructed by her in this matter."

Richard made himself nod, as if in contemplation of the event. He was too angry to think, which startled him. He looked at the man in front of him, who looked back calmly, not blinking. Years of trying to get a hold of both of them, and now this result. She sent a lawyer instead.

He gave another nod, to cover the growing silence. He needed very much to have time to think, to rediscover the options open to him, to try again for victory. He inclined his head to the knight on his left, Peter Gilfoylne, who looked back at him with a questioning air. Richard took in his slightly bulbous nose, and the unpleasant breath. Peter was looking at him, as if to ask what was his Grace's pleasure. Richard turned to the man on his right, Thomas Something or Other, the man's name kept escaping him. He looked back at the Bishop, and seeing Richard's questioning face, leaned in to whisper into his ear.

"We should assure ourselves as to his right to appear before us. Also, that they will appear before us if the so called danger is thus removed."

Nonsense. The danger would not be removed and he had no intention of indicating otherwise to them, they did not deserve him blackening his soul for them. But what to do with this development?

He raised his voice.

"While the absence of Dame Alice Kyteler is one that we view most grievously, we cannot but believe in our hearts that we are growing stronger in our view of her guilt and malfeasance. We therefore turn now to the case against William Outlaw," finished Le Drede. His voice was calm, him manner controlled. He fooled no one. There was small readjustment among the spectators, who sat up straighter.

"Bring forth William Outlaw."

Now this was new. While everyone knew William was now bound under the jurisdiction of the Court, no one had really believed he would attend. Would his physical state match that of Petra's? No one believed Le Drede would be brave enough. Still, all eyes turned towards the doors, waiting.

William stepped in, and stood before them. A gasp rose up. It was immediately apparent that no such bravery had repeated itself. He stood, tall, calm, with a polished air. The gasps however, were due to his clothes, for William wore the livery of Arnold Le Poer. He was aligning himself publicly and overtly with the secular power, and stating he was under their protection. Le Drede was seeing William's defences. To harm William was to harm the authority of the Crown, the very method Le Drede uses to operate. Surely he was thwarted?

It is nothing, thought Le Drede. It is a soiled vestment, a mere cloth. It is not chain mail against my sword, it is not protection from my Church. He could have worn it for the first time today. He is a liar, a cheater. He will not evade me and the truth I bring.

"Brother William," he spoke to the room, "I see you are nearly attired."

"I bear the livery of Arnold Le Poer," spoke William, his voice equally clear and loud. "It is clear to all whose interests I now represent and preserve."

"Such interests, while perhaps genuine, do not concern this court. Please step forward."

He moved to the place indicated, the place Petra had stood so recently before.

Le Drede watched him walk, and was conscious of only one thought. It was the beginning of the end.

William stood, calm, defiant, gazing boldly at him. The clerk of Dame Alice stood a few steps behind William. Unlike Petra, William would have protection. Le Drede let his gaze fall on the papers before him, while he thought.

William had the protection of Le Poer, and the legal protection of the Viceroy. Le Drede knew no physical harm would be permitted to occur, as much as he would like to hear the man's bones crack. So what could be achieved? Penalty of funds? Yes, yes a lot, but that would not sate Richard. An apology? If one was given, it would not be genuine, and worthless, without any doubt. So what? William signed, loudly enough to be heard, but Le Drede ignored him.

Let him admit the charges. He's fought again and again against any imputation on his guilt. Let him say that what is implied is true. Let him declare that that which was hidden is now made clear. Let William frankly concur with the charges. Let him agree to those, and still be so bold. Then Richard could chose to act as he wanted to in this court. He lifted his head.

"This court is aware of the difficulties as stated by William Outlaw, and we are grateful for your perseverance in this matter."

"However, the charge before this Court are those of the most grave and serious. These charges are severe to an extent that your inconvenience, or concerns over your personal rights, can and should be put to one side. Therefore, we will continue and turn our attention to the charges before the Court."

He looked directly at the young man in front of him.

"William Outlaw, you come before this Court charged with the crime of Heresy. This charge comes on foot of your excommunication for forty five days as demanded by secular law. While this law is not under any circumstances to be read as of greater priority or importance than ecumenical law, but as a courtesy to ensure that claims of unfairness or injustice that were levelled at this court, in a most intemperate manner, were not to be held to be credible."

He looked at William as he said all this. There was no change in the other man's face, he merely stood there, listening. He appeared neither angry nor afraid, nor defiant. Richard did not have time to give him full scrutiny. He continued.

"The charges of heresy are the reason you are called before this Court, William Outlaw. We hereby demand and insist that you hereby respond to these charges."

William nodded, calm at the question.

"Your Grace, I stand before you unable to respond, as I am not yet fully apprised, to the best of my knowledge. I therefore ask the indulgence of the Court to recall these charges."

"This request is the height of unusual, Master Outlaw."

"Nevertheless, I beg the indulgence of the Court."

Richard decided to avoid anger, as clearly he was being provoked. He merely glanced around the room, and seeing that there were no voiced complaints, nodded to the clerk of the court to continue.

The clerk, seeing this, roused himself to his feet. In perfectly pronounced Latin, the charges were read out again. William stood looking at the clerk, his face still impassive, still showing nothing. The Clerk was ending his intonation. Richard looked at William again.

"William Outlaw, we call upon you here again to answer the charges as already given."

"Your Grace, it would be my fervent wish to answer these charges. However, due to concerns that have arisen over my safety, and the safety of others, I am unable to do so. Therefore, I cannot and will not answer the charges at this session today."

The audience gasped. Le Drede looked at the man as the meaning of the words reached him.

"Explain yourself."

"I cannot and will not answer you today, as I will be without the right and proper protection I deserve. Therefore I will not answer."

A rumble went through the room, all those in attendance started.

At that moment, a beam of sunlight shone through the window, lighting on William's face. Even God Himself favours him. He leaned forward.

"Did you refuse to give any answer to the charges made here today?"

"I will not answer."

Another rumble across the room. Richard would not give up.

239

"These spells, that Petra and others have readily confessed, they are unknown to you?"

"I will not answer here." came the infuriatingly calm reply.

"Did your mother have anything to do with these?"

"I will not answer here, as I have already said."

Did any witchcraft, or heresy, occur, Master Outlaw, as has been described by Petra?"

"I will indeed give details to that question, and any question you care to put to me, but not here."

Richard sat back, slowly.

"It is simply not credible that a heresy as described should occur and that you did not know about it. This matter has been ongoing for some time. Numerous witnesses have give frank details of what they saw, indeed, what they themselves were involved in. Lest this Court forget, this family were held to be connected to a murder in 1306, but justice was prevented from being carried out then. Let it not be prevented now. My point is that a spell, spells, and heresy of the most grievous sort are alleged to have been carried out. These spells were held to be responsible for the great sums of money obtained by your House. Do you put before this Court that the spells were made by a third party? It is not credible that they would act in your favour without your knowledge."

William lifted his calm and clear voice, and it reached them all.

"If you have received a confession, or if a spell or spells were made, or confessions of a spell being made, then it was done so by a third party to my House. If a spell, or witchcraft of any sort was being carried out, the charge shows solely what they did; the actions were theirs, the intent was theirs. Surely my House or I could not be held responsible for what was done by a third party? That is a wholly unreasonable position."

"Why did you give help to those making the heresy? Why did you hinder so completely the work of those investigating the suspected Heresy, or indeed, the work of this Court?"

"What I have done, or not done, is not proven in any capacity. I have done nothing illegal."

"It is not your place to decide what is not illegal! You are not the decider of men's souls, nor do you bear authority in this Court! Do you expect us to believe as a credible proposition, that you did not know about the Heresy being conducted, or if you did know, that you would do nothing to facilitate it? You ask us to believe that you benefited from it, without doing anything to assist it?"

"My money was allocated as I wanted it to be. Do you suggest that I should somehow not do that?"

"Your money would be better served in the arms of the Mother Church!"

At this William openly snorted, and a few spectators stared at the Bishop. Did he seek all their funds as well?

The advocate of William, who had stood behind him throughout all this exchange, suddenly spoke up.

"Your Grace, it grows already late. We ask that the replies and deliberations be postponed until the first court date after the Festival of Saint Hilary."

Le Drede thought about the request, which would see the entire matter at rest until the 13th January 1325. The request, thrown in so casually in the middle of his interrogation, showed outrageous overconfidence. He considered the evidence against William. Petra had directly implicated him in protection Heretics, as well as relapsing against the faith. The case against him was much stronger than it had ever been before.

"It is pleasing to us to do so. We agree," he intoned. All in the room were still at the words, surprised. Even William gave him a look of alarm.

"To be sure of the accused, as the Church should be, while the business of the Faith is still pending, I hereby order William Outlaw to be taken to prison in the Castle in Kilkenny, keeping him there under strict security until the business of the Faith is completed."

The entire room froze, and the guards moved quickly to stand beside William. The Advocate opened his mouth to protest, horrified at the sight of his master being held, but Le Drede merely shook his head, silently. He spoke again, directly to William.

"You will have until Vespers tonight to get your House in order. Then you will be taken to the Castle."

He nodded to the guards.

"Take him to his House. And arrive back here at Vespers time with him in shackles."

A gasp of sheer impolite shock rose from the room, but Le Drede acted as if he did not hear it. He stood, and after a moment the room rose as one, to provide him with the respect he deserved. He left the room without looking back, confident finally that all eyes were on him.

Chapter Twenty Two

The three men left the Castle, along with the armed entourage of both William and Arnold. They made their way the short distance from the keep to the Kyteler House, with no talk between themselves.

The faces that they passed on the way there told the story of the Kytelers' new status. Some looked away, ignored those who they would have automatically nodded to before. Some stared at William in horror, falling back into doorways and alleys, afraid of the whispered evil that had infected him. And some were sneering, seeing only goodness in the fall of a House that had had mastery over them.

William gave no sign of seeing any of it. He kept his chin high and his eye above them all, and made no comment about it, to the others or to himself. Night was beginning to come in, the light was fading already and there was much to be done.

They entered the house with none of the usual calls out, for neither Rose nor Philip nor any known housemaid was to be there until later. Instead they made their way to the inner chambers, where they could be free to speak and write and plan, and shut the door behind them.

The door shut, all strangers' faces removed, William looked at the two men about him.

"Well?"

"It went extremely well. In this way the Court is held over for months while we campaign on your behalf. Your detention will be over in a matter of hours, once you have paid the gaoler. We grow stronger every day in Dublin and will soon remove Le Drede. We have many opportunities for success and no cause for distress."

William turned to the Advocate, who spoke without hesitation.

"While Sir Arnold speaks knowledgeably and with good reason, I fear there is more cause for alarm here. Le Drede, while despised abroad is roundly regarded as a reformer here. Gaining the trust or the services of those in the gaoler is by far no longer a surety.

We must prepare for the risk that you may not be free of gaol immediately."

Arnold snorted at this, but William looked at the other man.

"If I am held captive, what recourse is open to us?"

The Advocate thought hard for a moment, then nodded to himself.

"Our influence is greatest abroad, not locally. We have to strengthen our influence immediately, perhaps by application to the King, the Viceroy, as well as the Estate of Gilbert de Clare and the other interests that are in your control at the moment. There is silence so far from your mother, we may forego that channel for the moment."

William thought silently for a moment, neither man interrupting his thoughts. He looked at Arnold.

"Do you advise anything further?"

Arnold replied, "We should also use the names in the Kyteler loan book to perhaps insist on early repayments, stating your current circumstances as the cause. If we stir up enough people, we will be able to raise more that will clamour on the prison walls for your release."

William stared at them. They proposed his incarceration with a calm that was nonsensical to him. He wondered if somehow he could no longer trust them, then rejected that thought as one born out of fear. He looked away, telling himself to ignore his emotions and to concentrate on the problem at hand. Incarceration was a result that could devastate his campaign to be rid of the charges against him, would improve the campaign of Le Drede, and encourage his enemies to believe the House of Kyteler had fallen. There must be a way out of the problem, he told himself. How could he use the fact he was in prison to his advantage? He would be held completely in the custody of Le Drede, at his mercy and apparently unable to decide his own agency. How could this aid him?

William leaned against the table he was standing beside, suddenly tired. The weariness that came over him was startling in its speed, and he wondered if his humours were affected by the shock. No matter if they were, they would have to continue on with him. He looked at the two men, their faces lit only by the firelight. He had a sensation of too many whispered conversations, of too many secrets, of longing to feel fresh air on his face and to have an open hand. He was being like his father then, had he known it.

Just then there was a knock on the door.

All three men started. Was the Bishop sending his men early? They looked at each other in indecision, then William nodded at the clerk. The older man moved to open the door.

Before them stood the advocate, the unknown man who had been at the table with Le Drede when they arrived there that day. He stood, calm and unruffled, and unaccompanied by any staff who might announce him.

"Good evening Sir," said William. "I bid you welcome to this house, though you seem to have made welcome in it all ready."

"I have intruded beyond the call of good manners, I readily admit," said the other man, with a smile at this clever cheek on his part, "but I am bid by all good duty and loyalty to a rightful cause, and so ask your favour or leave to be heard for but a few moments of your time."

William frowned at this nonsense. The man spoke perfect French, but there was an accent there that he was not familiar with.

"Time, Sir, is something that I have little of, especially on this night of nights.

"Come in. Speak. We will listen."

The others looked at each other as William let the other man in. He was not sure himself why he did let him in. Tonight he faced jail, for who knew how long. What man would, faced with such a fate, not turn his face to unexplored windows of opportunity?

The man entered the room. He looked for a moment at the other three men, nodding gravely to each. There was a sense about him, however, of having no real fear of them. He knew he was already victorious, in this battle as in others. William recognised the attitude, he was speaking to one who was used to winning, and who had probably never really lost anything before. He felt himself relax somewhat at the realisation; perhaps all was not lost. He did not yet let himself hope, however.

There was a brief pause. The other man looked at the three faces staring back at him, the night light from the fire making the shadows of his eyes dark. He took a breath, and then started.

"Gentlemen, allow me to introduce myself. My name is Sir Richard Gile, and I am here to speak to you on behalf of the Archbishop of Dublin. I have been asked to resolve the matter as quickly and as satisfactorily as possible."

Sir Arnold frowned.

"What does that mean? Can we count on the Archbishop for support?"

Sir Richard looked briefly pained at the interruption.

"The Archbishop is placed into a unique position. His views of both the character of Bishop Le Drede and of the current litigation in the name of the Mother Church are very much at odds with those of Le Drede. Despite this, however, he has very little authority to act here."

"Why is that?" asked William.

"Le Drede's appointment was not as a result of the regular appointment structure as is usually the case, where the appointment is recommended by either the Archbishop or the Royal Viceroy. Instead, Le Drede is visited our Isle solely at the pleasure of, and under the authority of His Holiness the Pope. Therefore, to seek the removal of Le Drede, or to even publicly oppose him, is to invite enormous risk of reprobation. The Archbishop cannot move against him."

"So we are to be without help?" snarled Arnold.

"Indeed no, nor does the Archbishop seek to convey that impression," replied Sir Richard, smoothly. The slight smile had never once left his lips. "I merely hope to convey the complexities of the matter from the Archbishop's perspective. No, instead the assistance the Archbishop can offer you must be by necessity quiet and unseen to the world at large. Any such protection provided must be on that basis. Do I have your agreement to this point going forward?"

Sir Richard looked around him at the three men. The clerk and Sir Arnold as one turned to William to see his response. The fire crackled quietly in the room as he thought. I am asked to accept assistance, he thought, on condition that I do not reveal I receive it. And I do not yet know what the help itself is yet. No matter!
He gave a terse nod.

"Excellent. The Archbishop is prepared to arrange for the following; you and your House will accept a finding of guilt by way of aiding and abetting others in the carrying out of Heresy and mischief, thereby avoiding the greater charge of Heresy yourself. You will admit this in Court. You will publicly sign a confession to this in Court. You will accept the sermon of the Bishop on this charge and you will carry out any penitence he sees fit to impose upon you on this charge. And when you have gone through this day, and had all said to you that the Bishop will say to you, you will walk free from the Court."

"What of the financial penalty that may be imposed by the Bishop? Will it go forward?" asking Sir Arnold, meaning the right of the Church to impose a penalty on future generations of those found guilty. If this was the case here, William's grandchildren may yet in the future be asked for funds for their Grandfather's sins.

"Any such penalty may be considered that which is the business of others," replied Sir Richard. "You may consult the Archbishop to confirm if any such payment is necessary."

We pay nothing. William looked at him, and Sir Richard looked blindly back. Ignore it, he thought, give it no mind. Walk out and give no thought to any penalty they may impose. If Le Drede was to know about this, he would never stand for it. Le Drede, however, is never going to know about it, is he? He is for another fate.

William paused again, the fire light stretched tightly on his broad face.

There was another knock on the door. All three men looked at it with a more resigned air; there could be no mistake what news it brought now.

"In," called William.

The door opened and Philip, now so old, appeared.

"My Lord, the Sheriff's men have arrived."

"I am nearly finished, Philip. Tell them I am in the house and will be with them with all speed."

Philip paused, worried, but did not argue. He merely withdrew again and shut the door. They could hear his slow tired step up the stairs. William turned again to Sir Richard.

"Our time here grows short. I have but a few more questions. What certainty do I have that you will be able to convince the Bishop to carry out the conviction as you have described?"

"I have the authority of the Archbishop in this matter, plus there is no chance of failure here."

247

Again that certainty, thought William. A dire fate awaits Le Drede.

Above them they could hear the shouted response from the Sheriff. The men upstairs were not happy to be kept waiting. There were the sounds of footsteps thumping down the stairs.

"Just one more question," said William. "How are we to save Petra, the maid of this House?"

The thumping on the door continued behind them, as the face of Sir Richard showed surprise. He spoke quickly, in a hurried, worried tone.

"Oh no, Sir William, no. There can be no assistance for Petra." William stared at the man in horror.

The thumping on the door became more insistent.

"Open up!" roared a voice outside. "In the name of His Grace Bishop Le Drede!"

"There is to be nothing for Petra? We are to let her die?"

"No, Sir William, not at all. She cannot be saved if you are to be saved. She is to be sacrificed for the pride of the Bishop, a sacrifice that must be made. She must be lost."

William blinked, stunned. He had always presumed that some effort on his part would remove her from danger. This was not to be? The thumping on the door continued behind them, shards of wood beginning to fall away.

"You cannot save her William!" hissed Arnold. "Do not try!"

Petra, to die? She will die, he thought, suddenly thinking like his mother, the cold part of his mind racing. She will die, and it will be a terror on my heart. But we will pay no money. We will live on. The House will continue. She will die, but she and only she, and she is but a maid. She will die.

He gasped at himself and then spoke.

"God forgive me."

Behind them the men rushed in.

The neighbours were ready to witness the event, and they had been standing outside, silent but with some mirth, for some time. They held lit torches, and some of the less dignified began to jostle so that they could see better than others.

There had been great excitement when the men had come to take Master Outlaw to prison. A low murmur had spread through the gathering crowd when the men had first been seen, in their long rows, coming down the narrow Kieran's Street. There had even been a brief cheer. But most of the spectators were for now content to merely watch.

The crowd did not have long to wait. The leader in charge had been conscious of them waiting outside when he made his demands, and had hurried the arrest of William as much as possible in an effort to appease the crowd. There had been, in the man's mind, a brief awareness of the wealth of the house, with thick tapestries on the wall. But he had felt the drama of the moment, and had broken the door down with a passion that was affected, but he felt necessary.

Therefore, the crowd suddenly saw action after the entry of the men. Firstly the leader of the watch came out, with two men behind him, flanking him. Then Master Outlaw was brought out, and the crowd grasped. He was not yet in shackles! His hands were to be very firmly pinned together with an iron clasp used for such things. It was a punishment used only on the lowliest criminal, and only while in prison, but was to be used on Master Outlaw on the Bishop's instructions. He was making every effort to bring the other low. They watched to see what happened next.

The men, prisoner and captors alike, moved around the door while they all prepared for departure. A cloak was thrown over William's shoulders, for which kindness he gave a business-like nod. The crowd were conscious of a waiting, a breathless watchfulness that made each of them silent. They did not speak. Their mood was changing. The mirth was gone.

The front door of the House was still open, its light showing on all of the men's faces. Philip stood in the doorway, waiting for some sign that all would be well, or even further instructions from his Master. His fretful nature was now unabated. William ignored him, instead exchanging a few quiet words with the leader.

The crowd across the street were growing in number, the news having reached the taverns.

They waited.

The men were ready. William lifted his chin for a moment, and then thrust out his wrists. The shackles were cumbersome and awkward, and at the sight of them the crowd gave the first sign of malevolence. A slow, sly cheer went up, and then another. A few people took steps forward, shortening the distance. Get him.

William looked over at them, as if seeing them for the first time. What was this?

The sly cheers were fading away, and replaced by a gasping hunger for the rest of it to be delivered. For punishment. Long overdue.

The Master gave the nod. William was still looking at the crowd, frowning. What were they...?

The men set off.

That was the spur for the crowd.

Screams abounded about them, as the crowd split into two, one on each side of the entourage. Yells and catcalls filled the torchlit night, and each voice added to the screams and yells of hate.

"BASTARD!"

"Your mother will burn!"

"EVIL ONE!"

"You will DIE, unholy one!

"KILL HIM!"

"DIE!"

My God, thought William.

The stones were flying too, with vicious speed that gave no chance to avoid them. Spits were flying through the air too, on William, on the men, on them all. The men crouched down, hands over their faces, to protect themselves. One stone hit William on the shoulder, and he gave a grunt of pain. Another hit the leader on the face.

More! More of them! More of them come to get him! Up ahead! A swarm was appearing, another fifty of them, a herd of the scum seeming to appear, pouring out like mud from the Butterslip lane. They were converging, swarming over to them, without warning. William saw that all of them stared at him, and all stared in hatred. All the army men were alarmed, scared at this new event. Stones flew, and hit one of the men on the face. He screamed in pain and the sound excited the crowd more.

"KILL HIM!"

250

"Keep them back!" cried the leader, giving the men a legitimate excuse to panic. All of them unsheathed their swords, including William, even with his hands shackled. Stones flew through the air, hitting all and sundry, and the screams sounded as if from the truly insane. William stared around him in horror at what had appeared around him. He had no idea before now of the hatred that had waited for him.

More. There were more waiting in Rose Inn Street. All of the savages had a blood lust about them, and they rushed up Kieran's Street with unthinking rage about them.

"Jesus save us!" cried William in horror, and saw mirrored in the faces of the army men the fear he felt.

"Get him to the Castle!" shouted the leader, readying his own sword.

The men about him copied the action, sweating and swearing in fear. The troop as one broke into a trot, the leader running down the street first, all of them following, the mob on their heels.

"Stand BAACK!" he roared, and they met the oncoming crowd from Rose Inn Street. He cut down the first two men he met, and stabbed two more, pushing the troop further up the street. Quickly they made their way into Rose Inn Street.

"Keep ready!" he called over his shoulder, seeing that all of the men, including William, were still with him. The crowds there hung on to each side of the street, seeing the blood on the swords and the look in the army men's' eyes. The mob behind them were cowed back a few feet as well.

They trotted up to the beginning of the Parade, keeping their swords pointed at the mobs snarling about them.

Oh dear God, thought William, seeing the beginning of Hell.

The mob were preparing a fire. In the Parade, a huge bonfire to burn him. They were all waiting for him, two hundred strong of the poor, standing there, ready to rip William limb from limb with their hands.

"THERE!" came a scream as they saw him. The crowd began to rush towards them.

No!

The troop readied itself again, all raising their swords.

"MOVE!" called the leader.

251

Each of them got in a blow, fighting back hard. William got an invalid struck clean through the throat. Another moment saw a girl sliced through the waist. The madness was all about. People flung themselves clean on the swords to die. All of the men about him fought to save themselves and him. They slowly, inch by inch, made movement up the Parade. Most of the crowd were unarmed, and desperately weak and frail. But so many of them but they could not but be killed to save the others!

The men were nearly there. They were nearly in sight of the guards. The leader gave up a shout, though they must have been visible already. They struck on and on, striking more and more of the crowd who came at them. The sheer volume of the screams was terrifying to William, he had never heard the voice of the people before. There was a terrifying smell of blood. William saw, no, heard the gurgle of a man stumble away from some weapon used on him, the blood filling the lungs and the throat.

Here were the gates, nearly before them. They were nearly there. They were nearly safe. A boy tried to lunge at William, and had a sword on him for his trouble. He screamed and held the sliced hand to his chest, horrified.

"OPEN THE GATES!" screamed the leader, fighting now with all his might.

Slowly the gates began to creep open.

"OPEN THE GATES!"

They were there. They were safe. The men and he rushed in, not looking behind him. Someone, one of the men, was left behind. He almost made the gate as it closed, and his face was the last thing William saw before it shut. The man was immediately set upon by the crowd. All those inside the gates could hear the screams and cries of him, as he received William's punishment. William stood there, panting in the vacant blackness. He had nothing left in him. There were wild thumping on the gates for a while, and he stood there, with the other men, too alarmed to be aware of themselves, listening to it. After the longest, far too long a time, it faded.

There was a streak of blood, not his, on his clothes. His sword was in his hand, bloody. He had no thoughts, for a while. And then he had only one thought. In the sad sickness of being numb, in the sad sickness of it all, he could only remind himself that he was not ever going to be safe again. His days of his life were to be short. He would not live long. He would soon die, as surely as if a stone had been pushed over his tomb already. And then he saw it. He saw, finally, that his mother had been safe all along. As she had made it so, had known it would be so. Expect nothing less from Alice Kyteler.

Chapter Twenty-Three

Whatever evil spirit roamed the streets and alleys of Kilkenny, it had much material to delight itself once Petra's sentence was announced. Children, giggling their high laughs, mimicked the torture of the Maid, ending their games with a faux burning, chanting and laughing at whichever one of their playmates 'burned'. Women, gossiping furiously with vigour and delight, told each other over and over of the evil ordeals that the Kyteler house had long been known for. The acts and depravities were soon a matter of history. Society ladies found much need to discuss the weather and the recent resurrection of the crops, after years of appalling rains; anything rather than the disgraceful events all about them. Men gazed fearfully at the cathedral, its force of judgement now a matter of record for them all. Heresy might well exist in the hearts of a man unknown even to himself, only to be discovered by the hot brand of the Church. Others wondered aloud how much wood was necessary to properly burn a human body. Less wood than it took to burn a House, which make no mistake was what was happening. And for those with interests, financial interests, commercial interests, interests that might well be lost, Le Drede's act caused them to drink their mead, to fall silent, and to ponder the threat that one simple man could cause them all; And to silently decide that the threat was too large to countenance.

And Rose, safe and ignored and returned to the House, was washing her hands in a bowl of water in the fire. She remembered again hearing the verdict, and found herself examining her hand. She saw the solidity of it, the lines and the form of it, the sheer expectedness of it; it was her hand, part of her, she gave it no thought neither in the morning light nor during her prayers in the dark. Yet this part of her could burn, could be put into the flames, made to crackle and curl and blacken. That was what was to happen to Petra, what was to befall her. It would befall not just her hand, but also to her hair, her face, her belly and legs and all of her. Rose put her hand to her mouth, clamped it and pressed on it, so that the cry might not come. She was to lose her sister, sister in deed if not in blood, and it would be by the spilling her blood that Rose would lose her. She was only barely aware, in the beginning of her grief that she was stepping away from Petra. She was trying to forget her memories, to detach from the woman of her memory, to make of her a thing apart. Petra was already starting to die for her; a most necessary thing, considering what was about to happen.

The crowd had already been there for days, scavenging, hungry creatures, coming from the smaller towns and hamlets to see what would unfold. The wealthy townspeople naturally despised them, and on the day in question made great efforts to obtain better seats on the second floor of buildings surrounding the Thosel, or Town Hall. All of them, however, took a festive attitude to the proceedings, watching the town hall for any and all signs of movement. Hawkers and food sellers began their fires in an effort to prepare their wares for the public.

A day before the burning, when William had been taken from the Houses and had to fight his way to his prison in the Castle, a pyre had been built to accommodate the penitent soul it now expected. And now, on the day itself, it stood waiting beside the town hall. Every so often some priest or underling would appear and check and recheck the large scaffolding prepared at the front of the building. The crowd would hush and watch avidly any and all movements, wondering aloud when the event proper would start.

Soon there were even more signs of life. A platform had been prepared for the Bishop and the laity, as well as the noblemen of the surrounding area. A few knights and their wives made their way up to the platform, to be commented on again by the public watching. Just like the Inquisition courts in France! More than one chest was proudly puffed up at the comparison with their small little town and the great events abroad.

Eventually the laity and the Bishop made their way out to the platform. The Bishop was dressed in the most perfect white and gold vestments. They were a gift from a French family, and he had saved them for use on special occasions.

The crowd had been getting restless. As soon as the Bishop arrived, however, he stood at the platform, and addressed the crowd of about five thousand.

"Children of God!" he called out. He made to go on, but the screams of the crowd forced him to wait. Eventually he continued.

"Look upon the mighty vengeance of your Lord Jesus Christ and tremble! For it is only through our Lord that we may receive salvation! It is only through the Glory of His most Holy Church we may cast out the damned and raise ourselves up to the status of saved souls!"

The crowd roared its approval.

He allowed them a moment to compose themselves, and continued.

"I myself have been persecuted! I myself have suffered the unfair burden of unjust accusations! I, like the early Christians, have been thrown to the lions in the Coliseum in Rome, where my faith, and only my faith, was enough to guide me and give me comfort! But I did not falter! I did not stray from the path! I gave myself and my safety up to the quest to save the souls of those around me, no matter what obstacles or burdens should be placed before me! For the Lord is with us! We will not fail! We will overcome our enemies and sail forth into victory!"

The crowd did not allow any more, but let forth a mighty cheer that went on and on for several minutes. Hysteria reached them; the devil was everywhere! They must protect them and their loved ones, they must align with that which could save them! They prayed and screamed to the bishop to save them, to forgive them, to guide them from the valley of darkness.

He judged the mood at the perfect pitch.

He gave the nod to bring out the prisoner.

The guards were well primed. They moved with deliberate slowness. The woman was held on both sides by the men, and at her appearance in the morning light a great hiss rose up from the crowd. This moved quickly in to cries of hate and disgust, yells of savage threats and of terrible insults. The crowd had to be kept back.

William was not alone in his cell, but he was not aware of anyone else at that moment. The sounds of the roars of the crowd could be heard throughout the silent Castle. He looked at the small glimmer of light coming through the window. The screams, he told himself, do not mean she burns yet. She does not burn yet. She is as yet unharmed.

Philip stood far back in the crowd, afraid to go closer. He could see the small, crouched figure being hauled up towards the scaffolding, but could not keep his eyes on it. Instead, his gaze was drawn to the hysteria around him. There were people yelling and screaming at her, all of them yelling for her death.

Slowly the three figures moved from the Town Hall to the kindling. Cries and yells travelled with them all the way along. At one point a woman pulled herself out of the crowd and spat a phlegm filled spit on Petra, which hit her face and slowly travelled her skin until dripping on to her neck.

They had shaved her hair, Philip saw.

Rose was there too. She was to the side, but closer, much closer, and she stood as near to the stand containing the nobility and the priests as she could. There she could not see Petra's face, but she could see the scaffolding at an angle, so that she had an excellent view of the wood, and of Petra to her ankles.

Petra looked stupid and unaware, not taking in what she saw. Nevertheless, when she got near the pile of wood, she could not but pull at the arms that held her. A faint whimper escaped her lips.

"No... no!"

At this sign from her, the crowd hooted and jeered.

"Hey ya devil's whore, will he save you now?"

"Will he save your soul now?!"

Petra did nothing in response. Almost despite herself, she tried to move her arm away from the man on her right as she moved, but she found herself stuck fast.

They were at the pile. A small platform had been built so that she could be tied to the pole properly. The men lifted the now thin woman easily. Despite her resistance, she was not panicking. You have to be aware of what is coming to panic. Instead she merely whimpered slightly.

Rose whispered quietly, unheard, to the men carrying Petra. "Please, for God's mercy, let not ye do this thing."

One of the men spoke to Petra, unheard by anyone.

"It is for God's mercy, and for your soul, we must do this thing."

The last rope was tied. Petra was stuck to the kindling fast and now didn't hold any hope of escape. Her head lolled to the front.

The men lowered themselves from the pile, and a few extra bundles were cast on.

She was not aware of what was happening. She struggled weakly with the ropes, but not in any real way.

They lit the torch, and looking at the Bishop, awaited his nod before they lit the pyre.

The Bishop paused, considered, and stopped. He looked at her for a moment. He lifted his head to speak to the crowd.

Rose saw Petra's feet suddenly jerk, as if she was suddenly standing upright for the first time. Rose frowned, as a possibility crossed her mind. She continued staring at those feet, trying to be wrong. No, she thought. Surely God could not be so cruel as to restore Petra at this time? The idea that she should be in her right mind to see what was coming was horrible. Surely the horror of what was about to happen was not going to be made worse by the creature seeing all at her death? Surely not? She held her breath, staring in horror at what she saw.

The Bishop gave his nod.

The guard threw the torch as high as he could, above the crowd's heads, and all watched as it travelled into a smooth arch, landing straight and true onto the pile of kindling.

Petra screamed in terror as he drew back his arm, her eyes seeing, her mind comprehending.

Rose screamed.

The flames grew high immediately, burning the lower piles. Petra couldn't be heard to say anything, because the crowd were screaming in delight and hatred.

After a few minutes the flames had reached higher. Rose saw them begin to reach Petra's feet, which were unclad, and threatened the drab skirt she had on. The crowd's noise abated for a moment.

Petra's voice sounded loud and clear across the crowd.

"Save me!"

The crowd silenced for a moment, staring at her.

"Someone save me please!"

The mood of the crowd began to turn in pity at what it saw.

Petra tried to escape the fire growing towards her.

"Repent!" came a cry from the crowd. If she repented she could die by the sword while still on the pyre. The call was taken up by others in the crowd.

"Repent! Repent, Petra, and be saved!" they called. Petra merely struggled against the ropes, beginning to scream in pain.

Rose could not but try to move forward, but the crowd and the guards were holding all back.

Philip, yards away, heard the scream of Petra, and froze in horror. He was unable to move, and the crowd pushed him further and further back as it rushed to the spectacle.

Petra turned her face away, and did all she could to move her feet away from the flames, moving them this way and that. Now and again, she gave up a call.

Rose tried to get to her, but they were all kept further back.

"Save me! Help me!"

She gave another cry.

"HELP ME!! PLEASE!"

The crowd, hearing no repenting, turned again. Her cry for help was parodied.

"Save me! Save me!" yelled a small child.

"Save me!" cheered the mob, and laughed.

Rose looked at the Bishop from within the mob. His face was alert, but horrified. He did not look away, however.

The flames were now at the top of the pile. Petra's dress was on fire.

Her voice was growing ragged in the smoke. She was fully filled with hysteria now, she was screaming to all to save her. The crowd no longer replied, but instead merely pushed and pulled itself to and from the pyre.

The flames were truly at her feet now. They burned up her dress. The smell of flesh burning reached the crowd, who moved back and forward in repulsion. She was screaming in earnest now, begging all to help her. The flesh on her feet was gone, and the flesh on her torso was next. The guards were kind, they loaded up the fire with more so that the smoke should overpower her quickly.

Petra had lost the power of words, screaming as high as she could against the most awful pain. She called out to Alice, to Rose, to

William, to her own mother, to all who could hear, to help, help, help her.

Philip, hearing his name being screamed, spun his face away, and with his back to them all, burst into tears of deserving despair.

The smoke rose high in salvation, and was sucked into Petra's lungs. Her face, black with the smoke, fell forward, as death finally came. The crowd gave a low moan at the sight.

The flames made full use of her body now, covering all of her, feeding off the arms and legs of the woman, curling and blackening the skin, taking the hair off her eyebrows and lashes, pulling back the lips and skin around the eyes, until the skeletal frame broke and slumped further down the pole.

The crowd gave out another low moan at the sight. It was true that she was unholy. Otherwise why did God not come down and save her, if she was innocent?

The Bishop sat still and quiet throughout the entire spectacle. He did not speak to anyone else while she burned. Instead, he watched with a silent, resigned grief as she was put to the flames.

And at the end, he sighed, genuinely tearful and upset. God in His infinite wisdom have mercy on the maid. He had a terrible feeling of failure that he did not clearly understand; he only knew he felt a grief that he could not fathom.

He rose up on the platform, and raised his right hand. Those on the platform with him fell silent, and after a moment, so did the crowd.

"Let all testify that God's will was done here today. God is Good."

He turned from the fire and walked back into the town hall where his carriage was waiting for him, the servant priest silent, to match his mood. Richard settled himself into the carriage and shut the door. He sat there for a long moment, his heart full. What was he to say? What was there to say?

"Home," he said quietly. The carriage moved away. For a moment the business of the evening awaited him, the papers he would be expected to review, the petitions he had before him. The comparison brought the horror of the burning into sharp contrast. He burst into tears.

Chapter Twenty-Four

Rose wept in the hall, the door slammed safely behind her. Philip sat at the table, his own tears now to deep to reach.

She tried to talk, to speak of what was behind her eyes now and forever, but the words would not come.

Philip said nothing, but merely looked at her crying. His own gaze drifted to the fireside beside him as he saw his own memories. Then he realised what he was looking at and looked hurriedly away.

There was no one but the two of them in the house now. It was not clear when William was expected back, but it would be soon, it seemed. The house was empty, silent. The greatness of it was lost, somehow. All the treasures were there, but with no one to see them, what importance did they have?

Philip found everything was a reminder of Petra. The house was made by her, he thought, there was nothing there to see if she was not there. There was the beginning of anger within him, he thought, but he rejected it out of weariness. It was too late now. There should be no more fires lit in the house, he thought. There should only be ice in the house, spreading through the rooms, making white the windows, like the eyes of the dead. Silence should fill their ears and blackness their eyes. They should never speak again.

Rose looked at him from across the table. He is dying, she thought. He is useless for his role and he has no where else to go. He will die soon, and his death will leave me with something else to do. She felt the lines on her face deepen. She joined him in the silence.

Then there was a knock on the door.

Le Drede reached his Palace just before nightfall, but not by much. He had regained some of his composure, and his face and eyes were dry. He had briefly reviewed his conduct throughout the affair, and found it flawless. Once done with that, he had spent a few moments gazing out of the window, seeking new sights for his eyes. Then he had firmly turned his thoughts to the future obligations upon him. He would need to ensure that the prison stay of William Outlaw was indeed a proper penance; there would need to be a limit on the

261

visitors and on the rights granted to this supporter of heretics. Le Drede did not stoop so low as to compare his own stay, and the privileges granted to him, as being on a par with William. There was a real necessity for the law to be reinforced upon William, now that the evidence against him was so black. The two cases were not the same.

Le Drede looked out on the landscape again, growing dark. This was now the earth without the Maid Petra. She had died in the most terrible way, died in flames in the eyes of the Lord, and was now being judged by her Master. Yet the world was still here. She may have imagined her life as being of the Universe, that the Universe would end when she was gone, yet here it was, continuing, existing, without any reference to her at all. Le Drede found himself wondering what the world would think when he was gone. As the carriage pulled into the gates of the Bishop's Palace, he hoped it would find him worthy of the Church; that he had always protected it.

When they finally came to a rest in front of the house, he saw that there was someone there waiting for him. He could see another carriage standing in front of the house, the driver standing by the horse. He frowned slightly at this. If he had a visitor, why was the carriage not brought to the back of the house? Why had the driver not even dismounted from his perch? He looked at this, puzzled.

"Your Grace?" asked his own driver, waiting for him to get down.

Richard nodded and then got down. He approached the door, wondering who was waiting for him inside.

The door opened to allow him entry as he did so. His houseman stood looking at him, eyes wide.

"Your Grace, you have a visitor!" he cried.

Le Drede wondered why he sounded so afraid.

Rose sat looking at Philip, upon hearing the knock on the door. Philip did not say anything, merely sat there looking over her shoulder at the door behind her.

The knock came again.

"What should we do?" pleaded Rose. They could easily be set upon by the townspeople. They might even have a single inflamed mad soul set upon their death. Even the Bishop might have decided that they were now to be made to give evidence.

Philip said nothing for a moment. Then he stood up quickly.

"We find out who it is before we open that door," he said, decision clear in his voice.

Rose turned in her chair and watched as he slowly approached the door. He put his ear to it and called out.

"Who is there?"

She heard a muffled response.

"I said who is there?"

The voice sounded out again, but to Rose it was still unclear. It seemed Philip was able to hear it, however, as he suddenly undid the latch.

Rose wanted to stop him, to say he should tell her who it was first.

But the door was already unbolted and swinging back, it revealed William.

He burst in with a sense of the fugitive, looking over his shoulder as he entered to see if he was noticed. He was alone. He was unharmed.

Philip let him in with a sense of sad resignation. A thought came to him, and it shocked him. What did it take to remove them from the earth? Why was it always those around them that suffered for their sins?

Philip kept his back to the room, his hands on the door, as he thought this thought. Then, shocked, he asked himself what did this meant. Was he seeking the end of the House of Kyteler? He locked the door.

He made his face placid and untouched again and turned around.

William was speaking to them, his back to the door. Philip moved so that both of them were looking back at him.

"It is obvious we must quit the town, I do not know for how long," William was saying. "This is not a running away, nor do I intend to let the battle end here."

He paused, and looking down inhaled slowly. He looks exhausted, thought Rose, but there is something else...

He believes defeat is now possible, saw Philip. He has heard the scream of the crowd and saw the smoke of the fire, and is disheartened. Philip knew that his duty was to encourage the younger man, to give him succour for the remaining days ahead; else how would any of them be secure?

He would speak. He would open his mouth in a moment, while the Master was not speaking, and give support.

William lifted his head, and spoke again. Philip let him, the seconds ticking away. With each one, his duty moved away from him, stretching longer and longer until he stood in silence in front of the man. He knew his duty, he did. He simply found that he had no intention to carry it out. He felt that he would be able to do it tomorrow. But today, he had watched the fire take the Maid, (not true, Philip, not true, you turned at the last minute, didn't you?) and he was not able to do it today.

William went on.

"We will leave, and quietly. We will take all that we can with us, leaving nothing of worth behind. We will be gone before long, as quickly as we can."

He stood, paused, and inhaled again, gathering composure.

"I do not know when we will be back. We may have to quit the city to be safe. Therefore, take all that you can. I will call on you shortly," he said, finishing.

Rose immediately offered him food and mead, to which William agreed.

Philip quit the room, glad of something to do. He closed the door behind him, seeing Rose offering cold meats to William as he did so, and quickly shut the door.

William looked sadly down at the food, and began to eat.

Le Drede stood alarmed in his hallway and looked at the other man.

"Well, don't just stand there," he said, "Tell me who is my visitor?" he said, gruffly. He was still sad from Petra earlier, he saw, and so strove to compose himself.

The other man was not so composed.

264

"Your Grace, he does not give his name, but states he is of Archbishop Bicknor's service, and that he comes with instructions for you."

A visit, now, from the Archbishop. It came the day of his greatest triumph, a show of victory in the town for the Church against those that would destroy it. He was not so naïve, however, that he would believe that he would receive congratulations on this day of days. He would, instead, be forced to fight a battle even now.

He stood straight up, and looked back at the servant.

"Bring me to him," he commanded.

The other man led the way to the main reception room, and opened the door. Richard looked again on the face of Richard Le Gile, and found that he was not surprised. He looked to the servant who had escorted him.

"Bring me food."

"Your Grace is most kind to see me at home on this day of days."

Le Drede found himself filled with weariness upon hearing this opening gambit. He wished that he could be alone and away from this. He lifted his head to Sir Richard.

"How may I be of service?"

He is tired, and thin of resources in terms of his character, thought Sir Richard. This will need tact.

"I bear a missive from Archbishop Bicknor, who bids you good tidings," said Sir Richard. He took from a bag a letter with the seal of the Archbishop showing.

Le Drede took it in his hand.

"I thank you for this."

The other man spoke quickly.

"I regret that the matter cannot be delayed, your Grace. I am obliged by the Archbishop to request that the missive be read immediately."

Le Drede looked at him for a moment. Oh, just read it and get rid of the man. Let the house be empty of requirements to me for one evening at least, he said to himself, and slicing open the seal, let his eye fall over the words.

He gasped, the sign Sir Richard had been waiting for.

"Is all well, Your Grace?"

Le Drede reread the letter again, his heart beating fast. But this was outrageous, surely! He was to present himself in Dublin, to answer charges of corruption? If findings were of a serious nature, he was to continue on to the Papal Court? What nonsense was this!

But then a thought; no such attempt was made by Bicknor, that complaining cleric, before. There must be a move against Le Drede by others here in Ireland, others that had power and politics and influence on their side-

Sir Richard lifted a sardonic eyebrow to him, waiting.

"Due to the poor conditions of the roads, and the impossible nature of securing my safety and that of my staff, I regret it is not possible for me to travel as the Bishop wishes at this time."

Sir Richard did not waste a moment.

"I am instructed that you are to be brought safely and quickly to His Grace's presence at the earliest opportunity, and that you are to receive His Grace's guarantee that you will reach his presence safe and sound."

Le Drede heard this and stared openly. They were determined against him. There was no other explanation. They had no hesitation in insisting that he would travel whether he liked it or not, and would brook no objection. There was only one conclusion.

He was all done.

They must have written to the Papal Court, to the Pope himself, denouncing him to all that could read in an effort to avoid all he was doing here. What nonsense had been portrayed to His Holiness? Le Drede was sure once he was in front of the Pope he would be able to call any inquiry to a halt, he still had his supporters there. But to go, now? While William was in prison and the city laid before him like a jewel for his enjoyment?

Suddenly he remembered the letter that he had received only yesterday, before Petra died, with the Papal seal. There must have been a warning there, some hint of what was coming that would allow him to prepare and be ready, if he was vigilant. He always had been before. But he hadn't read it, had he? Instead he was now facing Sir Richard unprepared and surprised.

He closed his face of any emotions.

"I will, of course, comply in any and all ways possible. I will require several hours to ensure my duties are finished here, but will be ready to depart before Vespers."

Sir Richard knew not to labour the point. He merely inclined his head in thanks.

Le Drede turned from him and headed, without a word to anyone, to his private chambers. There, he bid the servants away and shut the doors, where he might be alone.

He fell on his knees.

"Oh Lord, let this not be so, let there be justice, oh Lord please..." the words flew out of him, as he prayed to the small altar there, as he threw his panicking eyes upwards, hoping for succour, hoping for leeway out of this disaster...

Come, Richard, said a cold, sneering voice in his head. We do not win battles this way. Did you win against the Kytelers by keeping a hot head? Did you win against Sir Arnold, when he threatened you when you carried the Host in the courtroom, by falling to fear like a woman and pleading for mercy? No. And you will not now.

He sat slowly back on his heels, and then stood up and away from the Altar.

We think, said the voice. We take the time to do so and we think. Sit on the bed, and think. Le Drede followed his own mind's instructions as if they came from another. He sat on the bed and marshalled his knowledge of the facts. They were all against him in Dublin, the Archbishop especially. He no doubt had written against Le Drede to the Pope himself. The papal Court, however, was a slow moving thing, and could not be made to turn quickly in a changing tide. Le Drede would still have friends there. He would be better there, than in Dublin, where the vipers grew around him. He would be best to make his way to Avignon immediately, with all speed, to ensure his safety. His safety! That which was to be so assured by the Archbishop! He snorted at the thought, and felt better.

No, he would not go to Dublin. He stood up, calm now, and ready. He would go to Avignon, his real home, and allow himself to put the case of what was to be done here to the Pope. He would outdo them all. And while he was gone, he would have the satisfaction of knowing William Outlaw was away in prison, at his mercy until he got back.

Le Drede bowed politely to the altar, and then left the room, barking orders to servants.

William packed the last of it onto the carriage, the old one that had been used by his mother, and was now being used in the yard at the back of the house. It was long past Vespers; it felt as if dawn was coming. Rose sat in, while Philip sat on another carriage that was not decorated in any way; the less decoration the better, it was thought.

William ensured that the ropes were tight, as much as he could. He did not want to have anything fall out, nor did he want to stop for anything either. To pause, for any length of time, would be dangerous to a heart stopping degree. A thought occurred to him; that the Kytelers should be afraid in Kilkenny! He wanted to grow hot with the slight that that did to him, but made himself remain cool.

He looked to the others and saw that they were ready, that they were waiting for him. He called out to them.

"I'll go shut up the House," he called, and turned away.

The house is long shut up, thought Philip, and tried not to think.

The kitchen was empty, and the fires gone out. He had not known it to be so in all his years. The storeroom that had always been full was now empty. He went into the study and ensured that the money was safely removed, that all possible documents were now gone. The silence there made him look around. Always this had been the place of discussion, the place where strategy was founded. Now, no voices spoke.

He frowned, and left the room, no longer sure of what he hoped to achieve by his tour of the House. He walked up the steps to the reception room. The front door, with its steps down was in front of him. There, at the table, the great ones had sat with them. All the complements and favours that were to be given! All burnt up and gone now. He looked at the fireplace that Petra and Rose had tended, like all the others. Empty and gravelike, now. He looked for a moment around the room, seeing all his life there. Here was where he had made a mark with a knife, when he had been fooling and foolish and not looking where he was at five years old. Here was where he had sat, when he had first heard his mother's request to speak to him, giving him news of Adam Le Blund. What a mistake that was! And there was where Philip had told him, again, of Adam.

He turned and walked up the stairs to the bedrooms. Having them cordoned off from the rest of the house was an unimaginable expense, and many had found it strange. William thought his mother had done it so that she may have a private face from her public one. It certainly had proved useful, he thought.

There had been the tapestry in red that his mother had loved so much. It was now safely put into the carriage, but the wall seemed to bear its imprint. She had wanted that for so long, someone had told him. His father had never enjoyed its colour; he had thought it too rich. But she would not rest until she had it. He walked on to his room, blank of his life now. Then on to the room his mother used.

There, beside the fire, had she told him of her impending marriage. There was her desk, where she had written and planned for the House with all the wit she had been given. There, from that window, had she seen the world and seen what she wanted. The silence of the room seemed to carry her still. He looked around at the bed, the table and the seats, seeing her there still. Her presence impressed itself upon him once again, as it always had.

"This House died when you left it," he said aloud to the room, accusingly.

It looked back at him in silence.

What had he expected?

He stood for a moment more, and then turned and left.

Le Drede stood outside the Palace, readying himself for the journey ahead. He had informed Le Gile that he was to join him in the city, but of course would do no such thing. He instead would head for the coast, gaining passage to France and then on to freedom and justification. He would be vindicated, of course, but he would need to take the long road before that would happen.

He sniffed the air. Dawn coming. He looked at the carriage, with all the documents of the trial and of other matters, his personal possessions (thank goodness the Order had seen sense in this matter!) and all that would be necessary to ensure his safe passage, had been made ready. He was tired but he could sleep on the boat. He knew he should not wait, but just for a moment, a mere moment...

He thought about all that had happened. He thought of the Cathedral, and the Castle, and the Town Hall. He thought of the Synod and of the trial, and of all involved. He thought of Arnold, and his attack on Le Drede in the Courtroom. He thought of his imprisonment in the Castle, of the injustice suffered there, and of his procession through the town. He thought of the nonsense he was made to suffer by Dublin, and he thought of the wisdom he was soon to rejoin in Avignon. And he thought of the Maid Petra, of the Maid Petra that he had burned, and he prayed briefly for her soul and wished her Heaven.

The others were waiting. He took the hand of the servant and let himself be helped into the carriage.

William and Philip slowly led the carriages out of the City gates as dawn rose. They slowly and carefully made their way down the path, not speaking to each other, no thoughts except the guiding of the horses over the rough terrain. Behind them a column of smoke still rose into the paling air. Rose did not let herself look behind her, convinced that to do so would mean disaster. She kept her back straight and did not look left or right. She felt somehow as if she would never see the City again; that she was leaving, that they were all leaving, never to return again. She did not look back.

They slowly made their way to the homestead of William, a good three hours journey for them, as they were so heavily loaded with goods. They saw few on the roads, thankfully. However, at one point, William thought he saw a carriage, horribly like Le Drede's, somewhere in the distance. It was not going their way, if anything it was headed away from the City towards the coast. But if it was Le Drede's, that would explain why it would pause, exactly the same way he had done, and sit, as if looking back, for a long moment.

Can it be? thought Le Drede. Is he free and unfettered and free to go home?

Is he leaving the Diocese? thought William. Is he to be gone and not to return? He remembered, like a distant memory, Le Gile telling him in his study that Le Drede would not be back. And now here is his carriage, thought William, heading towards the coast, heading away from all of them and the trouble he caused.

The two carriages sat there, paused, and looked at each other across the land.

Chapter Twenty-Five

Alice Kyteler sat safe and well in the House of her friend the Viceroy, and ate. She had almost no teeth left in her head, and so the chicken piece she chewed was small in size. She was grey but hid it well in her headdress, and her hands were still untouched by hard work, as benefited a lady of her stature.

She glanced around her at the room she was in. Sure it was a fine enough room, but it was not her own, and she was now eager to be off and enjoying her own house again. She was too old, she felt, to be away from her own fireplace for long. Not that she was ungrateful to the Viceroy for granting her a stay here. The time had passed most agreeably. But she was soon to hear, no doubt, that the local trouble down home had dissipated, thus allowing her to make her way back to the rightful home she had built up. She was eating alone today, as the Lord were out, due back at any moment. She had been expecting news from home, and so had remained here instead.

She finished her meal and wiped her hands of grease, pulling her shawl closer to her. These days, she had felt an inner coldness reach her that she had never felt before. Despite her attempts to ward it off, it never yet had left her. Old age, she supposed.

There was a knock on the door, and the maid came in to remove the tray. Alice sat beside the fire, willing the heat into herself. She looked up when she realised the maid was still there.

"There is someone here to see you, a messenger, ma'am," said the maid.

Ah yes, the news of home. Maybe she could come home now. She nodded, and the maid existed, to return shortly with a man.

He entered the room panting, clearly fresh from his exertions getting there. Alice looked at him, frowning. What was this?

"Dame Alice, I am bid by your noble son, Sir William, to bring you news."

Alice held out her hand for the letter, which was pulled out of the man's tunic and placed into her hands. She looked at him for a long moment, and then opened the seal.

Her eyes flew down the page and then, stopped, went back, read more slowly. At one point she stopped, looked into the fire for a few moments, and then went back reading. As she continued to read her hands began to shake, and she hunched over the letter as if to limit its harm. Each word killed her House in her mind, each image it conjured destroyed her work of her life. She sat there, the last word in her mind echoing over and over. She did not have words herself at that moment, she did not have any help for herself to say what she wanted to say.

"My lady?" asked the maid. "Are you all right?"

Alice said nothing, merely sat, shaking by the fire, her head bowed into her lap with emotion. She could not speak.

The maid, alarmed, heard the sounds that indicated the Master was back. She hurried herself and the messenger from the room and, finding them, briefly informed the Master that the Dame Alice had received some very bad news. Some very bad news indeed.

The Viceroy found her still in the same position by the fire. He was horrified to find the noble lady he had left two hours ago now reduced to senility.

"My Lady what ails thee?" he asked.

For a long moment there was no response. Then a hand, gnarled and twisted, thrust out the crumpled letter to him. He read it quickly, with a gathering sense of horror. What she must be feeling?

He pulled up a chair as close as he could, and spoke quietly into her ear.

"Know that she died, it said, a quick death, that would have spared her the worst of her pain. Know that she was a good woman, under a false charge, and that her soul was never in any risk of damnation in any sense. Know that-"

"She was of my House," whispered Alice, her voice a grasping hiss.

"Your House?" asked the Viceroy, not understanding.

"My House," said Alice, her voice still low, as if coming from the depths of her. "She was of my House."

The Viceroy tried to make sense of this, but could not. Alice slowly lifted her head, and looked at him.

"She was of MY HOUSE! This woman was of my House for years! All knew of her as my maid! He took her and killed her and made her an example so that ALL SHOULD KNOW that the House of Kyteler was no more!"

273

The Viceroy sat back in his chair, alarmed. She was up, moving away from the fire, shawl thrown to one side, her body rigid as a ratter with fury. She was standing before him, her hands in fists of rage, her eyes mad with anger as she screamed.

"She was of MY HOUSE! The insult, the trespass, the grave injury done to the status of the Kyteler House!" she screamed, pointing a finger at the Viceroy as if accusing.

"But,"

"The collapse of our authority! The desecration of all that had been built up, fought for over the years! Our standard is no more! Our victory is no more! We are nothing! We…-"

She stopped, her hand flying to her throat. She was choking, gargling in her throat, and her face went red as she tried to breath. She collapsed on the floor.

"Dame Alice!" cried the Viceroy, who rushed to her side.

She was convulsing, eyes white, her body made furious and jerking. He rose to his feet to get help, and so it was that she was alone when she died. Her heart beat faster and faster with fury and will, until it alone could no longer keep her alive. She remembered something, some brief last moment, some decision made, that was important, but she was not able to see it now. She could not see anything now. She felt her heart stop for a moment, and then another, and then again.

And then stop.

Alice Kyteler breathed her last breath, and was no more.

Chapter Twenty-Six

The two carriages, paused across the way, began to move away from each other. William was not sure if he moved first or if Le Drede did, but somehow he found himself back on the path, moving away from Le Drede, with the other carriage now out of sight. He did not know what to make of what had just happened. He preferred not to think about it. About any of it.

Le Drede let the carriage move him away from his prey, let the other carriage move away from him into safety and into security, back into the den of malevolence he had found them all in. He sat back in his own carriage. What had just happened? Had they seen and not seen? Had he been mistaken?

He did not know. He did not know anything anymore. Nothing seemed clear to him.

I am tired, he told himself, closing his eyes. I am merely tired. I will rest, and regain my strength, and continue abroad what I could not do inland. I will carry out God's wishes, and make anew the Church here. He thought for a moment of a particular scenic spot in Avignon that had always restored him, and a smile came over his lips. Home. He would go home. The thought gave him comfort when nothing else could. He would be at home, and be free for a while from it all.

And as he planned, he kept his eyes closed.

The End

About the Author

Claire Nolan was born in Kilkenny, Ireland, in 1973, the fifth child of Pat and Ann Nolan. Despite years of writing as a child and adult, it was only upon reading a famous, hugely bestselling historical novel of utterly dreadful quality that she felt spurred on to write her first published work. Writing in the evenings and on the weekends, she slowly produced what is now The Stone.

Claire is open to your feedback on the slightest whim. You can contact her at **thestonenovel@gmail.com**, or at her website: **www.clairenolan.com**.

About the Painting

The painting on the cover of this novel was painted by artist Paddy Shaw in 2003, after he came across the story of Alice Kyteler in a library. After the painting was exhibited in New York and Japan, he donated it to the famous Kytelers Inn, in Kilkenny, in 2009.

Meanwhile, in 2005, Claire Nolan started writing the first draft of The Stone, which went on to be published in 2008.

Mr. Shaw had never heard of the novel you currently hold in yor hands, The Stone, nor had he ever heard of Claire Nolan. None the less, the painting he donated is believed to carry a strong likeness to the author. It could be put down to just one more strange event surrounding the sad events of Dame Alice Kyteler and her maid, Petra.

Lightning Source UK Ltd.
Milton Keynes UK
177636UK00001B/25/P